THE CURSE DEFIERS

THE CURSE DEFIERS

BOOK THREE OF THE CURSE KEEPERS

DENISE GROVER SWANK

47NORTH

Published by 47North, Seattle

www.apub.com

Amazon, the Amazon logo, and Amazon Publishing are trademarks of Amazon.com, Inc. or its affiliates.

ISBN-13: 9781477825679
ISBN-10: 1477825673

Cover illustrated by Larry Rostant

Library of Congress Control Number: 2014908009

Printed in the United States of America

To my daughter Emma, whose stubbornness simultaneously exhausts and inspires me.

THE CURSE DEFIERS

∴ CHAPTER ONE ∾

I felt the demon before I saw it. The mark on my palm tingled slightly, and the tattoo on my back began to burn.

"Curse Keeper." The low voice floated in the wind.

I sighed. Yep. A demon. No one knew my recently initiated title except for the spirits and gods of the Croatan Indian tribe, along with five other people. I was Elinor Dare Lancaster—otherwise known as Ellie—multi-great-granddaughter of Ananias Dare, one of the original colonists from the Lost Colony of Roanoke. Only the colony wasn't lost anymore. The entire thing had reappeared out of thin air a month and a half ago. The reappearance was the signal that a four-hundred-year-old curse had been broken, cracking the gate to Popogusso—the Croatan word for hell—and releasing a slew of spirits, demons, and gods that had been locked away by my ancestor Ananias and Manteo, the son of a Croatan Indian werowance. I was one of two Curse Keepers, a title passed down from generation to generation. While I was the Dare Keeper, Collin Dailey was the Manteo Keeper. And it wasn't a coincidence that the curse had broken while he was on duty.

It had been a week and five days since I'd heard anything from the spirit world, which was one week and four days longer than expected. Collin and I had destroyed two demons over three weeks ago, and while there had been a few minor metaphysical encounters since, the spirits had been keeping surprisingly quiet, particularly considering Collin's claim that they considered us fair game now that they knew we could and would destroy them.

Part of it was undoubtedly because I had the protection of the god Okeus. And many of the spirits still needed to regain strength after their four-hundred-year-long incarceration. But even though I hadn't seen or heard much from them, I still sensed them. They were growing restless, causing an itch in my palm that wouldn't go away. So although I wasn't happy that I was about to face a Native American spirit, I wasn't exactly surprised. But I had just gotten off a double shift from my waitressing job at the New Moon restaurant and it was close to midnight. I had to walk home, and I really wasn't in the mood to deal with a cranky supernatural being. And from past experience, they were *always* cranky.

The demon seemed to be waiting for me to take the lead. Since I didn't know what I was dealing with, I decided to ask the question that would help me most in the long run. "Who are you?" Surprisingly, I've found that most supernatural creatures are eager to identify themselves to me. Maybe it's an ego thing.

The demon's answer was to appear in the middle of Sir Walter Raleigh Road in downtown Manteo, North Carolina, population twelve hundred. I had encountered giant badgers and a golden deer. A huge horned water snake and a panther-reptile hybrid. That didn't even take into account the multiple gods with whom I'd dealt. But after all of those encounters, I still wasn't prepared for the figure that appeared in front of me.

An old woman.

I blinked. Yeah, an old woman.

She looked like someone's grandma. She was slightly over five feet tall and she couldn't have weighed much more than a hundred pounds. Her face resembled a prune, and she had bushy gray eyebrows and a hooked nose that looked like a bird's beak. Her hair was long and scraggly and pure white, hanging past her shoulders. Dressed in a faded blue housedress, she was leaning over a plain wooden cane. The only thing about her that clued me in on the fact that she wasn't on her way home from bingo was her glowing red eyes.

Yeah, a demon.

I flexed my wrist, preparing to hold up my right hand. I could use the mark on my palm—an intersecting circle and square—and say the words of protection that would send the bitch away. Not permanently, but for at least a few days. I needed Collin with me to send it back to Popogusso for good, and that was something he wasn't willing to do. I was on my own.

"What do you want?" I asked.

"I am here to tell your future." Her voice sounded like she'd smoked two packs of cigarettes a day since she was fourteen.

A shiver of fear crawled up my spine. Nothing this woman could say would be good news. "Thanks, but I'll pass. Knowing my future is a lot like knowing what all my Christmas gifts are before I open them. Why spoil the surprise?"

Her glowing red eyes shined brighter than flattened pennies. "You are the vessel that will determine the fate of the world. You will either save it or destroy it. And it will happen soon."

Oh, shit on a brick.

"Are you sure that's not *Collin's* future?"

The old woman's eyes narrowed as she pointed her cane at me. "Do not mock the Fates."

Fates. Old woman. Was she one of the Greek Fates? Weren't they a set of three? And if I remembered correctly, they always traveled with yarn and a pair of scissors. There was no sign of either, not even a loose thread on her worn housedress.

"Is there anything else? Any love notes from Okeus?"

She smiled, and it was far from a pleasant expression. "You will see the Great One soon enough."

I almost snort-laughed. Was that what he was calling himself these days? Since Okeus had made it all too clear that he wanted to be my baby daddy and she'd called me a vessel in her premonition, seeing him was the last thing I wanted to do. "Tell Okeus that I'm pretty busy. I'll let him know when I'm free."

Rather than answering, she disappeared, replaced by a flame that shot into the sky.

I needed to talk to David. Stat.

I hurried the rest of the way home. Until a couple weeks ago, home had been my apartment behind the restaurant where I worked. But now I was back in the home where I'd grown up, one of two houses on the property. One house was our family residence and the other was a bed and breakfast my father had owned until his death a month and a half before. Daddy had suffered from Alzheimer's for several years, so my stepmother, Myra, had been left with most of the responsibility for the inn, along with her part-time job at the Fort Raleigh National Historic Site, the location of the no-longer-lost colony. I'd helped by working without pay around my waitressing shifts and providing financial support whenever I could. But the B&B had lost money for years, and the property was in so much debt I wasn't sure we could ever get out of it. Even with the recent boom in business. Everyone wanted to see the reappeared colony. And since Myra had moved to Durham two weeks ago, I was stuck running the inn. Thank God David was so willing to help me. Him and our part-time—now full-time—employee, Becky.

As I walked up the path to the house, I stumbled, then groaned in irritation. I had tripped a lot over the last week, which made me wonder if all my demon-related injuries had affected my gross motor skills.

I slipped in the side door to the house, checking out the Native American symbols scrawled in charcoal around the perimeter of the door. Collin hadn't been by for several days to put his mark on the door, so the marks needed to be redone. I decided I'd redo them in the morning in the hopes that my own power would be enough to protect us.

A soft light glowed in the office, and I found David hunched over a book, a legal pad and a coffee mug next to him. When I pushed open the French doors, he looked up, pulled his reading glasses off, and gave me a soft smile. "How was work?"

Every time I saw him after we'd been apart for more than a few hours, the sight of him stole my breath away. Dr. David Preston was a gorgeous man. He was tall and broad shouldered, with sexy dark hair that begged my fingers to touch it. His warm hazel eyes looked at me with a combination of love and lust. It was no wonder he had a mile-long waiting list of attractive college girls dying to get into his intro to history courses back at the University of North Carolina in Chapel Hill.

I sighed. "Exhausting. Frustrating."

"Is your new boss still being a wanker?" he asked in his sexy British accent. David was a UK-born history professor who specialized in Native American studies. Talk about an anomaly. But he was *my* anomaly, and the thought warmed my insides.

My mouth lifted into an amused grin. "That's putting it lightly. Though my crash course in British slang had led me to believe a wanker was a man."

He shrugged, his eyes twinkling with amusement. "I don't discriminate."

After I'd sought out David's help over a month ago to get information about the Croatan spirit world, he'd taken a leave from UNC, extending his research sabbatical at the colony site so he could study Manteo's hut. While helping me, he'd pursued a romantic relationship. I'd tried to keep our partnership professional, but he had been impossible to resist. I still wondered at the wisdom of being involved with him with so much danger lurking around. Making him my boyfriend painted a bull's-eye on his back. Still, I knew his physical safety wasn't the only thing at risk.

For one thing, Collin Dailey was the other Curse Keeper, my true partner, not that he believed in helping me much. But mostly, I worried that I'd never give David everything he deserved. Dr. David Preston was a kind, thoughtful, incredibly intelligent man who had devoted his time and attention to helping me discover everything I needed to perform my duties as a Curse Keeper. Granted, he wanted to help me protect humanity, but his devotion ran much, much deeper.

He'd already confessed that he loved me. I hadn't reciprocated yet. Maybe it was because there was too much going on to fall in love with someone, although I suspected it had more to do with the fact that I'd bound my soul to Collin's during the short week we'd been together while trying to reseal the gate. Of course, Collin had been set on keeping the gate open the whole time and had only fooled me into thinking we were closing it. In any case, we'd had a brief, highly intense, sexually charged fling and had inadvertently bound our souls together. If Collin had his way, I'd probably be in his bed at this very moment, and if things had gone differently, I would have been eager to comply.

Only Collin had betrayed me by opening the gate and releasing countless supernatural beings, a good portion of whom, on their way streaming out of Popogusso, had vowed to make *me* pay for my ancestor's crime. My father had died as a sacrifice, and I was on the supernaturals' most wanted list. While Collin had offered me his own twisted form of apology, I wasn't sure I'd ever be able to forgive him, let alone forget. Especially since he'd pledged himself to Okeus, the malevolent Croatan god.

No, I'd decided a month ago that David Preston was an honorable man, of whom my father would have approved. I loved him in my own way, and we had a very healthy sex life. It wasn't the highly intense connection I had experienced with Collin, but it was deeper and, more importantly, it was full of trust. I could trust David implicitly with everything. I couldn't trust Collin with anything.

David set his glasses on the desk and scooted his chair back, motioning me around the desk. I obliged and he grabbed my hand, pulling me onto his lap so that my legs were hanging over the arm of the chair. He placed a soft kiss on my bottom lip. "You look exhausted, love. How about we go to bed?"

I sighed with a combination of exhaustion and contentment. "That sounds wonderful, but I'm almost too tired to climb up the stairs."

"Then I guess I'll have to carry you," he said in a husky voice, lifting his hand to the back of my head and pulling my hair free from my ponytail.

"Then maybe I shouldn't have had that piece of cake on my break. You'll never hoist me up the stairs now," I teased. Then I heaved a sigh. I hated that I always had to steer our conversation back to serious topics, but David had a right to know what was going on. "Something happened on the way home."

He stiffened slightly. "And what was that?"

"I met a demon in the middle of the road." I shook my head and grimaced. "That sounds like the beginning of a bad joke."

His eyes widened and he ran his hands up my arms, checking me for any injuries. "Are you okay?"

"I'm fine. There was no confrontation. Not really." I couldn't blame him for worrying. Some of my recent encounters had left me physically injured. David too. He still had a slight limp from our battle with the two rabid spirits Collin and I had ultimately destroyed.

"Then what happened? Which one was it?"

"That's the odd part," I said. "I asked her for her name and she never gave it to me. They always seem eager to identify themselves, like their names are their calling cards."

"*Her?* You knew it was a female?"

I wasn't surprised by the question. Most of the spirits I'd met were animals. "It was an old woman. I would have thought she was just any old woman, nothing special, if it weren't for her glowing red eyes."

"What did she look like?"

I described her, but David's brow stayed lowered, his mouth pursed. I could tell that he didn't recognize her from his research. "Did she say what she wanted?"

"To tell me my future."

"*What?*"

"I told her that I didn't want to hear it, but she pushed on anyway."

"And what did she say?"

I took a deep breath. "She said I was a vessel that would either save the world or destroy it, and that it would happen soon."

He sagged back in his seat, his arm still around me. "Bollocks."

"Yeah. Exactly."

"Did she mention Okeus?"

A shiver ran down my spine. Obviously, David's thoughts were headed in the same direction as mine. "No. I asked her if she had a message for me from Okeus, and she said I would see the 'Great

One' soon enough. As though he wasn't enough of a pompous ass without the new title."

His hold tightened and he sat up, burying his face into the crook of my neck. "I'm trying to figure out a way to protect you."

I lifted my hand to his face, my thumb lightly stroking his cheekbone as I stared into his hazel eyes. "I know." I gave a half shrug. "But maybe there isn't one. Maybe I'll just have to be on high alert for the rest of my life to avoid getting ravaged by him." I couldn't bring myself to say "raped." Okeus had indicated at our last meeting that forcing himself on me was option number two if I didn't willingly comply. "You would think the tattoo of Ahone's mark on my back would protect my uterus along with my Manitou."

"Alas, they are two very obviously different things. While your soul is *yours*, your uterus could harbor a life with its own soul."

"I love how we're rambling on about my uterus. It's so romantic. Just what you want to do with your boyfriend. Next thing you know, we'll be discussing my menstrual cycle," I grumbled.

"That might not be a bad idea," he said. "Maybe you shouldn't leave the house when you're ovulating."

"I'm done with this conversation." I started to get up, but he pulled me back down. "Besides, I'm on the pill now. Ovulation isn't an issue." But could that stop a god? How much control did Okeus actually have over worldly events?

"Maybe we can convince Okeus that you won't provide the perfect baby for him."

I laughed, leaning my forehead against his. "You mean like how irresponsible I am and what a terrible mother I would be?"

He placed a gentle kiss on my lips, then looked into my eyes. "No, more like trying to convince him that you're incompatible DNA-wise."

I groaned in frustration. "DNA was never the issue with the other women he used, David."

He shook his head slowly. "I completely disagree. Okeus seems to think he was too powerful for the women who gave birth to his monstrosities. He thinks your Curse Keeper blood and power, along with the fact that you're a witness to creation, will make you strong enough to give birth to a child who inherits both your powers. But what if we can convince him that he's wrong?"

I gave him a blank stare. "You want to convince a malevolent, egotistical, arrogant god that he's wrong?" I climbed out of his lap and shook my head. "Good luck with that, David. I'm going to bed."

He stood and grabbed my hand, twining our fingers together. "Ellie, don't get frustrated with me," he said, sounding tired. "I'm doing my best."

I felt like a bitch. After being out in the heat all day working at the colony site, he'd returned home to help with the bed and breakfast. Then he had spent the rest of the evening researching for information to help me. I locked my hands around the back of his neck and rested my cheek on his chest. "I'm sorry. You deserve better."

"Ellie." He tilted my chin up so I was looking into his face. "We're both exhausted." He paused and his eyes turned serious. "Why don't you quit working at the restaurant? My university salary isn't a lot, but it's enough to cover our expenses here. Especially if I sublet my house in Chapel Hill."

I released a heavy sigh. "We've discussed this before. You don't owe me anything. I can't let you do that. It's bad enough that you're working at the inn when I'm not here. Not to mention the money you spent buying back my father's pocket watch."

"You're protecting humanity," he said with a small smile. "The financial strain shouldn't fall squarely on your shoulders."

"And it shouldn't have to fall on yours either." My voice rose in frustration. I needed to be quieter. Several researchers visiting the colony site were staying in the main house, and I didn't want to wake them.

"Ellie," he whispered gently. "It's okay."

I took a deep breath and pressed my cheek to his chest again. Just his tender voice helped center me. What would I ever do if he grew tired of me and my crankiness? I'd become so dependent on him in such a short time. I didn't know how I'd survive without him. My boss at the New Moon was awful, and I'd have loved nothing more than to quit. Still, being totally dependent on Collin had bitten me in the ass. Granted, this situation was totally different, but it was difficult enough to accept that I needed David so much emotionally—I wasn't sure I could give up my financial independence too. "I need to take care of myself."

He stroked the back of my head. "I know, love. I know. But you're getting worn out and you haven't even really had to battle anything yet. Just consider it, okay? You would have your hands more than full with the B&B."

"Okay. I'll consider it."

"Let's go to bed."

I nodded my agreement and we headed upstairs to my childhood bedroom. When I let go of my apartment and moved back home, David had suggested we sleep in Myra's room, but her things were all still there, awaiting her return in December. But I knew deep in my gut she wouldn't be back. She'd just started her dream job at Duke University—working in the history department—and had begun a relationship with one of the professors. Myra had spent the past several years caring for my father as his illness slowly stripped him away from us, so I was grateful that she had found happiness and love. She was also so much safer two hundred miles away than she would be at home. But I missed her like crazy, even if she'd been avoiding my calls lately.

After I stripped off my clothes and put on a short nightgown, I climbed into bed, snuggling into David's side.

His fingers lightly stroked my arm. "Ellie, I think you should stop taking guests in the main house, even if they are researchers."

I propped up on my elbow, searching his face, which was spot-lit by the full moon. "But we're bringing in extra money."

"I know, love, but let's be honest: it's a drop in the bucket. You said yourself you're about to go into foreclosure. What if you lose the house before finding all of the clues your father left? It's next to impossible to search when there are guests staying here."

A heaviness weighed down on my chest. He was right on both counts.

"Not to mention there's someone on the other side of this wall behind us." He laughed softly. "We have to make sure we're quiet if we want to be able to face the guests the next morning at breakfast."

"Very funny."

"You have to admit we were much more liberated in our sex life when we were living in your flat."

"My bedroom was on an outside wall."

"Exactly," he teased, lifting the edge of my nightgown. His hand slid up, over the z-shaped scar on my abdomen, tracing the under-side of my breast. "Before I forget, one of the boarders said he smelled something bad in his room. Maybe we should get someone out here to look for rodents. It could be a dead mouse or maybe a squirrel or bird that got trapped in the attic."

"Great," I grumbled. "Just what I need. To spend more money."

His fingers soon distracted me from my financial woes and had me panting with need. His lips skimmed along my neck and up to my ear. "What do you think about going out of town for a few days?" His voice was low and husky.

My eyes widened in surprise. "You're seriously suggesting a vacation? Now?"

He laughed again as his hand concentrated on making me squirm. "No, not exactly a vacation. More like a change in scenery."

"I'm listening," I forced out, trying to focus.

"You know how I've asked several of my colleagues to keep an eye out and an ear open for anything about the Ricardo Estate? Well, I heard back from one today."

I grabbed his hand to stop his torture. "What did he say?"

"*She* e-mailed tonight to tell me she'd been invited to see a collection of antiquities, and it was all very secretive."

I bolted upright. "Is it what we're looking for?"

He rolled to his side and propped his head on an elbow. "She can't be sure. She already went to see the collection in Charlotte. She said it was mostly an assortment of weapons and pocket watches. It didn't contain the candlesticks or other paraphernalia that you saw in those photos from Marino's guy."

"So it's not the estate?"

"Not necessarily. She says she saw a watch similar to your father's. I sent all of my colleagues a photo of it when I put out word about the collection."

"The four-century-old pocket watch?"

"Yeah."

That didn't make sense. "So if it *is* the Ricardo Estate, what happened to the other stuff?"

"I don't know, but there's something I should mention about Allison." He paused and waited for me to meet his eyes. "She's a history professor at Chapel Hill and she's an expert on old weaponry, particularly from the Middle Ages. The curators of the collection asked her to examine one of their swords."

"Swords? And isn't that the wrong time period?"

"She says they told her this particular sword was rumored to have been blessed by priests for a knight to carry into the Crusades."

I shook my head. "I'm confused. What would that have to do with the curse?"

"Ellie, the sword was blessed to fight *demons*."

A chill ran down my spine. "Oh, shit."

"She took several pictures of the sword. And she says she has something she thinks I'll want to see."

I fingered the gold band on my right middle finger. "What is it?"

"She wouldn't tell me."

"And you want to go see it?"

"If you're open to it. I won't go without you. I'd be sick with worry the entire time I was gone." He pulled me back down to him and placed a sweet kiss on my lips. "And I thought I'd check on my house. I haven't been back in over a month. You'll get to see where I live, and I can pack up most of my things so we can start renting the place out. Maybe we can stop and see Myra too."

I only hoped Myra would *want* to see me. "That sounds like a good idea."

His hand resumed its previous task on my breast. "So we'll go?"

"I'll have to get off work."

"If your boss won't let you off, then quit."

"David."

His mouth replaced his hand as his fingers glided over my abdomen and between my legs, making me squirm. "Promise one way or the other that you'll get off work."

"You fight dirty." But he didn't have to convince me. Wild horses couldn't keep me from going to Chapel Hill this weekend. If Allison had seen a sword capable of killing demons, I needed to figure out how to get it. And if I had to quit my job to go, maybe that was the catalyst I needed to get me out the door of the New Moon for good.

"When it comes to your safety, I'll use *all* my resources to protect you." Then he proceeded to show me how talented some of his resources were.

Long after David fell asleep, I lay awake in his arms. My mind returned once again to the old woman's premonition, and a feeling of dread weighed down my limbs and kept my eyes open late into the night.

∿ CHAPTER TWO ∿

"You can have Saturday off over my dead body," Phoebe, my new boss, said, brushing past me and heading into the back room.

I stood in the middle of the dining room of the New Moon ten minutes before we opened, wondering how that could actually be arranged. Phoebe and I had butted heads ever since I showed up two minutes late for our first mandatory staff meeting right before the reopening of the restaurant. While Marlena, my old boss, had believed in firm authority, she'd also possessed a heart. Something Phoebe Willington seemed to be without.

A sudden wave of grief and guilt washed over me. The two emotions were usually hand in hand when I thought about my old boss, who had also been my friend. She'd died because of me, because I'd refused to side with Okeus.

Now Marlena's husband was a widower and her three children were motherless. The only thing I could possibly do to make things right was to make Kanim, the bastard spirit who had killed her, pay. Only I hadn't seen Okeus's messenger spirit since Collin opened the gate at our ceremony, and I didn't know where to look. Collin had given me a map that documented the sanctuaries of a dozen Croatan spirits, along with the gate to hell—a location with which I was all too familiar. But there was no mention of the wind gods, Okeus and Ahone, or either of their messengers. David and I had visited at least half the marked sites, but always during the day. They were difficult to find since the landmarks had all changed, not that we could get too aggressive anyway. No sense flushing them out if I didn't have the means to permanently destroy them on my own. Perhaps that would all change if we could manage to secure this sword.

I followed Phoebe into the back, my voice firm. "Look, Phoebe, I know it's short notice—"

She turned to me with blazing eyes. "You're damn right it's short notice. Not to mention it's on the weekend. You already have Sunday off."

"I wouldn't ask if it wasn't important."

She shook her head. "You already have special privileges. No one else gets away with only working day shifts."

"That's bullshit and you know it. You made me work last night after I worked all day."

"And that's because Nina quit. It was a special circumstance."

"That seems to happen every week. And whose fault is that, Phoebe? Maybe if you were nicer, your employees would stick around for longer."

She put both hands on her hips. "If people bothered to do their jobs, they might keep them. And as for the answer to your question . . ." She lifted her eyebrows, her eyes bugging out like a pug's. "It's a firm *no*."

I reached for the knot that tied my apron behind my back. "Then I quit."

Her eyes narrowed. "Do you think I'm bluffing?"

"I don't care if you are or not." I pulled the apron over my head and spiked it onto the floor. "I've worked my ass off for this job, but dealing with your attitude just isn't worth it." I grabbed my purse off the desk and headed for the back door.

"Fine!" she huffed, throwing her hands into the air. "You don't have to work the night shift anymore. Ever."

"No shit, I don't," I said. "Because I just quit."

I stormed out the back door and walked until I got to the parking lot of my old apartment, sucking in deep breaths.

What had I done?

I pulled my phone out of my pocket and dialed my best friend, Claire.

"Ellie, I thought you were working today," she answered. "Is everything okay?" I didn't usually bother her when she was at her housekeeping job at the Tranquil Inn, so she knew it had to be important.

"Actually, I don't have a job anymore since I just quit."

"You did *what*?"

"I think I'm going to hyperventilate." I walked over to the wooden steps leading up to my third-floor apartment and sat down, running my hand through my hair.

"Ellie, it's just a job and your new boss is a bitch."

"But it still paid the bills. And Darrell's Restaurant will never take me back after all the times Tom showed up to question me while I was working." We'd grown up with Tom. That, along with his respect for my father, was why he cut me some slack even though there was plenty of evidence that I was tied to the strange things happening on Roanoke Island. Still, his patience was wearing thin. Especially when his intuition told him I knew more than I pretended to know. Too bad he was right.

"I thought you said David *wanted* you to quit."

"He does, but this means I'm totally dependent on him. I'm

supposed to be a strong, independent woman and now I'm just what Collin thought I was when he first showed up at the New Moon."

"An easy mark?"

"No! An opportunistic gold digger. Now David will end up paying my bills and helping float the inn."

"Oh, Ellie. There's a difference. David loves you and wants to help you."

"It's still not right."

"Okay," she murmured. "So you'll get another job. It's not the end of the world. Now tell me what's *really* going on."

My head jerked up in surprise. Sometimes I wondered if Claire knew me better than I knew myself. "Something's wrong with Myra."

"With her new job?" she asked, surprised.

"I don't know. She was fine until the day before she left, and then she started to act . . . distant. She hasn't called me in over a week, and she acts like I'm bothering her whenever I call her."

"That doesn't sound like Myra at all. Could she just be nervous about her new job? She hasn't taught in a long time and classes started this week."

"Maybe." But she'd never blown me off before, no matter how busy her schedule. "David and I are going to Chapel Hill this weekend. I think I'll drop by Durham to see her."

"Are you going there to pack up David's house?"

"Yeah, and one of his colleagues might have some information about the Ricardo Estate."

"Really? That's great." Her voice lowered. "Listen, I've got to go. I think my boss is coming down the hall. Are we still cleaning your apartment after I get off work?"

"Yeah, see you at three." I hung up and glanced up toward my apartment. Now that I didn't have a job, I could go up and clean it myself. But I'd only seen Claire twice since her return from her honeymoon in Charleston, and I couldn't ignore the fact that she'd been acting different too. While she hadn't blown me off, she *had* been more subdued than usual.

With nothing to do for several hours, I went back to the inn to help Becky. I called David to tell him that going out of town wouldn't be an issue since I quit my job. I hung up as I walked into the inn, finding Becky at the office desk.

She looked up in surprise. "Ellie! Why aren't you at work?"

I shrugged. "I guess inn keeping is my new full-time job."

Her face fell. "Does that mean you don't need me full time anymore?"

Oh, crap. I hadn't considered that. The inn could barely pay her salary and the mortgage along with the other expenses of running the place. But I couldn't count on being here all the time with my new Curse Keeper responsibilities. "No. I still need you. Tell me what still needs to be done today."

Relief washed over her face as she told me what she'd accomplished while I was gone.

After I did laundry and some long-overdue deep cleaning, I realized it was almost time for me to meet Claire. I grabbed a bottle of water and stepped out into the August heat to walk to my apartment.

When I stepped onto the third-floor landing, I stared at the now-bare front door. It looked naked without all the symbols Collin and I had marked on it.

Claire was waiting for me in one of the plastic chairs on the front porch, watching me with a wistfulness I hadn't expected.

"I forgot about those chairs," I said as I moved toward her. "I'm not sure I want to drag them several blocks to the house."

Claire shrugged, lifting a bottle of beer to her lips. "Toss 'em in the Dumpster. They cost less than ten bucks at Walmart, not to mention they're tacky."

"What are you doing outside? You have a key."

She stared at the door for several seconds. "It's too sad and creepy in there now that it's empty."

"Creepier than my father's house?"

She cocked an eyebrow, her dark brown eyes bright with amusement, but there was some heavier emotion behind them. "That's a telling phrase right there—your *father's* house."

I released a sigh. "You know what I mean."

"Why are you doing this, Ellie? You hate that house."

"I don't hate it. It just makes me uncomfortable."

"Well, no shit!" she shouted, waving her hand in the air. "Maybe you should listen to your instincts. Your mother was murdered there. You recently found out that the killer had you trapped in your closet. You were eight years old, Ellie. Eight!" she said, her eyes blazing. "Why are you doing this?"

"Because someone needs to take care of the inn."

"That's bullshit. What's the real reason?"

"Because Daddy hid notes to me in the house and I have to find them."

"And have you found any since you banished those evil badgers?"

I scowled. "No." I turned toward the door and put the key into the doorknob. "We need to clean my apartment. I want to be home when David gets back from work."

"Ellie. It's me, Claire. I know you better than probably anyone alive. What's the real reason?"

Tears filled my eyes. "I let him down, Claire." My voice broke. "I have to try and save it."

She leaned forward and grabbed my wrist, guiding me to the chair next to hers. Then she reached under her seat and grabbed a paper bag that I hadn't noticed. After pulling out a second bottle of beer, she popped the top off and handed it to me. "Here."

I took a long sip, then placed the cold bottle against my chest to help me cool off. "You came prepared."

She took a drink from her bottle and shrugged. "I was going to make you talk one way or another. Getting you drunk was Plan B."

"And Plan A?"

She grinned. "*Asking* you."

I chuckled softly and took another drink. Claire was right. She knew me better than anyone. Being best friends with someone for fifteen years wasn't for nothing.

"You seriously think you let him down?" she asked.

"Of course I did. In every conceivable way. I refused to relearn the curse after Momma's murder. If only I'd listened to him—"

Her hand covered mine, her eyes pleading. "Ellie. Enough. We've rehashed this every which way left of Sunday. *Woulda, coulda, shoulda.* We all have things we wish we'd done differently, but what good does it do us to dwell?"

"Maybe Marlena wouldn't be dead right now if I'd known enough to figure out what Collin was up to. Maybe Daddy would still be alive too."

"That's bullshit and you know it." She took another drink. "How in the world could you have stopped Okeus's lackey from killing Marlena? And Ahone demanded a sacrifice—your father. All the knowledge in the world wouldn't have prevented either of their deaths."

"I have to blame someone, Claire."

"Fine, then blame Collin. Blame Okeus. Blame Ananias Dare and his cohort, Manteo. But stop blaming yourself, because that's just bollocks, as your Brit likes to say."

I grinned. "I'm quite fond of my Brit."

"No wonder. He's hot and he's great in bed."

My mouth dropped open in protest. "I *never* said he's great in bed."

"I know. I'm reading between the lines. You've told me all about all the awful experiences you've had. The fact that you won't tell me a thing about sex with David speaks volumes."

"I never told you about sex with Collin either."

She lifted her beer bottle in salute. "Exactly."

I laughed and we drank the rest of our beers. Once we were done, Claire pulled out two more bottles, then stopped, her gaze drifting down the landing toward my neighbor's door.

"What are you looking at?"

She shook her head and handed me the drink. "Nothing."

"We're supposed to be cleaning," I said, taking the proffered beer and checking out the door that had caught her attention. Claire was lying to me, but for the life of me, I couldn't figure out why.

"Your apartment isn't going anywhere," she said, but she didn't sound happy. "I seriously think you should reconsider."

"It's too late, Claire. My landlord has already rented it out."

We were quiet again, the silence more heavy this time. "Tell me more about your honeymoon," I finally said. "You've been home for two weeks and every time I ask you about it, you change the subject."

She shot me a grin, but she looked somehow nervous, a first considering that she was a chronic oversharer. "Now who's trying to get sexual exploit details?"

"*Please.* You're the queen of TMI. But that's not what I'm asking and you know it. Tell me about Charleston. You've been dying to go there your entire life and you finally got to go. What was it like? Were the ghost tours fun?"

She took another sip from her bottle. "We need to take care of your apartment."

"Claire. You and Myra have something in common: you're both acting strange. Her since she moved and you since you came back from your honeymoon. If I wasn't full of so much self-confidence, I might start getting paranoid," I teased.

She was silent for several seconds, her face turning pale.

Oh, shit. Something was wrong. "Did you and Drew have a fight?"

She shook her head with a wry smile. "No. Drew is perfect."

"Then what happened?"

She leaned forward, fear in her eyes. "Promise me that you won't think I'm crazy."

"Are you serious? You're one of the sanest people I know. You keep *me* sane. How could I think you're crazy?"

She nodded, pressing her lips together in concentration.

"So tell me what happened."

"Drew and I went on a ghost tour the second night we were there. The tour guide was lame. In fact, I was kind of bored. I kept thinking how I would have done it differently." I didn't find that surprising since Claire ran ghost tours in downtown Manteo. Hers were always quite entertaining.

"And which part of that is crazy?"

She took a long pull on her beer. "The Unitarian Cemetery was part of the tour, but we didn't even get to go in. The tour was at night and the cemetery was closed. When we were about ten feet away from the gate, something happened." She paused and chewed on her thumbnail. "One minute I was in the hot, muggy evening air, and the next a cold chill hit me, like I'd walked into a freezer."

Fear crawled up my spine.

"The closer I got, the colder it became. The tour guide's voice faded and a figure appeared. A woman. But she wasn't really there."

Oh, God. Were the demons going after Claire now? Had they actually followed my friend on her honeymoon? "Did she try to hurt you?"

"No." She swallowed, refusing to look at me. "She was wearing an old-fashioned dress, long and flowing, and her hair was pulled back. She was pretty, but she looked sad. She was watching me from the other side of the locked gate. As the guide started to lead the tour away, I approached the gate, and . . . that was when she spoke to me."

"What did she say?"

"She said, 'It's time to wake up.' Then she vanished into thin air."

"What does that mean? Wake up?"

She didn't answer my question. "I was pretty shaken up, but we were still on that stupid tour. Drew knew immediately that something was wrong. He even stood at the gate next to me, but he didn't see her—the ghost."

"You think you saw a *ghost*?"

She stiffened. "You don't believe me."

My eyes flew open in astonishment. "How can you say that? After everything that I've seen, that you've seen with me. Of course I believe you. I'm just scared for you. They're coming after you now." My worst nightmare was coming true. I should have made Claire leave Manteo like Myra. Everyone close to me was in danger.

"No, Ellie," she said, shaking her head. "She didn't want to hurt me. She was trying to help me."

That didn't make sense. "Why do you think it was a ghost? And what did she mean about it being time to wake up?"

She sucked in her top lip between her teeth. "When I was little . . . I used to hear things. Voices."

Something stirred deep inside my head. The flutter of a memory trying to break free. Then it dove below the surface, out of reach.

"I heard them when I was little, but soon after we moved to Manteo, they went away."

"Around the time Momma was killed."

Claire's face paled. "How did you know that?"

I shook my head, feeling light-headed. "I don't know." But I knew it was true.

"I told you about the voices when we were little," she whispered. "The day you told me about the curse after school. Your mother got a phone call that made her upset. She was crying. You'd told me the truth about the curse before she came home, and I felt like I should share something with you too. I hated to see you so upset. So I told you, scared to death you'd think I was crazy or lying, but you didn't. At least not that day."

I closed my eyes and leaned back against the chair. "The memory is there. I can feel it, but when I try to remember, it's like I'm reaching for water that's running through my fingers."

"After your mom died, I mentioned something about the voices I heard, and you looked at me like I was crazy. I figured you didn't want to talk about it."

"No, Claire. I don't remember it at all. It disappeared with all memories of the curse. I don't even remember Momma taking a phone call or getting upset. Before my dreams and everything started to come back, the only thing I remember about that day is that I told you about the curse while we were sitting under the oak tree at the side of the house."

"So you really *didn't* remember me telling you about the voices?"

I shook my head.

Her eyes widened. "I can see you forgetting everything about the curse, but why would you forget the other things? Was it trauma, or something else?"

"I don't know."

"Ellie, she said something else before she disappeared."

Oh, lord. After seeing the old woman last night and finding out that Claire could see ghosts, I wasn't sure how much more I could take. "What?"

"She said, 'You have to help her.'"

"What does that mean?" My voice rose. I was starting to panic and I didn't even know why.

"You *know* what it means." She leaned forward. "And why are you freaking out?"

"I don't know." I stood up and reached for the doorknob. "Let's get started. I need to finish up here soon so I can get home to David."

Claire followed me inside, where the emptiness of the apartment was still a shock to my system. "Ellie, why are you running away from this?"

I spun around and glared at her. "Why did you wait almost two weeks to tell me?"

"I was worried about how you would react."

"Why?"

She waved her hand at me. "Maybe this is why."

My anger faded and my shoulders slumped.

"Ellie, talk to me. Why are you freaking out?"

"I'm scared, Claire. I'm scared for you. If something happens to you—"

"Nothing's going to happen to me."

I shook my head, my anger resurfacing. "You don't know that! The more involved you are, the more at risk you are."

Claire closed the distance between us and grabbed my arms. "Ellie, I'm not going anywhere." Her eyebrows rose in mock surprise when I gasped. "What? You don't think I can see what you're doing? First sending Myra to Durham—"

"Myra wanted to go to Durham!"

"Don't tell me that you weren't happy to send her off."

Tears stung my eyes. "How can you say that? I love Myra."

"I know you do! And the way I said it came out wrong. I know you were trying to protect her, but I also know you've been trying to figure out how to distance yourself from me too."

"I love you, Claire. I have to protect you."

She shook her head. "Maybe I'm supposed to protect *you*. Just like David's trying to do. We're not Curse Keepers, but we have other ways of helping. And don't get it into your head that we're not meant to be involved. What do you think, that the professor whose help you were seeking just *happened* to show up in Manteo to work at the colony site? That I just *happened* to hear ghosts who know about you and your role as Curse Keeper?"

My mouth moved like a fish trying to breathe as I struggled with what to say.

"Things happen for a reason, Ellie. Yeah, Collin-fucking-Dailey won't help you, but that doesn't mean you have to be alone. Maybe *we're* meant to help you."

I shook my head, trying to make sense of her words. "How?"

"You need to listen to me. I'm telling you that you shouldn't be living in that house. There's a darkness there."

Sweat prickled the back of my neck. "I thought you just heard voices?"

Her face softened. "That was when I was little . . . now I can see things too. Like that ghost. Something changed after we got home from Charleston. Whenever I look at the house, it's covered in a hazy darkness."

"You're scaring me, Claire."

"*Good*. You should be scared. There's something dark in that house. Maybe that's why you've felt uncomfortable there since the curse broke. It's because you shouldn't be there at all."

I knew there was some truth to what she said. Ever since the curse broke, I'd felt something bad in the house, mostly in my bedroom. But over the last week, I had felt something ominous in *both* houses. As long as David or someone else was with me, I could handle it. But I couldn't bear to be there alone. "What am I supposed to do? I gave up my apartment. I have nowhere else to go."

"Ellie, you're about to lose the house anyway. Find somewhere else to live. And whatever you do, don't stay there without David." Claire hesitated. "She says you need him."

"*Who* says I need him?"

She sucked in her top lip. "I see ghosts all the time now. When you asked me what I saw outside that other apartment just now, it was a ghost. An old guy wandering around in his bathrobe, holding a newspaper and a cup of coffee."

My eyes widened. "Mr. Murphy. He liked to walk around in his robe. He died about two weeks after I moved in here. That was four years ago." I took a deep breath. Why was this freaking me out? After everything else I'd seen, ghosts should have been nothing.

"He's pissed that someone is living in his apartment. He says she doesn't keep it clean enough."

I stared at Claire, wide-eyed. "How many do you see?"

"Some days one or two. Yesterday I saw ten."

"And you're not scared?"

"No. Unlike your demons, the ghosts seem harmless. But not all of them are fully formed. Some are blobs—kind of like when we saw Kanim. From what I can tell, the longer they've been dead, the more I can see of them."

"And the ghost that thinks I need David? Can you see her?"

29

"No. She's a blur, not even a blob yet. She started making sounds a few days ago, and yesterday was the first time I could string the words together. But I've figured out enough to know that she's worried about you and wants you to leave."

"How do you even know you can trust the voices, Claire? What if this person is somehow working with Okeus?"

"I just know that we can. Call it instinct."

I headed for the kitchen and started opening cabinets to make sure they were empty. "Well, then you must be happy that David and I are heading to Chapel Hill for the weekend."

"Relieved." She leaned her hands on the bar. "Then you can find somewhere else to live when you get back."

A movement in the open front door caught my attention.

"Why are we looking for somewhere else to live?" David asked.

I bugged my eyes at Claire in warning, then turned to face David. "What are you doing here?"

"I missed you." He moved toward me with a mischievous grin. "I wondered what was taking you so long, and then I saw the empty bottles on the porch."

"Busted," Claire said with a laugh.

David pulled me into a hug. "I figured I'd come and help, and then we can grab something to eat before heading back." He looked over my head at Claire. "And why do we need to find somewhere else to live? And no, I'm not so easily veered off topic."

I'd discovered that firsthand when David started asking questions about the marks on my door a month ago.

She glanced from my pleading face to David's. "Oh, you know. It has to be difficult for Ellie to live in the house where she grew up."

"You mean the house where she suffered a horrible trauma?" David was quiet for several seconds when Claire didn't give him an answer. "We'll definitely keep that in mind. Now what do we need to do to finish up here?"

We spent the next half hour cleaning. When we were done, I stood in the doorway and spent a moment surveying the only place that had ever been completely mine. I had to wonder if Claire was right. I knew I should tell David the whole story—that she *wanted* me to tell him—but there was someone I needed to talk to first. I hadn't seen him in weeks, and just the thought of it made me nervous.

Before I left for Chapel Hill, I needed to talk to Collin.

↶ Chapter Three ↷

The next morning I texted Collin. It felt wrong and underhanded, but I knew it was the right thing to do. Although I had a hard time convincing myself of that fact since I was hiding my plan from David. We had promised not to keep secrets from each other. I justified my decision by telling myself that I'd tell David everything after I talked to Collin. For some reason, I felt the need to get his take on the situation before putting it out in the open. If Claire really could see ghosts, if they really did want her to help me, it might be a game changer.

Of course, I ran the very real risk of Collin refusing to tell me anything at all. But he knew much more than I did about demons and spirits, and his expertise in the supernatural might extend to ghosts. It was worth asking.

I composed the text after I put two breakfast casseroles in the oven and quickly sent it before I could change my mind.

Something's come up. I need to talk to you as soon as possible.

I wasn't sure the last part of the second sentence was necessary, but I wanted answers before we left for Chapel Hill later in the afternoon.

David walked into the kitchen and poured himself a cup of coffee. "Is Becky okay with running the inn this weekend?"

I shoved my phone into my jeans pocket. "Yeah. She's happy to do it. She really likes the added responsibility."

He kissed me and then looked around the kitchen. "Anything I can do to help?"

"Nope. Got it under control. It's not so humid this morning. If you want, you can take your coffee out to the front porch before you leave for work."

His forehead wrinkled. "And leave you in here working? Not likely. Besides, I'll have plenty of time outside today." He sat on a stool in the corner and studied me for a moment. "I've been thinking about what Claire said. Have you called Myra yet to arrange a time to meet her?"

"No," I murmured, not looking at him. "I haven't had a chance." But that wasn't why I hadn't called. Considering the way she'd been brushing me off lately, I was worried how she would react to a suggested visit. What if she'd decided she preferred her new life without me? I wasn't sure I could bear it.

"And Claire said a lot of things," I said, wiping a counter and avoiding eye contact. My guilt over texting Collin was already eating at me. "Especially after Drew joined us for dinner and she and I split a bottle of wine."

"I really like Drew. He seems like a good bloke."

"Yeah, I like him too. We've been friends for even longer than Claire and me. Did you know that Drew's had a crush on Claire since she first moved to town in the third grade?"

"You've mentioned that about ten times, and I'm talking about when Claire said we should find somewhere else to live." He quirked an eyebrow before taking a sip of his coffee. "I'm on to you, love. I know when you're trying to steer the conversation in a different direction."

I rested my butt against the counter to watch him. "She's just being a protective best friend."

"I know. But I can't help wondering if she's right."

I released a heavy sigh. "David."

"No, hear me out. I know you hate your bedroom, but we're staying in there anyway since you refuse to invade Myra's room. Let's give the boarders notice, search the house from top to bottom again, then put the property up for sale."

My muscles tensed. "You want me to give up on it just like that?"

He cringed. "I didn't mean to put it so flippantly."

"This house has belonged to my family for over one hundred years. My father did everything he could to save it. What would he think of me if I just left?"

"Ellie, the way I see it, you have two choices: you can either be an innkeeper or you can be the Curse Keeper. The inn is a distraction for you. You constantly worry about money and making sure the guests are happy. It's draining you. You can't deny it."

I stayed silent.

"If your father were here right now, you *know* which one he'd choose."

I pushed away from the counter and moved to the sink. "I don't want to talk about it."

David got off his stool and pressed his chest against my back. "I'm sorry. I don't mean to push you. You don't have to make any decisions now. In fact, let's use this weekend to try to distance ourselves from all of this as much as possible."

"While we go to Chapel Hill to talk to your colleague about a sword that kills demons," I said dryly as I spun around to face him.

"Point taken." He kissed my forehead but then drew back. "There's something I need to tell you."

My gaze lifted to study his face, my stomach knotting. "Conversations that start with 'there's something I need to tell you' never lead to anything good. Should I be worried?"

A soft smile spread across his face. "Ellie, how can you doubt that I love you? I know I haven't said it since—"

Since he had told me several times without any reciprocation. "Stop." I put my fingers on his lips. "You don't have to say it. It's just that I'm not the easiest person to live with. If you decided—"

"Ellie, I love you. I promised you that I'm not going anywhere, and I meant it. Please rid yourself of any worry to the contrary."

"Okay." I gave him a gentle kiss. "So what did you want to tell me?"

"About some research I've dug up. As I mentioned last week, I expanded my search to include possible fringe group interest in recent supernatural activity."

"You mean the crazy conspiracy theory people?" I asked skeptically.

"Yeah, the people who aren't afraid to think outside the box."

"And I take it you found something?"

"Maybe." He paused. "There's a group called the Guardians. They say they've been around for hundreds of years. They've been preparing for a surge of demons to be released upon the earth."

"You mean the apocalypse."

"Think about it—the breaking of the curse could be seen as the apocalypse by a lot of people."

"If you ignore the fact that half the people on the earth didn't disappear in the rapture."

"Many fundamentalist Christians estimate that only a quarter of the population would be raptured."

My eyes narrowed. "The fact that you can spout that without blinking an eye scares me more than a little bit."

"It's on their website. And this group doesn't believe in the rapture anyway. Not all Christians do, you know."

I'd spent a fair amount of time in church growing up, and we'd never been told anything about the rapture, but demon attacks hadn't come up either. "You must think there's something there if you're mentioning this group."

"I had to do a lot of digging, but I finally found out where they're from." His eyes turned serious. "Ellie, they're based in Charlotte." Just like the stash of antiquities that might be the Ricardo Estate.

I felt like I'd been kicked in the gut as I backed into the counter behind me. "That can't be a coincidence."

"I agree. There's been an upsurge in online activity for the group. As well as mention of new interesting developments in the last month or so." He paused. "I'd like to stay for a couple extra days. I want to go to Charlotte on Monday to look into this some more. Do you think Becky will be okay with taking point at the inn while we're gone?"

I nodded, my stomach churning. "Yeah."

"Are you okay? You look like you've seen a ghost."

His words reminded me of Claire, which in turn made me think of my text to Collin. Guilt quickly replaced my shock. "This is good. It's our first solid lead on who's in possession of the Ricardo Estate." I shook my head. "I don't know why I'm so upset."

"It's understandable. After all, we think there's a tie between the people behind the Ricardo Estate and your mother's death." He gripped my shoulders and lowered his gaze to my eyes. "Word of warning, love: the closer we get to the truth, the more difficult this is going to get, emotionally and otherwise."

"Yeah, you're right." I smiled up at him. "I'm fine. I promise."

"How about you let Becky do the rest of the work today? You could use some time to relax. I'll be back by three. If you're ready to go when I get back, we'll have plenty of time to get to my house before dark so you can mark the doors."

"Oh." I hadn't considered that. Sloppy on my part.

He gently kissed my lips, his tenderness catching me by surprise. "I think I'll take off for work now and get an early start. Come out to the site if you'd like. Text me first and I'll meet you at the entrance."

"Thanks. I'll think about it."

"And don't forget to call Myra. I know her behavior has been upsetting, but she's probably just distracted by all the changes in her life. I'm sure she'll be thrilled to see you." My eyebrows lifted in surprise and he shot me a grin. "Like I told you, I know you by now. *Call her.*"

As I watched him go, I thought about his parting words. He was right about Myra. I decided to give her a call and leave her a message if she didn't answer. A small part of me hoped she wouldn't. It would hurt too much if she rejected me.

Myra answered on the third ring. "Ellie, what a surprise." While she didn't sound like herself, she didn't sound as cold as she had recently.

"Hey, Myra. How's the new job going?"

"Oh, you know . . . keeping me busy."

I waited for her to ask about my life, but she stayed silent. Trying to keep the disappointment out of my voice, I said, "David and I are coming to Chapel Hill this weekend. He's meeting with a colleague to discuss some things. I thought maybe we could come see you. I'd love to see your new apartment."

"Well, I'm fairly busy this weekend."

Tears burned my eyes. Myra might have been my stepmother, but she'd spent more years with me than my biological mother. Myra had been the one to help me navigate the minefields of middle school and high school. She'd always sworn that while I may not have been born from her body, I was part of her heart. And now she wanted nothing to do with me. "Myra, have I done something to upset you?" My voice broke. I couldn't help it.

She paused for several seconds before her voice lowered. "No, Ellie. I'm sorry. I've been insensitive. I just have a lot going on." Her words were gentle and soft. "Of course I'll make time for you. Why don't you call me when you get to Chapel Hill and we'll figure out a time."

"Okay."

"I have to go. We'll have a nice chat this weekend. Bye." She hung up and I stared at the dead phone. Why hadn't she told me that she loved me? I shook my head. She was probably on her way to a class or something. I was making too much of this.

To get my mind off Myra, I decided to figure out my day. One, I needed to talk to Collin, and two, I needed to reexamine my treasure chest of trinkets—which included Daddy's pocket watches and the gold engraved ring I wore, which I'd found buried under the oak tree in the yard. It couldn't be a coincidence that my mother had been murdered a week after being asked to examine the contents of a collection called the Ricardo Estate. Especially when I took into account that a thug in Buxton thought I was part of something he called "the Ricardo deal." His goon had cornered me after finding my father's pocket watch collection and showed me a photo of an almost identical watch from the Ricardo Estate. Now David's colleague had recently seen a watch similar to Daddy's.

Coincidence?

My mother's death had happened years ago, so figuring out the circumstances seemed less important than wrestling actual demons, but as David had pointed out soon after agreeing to help me, there weren't any coincidences in this thing. And while her murder was a long time ago, she was my *mother*, and it was difficult to let go with so many unanswered questions. I needed closure. Nevertheless, I was clueless about how it all wove together. I hoped we'd get more answers this weekend.

My cell phone dinged. I picked up the phone and nearly choked when I read the text message.

I'm always here for you, Ellie. When?

What a fucking lie. He knew so much about the curse and its background, yet he refused to share any of that information with me. Instead, he used it as bargaining material, parceling out little bits at a time. But I had to admit that he seemed to have experienced a change of attitude the last time we saw each other, at Claire's wedding reception. He'd given me the map and he'd given me his blessing to be with David. Maybe he'd changed.

In person. Anytime today.

His answer came seconds later.

Noon. The foot of the Nags Head Pier.

I stared at my phone for several seconds, wrestling with my conscience. David wasn't the jealous type, and he'd actually called Collin to ask for his help when we were fighting the demon badgers Ukinim and Ilena. The cold hard truth was that I'd probably be dead if Collin hadn't helped us. I knew David wouldn't have a problem with me meeting Collin, so why didn't I want to tell him?

Okay

Despite David's suggestion that I take the day off, I spent the rest of the morning helping Becky clean the rooms in the inn and tidy the bathrooms in the main house. I just couldn't lie around while she was working. It didn't seem right, even if she was getting paid. Plus, working helped keep my mind partially busy. At eleven thirty, I checked my reflection in the mirror. I was wearing a pale-green sundress that made my hazel eyes greener than usual, and my long dark red hair was arranged in a loose French braid. My makeup was minimal—some mascara, a little bit of eye shadow, and blush. The brightness of my gaze gave me second thoughts. My bond to Collin was strong, and I found it difficult to resist him when he pursued me. I just needed to keep David first and foremost in my mind while the two of us were together.

The traffic wasn't bad crossing the bridge off Roanoke Island toward Nags Head, so the trip was short. The closer I got to the ocean, the antsier I became. My bond to Collin wasn't the only pull I had experienced since the curse broke. The ocean called to me, begging me to touch it. As the Dare Curse Keeper, I was the daughter of the sea. I had always been drawn to the ocean, ever since I was a girl, but after the breaking of the curse, the pull was irresistible at times.

I arrived five minutes early and parked in the public lot, where I was surprised to see that Collin's beat-up old pickup truck was already in a space. After locking my purse in the trunk, I walked toward the pier.

Collin was waiting at the edge of the parking lot at the entrance to the pier restaurant. I stopped in my tracks, the sight of him sending an overwhelming yearning shooting through my body.

I still wanted him.

I'd been drawn to him from the beginning. It had been hard to admit that to myself when we first met; he'd acted so egotistical and arrogant, making no secret of the fact that he couldn't stand me. But my attraction had taken root the moment we saw each other.

He had felt the same undeniable draw, and when we finally slept together, Collin Dailey had been imprinted on my very soul. But our connection was more powerful than that. He was the literal other half of me. I was the daughter of the sea and he was the son of the earth—the yin and yang of the curse—and I couldn't help but wonder if our strong mutual attraction was a chemistry that went back to the curse itself.

He watched me, his face expressionless. He carried two bags and had a blanket tucked under his arm. His dark hair was shorter than the last time I'd seen him, and he was tanner too. Short stubble covered his face. He wore a pair of khaki shorts and a V-neck white T-shirt, and he looked sexier than I'd ever seen him.

Turn around and go home, Ellie.

That's what I knew I should do, but my feet disagreed, and I took several steps toward him, stopping several paces away.

"You look beautiful, Ellie."

I swallowed a burning lump in my throat. This was why I couldn't be around Collin very often—not because of how drawn to him I was, but because I knew I could never be with him. David wasn't the reason for that; Collin himself was. "Thank you." I forced a smile, my eyes tearing up. "You look good too."

His mouth pinched and I could see an inner battle wage in his eyes before he reached out his right hand—the circle and square burned into his palm clearly visible—and took my left hand, linking our fingers together. "Come sit with me."

I nodded my consent and we walked fifty feet south of the pier until Collin stopped and released my hand, then set his bags down and spread out the blanket.

"Have a seat, Ellie."

I kicked off my flip-flops at the edge of the blanket and walked to the center, tucking my legs to the side as I sat down. Collin lowered himself next to me, grabbed one of the bags, and pulled out two foil-wrapped sandwiches.

He handed me one, flashing his cocky Collin grin. "I knew I could get you to eat lunch with me if I held out long enough."

I took the sandwich and released a soft laugh. "I didn't know you'd been trying."

He was reaching into the bag again when he stopped mid-gesture and looked into my face with a sadness that ripped my soul to shreds.

"And I didn't say lunch," I said. "Just that I needed to see you."

He shrugged. "So I improvised." He pulled out two bottles of water and set one next to me.

I opened the sandwich and the smell of a bacon cheeseburger filled my nose, making my stomach growl. I took a bite and couldn't contain my groan of appreciation.

Collin laughed. "They say the way to a woman's heart is through her stomach."

I shook my head and chuckled. "That's a *man*."

We looked out onto the crashing ocean waves for several seconds in silence, both eating our sandwiches, so much like our last night in Morehead City. The night before everything fell apart. I had expected to be more anxious around him. I'd expected more animosity from him despite the fact that the last time we'd met had been on civil terms. What I hadn't expected was this sense of peace. My yearning was still there, but this time I had it under control. It just felt good to be with him.

"When was the last time you were in the ocean?" he asked, keeping his gaze on the horizon.

"Last week."

"You need to visit it more, Ellie. It's a part of you now." His voice was soft and noncondemning.

"It's hard to get over here, even though it's just a fifteen- to twenty-minute drive. When you take into account that I lose anywhere from fifteen minutes to an hour when I zone out every time I come . . ." My voice trailed off in frustration.

"You wouldn't spend as much time in the water if you came more often. It gives you power. And if you're losing that much time, you're using more energy than you're getting."

"This Curse Keeper gig didn't come with an instruction manual, Collin. At least not for me." Ordinarily it would have come out as an accusation, but today it was laced with exhaustion.

Collin's hand covered mine. "I know."

His touch was comforting, and although I knew I should pull away, I couldn't make myself do it.

"I've been thinking about what you said when I took you out on the boat, about me keeping things from you so you'd keep coming back to see me." He paused, then stared into my eyes. "I think there might be some truth to it, but it's more complicated than that." He offered me a wry smile. "I've partially done it to protect you."

"Hiding things from me won't protect me. It puts me in more danger. I have no idea what to expect, and that could get me killed."

Collin stiffened and started to say something before stopping himself. "Why did you want to see me?"

He changed the subject. He still wasn't willing to fill me in on everything. Bitter disappointment seeped into my blood. "Do you know anything about people being able to see ghosts?"

He hesitated. "Why do you ask?"

My anger, dormant for longer than I'd expected, rushed to the surface. "For once would you just answer a *goddamned question*?"

His jaw clenched and I wondered if he was going to get up and walk away, but he blew out a breath instead. "Yes. I've heard of it. But contrary to what people believe, it's not that common."

"Are the ghosts good or bad? And how would someone know if they were ghosts and not spirits or demons?"

"I told you the first day you asked about good gods and bad gods that there's good and bad in everything. People included. There are a lot of shades of gray, Ellie. Take Ahone."

Pissed, I started to get up, but Collin wrapped his hand around my wrist and pulled me back down. "For Christ's sake, you asked me a question, and then you start to storm off when you don't like the answer. Did you ever consider you might actually know more if you stuck around and listened?"

I sat back down and took several breaths to settle my anger, part of which was directed at myself. He was right.

"Okay." His hold on my wrist loosened, but he didn't let go. "Ahone isn't all good, Ellie. He made you sacrifice your father, for fuck's sake."

My simmering temper exploded again and I turned to him, livid. "That was your fault, Collin! You broke the curse! Daddy never would have died if you had left things alone."

A tourist family gave me curious looks as they walked by, but kept moving.

Collin watched me and waited until they passed. His face softened. "You asked me why I broke the curse. Do you remember what I said?"

My anger clung to me like a familiar friend. "You said you wanted it done! That your family had paid the price, but you didn't give a shit about my family."

"Ellie." His voice lowered and there was no anger in it, only regret. "Did you ever wonder why I walked into your restaurant that day? Or how I knew where to find you? Did you wonder how I had the henna supplies ready the day I took you to Buxton?"

My mouth opened and then closed without emitting any sound.

"I didn't just come up with this on my own, Ellie. Granted, I hated the fucking curse, but I never considered breaking it until about two months before I did."

I blinked, amazed that he was finally opening up to me. "What happened?" I asked, my voice breathless.

"Something came to me one night while I was out on the boat." He paused and glanced out at the water. "I had already forked over a ton of money on repairs for the engine, and Marino wanted me to work some big job. I'd been resisting because I was trying to distance myself from him." He swallowed and let go of my wrist. "This ball of light appeared and told me that I could change things. That my family had been punished because of the deeds of my ancestors and that we didn't need to suffer any longer. It told me that I could make things right. All I had to do was break the curse."

"But—"

Collin turned and put his finger on my lips. "Shh. Let me finish. Then you can ask questions."

My lip tingled where he touched it and fire raced through my body. My breath came in rapid bursts as Collin's finger lightly slid along my bottom lip, his gaze pinned on my mouth. It took every ounce of restraint in me not to close the distance between our mouths. It couldn't have been more than a foot.

David. Remember David.

My expression must have changed because the longing in Collin's eyes turned to resignation. He dropped his hand and turned back to face the water. "I didn't listen at first. My job was to *protect* the curse and keep the gates closed, but the seed of doubt had been planted. And I began to wonder: What if the curse was broken and I didn't have to spend the rest of my life stuck around Roanoke Island? I could go anywhere I wanted. I could start over where Marino would never find me. After that, it was easy."

I watched the emotion battle in his eyes.

"A month or so later, the ball of light returned with its whispers about how I could make things right. This time I was willing to listen. It told me that all I had to do was find you—I already knew we had to touch our right palms together. Then the curse would break, cracking the gate open, and after six days I could seal it so that it would never open again. And the curse would be done. Forever. The light told me that I would need to protect you until the ceremony because you didn't have the mark of protection that the Manteo line wore. After the ceremony, you would be safe."

Collin ran a hand through his hair, then leaned his forearm against his upright knee. "I still wasn't sure. It went against everything I had been trained to do and believe." He sighed and closed his eyes, then slowly opened them. "That's not entirely true. My father was the Keeper before me. He was angry about his fate, and he always swore he'd break the curse someday. Then he disappeared when I was ten. He just vanished, and my mother didn't take it well. She was in and out of mental health facilities and my brother . . ."— he turned to me, his eyebrows lifted—"*Conner* and I were passed around from family member to family member when she was away."

I stared up at Collin in disbelief. I couldn't believe he was sharing so much with me.

His hand rested between us on the blanket. I placed my hand over his and he flipped it over, lacing our fingers together. I could feel strength from my body flow into his, and we weren't even touching marks.

Our power had grown.

Collin's eyes widened slightly in surprise before he continued. "I decided to get advice from my grandmother, who was the Keeper before my father. After he left, she took over responsibility for my training, teaching me everything I needed to know. She was only the third female Keeper in the Manteo line, but when I was younger, my father told me that she was the wisest of them all. I suspect he was right. She has much wisdom about the curse and life in general. She instructed me with a firm hand and made sure I believed in the importance of our task. So I went to her and told her about the ball of light. She told me not to trust it." He laughed. "Of course, I talked myself into believing it in spite of her warnings. The ball of light was telling me things I wanted to hear. So I went to Conner and asked what he thought. He told me that if I was conversing with talking balls of light, I was crazier than our mother. But I think a tiny part of him believed." He grimaced. "Or was afraid not to believe. Rosalina was Conner's girlfriend and I knew she had access to henna supplies. After the wind god Wapi almost stole your Manitou, I knew I needed to step up to keep you safe. So I went to Rosalina. Conner had already warned her that I was going to come by for supplies, so she had them ready.

"By then I knew I'd fucked up and fucked up big, but the gate was open and I only had to keep you safe until the sixth day. Then we'd shut the gate and that would be that. But when Wapi attacked you in the ocean, I knew that the ball of light had lied."

"What did you expect, Collin?" My tone was hateful and condescending. "Okeus is a liar. He'd do anything to get what he wanted. Besides, you told me that Okeus bribed you to keep the gate *open*, not closed."

Collin stared into my face with more patience than usual. "Okeus is a *god*, Ellie, and gods are by definition self-centered, egotistical beings who will do whatever they have to do to get what they want."

"You're defending Okeus again? After everything you just told me?"

My hand was still linked with Collin's and he grabbed my other hand, searching my eyes. "After you had your vision of creation in the ocean, you told me the gate wasn't thrown open all the way when you and I met, that it was only partially open and only a few spirits were let loose."

"So? Okeus lied again. Why are you surprised?"

"*Ellie*, you told me who escaped that day. Okeus hadn't."

The blood drained from my head. "What?"

"You told me that two spirits and one god escaped when we cracked the gate. Who was the god?"

"Wapi," I whispered, horror washing over me.

"The ball of light came to me *before* the curse broke. Before the spirits and god were released. Four hundred years ago only one god escaped being trapped in Popogusso by the curse, and he ascended to the heavens to wait for hundreds of years. You saw it in your vision." His voice was low and insistent. "Who was it, Ellie? Who convinced me to break the curse?"

My mouth gaped in dismay and the edges of my vision went black.

"Ellie, who was the god who escaped being trapped in Popogusso with all the others?" he asked again, more insistent.

Tears stung my eyes and I shook my head. "No." Everything I'd been led to believe was an outright lie.

"Who deceived me and told me that you would be safe when you are anything but? What sick and twisted god withheld his mark from you until you finally came to me and I took you out on the ocean?"

My mouth opened, but I couldn't make the word come out. If this was true, what did it mean? Not *if* it was true—I knew in my gut that it was. I'd seen the proof of it. Only I'd been too stupid to put all the pieces together.

Sympathy filled Collin's eyes. "You know. I can see the horror in your eyes, but you have to tell me, Ellie, you have to tell me who betrayed you. Who betrayed us both. Which god *really* wanted to break the curse?"

My shell of control was cracking. The black edges were creeping into my peripheral vision.

"Ellie, who *really* destroyed your life and killed your father?"

"*Ahone.*"

Chapter Four

I was in the upstairs hallway, my pretty white princess nightgown billowing around my legs. I clutched Bunny to my chest, terrified.

I could hear my mother crying downstairs as the rain beat against the windows. A crash of thunder made the whole house shake.

"I'm going to ask you nicely one more time: Where is the ring?*" a mean man asked Momma.*

"Do you want my wedding ring?" my mother asked. "Here. I'll give it to you."

A man slapped her and she cried harder.

I knew I had to help Momma, but I was terrified.

"Amanda, I thought you were smart. Isn't that why Higgins asked you to come to Charlotte?"

"I don't know what you're talking about."

"I'd hate to cut up that pretty face. All you have to do is cooperate."

I couldn't let the man cut Momma. I ran to the staircase and set my foot on the top step, but an older man's voice stopped me. He whispered in my ear, "No, Ellie. Don't go downstairs."

Ahone.

"Ellie." Collin's insistent voice filled my head.

My eyes blinked open and I was blinded by the sunlight glaring in my eyes. A shadow crossed over my face and Collin's worried face blocked out the sun. I was on my back and he was leaning over me, his hand by my shoulder, bracing his body. "He was there," I whispered in horror.

Collin shook his head in confusion. "What are you talking about?"

"Ahone. He was there the night Momma was murdered."

Collin's eyes flew open in astonishment and he gently helped me sit up, keeping his arm around my back for support.

"Ahone was there! He told me not to go downstairs. He wouldn't let me help her."

"Oh, fuck."

I leaned my head against his shoulder and closed my eyes, trying to remember every detail. It was all still there, perfectly preserved like a DVD on pause; all I had to do was rewind it. "The man wasn't there for me. He was there for a ring." I looked up into his face. "She told the man who broke into our house that she didn't know about the ring." I shook my head. "She was lying to him. I *know* it, deep in my gut. But how do I know she was lying when I don't remember anything else?"

Sorrow filled his eyes. "I don't know, Ellie. Maybe you know from your memories, even if you can't access them."

"He told her that he thought she was smart and that was the reason Higgins asked her to come to Charlotte."

His face paled. "Charlotte?"

The pieces were starting to fit together. "My mother saw the Ricardo collection a week before she was murdered. She was murdered because of a *ring*, the ring I found buried under my oak tree, the one I'm wearing now"—I held up my right hand and showed him the ring—"not because that man was after me."

"*Your mother saw the Ricardo Estate?*" His arm dropped away from me as his back became rigid. "You told me you thought there

51

was a connection between the estate and your mother's death, but I didn't understand how you'd made that leap." He watched me for several seconds, terror washing over his face. "Why didn't you tell me?"

"I only found out a couple of weeks ago. From a friend of my parents."

Collin leaned forward, looking like he was about to be sick. He squeezed his eyes shut. "*Fuck.*"

"Why are you so freaked out?" Collin was always in control when it came to the curse and all things supernatural. The only time I'd seen him panic was after Wapi attacked me in the ocean. He'd suddenly realized the danger I was truly in from the gods and demons and was hit by the full impact of what he'd done *to me.* So what had him freaked out now?

He glanced over his shoulder at me. "We're just pawns in some monumental game. He's been planning this for centuries." His voice sounded strained.

I wanted to argue with him, but I knew he was right. I just didn't know what to do about it. "So Ahone let that man kill my mother?"

Collin shook his head and turned away. "I don't know, Ellie." He ran a hand over his scalp, refusing to look at me. "Maybe . . . Probably."

In light of everything else, I didn't doubt it.

"Then Ahone killed my mother *and* my father," I whispered as the horror washed over me. "He took them both from me. *Why?*" Tears slid down my cheeks.

Collin grabbed my hand, linking our fingers and holding tight, still staring out into the ocean. "I don't know."

We sat in silence, watching the waves together. Tears burned my eyes. Ahone was a monster too. "I have his fucking mark on my back. I want it off!"

He turned to me, pity in his eyes. "It's too late. You've been picked."

"Oh, God, Collin." My voice cracked as I desperately tried to keep control, but panic was overtaking my senses. "I feel so disgusted and used and—"

"Betrayed." His voice was full of resignation.

"Yes. *Betrayed.*"

His mouth twisted into a sad smile. "I know exactly how you feel."

I should be angry. Where was my anger? But all I felt was a numbing iciness. "Why? Why would he do this?"

"I don't know. He's a god. Was he bored? Was it fun for him to set this all up? But you can't trust anything he says or does."

Collin was right, and part of me hated him for that. He'd tried to warn me, but I'd refused to listen. "What about Okeus? Are you suggesting that I should follow him instead?"

"No. He's just as bad, although maybe Ahone is worse. Okeus was still trapped after the curse broke, but he sent his messenger to me. Kanim told me that Ahone had used me, just like Ahone had used Manteo years before to create the curse. If I pledged myself to Okeus, he said, I would be rewarded for my loyalty." He looked away. "At least Okeus is fairly up-front about his deviousness. Ahone masquerades as a kind, benevolent god."

Tears welled in my eyes and my throat burned, but I was too shocked and devastated to cry. What little I knew about the curse was all a lie, which meant I knew absolutely nothing.

Collin stood and reached down for me. "Come here."

"What are you doing?" I asked as he pulled me to my feet and started for the water.

"You need the ocean."

I dug my heels into the sand. "No. It's from Ahone. I don't want any part of it."

"Don't be stubborn, Ellie. You need it whether you want it or not." He continued to drag me. "And it may have been Ahone's idea to invest us with the power of the earth and the sea, but they belong firmly to us. Especially you. You're the witness to creation. And there's no way he could have given that to you."

"How do you know that?"

"Ellie, you saw it yourself. You were present at the birth of the gods. They have no control over that part of you."

I still resisted. I knew it was stupid, but to go into the ocean felt like accepting what Ahone had done, and there was no way I'd ever accept it or him again.

Collin stopped pulling and I fell against his chest. He took advantage of me being off balance and scooped one arm around my back and the other under my knees, picking me up and holding me to his chest.

"Put me down, Collin!"

He was in the water in only a few strides, walking farther out until the waves hit his waist and he dropped my legs into them.

The power hit me as soon as my toes touched the water. I started to fall as the onslaught of power shot through my entire body. This was my most intense experience yet, and I struggled to stand once my feet hit the sand.

Collin wrapped an arm around my back and pulled me to his chest. "Fuck, Ellie. You've been without the ocean for longer than a week."

But I was too overwhelmed to answer. Before I realized what he was doing, his right hand reached for mine, pressing our palms together.

The Manitou of every living thing filled my head at once, and I felt like I was drowning in the sea of life. Collin and I were even more powerful than the last time we'd joined our marks. His emotions pushed through our connection—guilt, worry, love. Deep love and deep lust.

I looked into his face and wasn't surprised to see that his eyes were dilated and filled with intense longing. His mouth hovered over mine, waiting for me to close the distance of an inch. I stretched up on the balls of my feet, but I sunk into the sand when I felt something else seep through our connection.

Deception.

Even after his confession, he was still purposely hiding things from me.

"Don't fight it, Ellie," he groaned, and his mouth covered mine.

It was all too much for me to resist. Getting lost in the intensity of the experience, I wrapped my free hand around the back of his head as his tongue coaxed my lips apart and explored my mouth.

I wanted him. All reason fled and my only thought was to be with him in every sense of the word. Nothing made me feel so complete as when I was one with Collin, and I was desperate to feel whole again. I reached for the button of his shorts . . .

Suddenly I felt myself falling into a dark abyss.

I was in the valley where I'd seen my father weeks ago, only now the sky was overcast, tinting the scene a dingy gray. The flowers were wilted and dying, and the air was thick and heavy and difficult to suck into my lungs.

"I wish we were meeting under different circumstances."

I'd recognize that voice anywhere. I spun around, my heart racing. Okeus sat on a tall-backed wooden chair that resembled a mini throne. The tall grass was trampled flat underneath the chair and in a three-foot circle around it. He was dressed in modern clothes again—a pair of dark gray dress pants and a pale-gray dress shirt tailored to fit his toned body, the first two buttons of the collar open. His black hair was cropped short, and his piercing, dark, almost black eyes were pinned to my face. "Ellie, come speak with me." He gestured to the path of flattened grass that led from me to him.

"I don't want to be here. Send me back." I spun around in a circle, looking for an escape. The last time I'd met Okeus like this had been in a dream. The only reason I had escaped was because I'd screamed for David, who had woken me up and saved me. Who would save me now?

Okeus crossed his legs, his mouth twisting in irritation. "There's no need to be so dramatic, Ellie. I don't plan on stealing your virtue today, although I have to wonder how much virtue you actually possess." He placed both hands on the arms of the chair and grinned. "You were about to fuck Collin on a public beach in front of families with children."

Horror flooded me. He was right. What had happened to me?

He shook his head and tsked. "No need for shame, Ellie. It's not surprising. You and Collin were handpicked for one another. The perfect match in every way." Okeus stood and took a step toward me. "Did you know your mother had five miscarriages before giving birth to you?"

"No." I knew my parents had experienced infertility issues, which explained why Momma was in her late thirties and Daddy in his forties when she got pregnant with me. But I didn't know about the miscarriages.

"Do you know why?" He looked amused.

I shook my head. But the truth hit me as soon as he opened his mouth to gloat.

"Those pregnancies were unacceptable. Three were boys, which automatically ruled them out since Collin isn't gay. One of the girls was deemed incompatible. She would have been too meek and Collin wouldn't have given her the time of day. The second would have developed leukemia at age six, then died ten years later. Finally, there was you." He grinned and took several steps toward me, stopping two feet in front of me. "And you were *perfect*. A fire that would catch his interest. A stubbornness to keep him on his toes." Okeus lifted his hand to my cheek, running his fingertips down to my jaw. "A beauty that would draw him to you. The fact that you are a witness to creation was a lucky coincidence."

I resisted the urge to wrap my arms around myself. My thin sundress was soaking wet and clung to every curve of my body. "There are no coincidences in any of this."

His gaze fell to my right hand. "Take that ring on your hand. If only you knew its history, its intended purpose."

I curled my fingers into a fist.

A devious grin spread across his face. "No coincidences? Are you so sure of that? Granted, many things have been finely orchestrated, more nuanced than you can imagine, but even Ahone can't control the Manitou. It is a force greater than all of us." His knuckles slid down my bare arm. "He *could* control your characteristics. Your personality. But he couldn't bestow you with your pure soul. That was out of his control, as hard as it must be for the *creator god* to accept. But you can be sure that once he realized his good fortune, he chose to use it to his advantage."

"For what purpose? I could have been anyone and all Collin had to do was grab my hand to break the curse."

A grin spread across the god's face. "Now *there* is a good question. But there's no arguing that you were meant to be Collin's, Ellie."

This was surreal. "I thought you wanted me for *yourself*."

"What I need from you is easily enough given. I'll impregnate you. You'll gestate my child, then give birth. If it's successful, we'll repeat the process."

Disgust nauseated me. "You're such a romantic. A girl needs a little wining and dining, you know."

He lifted his eyebrows with a half shrug. "I tried that last time and it didn't work. I've decided to take a more direct approach."

"Sorry. Still not interested. And why would you care if Collin and I get together?"

"Ellie, Ellie." He shook his head, smirking with amusement. "How easily you forget. Why *would* I care if you were perfect for Collin? It's all part of Ahone's game."

Okeus lifted his hands from his body and shrugged, his grin fading. He began to slowly circle me, but I was too paralyzed with shock to stop him. Why would Ahone care if Collin fell for me? He wanted Collin to open the gate, but obviously there was more to it, though I had no idea what it meant.

"You needn't feel shame for your intense attraction to Collin. Ahone created you to be drawn to each other. Throw in your Curse Keeper bond and your souls' strong connection . . . well, I'm not sure why you fight him. It's a waste of energy."

Obviously he had brought me here for a reason, and it had to be more than just an opportunity for him to gloat. "What do you want, Okeus?"

He stopped in front of me, his forehead wrinkled with a mock scowl. "So *impatient*." He turned away and walked back to his chair, sliding into his seat with a graceful flourish. "You came to Collin with questions, did you not? I would like to give you answers."

"Why would you help me?"

He sighed, rolling his eyes in boredom. "To prove to you that I have no hard feelings over our last encounter, nor over your foolish decision to choose Ahone instead of me."

I shook my head, my eyes narrowing in suspicion. "No. You're not altruistic. You want something in return. Even if it's a long-term payoff."

He shifted in his seat. "Ellie, you know what I want. Perhaps you'll be more compliant if I make a goodwill gesture."

I clenched my fists at my sides. "I'll never agree to become pregnant with your child, so you might as well send me back now."

His elbow rested on the arm of the chair and he set his right cheek on his upraised fist. "I think I'll overlook your rude and shortsighted request and help you anyway." He sat up slightly. "I believe you want to know about your friend's ability to see the souls of those who have yet to cross over to the spirit world."

My mouth gaped. "Claire?"

"Yes, her. And the answer is yes, there are some who possess this gift. You can use your friend to your advantage."

A cold chill shot through me. "Did Ahone set her up too?" I was already positive that Ahone was responsible for bringing David into my life; was it too much to think he'd involve Claire in his plans too?

"No, I suspect not. She has the potential to be useful in sniffing out his deceptions. The souls of the departed are not easily fooled."

My father instantly came to mind. The last time I'd joined hands with Collin in the ocean, I'd seen my deceased father, who had given me a message from Ahone. My back stiffened. "Are you calling my father a fool?"

"Did Ahone send your father to you after my plan failed?" Okeus laughed, shaking his head. "So unoriginal."

"The man with you was not my father."

Okeus shrugged like it was nothing of concern. "Your father believed I was evil incarnate. Besides, Ahone took your father's soul. It *belongs* to him, thus Ahone controls him. He is not a normal spirit." His expression darkened. "You would be wise to remember that in any future encounters."

Would I see Daddy again? How much would this revelation cloud my perception of him?

He paused, turning serious. "Your friend will help you navigate the waters of what to believe and what not."

I shook my head in disgust. "Let me guess. All the souls will tell her that you're the good guy and Ahone is bad."

He laughed again, this time more genuine. "You are a fearless creature, aren't you? Most beings tremble at my feet."

"Cut to the part when you tell me that you'd never try to get Claire to dupe me like that."

His mouth lifted on one side. "The answer to your question about good and bad isn't so simple, Ellie. There is no perfect good or bad. *You* are neither completely pure nor completely evil. Your level of selflessness or self-centeredness varies from day to day. Some days Ahone will want something that is for the good of his creations. Other days he will want something that benefits him and his own needs and desires." He gestured his hand toward me. "Just like creating and using you."

As much as I hated to admit it, I knew he was right. I'd been stupid to blindly accept Ahone, but I'd seen no other choice at the time.

"All is not lost, little Elinor Lancaster. Your friend is now your shield of truth. She will be your counsel." His mouth lifted into a smirk. "And yes, sometimes she will counsel you not to trust me."

"Why are you telling me all of this?"

He leaned back his head and gave me a calculated glance. "To prove to you that I have something of worth for you, just as you have something of worth for me." His eyes narrowed and glowed red. "Do not think for a moment that if I grow weary of waiting, I won't take what I want when I want it." His eyes returned to their usual dark brown. "But for now, I will remain patient and wait for you to change your mind."

"Why do you seem so certain that I will?"

His eyes twinkled. "Because I know something about you. You love deeply, and *that* is your greatest weakness."

Suddenly, I was whisked back into the ocean, Collin's left arm supporting my dead weight. Our right hands had broken contact. He was still standing in the same place, but we'd gathered a small crowd of curious onlookers.

I looked up into his worried eyes.

"Are you okay?" he asked, helping me regain my footing.

I nodded. Three times now I'd joined marks with Collin in the ocean, and three times I'd had some type of vision involving the gods. But each time I'd been completely unaware of my surroundings, leaving me utterly vulnerable. I might have been the daughter of the sea, but I wasn't sure it made me invincible to drowning, as ironic as that seemed. I couldn't ignore that Collin had protected me each and every time. Didn't that constitute a type of trust?

But while I might have been able to trust Collin to protect me when he was with me, there were too many other things I couldn't count on him for. One constant with Collin was his secrets. "Did Okeus tell you to bring me out here and press our marks together?"

Guilt flickered in his eyes.

I jerked out of his hold. "Why couldn't you have just been honest with me?"

"Do you really think you would have agreed to come out here if I had?"

"I don't remember agreeing in the first place!" I shouted.

"Ellie, you're making a scene."

The crowd had begun to grow, the families staring at me like I'd grown a second head. I rolled my eyes in disgust. "Leave it to you to turn this around and blame everything on me." I stomped out of the water, Collin following close behind me. Our connection was even stronger now and I could literally feel his presence. What would it be like if we were together all the time?

I stopped at the blanket and bent over to pick up my flip-flops. I had to get away from him. The draw I felt to him was too strong. I could barely stop myself from turning around and throwing myself into his arms, begging him to take me right there, in front of everyone. But another part of me hated every fiber of his being. He was the reason why my life was utter hell. I couldn't ignore his betrayal and dishonesty, even if Ahone had tricked him.

He stopped next to me, clenching his hands into fists at his sides. "We're not done here, Ellie. We have more to talk about."

I gritted my teeth, trying to keep my hands to myself. "Well, *I'm* done."

"You are such a hypocrite," he sneered in disgust. "You always accuse me of hiding things, but here I am offering you information and you're running away. *Again.*"

"I can't, Collin." I looked up into his face, pleading. "Don't you see? I can't. I need to think. And I can't do that around you."

He shook his head, his irritation palpable. "You can't run away from this. *This* is our lives now. We're pawns being manipulated by selfish gods, and that means everyone and everything in our lives is vulnerable to them. Is that fair? Hell no, but there it is nevertheless. The sooner you accept it, the sooner you learn to adapt and roll with whatever these bastards throw your way, the better off you'll be. I want to help you—I'm begging you to let me help you—but you rebuff me at every turn. Decide right now, Ellie: Do you want my help or not?"

My mouth dropped open in shock. "Are you saying you won't mark my doors anymore if I say no?"

"Do you even *want* me to? You keep telling me that I've ruined your life, but mine's been ruined too. Do you think I want to go to

Manteo every couple of days to mark your door? Did you ever once think that *I* may need protection?"

The blood drained from my head. Finding out about Ahone, seeing Okeus, listening to Collin say he didn't want to mark my doors anymore—it suddenly felt like I was drowning. I sank down to the blanket, too numb to know whether to be angry or sad.

"What do you want from me, Ellie?"

I slowly shook my head. "I don't know."

"Well, I *need* to know."

I nodded. He was right. He'd been screwed by this whole mess too. He was an easy scapegoat, but I wasn't guiltless in this either. I searched his dark brown eyes, again resisting the urge to touch him. "After what Okeus told me, I need some time to think. I'm sorry, but I do. I just found out my entire existence can be attributed to the gods' ulterior motives. I need to sort this out in my head."

He studied my face, and some of his guard fell. "Okay."

"You're not going to ask what he said?"

"No."

My shock was wearing off, replaced by a profound sadness. "I'm going away for the weekend." I paused and picked at a fold in the blanket, avoiding eye contact. "We're going to Chapel Hill. David dug up some information he wants to check out." I still didn't trust Collin, so the less he knew about our trip, the better.

"Are you sure that's a good idea?"

Part of me wanted to rise up and fight him. Who was he to ask me that? Was he doing it out of jealousy? But I was so tired of fighting with Collin. I lifted my gaze to his face.

"You'll be a couple hundred miles from the ocean, Ellie. What happens if you need it?"

"I've never really needed it before. I'm sure I'll be fine."

"You *have* needed it," he said softly. "What about the times you drive here before even realizing what you're doing? You'll be weaker that far away from the ocean, so be careful if you face any demons or spirits."

I lifted my mouth into a lopsided grin. "I thought you weren't going to help me anymore."

A soft smile spread across his face. "I'm waiting for your decision. Until then, I'll keep with the status quo."

The thought of banishing Collin from my life was inconceivable, like cutting off an appendage. But I couldn't resist him if I kept seeing him on a regular basis. So what was the answer?

One thing was certain: my life was a freaking mess.

↭ Chapter Five ↭

My clothes had dried by the time I got back to the house, but the dried salt on my skin felt disgusting. As I walked up to the house, I stumbled and then spun around to see what had made me trip. That was the fifth time I'd felt my foot catch on something by that exact spot on the path, but nothing was ever there. I was not only losing my mind but also my coordination.

Grunting in frustration, I let myself in through the side door and checked the kitchen before climbing the stairs and heading for the bathroom. I stood in the shower, letting all that I'd discovered marinate in my head. I couldn't change the fact that Ahone had been setting me up since before my birth. I couldn't change the fact that Collin and I had been created to be—what? Partners? Lovers? What was Ahone's end goal? But it didn't mean that I had to sit back and accept it.

I stayed under the spray a long time, resting my head against the cool tiles. The shock was wearing off and anger was seeping into the cracks, filling the marrow in my bones with simmering rage. My life was part of some elaborate game. My mother had died for the amusement of a bored god. Was my father's dementia part of the plan too? To keep me from having the information to stop Collin?

Daddy's death most certainly was. I knew what Okeus wanted from me, but what about Ahone?

My defiance swelled. I was done playing into the gods' hands. The path they had chosen for me might or might not be inevitable, but it didn't mean I'd go quietly along like a sheep to the slaughter. I would go kicking and screaming.

But I didn't want to waste my energy on anger. Collin was right. This was my life, and I needed to figure out how to deal with it. I didn't have to accept the gods' plans, but lashing out in a blind rage wouldn't help either. I'd figure out my own path. I lifted my face into the shower stream, letting the now-cooling water roll down my body. I needed to stuff my anger back inside, but that was going to take more than a few minutes in a shower. And one thing I didn't have was time. I'd been with Collin for longer than planned, and David was going to be home in less than an hour. I still needed to pack.

Reluctantly, I got out of the shower and dried off. Thoughts whirred through my head as I got dressed and packed several days' changes of clothes. I should never have gone to see Collin. At least not right before my weekend with David. Now I felt guilty and dirty. Sure, Collin had been the one to kiss me, but I'd welcomed his embrace and had been about to pursue more. I could attribute part of my reaction to him as part of our magical bond, but how much was really out of my control?

I should have told David I was planning to see Collin. And I should also have told him about Claire hearing voices. Why had I felt the need to keep both things to myself? I was afraid to answer my own questions.

Collin's concern about going too far inland was sobering. What if he was right? What would happen to me if I used energy to send away a demon or god while I was so far away from the water?

I was in the bathroom packing my makeup bag when my phone rang. I raced into my room to grab it before the caller hung up, expecting to see David's name on the screen. My stomach dropped when I saw that it was Tom Helmsworth.

After taking a deep breath, I answered. "How's my favorite Manteo police officer?"

"I need to talk to you, Ellie." He was using his serious voice. The one that told me I was in trouble . . . but for the life of me, I didn't know why. The spirits had laid low for the past few weeks, which meant that I had done the same.

"Well, I've missed you too, Tom, but it's going to have to wait. I'm about to go out of town for the weekend."

"Well, then it's a good thing I caught you before you left." His tone was far from friendly.

"Actually, Tom, I don't have time to chat. David's supposed to be home in less than thirty minutes. I'll be back on Sunday night, so we can talk on Monday." I almost added, "before I go to work." At least that wasn't an issue anymore. Too bad it didn't make me feel any better.

"Actually, Ellie, if you leave town before you talk to me, I'll put out a warrant for your arrest."

I sank to the edge of the bed, feeling light-headed. "*Why?* What did I do?"

"You didn't do anything, Ellie." He sounded exasperated. And tired. "I just need to talk to you."

"Then why can't it wait until I get back?"

"Goddamn it, Ellie. Will you just do as I ask for once?"

My irritation was back. "Maybe I would if you asked nicely."

"We both know *that's* bullshit," he grumbled. "You have thirty minutes to get your ass to the Manteo police station or I'm going to send someone to pick you up."

I started to tell him off, but the dead silence in my ear told me he'd hung up.

Damn it. I didn't have time for this, for any of it. If Tom wanted to talk to me, it could only mean one thing: the supernatural world was up to some serious shit again. The last time he'd grilled me was when the demon badgers had started ripping out dogs' hearts before moving on to humans.

I grabbed my weekend bag and took it downstairs with me, setting it by the side door before heading outside. I needed to tell David, but he would be worried. I had to admit that I was more than a little worried myself. But I'd kept enough secrets from him for one day. And if this made me late, I'd have to tell him what was going on anyway. I typed a quick text and hit send.

I need to talk to Tom Helmsworth before we leave. Don't worry— it's just a chat. I'll be home as soon as I can.

I hoped to God the chat part wasn't a lie.

I considered driving since it was a hot and humid August afternoon, but the car would have barely started to cool down by the time I pulled into the parking lot of the police station a few blocks away. Ten minutes later, I walked into the building a hot sweaty mess and approached the receptionist's desk. I lifted my heavy braid off the back of my neck. "I'm here to see Tom Helmsworth."

The elderly female receptionist eyed me up and down, frowning slightly, as though she found me lacking. I knew I was a mess, but I couldn't be *that* bad. "*Officer* Helmsworth will be with you in a minute."

"I'm kind of in a hurry. Could you tell him I'm here?"

Her mouth puckered and she looked down her nose at me while she picked up the phone. "Officer Helmsworth, someone is here to see you. She didn't give her name." She paused. "Yes, that's her." She hung up and offered me a tight smile. "He'll be here in a moment."

A few seconds later, Tom appeared in the doorway holding a stack of files. Tom was a good-looking guy with dark hair and a toned body. We'd gone to high school together, although he was a couple of years older than me—making him twenty-five—but the last month had been hard on him. Dark circles underscored his eyes, and I even noticed a few crow's-feet. "Come on back, Ellie." At least he sounded a little less cranky than he had on the phone. He led me to a room and pushed open the door, motioning me inside. "Thanks for showing up so quickly."

"Well, when you put a time limit on my arrival, I considered walking in twenty-nine minutes and fifty-nine seconds after your call, but I actually have things to do."

He scowled and I wondered why I was being so hateful to him. Tom was just trying to do his job, and he wasn't wrong in thinking that I had some connection to all the odd things that had happened since the reappearance of the colony. I just wasn't sure how safe it was for him to know about it.

I entered the room and was taken aback when I saw that it was an interview room with a table in the middle and two chairs, one on each side. My heart lurched and my breath stuttered. "Am I in trouble?"

"Ellie, I just need to talk to you, and you haven't exactly been cooperative in the past. This time we're going to have an official interview." He waved to the chair. "Why don't you take a seat."

I walked around the table and slid into the metal chair, folding my hands on top of the table. I tried not to look nervous, but I wasn't sure how effective my strategy was. "What do you want to know?"

Tom sat down across from me, setting the files to the side of the table. His face was devoid of any expression. "Other than the usual public drunkenness, petty theft, and vandalism, things have been quiet on Roanoke Island for several weeks. Until this past week."

I shifted my weight to the side, keeping my eyes on his face. So far, he wasn't giving anything away.

"This week there have been four deaths in town—one every night for the last four nights. All four patients were ill, but none of them was in serious condition on the morning that they died."

Tom was quiet for several seconds and I realized he was waiting for me to respond. "Is this some kind of flu like H1N1? I'm not sure how I can help you with that. Shouldn't you call the health department?"

"The health department has already been notified. They were the ones who contacted us."

"I'm still not sure why I'm here, Tom." For once, I was genuinely confused. I had no idea how or why he was connecting this problem to me.

"The patients were all ill with some minor condition." Tom slid the stack of files to the center of the table. "One had strep throat, another had bronchitis." He spread out the stack as he spoke, four manila folders with a note paper-clipped to each file. "The third victim had food poisoning and the fourth an abscessed tooth. They were ill during the day, but not deathly so, at least not until the sun went down."

A chill started at the back of my neck and crawled slowly down my spine. It didn't escape my notice that he'd called the third patient a victim. "Then what happened?"

"Then they deteriorated quite rapidly, hallucinating and screaming and thrashing in pain. Within two hours they were dead."

I sucked in a breath. If there was some kind of deadly virus going around, I was glad David and I were leaving town. "I'm still not sure what this has to do with me, Tom."

"After the second patient died, the coroner became concerned and did an autopsy." Tom leaned his forearm on the table, leveling his gaze with mine. "And what he found is the reason why you're here."

I resisted the urge to ask. Tom would tell me soon enough, and he seemed to be making a production out of it.

He waited for a long moment, a flicker of disappointment flashing in his eyes when he didn't get a reaction from me. "The patients had no hearts."

All the blood in my body instantly pooled at my feet. Could the demonic badgers be back? They had eaten out their victims' hearts after ripping their abdomens open. Collin had assured me they were gone forever, earning us each a new title: destroyers of life. "Did they leave their houses? Were their abdomens ripped open?"

He pressed his lips together as he fingered the edge of one of the files. "No. That's the strange part. Two of them never even left their houses. Two went to the hospital. One died on the way; the other died in the ER." He opened one of the folders, exposing a photo of the naked body of a little boy.

I gasped, choking back a sob. "A kid?"

"Yeah, a kid." He pushed the file closer to me. "Notice anything?"

"Are they all kids?"

"No. Just this one. One was a middle-aged woman and the other two were elderly."

I looked away. "I don't want to look at that, Tom."

Tom banged the table and I jumped.

"Look at it, Ellie. This kid's heart is missing. *Gone.* Do you notice anything strange?"

I forced myself to look at the five-by-seven photo, trying not to focus on the boy's face. I couldn't stop myself. He was seven or eight at most, with dark brown hair and freckles scattered across his face.

He had a tan line at his waist and his lower thighs, most likely from a swimming suit. "What am I looking for?" I started to cry. "I don't know, Tom."

His voice softened. "Ellie, I'm sorry. But look at the photo. His heart is gone." He asked again: "Do you notice anything strange?"

I forced myself to look again, which is when it hit me. "There's no wound where it was removed. Is there one on the back?"

"No."

I shook my head, my tears drying up. "But how . . . ?"

"Exactly. *How.*"

I lifted my face and stared into his eyes. "Tom, I swear to you. I have no idea what's going on. I didn't even know anything about it until you just told me." But if something evil was killing children, I didn't know what it was or how to stop it.

He closed the file. "It's okay, Ellie. I believe you."

The image of the little boy was burned into my brain, and I knew I was about to lose it. "Can I go now?"

"In a minute. I want to ask you a few more things."

I nodded. "Okay."

"One of the deaths, the elderly woman, happened two blocks from your house."

"Two nights ago?" I asked.

Tom jerked upright. "Yeah, how did you know?"

Crap. I couldn't tell him about the old woman who'd told me my future. Was she the one who had died? Could she have been a ghost rather than a demon? "I was walking home from work. I saw the ambulance."

He sighed in disappointment. I'd guessed about the ambulance. "What else do you want to know?"

His voice lowered. "Ellie, I'm begging you. If you have any idea what might be doing this or how to stop it, either tell me what to do or make sure it's taken care of."

My head jerked up in surprise. "*What?*"

"Whatever was ripping out people's hearts before suddenly stopped, the exact same night when we found some strange things out at Festival Park. There were circles with candles, salt, and markings very much like the ones you make on your doors. We also found gigantic claw marks on a tree that had been knocked over, along with extensive damage to the *Elizabeth II.*"

We'd been sloppy to leave so many signs of our fight in Festival Park, the re-creation of the first English settlement in Roanoke, that night. We'd been sloppy about a lot of things. David had been certain I was a conjurer and could send the demons back to hell on my own. We'd made a temple of sorts for me, creating seven circles consisting of tribal markings, candles, and salt. I had stood inside the circles and recited the Cherokee chant David had been so sure would end the lives of the badgers. He had been mistaken. I had lured the demons away from David and onto the replica ship. We would probably both be dead if Collin hadn't shown up to save us.

"I think you did something that night. I don't know how you managed it, but I think you made that wild animal go away. I'd prefer if you would tell me what's going on so trained professionals can deal with the situation. But I also know how stubborn you are. So if you refuse to tell me, but you can make this thing go away, please do what you can."

My mouth dropped open in shock.

He gave me a wry smile. "Not what you expected?"

I took a deep breath and released it. "No."

"I have to warn you, this isn't officially sanctioned by the Manteo Police Department. It's off the books."

I shook my head, wiping the tears from my cheeks. I was both shocked by his change of attitude and grateful for it, but there was one problem. "I swear to you, Tom. I have no idea what this thing is."

He leaned across the table, his eyes piercing mine. "Then find out. And take care of it."

⤳ CHAPTER SIX ⤳

Tom insisted on driving me home. I considered refusing, but I was still shaken from seeing the photo of the little boy. Besides, I suspected that the air-conditioning in his squad car got cool pretty quickly. It was better than walking in the heat.

"Are you going to let me ride in front?" I asked as we walked across the parking lot.

"This time," he said, opening his car door. He glanced over the top of the car and winked at me. "Don't get too used to it."

I slid in the passenger seat. It occurred to me that I'd been in this exact car a month and a half ago when Tom found me in the botanical gardens shouting at Okeus. "Who says I plan to?"

He put his key in the ignition and shot me a weary gaze. "Call it a crazy hunch, but I have a feeling this won't be the last time we're thrown together."

I was envious of his AC by the time we pulled up next to my house. I considered sitting in front of the blasting cold air for several seconds, but David burst out of the door, his face contorted in anger.

"Shit. Your boyfriend's pissed," Tom muttered as he climbed out of the car, readjusting his belt.

I opened my car door as David started shouting, "What is the meaning of this? On what grounds did you bring her in for questioning?"

He charged toward Tom, but I jumped in his path and grabbed his arm, holding him back. "David, it's okay."

"Bloody hell, it is."

"Dr. Preston." Tom hooked his thumbs in his belt. "Ellie isn't in trouble. I asked her in as a consultant."

The tension in David's body faded, and he glanced from my face to Tom's. "What the bollocks does that mean?"

I dropped my hold on his arm. "Something weird has been happening, and Tom wanted to make me aware of the situation."

Confusion washed over David's face.

"I'll explain it on the way to Chapel Hill."

Tom narrowed his eyes, anger stiffening his shoulders. "You're still going out of town? Even after what I told you?"

I met his gaze without flinching. "And I told you I don't know what it was. We're going to Chapel Hill to get information. We'll be back Sunday night."

Tom didn't look happy.

"It's the best I can do."

The officer moved closer to me and lowered his voice. "People are dying, Ellie. Kids."

"I know." My voice broke. A few months ago my biggest worry had been scraping together enough money to help put a new roof on the inn. Now I was expected to save lives even though I had no idea what I was doing. "The only thing I know to tell you is that people can try to protect themselves by putting salt on their windowsills and across the threshold of their doors." I paused. "It should keep the evil out."

His eyes widened in disbelief. "You can't be serious? How am I supposed to tell people that?"

"It's all I have at the moment. If anything changes, let me know."

"I still don't like it."

My patience gave way to irritation. This day had sucked all the way around, and I was just about through with it. "Well, welcome to my world. There's a shitload of crap I don't like, but I don't have a say in any of it."

We had a stare-off for several seconds before Tom swore under his breath and looked away. He turned and climbed back into his squad car, leaving without another word.

"Did you actually tell Tom Helmsworth what's going on?" David asked from behind me. He sounded incredulous.

I stared in the direction in which the police car had disappeared. I had a sort-of ally in the police department now. I was still trying to determine if this was a good thing or a bad one. "No. But Tom's a perceptive guy, and he's figured out quite a few things on his own. He knows I had something to do with the badgers disappearing."

David put his hands on my hips and pressed his chest against my back. "It was inevitable, I suppose. As long as he's not blaming you." He paused. "I take it that something else has happened . . ."

I spun around to face him, and an unexpected wave of love and gratitude washed through me as I took in his concerned expression. I threw myself at him, wrapping my arms around his shoulders and holding him tight. My hormones might have been infatuated with Collin, but I needed *this* man. He was my rock, my stability. He was the support I needed that Collin wouldn't—or couldn't—give. But after what had happened at the beach—both with Collin *and* Okeus—I was suddenly terrified of losing David.

"Hey." He gave me a gentle kiss on the forehead and pulled away to study my face. "What's going on?"

"Can we just go? You have no idea how much I need to get out of Manteo."

"Of course, love. I've put your suitcase in the trunk already. Do you need anything else?"

Did I? The crushing guilt of what had happened with Collin was making me addled. I rubbed my forehead, trying to focus. "Um . . . I need to talk to Becky about overseeing the inn this weekend."

His hands ran up and down my arms. "I've already spoken with her. She's all set. She'll call you if a problem arises."

"Okay," I said, distracted.

"What did you and Tom talk about? It has obviously upset you."

I gazed up into his face. "Can we talk about it in the car?"

"Of course, Ellie."

He led me to his car and we drove out of Manteo in silence as I leaned my elbow on the armrest, staring out the window. Something was terrorizing Manteo, and I had to wonder if Tom was right. Was it wrong to leave at a time like this? David didn't need me to talk to his colleague, and he didn't need me to visit Charlotte with him. I wondered if I should stay and try to convince him to go without me, only the selfish part of me didn't want to be alone for that long. Even if it meant possibly saving people. What did that say about me? But the truth was I had no idea what was killing those people or how to stop it. David had more resources at his disposal to figure it out. I wasn't sure what good I could do if I stayed, and the truth was *I* needed David.

As he started across the bridge from the island to the mainland, I was struck with a new worry. How could I have forgotten about my agoraphobia, which was the curse's way of preventing me from traveling too far from Manteo and the gate to Popogusso at the edge of the Elizabethan Botanical Gardens? Of course, the curse had allowed me to leave the island before when fate required it.

David must have sensed my trepidation because as soon as we crossed the first bridge, he reached over and covered my hand. "How are you doing?"

"Okay so far." I usually felt an immediate pressure on my chest when I left the island. Since I felt fine, it appeared that this trip was sanctioned, but the question was by whom? Ahone?

My anger surged out of nowhere, but I pushed it back down. It wouldn't do me any good right now. I'd save it for when I needed it.

"What happened?" David asked.

It took me a second to figure out what he was talking about. "With Tom?"

"Of course, with Tom."

I knew I was going to have to tell him about seeing Collin, but I wanted to tell him about our newest adversary first. "Tom called and asked me to come in so he could tell me about some recent cases." Since Tom had told David he'd called me in as a consultant, I decided to keep the harsh tone of his phone call to myself. After I shared the information Tom had given me, I asked, "Do you have any idea what's doing this?"

"Maybe, but what I'm considering is Cherokee." He paused, his forehead wrinkling in concentration. "If it's what I'm thinking, it would mean that it's not acting completely in character."

"Yeah, well none of us seem to be acting in character lately, so we'll take that into account. And besides, you said Big Nasty is Cherokee, so why wouldn't this thing be?"

"Mishiginebig—or the great horned serpent—crosses multiple tribal belief systems. The Raven Mockers seem to be purely Cherokee, although it's possible that they were Croatan too and the information has just been lost to history along with just about everything else." His mouth twisted to the side as he considered it.

"Raven Mockers?"

"They haunt the deathbed of a victim and hasten his or her death. They add the years they shave off the victim's life to their own, which means they can grow to be very, very old. The victim never even knows the Raven Mocker is there, since no one can see them."

"They're invisible?"

"To everyone except for those with powerful magic. The legends say that the victims' families often report hearing the screaming of a large bird. Did Tom mention anything like that?"

"No."

David was silent for a moment. "You said the deaths came out of nowhere, and if the victims were in as much agony as legend has it, the families were probably too upset and preoccupied to notice."

"You said that if Raven Mockers were responsible, they were acting out of character. If it's them, what are they doing that's different?"

"The legend says that Raven Mockers go after the hearts of the elderly, but you said one of the victims was a middle-aged woman and the other was a kid. That's unusual."

I pursed my lips in silence. This was bad . . . and probably about to get much worse.

"Ellie, the old woman you met in the road the other day . . ." He cast a wary glance at me.

I shifted in my seat. "Do you think I saw a ghost of one of the victims?" I couldn't help but think about Claire and her newfound "gift." "The thought had occurred to me."

"No." He paused, looking serious. "It might have been a Raven Mocker. Legend has it that they sometimes tell a person their future . . . and that the predictions they make are set in stone."

"So if I'm to believe the message she gave me, I'm a vessel and will either be the salvation of the world or its destroyer?"

"A vessel can mean many things."

"Yeah." Maybe so, but my mind kept racing right to Okeus.

"One more thing about the Raven Mocker and its vision. I told you that they can only be seen by someone with powerful magic, but there's more to it. If they are seen, it's a death sentence for them. Once a Raven Mocker has been seen by someone with magic, they only have seven days to live."

"What?" That got my attention. "So if it was a Raven Mocker, it basically committed suicide to give me some lame prediction."

"There must be more to the message if it was willing to die to give it to you."

I wasn't sure how I felt about that. If Raven Mockers tortured their victims, that made them evil. So why did I feel badly that this one had given its life for me? "So all I have to do is see all the Raven Mockers and they'll all die? How many of them are there?"

"Honestly? I don't know. Some legends say there are countless. Some say the Raven Mockers are the children of Kalona."

"Who is Kalona?"

"Kalona is the equivalent of the angel of death."

I sighed. "*Of course* he is."

"He may be called an angel, but he's really a demon. If we can figure out a way for you to defeat a demon without Collin's help, you can defeat Kalona. And without their leader, the Raven Mockers will be lost. They'll crawl back into their holes until someone else takes control."

"That's a big *if*, David."

"You can do this, Ellie. And I think I know how." He squeezed my hand. "I know we're going to talk to Allison about the weapons she saw, but I also want to visit the library while we're there. There are a few books and documents I want to review, and one letter that I'm eager to reread. It tells the story of a Croatan conjurer who created two weapons capable of defeating demons."

"*Two* weapons?"

"A gold ring created by an Englishman, consecrated and carved with Croatan symbols by a Croatan conjurer. The other is a spear. I know there's more to the story, but I've forgotten. It seemed like an ancillary tale at the time. But I know the document is in the archives. Once we find it, we can figure everything out."

"You sound so certain that I can do this, that I can fight these things on my own."

His eyes widened in disbelief. "Ellie, how could I not be?"

We spent the next couple hours of the four-hour drive with David catching me up on the latest findings at the colony site. While he was most interested in Manteo's dwelling, there were thirty other buildings that had been inhabited by the colonists, one of which had been the home of my multi-great-grandfather, Ananias Dare, and his wife and infant daughter.

I considered telling him about Claire's reawakened ability and my new memory about Ahone, but I decided both were serious enough to require his undivided attention. We'd get into Chapel Hill early enough for me to tell him. But there was something else that couldn't wait.

My guilt over what had happened with Collin started eating me alive, getting worse the longer we were in the car. I needed to tell him. Now. David would understand why I had met with him, so I needed to just put it out in the open. "David, there's something I have to tell you."

David shifted uncomfortably in his seat. "Actually, there's something I need to tell you first. I've been trying to work up the nerve to bring it up, so I'm just going to come out with it."

My breath stuck in my chest. I wasn't sure how many more surprises I could take today. "Okay. What?"

"Allison's not just a colleague."

"Okay," I said, hesitantly.

David shot me a glance before looking out the windshield. "Allison is my old girlfriend."

"Your old girlfriend is a history professor?"

"Yes."

I felt like I'd been doused in ice water. It was hard enough to accept that David not only had a college education but a master's and doctorate degree, while all I had was a Manteo High School diploma and a Dare County food worker's certificate. But what had I expected? He worked at a university, and while plenty of students were interested in him, he would never get involved with one. Of course he had dated a fellow professor.

"I should have told you sooner."

My mouth dried up and I took a breath before answering. "Why didn't you?" I didn't want to think of the implications.

"I was afraid it could get messy"—he cast a glance in my direction before returning his attention to the road—"on *her* end, and I didn't want to worry you. I was the one to end our relationship, and I know she hoped I would change my mind. Given the circumstances, there's a chance that this lead will turn out to be nothing."

Great, just what I needed—a jealous ex-girlfriend to add to my list of adversaries. "I guess we won't know until we see whatever it is she wants to show you, right?"

He took a deep breath, then released it. "I have no reason to believe she'll be anything but professional. Allison was never overly dramatic or emotional. And I told her that you'd be with me. Still, I'm worried."

"The ex-girlfriend and the new one together in the same room.

I can see why you might be on edge," I tried to tease, but I wasn't any more happy about the situation than he was. I could only imagine how ecstatic Allison had to be about David's new, younger girlfriend.

"I would suggest I go alone, but this concerns you too and I think you should be there. That being said, if it makes you uncomfortable—"

"I'll be fine. And don't worry. I'm not jealous, David." And I wasn't, not really. I knew beyond a shadow of a doubt that David wanted to be with me, that I could count on him to always be there. And I believed him. I had no worries that he would dump me after meeting with his old girlfriend this weekend.

My biggest concern was that I wasn't good enough for him. This morning was proof positive of that.

"David, please. It's not that big of a deal. We'll handle it."

"Thank you, Ellie. I know we've only been together a short time, but I've grown very attached to you, and I don't want to jeopardize our relationship." He picked up my hand and kissed it. "I would never intentionally hurt you. I want you to know that."

Guilt gnawed at my gut. I didn't deserve this man, but I was going to do everything in my power to change that. I knew I should tell him about kissing Collin earlier. I just couldn't. "I do." I choked out.

"Now what did you want to tell me?"

I was a Curse Keeper because Ananias Dare had done everything in his power to protect his family, even if he'd inadvertently destroyed them in the process. I wouldn't destroy David. I needed him too much, in every possible way. But I had to tell him something about meeting Collin. I owed him at least that much. "I saw Collin at the beach today."

He was silent for a moment, and then he forced a smile. "It's okay, Ellie. He's the other Curse Keeper. I know you're going to see him sometimes."

"You don't want to know anything else about me seeing him?"

He hesitated again, swallowing before he answered. "No. I trust you."

Did he have reason to trust me? I'd only kissed Collin, but I'd wanted so much more. It killed me that my carnal need for Collin simmered under the surface of my subconscious no matter what the commonsense part of me wanted. I knew I should tell David the full story, but would it help anything? It would probably just hurt him without helping either of us. Still, I couldn't ignore the fact that burying my feelings meant that I was breaking my own cardinal rule for our relationship.

No secrets.

⌁ Chapter Seven ⌁

The sun dipped close to the horizon as David pulled into the driveway of a tiny bungalow. "Here it is," he said, opening his car door.

"It's cute," I said, climbing out and staring at the front porch covered in vines. Somehow I'd pictured him in a more contemporary house, not an older one with so much character. But after seeing the place, I realized it fit him perfectly.

David moved to the trunk and popped the lid. "Let's get the door marked and get inside before we stumble upon any nasty surprises."

"You think there's a chance that we'd find any spirits or demons this far from Manteo?"

He already had his bag slung over his shoulder and my bag in his hand. "Honestly, I don't know," he said as he closed the trunk. "But I'd rather not hang outside and find out."

He led me down a short cobblestone path to the stone-covered front steps, and I noticed that two wicker chairs had been arranged on one side. Several flowerpots with dead plants were in one of the corners.

"You had flowers?" I asked.

He cast a glance at the containers and shrugged before placing his key in the doorknob. "Yeah, they reminded me of my mother's garden back home."

"Do you miss your family?" His mother and father lived in London, and he saw them no more than once or twice a year.

"Sometimes. I was feeling a bit nostalgic at the beginning of the summer. I told you I was going through a rough patch."

He pushed the door open and stepped inside to turn on a light. A warm glow lit up the sheer curtains in the windows.

I grabbed a piece of charcoal from my purse and tossed the bag on the porch. David came back out, his gaze dropping to my hand. I lifted it and shrugged. "I came prepared. Why don't you go inside and I'll start marking."

He moved behind me, standing on the top step as if guarding my back. "And leave you out here alone? I'd rather not. Besides, I like to watch you mark the doors. It's like watching a ceremony."

I gave him a small smile, though his comment made me think of how I'd felt when I first saw Collin marking my door. "How many doors are there?"

"Two."

I nodded and then began, making the marks for the elements around the perimeter of the door, starting with the four corners. As I applied the signs to the door, I asked the moon to lend its protection through the night, for the sun to add its strength to the moon as it watched over us, for the air to protect us from the wind gods. And in the center of each edge, I placed my own symbol for water along with David's initials—the two people I was asking the elements to protect. In the very center of the door, I placed the new mark that Collin had begun to add, a diamond with an x in the center—the symbol that would keep the gods and spirits from invading our dreams.

When I finished, I stepped back and made sure it looked complete. The black charcoal marks on the red door were really going to stick out tomorrow in the daylight.

"What are your neighbors going to think?" I asked.

He chuckled. "They know I'm a professor of Native American studies. They probably won't think anything of it. Besides, we'll only be here two nights. Now let's go mark the back door so we can give all of my neighbors something to talk about."

He grabbed my hand and pulled me through the front door. Like the house itself, the furnishings weren't what I'd expected. There was a vintage sofa in the living room and a couple of armchairs arranged in front of a brick fireplace.

"The back door is off the kitchen." We walked through the dining room and into the small kitchen. David flipped on the overhead light, then opened an upper cabinet door and pulled out a flashlight. "There's a small landing outside the door. We both won't fit on it, so I'll muck about the yard while you do the marking. When we go back inside, we can both take care of the salt."

"Okay."

We walked out the back door and I started making the protective marks while the flashlight beam bounced around the backyard. When I finished, I looked around, the nearly full moon providing enough light for me to tell that the yard butted up to some woods. A small shed was in the back corner.

Realizing that I was finished, David came back and flipped off the flashlight. "Nothing looks amiss, so that's good."

"I can't wait to see everything in the daylight."

He laughed. "I hope you're not too disappointed. The grass is overgrown and the flowerbeds need weeding."

We went back inside and I poured salt on the window ledges in the front room while David worked on the back. When we were finished, I asked for the location of the bathroom, and David pointed me toward a short hall off the dining room.

"There are only two bedrooms and mine's in the back," he said, moving into the kitchen and opening a cabinet. "I put our bags in there. Feel free to make yourself at home. I'm going to figure out what I have for us to eat."

"Okay." I took my time walking through the dining room and down the hall, amazed by how comfortable and cozy David's house was. I closed myself in the small bathroom, which was covered in light blue tiles. The shower curtain and towels were white, making the room feel clean and fresh.

When I finished, I wandered back to David's room. He'd left the lamp on next to his bed, and my bag was sitting in a chair in the corner. The room was small, so the queen-size bed filled up most of it. The room was warm and inviting, with light tan walls and a dark red comforter on the bed.

I found David in the kitchen, standing in front of the oven with a frozen pizza box. He looked up with a grin. "The bad news is that we're having a three-month-old frozen pizza for dinner. The good news is that I have a bottle of wine that's even older."

I laughed. "Sounds good. Especially the part about you cooking."

David put the pizza in the oven, then poured wine into two glasses and handed one to me.

"I love your house," I said after taking a sip. "Are you still planning to give it up?"

He picked up his glass and rested his backside against the kitchen counter. "I don't see the point in keeping it. At least for the next few months. Subletting it to a grad student or a new professor seems like the best plan."

"What about your things? We probably won't have time to move everything out while we're here."

"I can pack up most of my personal items this weekend and store the boxes in the shed. I'll just rent it furnished."

"Are you sure you want to do that? You have some really nice furniture."

His eyes narrowed in concern. "What's this all about, Ellie?"

"I just feel so guilty. You're giving up everything, literally *everything*, for me."

He cracked an ornery smile. "Not just for you, Ellie. I'm doing my part to save humanity. You're just a fringe benefit."

I laughed. "So you're telling me that your decision to live in Manteo—with me—was made with purely altruistic motives."

He stepped toward me and pulled me into his arms. "Yes. Pure and utter selflessness." He kissed me, taking his time as his mouth explored mine.

But I wasn't so easily distracted. I pulled my head back and searched his face. "David, I'm serious. What happens when your sabbatical is up? It only lasts until the end of December."

"It's only mid-August. We have a few months to figure it out." He cupped my cheek. "Don't worry, Ellie. I'm exactly where I want to be."

"Back in your kitchen?" I teased.

"No, with *you*. Wherever you are is where I want to be, Ellie Lancaster."

We sat at his kitchen table and drank wine while we waited on the pizza. "What's your plan with Allison?" I asked, keeping my gaze on my glass.

David hesitated. "I'm supposed to call her in the morning to confirm, but last I heard, she can't meet with us until tomorrow evening. So I thought we could go by the library during the day to look at those resources I mentioned."

"Okay." Part of me was happy to hear we wouldn't see David's ex for almost twenty-four hours, even if she had potentially seen the Ricardo Estate. I needed to suck it up and be mature.

"The library opens at nine and closes at one on Saturday. I want to get there as soon as it opens so we don't run out of time. Afterward, we can go out to lunch and figure out what to do with the rest of the day." He paused and reached for my hand. "And then if everything is still a go, we'll meet Allison in the evening."

I nodded. "Yeah. Sounds great." I sucked in a breath, hating myself for what I was about to ask. "Why did you break up?" Talk about sounding needy.

He sat up straighter but didn't release my hand. "We dated for a year and Allison was ready to get serious and start a family. I cared for her, but I knew she wasn't the one."

"How long ago did you break up?"

He hesitated. "Last winter."

The timer on the oven went off and David hopped up to get the pizza out. I grabbed two plates out of the cabinet and rinsed them off and dried them before putting them on the table. When we sat down, I grimaced and turned to him. "I have a feeling this meeting might not go very well."

"Why?"

"From everything you've said, Allison obviously loved you. She's going to be able to tell how you feel about me. We've been together for a little over a month. You didn't love her after a year. That's not going to go over well."

He sat back, looking slightly alarmed. "What do you want to do? I really think you should be there. You might have some insight that I don't."

I had to admit that I wanted to see whatever it was that she had in her possession. "How about I go, but if things get too tense, I'll leave."

He nodded, but he didn't look happy about it.

We ate in silence for several seconds before I decided now was a good time to tell him about my recent discoveries. "Yesterday, when Claire and I were supposed to be cleaning, she told me about something that happened on her honeymoon."

He laughed. "She's not urging us to try another new sexual position, is she? Why she cares so much about our sex life is beyond me."

"No." I chuckled nervously. "Nothing like that."

"Why do you look so anxious? Should I be worried?"

"No, I don't think so." I told him about her seeing the ghost of poor Mr. Murphy at my apartment building and her experience at the cemetery in Charleston. "She used to hear voices when she was a little girl," I said. "They stopped right around the time of Momma's murder. Apparently she told me about it when we were kids, the day I told her about the curse. Only I don't remember her telling me."

His eyes widened. "Claire's ability to talk to ghosts is related to the curse?"

"I don't know. Maybe. All I know is that her ability has suddenly returned, and she says a voice is telling her that we need to move out of my parents' house, that there's a darkness there."

"How do we know we can trust this voice?"

"When Claire was a little girl, the voices used to say 'you have to help her.' Claire didn't know what it meant then, but now she thinks it means she needs to help me."

He looked skeptical. "I still don't know if this voice is a credible source."

I cocked my head. "It also told Claire that I need to stay with you."

A sly grin spread across his face. "I suddenly like this voice."

"Besides, Claire says she sees the darkness too. It could be nothing, but you know I don't feel comfortable there. Especially since Myra left for Durham."

"I know, love. It might be because you miss her so much."

While I had to admit it felt empty without Myra and Daddy in the house, I was sure there was more to it. I rubbed my greasy hand on a paper towel. "I've put more thought into selling it."

He looked surprised. "But you haven't found all the notes from your father. And what about it being in your family for generations?"

"Those are all still issues, but I trust Claire." I paused. "I trust the voice." I knew I should tell him that Okeus had said Claire could help me, but that would mean telling him more about Collin.

"Okay." He looked lost in thought. "Do you have any idea where you want to move?"

"I think I'd like to be closer to the ocean."

He was lifting his wine glass to his mouth, but he lowered it, his face expressionless.

"I know it's expensive, and we don't have to find somewhere that's oceanfront, but if I could find an apartment—"

"Ellie."

"—and real estate is cheaper since the last hurricane—"

"Ellie."

I stopped talking and started twisting my hands in my lap.

"I think it's a great idea. I don't know why I hadn't considered it before. If you're closer to the ocean, you can swim in it every day. The spirit world is getting stronger, which means you're going to have more and more contact with them. I think you're right. I think we should do it."

I released a heavy breath. "Thank you."

His brow furrowed. "Did you think I'd be upset?"

"It's so expensive. But if I manage to sell the house quickly, I can use what little money I get from the sale toward a down payment on a new place."

"Ellie, we'll sort it out. I think we should start looking right after we get back."

"There's something else."

"Something bigger than Claire's newly awakened ghost-whisperer ability?"

"Today I remembered something about the night Momma was murdered."

"You did?" He set down his wine glass. "When? What did you remember?"

"The man who was downstairs with Momma was looking for a ring. I think it was the one I'm wearing now."

David stared at the wall behind the table, concentration wrinkling his brow. "That would definitely tie her death to the Ricardo Estate."

"And there's one more thing about my memory." I waited until I had his full attention. "Ahone was there, and he kept me from going downstairs."

"*Ahone?* Are you sure?"

"Yes."

"This *is* a big deal. Do you remember anything else?"

"He told me that the man would hurt me." I bit my bottom lip. "David, if he was there, he could have prevented Momma's death. He's using me. He's been using me since I was a little girl. I think he knew I was a pure soul and he's been waiting for me to be ready. He was the one who convinced Collin to break the curse."

David looked skeptical. "That's a lot of suppositions."

"You're the one who said there are no coincidences when it comes to the curse."

"True enough."

I needed to tell him what I'd discovered. "When I saw Collin today, he told me that Ahone came to him as a glowing ball of light two months before the curse broke. He's the one who wanted Collin to come and see me."

"Can you trust him?"

"I didn't at first, but then he made a good point. All the other gods and spirits were locked behind the gate to Popogusso. It had to be Ahone. He was the only one who was free."

"And how do you know that Collin isn't lying to you, that he didn't come up with this plan all on his own?"

"Because I felt it through our connection. He's telling the truth."

He hesitated. "You touched marks today?"

Damn my mouth. But David deserved to know. "Yes."

He gave me a soft smile, but sadness filled his eyes. "You're the Curse Keepers. You were meant to use them."

I threw my arms around his neck. "I need you, David. You have no idea how much I need you."

He pulled me back and cupped my cheek. Disappointment covered his face. "I know, Ellie."

Those weren't the three words he wanted to hear, but I couldn't bring myself to say those *other* words yet. I dropped my gaze. "I can't trust Ahone. He's just as bad as Okeus, and I have no plans to align myself with him either, but now I'm stuck with his mark on my back and I'm not sure what that means. His messenger led me to believe that it meant I could go to heaven with my parents. But Okeus said my soul is bound to Collin's, so I'll end up in Popogusso with him. Which is it?"

David shook his head and said softly, "I don't know."

"I need to figure out how to do this without relying on Okeus or Ahone or even Collin. I'm the witness to creation. I must have some kind of power of my own other than the mark's ability to send away spirits. I want to find out what it is and how to use it. I want to make my *own* destiny."

"Perhaps Allison will have some information that will help us. If the Ricardo Estate really does have weapons that can kill demons, it will be a complete game changer."

"You're right and I hope it's true, but Collin pointed out that while Ahone gave us the power of the earth and the sea, he had nothing to do with the fact that I witnessed the birth of the gods. I can't help thinking that I can somehow harness my power as a witness to creation. I'm sure Ahone wanted to use it to his benefit, even if I'm not sure to what purpose. And we both know how Okeus wants to use it."

He pushed his plate away and sat back in his chair. "Okay, Ellie. How do you want to go about this?"

"I want to scour those books at the library for any kind of clue. Not only about any prophecies, but also for any mention of a previous witness to creation. Do you remember ever coming across something like that?"

"No, not offhand, but I wasn't looking for it then either. We're investigating texts anyway, so we'll just expand our search. But it might take all weekend. And then some. The books and documents in the archives can't be removed, but we have full access to them during library hours."

"Okay. Collin and I still have the power of the earth and the sea as well, but I'm not sure how to use the ocean either. Surely it involves more than being a power generator."

His mouth pursed. "And Collin definitely has the advantage there since he's the son of the earth. He can go anywhere to tap into his power. You're tied to the coasts."

"Exactly. Not very convenient, which is why I need to figure out how both sources can be used."

He nodded and I could see him thinking my ideas through. His gaze lifted to mine. "Yeah, it's a good idea. We'll start looking into it tomorrow."

I took a sip of my wine, feeling more in control than I had in a long time. It was good to take charge of my life and not feel like a leaf dangling in the wind. I watched the man across from me, reassured that he was the one for me. I gave him a sexy smile. "You haven't shown me the rest of your house."

He polished off the small amount of wine in his glass and set it on the table. "I take it that you have a particular room in mind." He stood and reached for my hand, pulling me to my feet.

"I most definitely do." I stood on my tiptoes, pressing my mouth to his.

"You're being very assertive tonight," he murmured against my lips, then grinned. "It's very sexy."

"You mean bossy?"

He lifted his head, still grinning, but his gaze was serious. "No, bossy insinuates that someone has overstepped their bounds. You're a bloody Curse Keeper, Ellie. I think you're right. There's more power available to you than you know. That makes you a person of authority. Hell, demons need to bow to your wishes."

I gave him a wicked grin. "Then I command you to take me to your bedroom and undress me."

He took a step backward, pulling me with him. "It will be my pleasure."

◦: CHAPTER EIGHT :◦

I woke up disoriented, barely registering the banging on the front door.

David bolted upright. "*Bollocks.*"

With a groan, I sat up, completely naked, and checked the time on the clock on David's nightstand. Three a.m. It had been too much to hope that I'd escape a nocturnal visit two hundred miles away from ground zero. Especially since my front door hadn't seen any middle-of-the-night action in a couple of weeks.

There was more banging on the door, followed by a moan. "Curse Keeper."

Climbing out of bed, I groped around in the dark for something to wear, finding David's button-down shirt on the floor where he'd thrown it a few hours earlier. Slipping my arms through the sleeves, I fastened the middle buttons as I walked to the front door. David was on my heels, tying the drawstring of a pair of pajama bottoms he'd pulled out of a dresser drawer.

"David, stay back. I don't know what's out there."

"All the more reason for me to be close at hand. You could be facing an entirely new set of spirits this far from the coast. If I recognize it, I can help you."

"No. All the more reason for you to take cover. Even if the spirit can't cross the threshold, it might be able to project its power."

"If you think I'm just going to leave you to face it alone, you've got another think coming."

I stopped at the front door. "If you're going to stick around to watch, at least go hide behind a sofa or something."

"Do you know how emasculating that sounds?" he asked, running his hand through his hair.

"David, please." Some of the fight left my words.

"Fine," he said, moving behind the sofa and crouching down. "Just *please* be careful."

I flashed him a grim smile before opening the door.

A three-foot-tall bird with a human head sat on the front porch. A wind god. I was used to regular visits from Wapi, the white-haired wind god of the north, but damned if I could remember which one this was. His hair was red and his nose was wider than Wapi's.

"Curse Keeper," he groaned.

"Hello, wind god of—sorry, I'm not sure which one you are."

The bird man screeched his displeasure. "You will fear Mekewi, god of the south, Curse Keeper. You will remember my name and it will strike fear in your heart."

I grabbed the edge of the door and leaned into it. "Well, *Mekewi*, I've had a long day and you're interrupting my sleep. How about you cut to the chase?"

He shouted something unintelligible, but the force of his breath blew my hair out behind me. "You do not give orders to a wind god!"

I waited a couple of seconds and then lifted my eyebrows in mock surprise. "Are you done with your fit now? Because so far this has been a huge waste of my time. Do you have something to tell me or not?"

"Do not trust the children of Kalona or their overseer. They wish to seek you out, but Okeus worries for your safety."

I wanted to ask why Okeus hadn't bothered to mention it the day before, but I didn't want to broach the subject while David was listening. "I'm an equal opportunist—I distrust all of you, so tell Okeus not to worry. I'll be on guard."

The bird moved closer until he stood only inches from the invisible wall between the inside and outside. "You have many enemies in the spirit world as well as out of it. One day, Okeus will be done with you. And then we will feast."

"Sorry. My Manitou is no longer fair game."

His grin was wicked. "There are other parts of you to devour besides your Manitou."

Then he vanished into thin air.

"You really need to quit taunting them." David stood up from behind the sofa. "He's right. Okeus's protection probably won't last forever. Then you'll be at their mercy."

"Not for long, I won't." A small part of me knew he was right, that mocking them was stupid, but I hated that they had the upper hand. I needed to show my defiance somehow and my mouth was the only way I knew how.

But not for long.

I slammed the door shut and strode past David to the bedroom. "I will never be at their mercy, because you and I are going to figure out how to defy them with magic."

I was amazed that I managed to get back to sleep. I usually couldn't after a confrontation with a god, but I realized I was becoming desensitized to them. I was also smart enough to know that that could prove dangerous. I could mock the gods and spirits all I wanted behind my protected doors, but I refused to live hidden behind them. Especially while people were dying.

When I woke up again, sunlight was streaming through the crack between the curtains hanging in David's window. He sat upright in bed, holding a cup of coffee, his computer in his lap. When he realized I was awake, he glanced down and smiled. "Good morning."

I arched my back and stretched. "What time is it?"

"Seven fifteen."

"I haven't slept this late in weeks." I sat up, propped my pillow against his headboard, and leaned back. "Why didn't you wake me?"

David set his cup on the nightstand. "You needed the sleep, and I loved watching you."

"Well, you obviously have coffee, but is there anything to eat?"

He leaned over and gave me a kiss.

"I was talking about actual food."

He pushed me back down. "Did I mention how sexy you looked standing in my doorway last night, wearing my shirt with nothing on underneath?"

I grinned. "No. You didn't."

His mouth covered mine as his hand slipped under the covers and up my shirt. "We have an hour and forty-five minutes and I live ten minutes from the library."

"Don't we have something more important to do?" I asked, my chest rising and falling in quick bursts.

A huge smile spread across his face. "I can't think of a single bloody thing."

"Well, all right then." I reached behind his head and pulled his mouth to mine, kissing him hard. A half an hour later, we lay in bed naked, our arms and legs tangled.

"As crazy as it is in all this chaos, I've never known such contentment as I feel with you, Ellie."

I sighed with my own contentment, even if it was tinged with guilt. David was the man I wanted. The one whom I had chosen. I'd be damned if some asshole gods thought they could control that part of my life. "I know exactly what you mean, but I want it to last. Let's go find some answers in your books." I sat up. "But first you need to feed me breakfast. I've worked up an appetite."

After we got ready for the day and stopped to pick up breakfast sandwiches and coffee on the way to the campus, David parked in the faculty parking lot at eight fifty.

"We need to stop at the coffee shop on the way to the library," David said as he took the key out of the ignition.

"We just got coffee."

"Oh, this isn't for us." He climbed out of the car, slinging his bag over his shoulder.

"Okay . . ."

As we started to walk across the campus, he shot me a sly grin. "This is for Penelope, the archivist I usually work with. I'm lucky she works on Saturdays."

"You're bringing the archivist coffee?"

"This morning I made a list online of all the books and documents I want to see and uploaded it to the system, but one of them is an older letter that will require more attention. This is my way of saying thank-you."

"What?" I laughed. "Your good looks, charming smile, and sexy accent aren't enough to get her to help you?"

He shot me an ornery look. "Penelope can see right through that nonsense."

"Then I can't wait to meet Penelope."

The coffee shop was in the bookstore, which happened to be on the way to the library. Once we reached the library, David logged on to one of the computers and printed out his list of requested documents before taking it to the desk.

"Well, Dr. Preston." A woman with graying dark hair beamed from behind the desk. "I haven't seen you in ages."

"I've been working in Manteo. At the colony site."

Her eyes widened. "What I wouldn't give to see that."

"Come over to the Outer Banks and I'll get you a visitor's pass and show you around."

She blinked in surprise. "You can't be serious."

"I'm totally serious; just give me a day or two of notice so I can get it pushed through the approval process." He set the coffee cup on the desk. "In the meantime, I hope you still like vanilla soy lattes."

"You know that I do." She grinned and took the cup, then glanced up at me.

"Ellie, this is Penelope Fisher, my favorite archivist." He winked at her, and an amused smile spread across her face. Then he motioned toward me. "Penelope, this is Ellie Lancaster, daughter of John and Amanda Lancaster. They both lived and breathed the Lost Colony before their deaths. John was well known for his work—"

"On the colonists and their relationships with the neighboring Native Americans," Penelope finished. "We have some of his work in the North Carolina collection."

My mouth parted in astonishment. "You do?"

"I attended one of your father's lectures twenty years ago when he came to Chapel Hill. He had some fascinating insights. He was a great man. I was sorry to hear about his passing."

"Thank you." I waited for the familiar lump in my throat when talking about my father's death and was surprised when it didn't come. Maybe I was getting desensitized to that too.

"Ellie's mother was an archaeologist who worked at Fort Raleigh.

She specialized in English artifacts dating back to the colonies. Ellie practically cut her teeth on anything to do with the Lost Colony, so you can appreciate her fascination now that it has reappeared."

"Of course," Penelope agreed. "Are you two here to research something connected with the colony?"

"Yes, but I'm studying Manteo's hut that was located on the site, and I need to research some books and letters that might help me interpret what I've found. And there's also an old letter I'd like to examine." David handed Penelope the printout.

She studied the list before looking up at David. "The books I can get for you right away. But it will take me a bit to get the letter."

"Thanks, Penelope."

"I'll bring the books into the reading room. Why don't you two wait for me there."

David nodded his agreement and led me into a large room full of wooden tables and chairs. The marble floor was set in a checker-board pattern, and tall arched windows lined the walls. The multiple gold chandeliers hanging overhead completed the impressive décor. Less than a dozen other people filled the room, not that I was surprised. Who wanted to spend a Saturday morning in the library the first week of school? Even one as nice as this.

"This place is amazing," I murmured.

He looked around with a grin. "One thing I love about it is that there's always plenty of light in here. I spent so much time in this room when I first came to Chapel Hill, I was grateful it wasn't some dark, dingy hole."

The archivist appeared ten minutes later with several books and set the stack on the table. "Give me about twenty minutes' notice before you want to see the letter. Then I'll take you back to examine it."

David smiled softly at her. "Thanks, Penelope."

"I've missed your face around here," she said with a wink before she left us.

"You haven't been gone that long," I murmured, sitting next to David.

"True. But I haven't been here in the library since last spring. As I mentioned, I spent a lot of time here when I first came to Chapel Hill. There were so many documents about the Cherokee that I could access from the archives. But I was also lonely and didn't have anywhere else to go. After spending so much time here, I got to know Penelope pretty well. She lived in London in her twenties and early thirties, so we had that in common. She felt sorry for me and started baking things and bringing them for me to take home." He pulled the first book from the stack. "I'm going to put you to work on this too. These books are older, but they're not rare and fragile. I'm not sure how much we'll find, but a few pieces of information here and there could help. If you find something that looks useful, let me know."

"Okay."

We spent the next hour and a half reading and scanning through the books before I found something that mentioned Ukinim, the malevolent badger. "David, look at this."

He leaned closer, reading the passage. "This is good. And a few more of the deities are mentioned as well." He reached for the book. "Do you mind?"

I gladly slid it over to him. "I'd like to read it when you're done, but go for it."

He scrawled several pages of notes and then glanced up at me with excitement. "I've got a list of twelve supernatural beings, some considered good, some evil. This is fantastic." Glancing down at his phone, he grimaced. "The library closes in two hours. I'll go tell Penelope we're ready to look at the letter as soon as possible. We can come back when the library opens tomorrow to review the rest."

"Sounds good."

He passed the book back to me and I read the material about the assorted spirits. There was a rabbit that watched over crops, a white crane that brought good luck, and a lizard that liked to play tricks on children. I read about a bear that brought destruction to those who offended the gods—I suspected I'd meet him at some point—and a large bird with razor-sharp teeth that liked to eat young men as they passed into adulthood. But the scariest was the Wendigo, a demon that possessed the body of a human before attacking and killing other humans.

"Have you heard of a Wendigo before?" David asked. I hadn't even processed his return, but he must have noticed I was lingering over that portion of the text.

"No."

"They appear quite a bit in folklore and stories. Most historians think the legend came from the northern Algonquian, who were known to perform acts of cannibalism on enemy tribes. But consuming human meat produced a psychosis in aboriginal tribes called Wendigo psychosis."

"So you think that maybe Wendigo aren't real?"

"No, that's not what I'm saying at all." He shook his head. "While there were cases that were attributed to psychosis, they happened after the disappearance of the colony. I think it's two different things, but I also think it's good to have all the facts and not jump to conclusions."

I nodded my agreement.

We had gone through six books by the time Penelope came back an hour later to tell us the letter was ready, apologizing for the delay. "We're short-staffed today." She collected the volumes and asked us to follow her into a small hallway with dim lighting. "Wait here a moment and I'll let you in."

Penelope carried the books down the hall and turned the corner as David cast an anxious look at the closed door.

I glanced at it too, now worried about what lay behind it. "Why do you look nervous?"

"I'm hinging a lot of hope on this document, Ellie."

"*What?* You didn't tell me that. Only that you thought you could get some useful information."

"I didn't want to give you anything else to worry about. In case it came to nothing."

I wanted to call him out for keeping something from me, but who was I to judge? My own guilt smoldered in my gut. "What do you hope to find?"

"I think this letter will tell you what you can do with the ring on your finger. I only hope it lives up to my expectations." He paused, fear filling his eyes. "Ellie, your life depends on me finding answers. What if I'm wrong? What if I keep failing you?"

My eyes widened. "David, you could never fail me. Even if we don't find anything useful in the letter about the ring, you still haven't failed me. Besides, we've already gotten information about a dozen other spirits today, not to mention your connection to Allison and her possible information about the Ricardo Estate. And what about everything you've discovered about the Guardians? I never would have known about any of it if not for you."

"But the possible connection to the Guardians is a shot in the dark. And it could be a coincidence that Allison saw a watch similar to your father's."

"Who's the one who keeps insisting there are no coincidences?"

"I know, Ellie." He grimaced. "I'm sorry. It's just that if you can't learn how to fight these things on your own, we're lost. It's almost too much to hope for that the information would conveniently show up like that."

"We could use a little convenience for once. But I understand what you're saying."

His voice softened. "You have so much faith in me. I just hope it's not misplaced."

I shook my head. "Don't think like that. I need you, David. And not just for this." I pointed to the door to the climate-controlled room. "I need *you*. When I feel like this situation is completely hopeless, you make me believe I can actually do it. That we actually have a chance."

"We *do*." He leaned down and gave me a soft kiss.

"That's just it," I murmured as he pulled away. "That's why I need you. You have enough faith for both of us."

Penelope cleared her throat as she reappeared. "I think you left out an important piece of information about Ms. Lancaster."

David laughed. "I didn't think it was important."

"Anything concerning your love life is important. Especially after Dr. Moran."

David stiffened slightly and cast a glance in my direction, but I offered him a reassuring smile. So Penelope knew about David's old girlfriend. It wasn't really a surprise, since they'd dated for a year.

She led us into the room, where a document lay on a tray on a metal table. "You know the rules. I don't think I need to go over them again."

David sat down in front of the document, already enthralled.

"I'm not supposed to leave you alone with this, but if I can't trust you, I'm not sure there's anyone I can trust. I need to go check on something, but I'll be right back."

David grunted his acknowledgment.

Penelope chuckled as she walked past me. "He gets like that

when he's reading these old things. I love when someone appreciates these antiquities as much as I do."

I watched her leave, then sank into the chair next to David's, worried about disturbing him. But he reached over and placed his hand on my lap for a moment before turning back to his reading.

Penelope came back in the room just as David sat upright, groaning. "This isn't it."

"What are you looking for?" she asked, moving closer and resting her hand on the back of his chair.

"I remember coming across a letter from an English settler, dating back to the late 1600s, that tells about a Croatan conjurer who created two weapons to defeat demons."

The archivist's forehead wrinkled. "What else did it discuss?"

"It seems like it was a letter sent from a man in the Albemarle colony to his sister up in Jamestown. It mostly discussed his daily life as a farmer, but he also shared this story with her."

"Hmm." Penelope murmured. "I may know where to look, but I'm not sure I can find it today."

"Okay," David said, disappointment in his voice.

"But there's another one that might be helpful too, and this one's easier to retrieve. I take it you're looking for something pertaining to the Croatan and a conjurer? It's another letter, from the same area, but pertaining to the proprietor Seth Sothel and his harsh rule over the colonists. It dates back to the 1680s if I remember correctly. I believe there's mention of a Croatan conjurer."

David's forehead wrinkled. "You would think I'd remember that."

"It's fairly new. Just added to the collection via a private donation a couple of months ago."

David shot me a look before turning back to Penelope. "It's definitely worth looking at. Thank you."

"No problem. Let me just put this away and I'll pull it for you."

David and I waited in the room while the archivist took the document away.

"Do you think it's a coincidence that the letter showed up right before the curse broke?" I whispered.

"No," was his terse reply.

"Why are you so upset?"

"I know I should be grateful that this might answer some of our questions, but I hate being a pawn of the gods."

Closing my eyes, I released a heavy sigh. "I know. And it's becoming more and more obvious that that's exactly what we are."

His hand covered mine again. "We're in this together." His touch was comforting, but it reminded me of my moment at the beach with Collin. If only I could sever my attraction to him entirely.

Penelope returned about twenty minutes later with the document. She set it in front of David. "Like I said, this is a fairly new addition."

"Do you know who donated the letter?"

"Not offhand. It came from a private collection and was the only letter donated. Usually they come in groups. It's also unusual in that we had little advance notice that it was coming. It's almost as though it just dropped from the sky."

David shot me a glance before turning back to the letter. "I'm eager to take a look."

Penelope nodded and then moved to the corner of the room to give us some privacy. David read for a couple of minutes before he sat upright, his eyes alight with excitement.

"Did you find something?" I whispered.

He turned to me and gave me a hard kiss on the mouth before leaning back, grinning with excitement.

"Ellie, this changes everything."

∿ CHAPTER NINE ∿

"What does it say?"

He cast a glance at Penelope, who was still standing in the corner of the room and was clearly dying with curiosity.

"It has the information we needed and so much more."

The words were obviously bursting to be released, but I could tell that he didn't want to talk about it in front of the archivist.

"So this letter was helpful?" she asked, prodding.

"More so than you can know."

"Well . . . ?"

"It talks about a Croatan conjurer who spoke to demons at the gate to Popogusso."

Penelope smiled. "So it's a legend."

David hesitated. "It reads as though this man witnessed the event, which of course is ludicrous," he added. "But it corroborates another story I've heard."

"From the other letter?"

The corner of his mouth quirked. "Yes."

"I take it that you still want to see it?" Penelope asked. "I can leave a note for Sylvia that you'll be in to view it tomorrow afternoon."

"That would be great. Thanks." He pulled out his phone and started to take photos of the text—flash off, of course—while Penelope watched. After he examined the photos, he told her that he was done and picked up his bag.

Penelope could obviously tell that he wasn't being straightforward, but she seemed to be willing to let it go.

"There's another document you might be interested in," she said as she started to take the letter away. She paused and looked up at him with a smug smile. "If you're interested in stories about Croatan demons and gods, that is."

David's head jerked up.

"I'm a resource, David," she said, using his first name. "Use me."

"You're right, Penelope. Thanks."

"It's a handwritten book of sorts, quite unusual. It tells the story of an Englishman and a Croatan warrior who had a confrontation one night. It mentions demons and the gate to hell."

"Why haven't I heard about this one either?"

She shrugged. "It's anecdotal. There's some argument over whether it's even legit."

"And what was the conclusion?"

"There wasn't one. The paper was determined to be old enough, but the ink that was used was unconventional for the time period."

"And what time period was that?"

"Mid-eighteenth century. The manuscript was dated."

"And I take it that I can't read it until tomorrow."

She grinned.

"Okay," he said. "Can you add it to the list?"

"You got it."

We left the room and David grabbed my hand, practically dragging me outside the library.

"Okay," I said, barely able to contain myself. "What did you find?"

"Let's go to my office. I want to upload these photos and show you."

While I could see the wisdom in that, and I knew we shouldn't be talking about this out in the open, I was dying to know. "So it's good?"

"It's better than good. It's the best we could hope for."

Thankfully, his office building was practically behind the library. He pulled his keys out as we climbed the stairs to the second floor and had the door open within seconds. The room was small, less than eight feet wide. There was a window with vinyl blinds in the outside wall, and a wooden desk sat against the wall, perpendicular to the door. There was a tall metal file cabinet next to the desk.

"I guess you get a proper look at it this time, huh?" he said as he shut the door behind us and sat in his office chair. He opened a drawer and pulled out a cord to hook his phone to his computer.

"It's so weird," I said, looking around. "I was with you the last time you were here. As you were getting ready to leave." I had come to see him two months ago. He'd been packing for Manteo at the time, though I hadn't realized that. At first he'd thought I was an overzealous undergrad who was trying to get into one of his intro classes. "I bet those poor girls who moved mountains to get into your class are beyond devastated to find out you weren't their instructor after all."

He laughed, sounding embarrassed. "I'm mortified when I think about how incredibly rude I was to you that day."

"You were pretty bad. But I'll let it go if you tell me what you found in that letter." The suspense was starting to eat at me.

I perched on the edge of his desk as he started the photo upload.

"Parts were a bit smudged, but I was able to make out most of it. The man who wrote this letter was a farmer from the Albemarle colony in northern North Carolina. He came down from Jamestown with a group who started a settlement along the Albemarle Sound in the mid-1600s. The note we found from your father said your ancestors went to Jamestown and then down to Albemarle with the initial colonists. In any case, this man—George—was part of a scouting expedition."

"So this George is one of my ancestors?"

He glanced up, shaking his head. "No, I don't think so, and I'll tell you why in a second." He picked up an ink pen and pointed the end at his screen. "It says here that there had been some skirmishes with the natives, and the colonists decided to take the offensive and scout for any hostile parties. They took three boats and set out on the sound. After a long day on the water, they landed on an island and started to look around, but something spooked George's friends and they took off without him. Soon after they left, the sun went down. George was worried, but he figured his friends would come back. There was a new moon, though, so he knew they wouldn't be able to retrieve him until morning. He decided to walk around the perimeter of the island and he came upon two boats—one obviously native, the other English. Worried, he pushed into the woods until he heard voices and saw a fire in the distance. While he was hiding in the trees, he saw a Native American man and an Englishman deep in the forest. The native was conducting a ceremony of some kind while the Englishman stood to the side and watched.

"There were multiple circles and markings on the ground. The native—George calls him a conjurer—had a spear in his hand, along with something else. He smeared his own blood on the objects, and then a huge storm rolled in out of nowhere. He said the trees shook violently, but the conjurer and the Englishman paid no attention, and the conjurer continued his chant. Suddenly something appeared in front of an oak tree—a gate." David scrolled to the next photo and enlarged it, then read: "'All manner of beasts and demonic creations were trapped behind the massive gate. The air was filled with wailing and moaning and screaming pleas to be set free.'"

My mouth gaped. "He saw Popogusso? When was this written?"

"1687."

"A hundred years after the curse? How is that possible?" I tried to make sense of it. "So he had to be on Roanoke Island."

"Agreed."

"You said this was good. There must be more."

David spun his chair around so he could look up at me. "George wrote that while the conjurer ignored the demons and spirits, the Englishman looked frightened. Then one of the demons—a man with black hair that was long on one side and short on the other, who was dressed in native attire—grabbed the bars and shouted at the men."

"Okeus," I breathed out in a gush. That was how he'd looked when he'd passed through the gate the night Collin let the demons loose.

David nodded and then turned back to the computer and pulled up another photo, reading the text on the screen. "He shouted, 'Conjurer! Give up this madness. Find your fellow Croatan brother, the Manteo Keeper, and have him join with the Dare Keeper to open the gate. If you do this, I will offer you great rewards.'"

"How did the conjurer have the power to expose the gate?"

"I don't know," David answered, deep in thought. "After reading the rest of this letter, it sounds like Ahone set the whole thing up." He turned back to the screen. "It says here that an older man appeared as the conjurer continued his ceremony. He had long white hair and a beard, and he told the demon behind the bars, 'One day you will be free, but not for long. Once the seal to the gate breaks open, I will set in motion a plan that will seal the gate permanently with you and your vile creations locked behind it forever.' Then the white-haired spirit chanted words and the spear and the other object in the conjurer's hand—a gold ring—began to glow so much that they lit up the forest. The demons started to scream and the white-haired man's voice rose above the noise, telling the Englishman, 'You now have a weapon to use on your own. And the other Keeper has one too. When you bring the weapons close to the gate of Popogusso, they will sing, and that's your sign that the weapon will allow you to send the demons back to hell.'"

"The weapons sing?" I asked. A thought tickled in the back of my head, a memory just out of reach. "The ring that sings at the gate of Popogusso," I murmured.

David sat up straighter. "You say that like you're remembering something."

I closed my eyes to concentrate, but nothing emerged. Shaking my head, I opened my eyes. "There's a memory there, but I can't reach it."

He snaked my hand and cradled it in his. "Obviously your memories have information we can use. Perhaps we should consider hypnosis to bring them to the surface."

I'd never thought of that before. "Do you think it would work?"

He searched my face. "It might be worth a try."

I released a sigh and stood, breaking free of his hold. "Does it say anything else?" A hint of irritation laced my words. I wasn't frustrated with David, though, just my own broken memory. I wasn't sure hypnosis was the answer. Did I really want a psychologist hearing my memories of the curse? I'd probably get a one-way ticket to the loony bin.

"It says the ceremony ended and the gate disappeared and the demons along with it, but the older spirit stayed and told the Englishman that one day the curse would break and his descendant would need the ring. That she was to stand next to the gate and recite the inscription on the band and reseal the gate. That her survival would depend on it." David looked up. "*Her*. All mentions of the Keepers on both sides seem to refer to them as men. Do you remember there ever being a female Keeper on the Dare line before you?"

I scoured my memory and shook my head, my breath catching. "No. Collin said his grandmother was a Keeper. She was only the third female Keeper in the Manteo line. But Daddy never mentioned a woman on our side."

David's mouth puckered with concentration. "It's not surprising that women would be the Keeper in the Manteo line. The Croatan were a matriarchal society. Although the conjurers were traditionally men."

"So the *her* could have been a Manteo Keeper?"

David shook his head. "I don't think so. Ahone told the Englishman—a Dare Keeper—that *his* descendant's survival would depend on it."

If the *her* referred to me, Ahone had predicted my birth over three hundred years ago. This had all been planned centuries ago. "Ahone had the letter sent here."

"You don't know that."

My gaze found his. "Yes. I do. It goes back so much further than I thought it did." It was past time to tell him about my chat with Okeus. I shouldn't have kept it from him for this long. "When I was at the beach yesterday, Collin and I joined hands when I was in the ocean. I had a vision of sorts. I was in the field where I saw my dad. Only this time, I saw Okeus."

"What?" he shot out of his seat and stood in front of me. "Why didn't you tell me? Did he try to hurt you?"

I understood his concern after my last encounter with the god. I shook my head. "No, he didn't, and I'm not sure why I didn't tell you. I didn't want to worry you, I guess."

"Ellie." The disappointment in his voice killed me.

"He told me that Ahone had orchestrated my birth. That my mother had experienced five miscarriages before giving birth to me."

He blinked in surprise. "Did she?"

"I don't know." I turned away and moved to the window. "I know my parents had fertility issues. They were older when I was born. It's not outside the realm of possibility."

"But why?"

I couldn't bring myself to tell him what Okeus had told me about Ahone wanting to create the perfect counterpart to Collin. "Who knows why they do what they do? Maybe he was waiting for a Keeper who was a witness to creation." I shrugged, hoping I was convincing. "Like I told you, Ahone was there the night my mother was murdered too." I spun around to face him, my face burning with anger. "He's a fucking god, David," I said. "He could have saved her that night, but he only saved me. He kept me hidden while I listened to her screams. I couldn't help her."

David's eyes widened. "What did you just say?"

I shook my head, fighting a faint feeling. Where had *that* come from? Was it true?

"Ahone *saved you*?" he asked.

I moved to the desk and sat on the edge. Too many things were happening and too many memories were rushing back to me before fading away just as quickly. I needed to get myself together. "It just popped into my head. I knew he kept me from going downstairs, but somehow I know he did even more to protect me. I just can't remember what."

He released a deep breath. "Wow. Okay. Ahone really wanted you alive. That's good."

"Is it? Okeus wants to use me because I'm a witness to creation, but at least he's semihonest about it. Ahone's a sneaky bastard who's trying to get what he wants without admitting to any of it. He was the one who told Collin to open the gate. He was the one who tricked him. Why would he want me to use the ring? For what purpose?" I'd spent a good part of the morning mulling it over while I scanned page after page, coming up with nothing.

Until now.

My eyes widened. "*The inscription*. He wants me to recite it at the gate. That's exactly what Ahone told my ancestor I needed to do." I shook my head in disgust. "I'm not giving that bastard what he wants. I don't think I should use it."

David's jaw dropped. "What do you mean you *shouldn't* use the ring? We just found out that it's real and you can use it on your own. Without Collin." He took a step back and ran his hand over his head. "Ellie, Ahone told the Dare Keeper that the ring would save your life by locking up the demons. No Collin needed. *Why wouldn't you use it?*"

"Because that's what Ahone wants, David! He's using me. I don't trust him, so I don't trust the ring either." I looked down at the vile thing on my hand. It had gotten my mother killed. I was certain of it. Was Ahone planning to sacrifice me as well? "I will never side with Ahone again."

"You're not seriously thinking about siding with Okeus, are you?"

My eyes narrowed. "No, of course not. I already told you last night that I don't want to side with either of them."

He shook his head in frustration. "If you won't use the ring for yourself, think about the lives of countless other people. Four people already died in Manteo because of the Raven Mockers, Ellie, and that might just be the beginning."

"*I don't trust him*. If I use it, I'm falling right into his plans, which we both know is *never* in my best interest. So if I use the ring, what price will I have to pay?"

"You already put his mark on your back, Ellie. You sold your soul to him. What else can he take?"

"You." Tears burned behind my eyes. "He can still take *you*. He's using me, yet he keeps taking things from me. He took my mother and my father. You might be next."

David heaved out a breath and pulled me against his chest, wrapping his arms around my back. "Oh, Ellie."

"I can't lose you, David. I don't think I could survive it."

He cradled my head against his chest. "I'm not going anywhere."

But I knew he couldn't promise me that.

Only one being could. And I was going to stop him if it was the last thing I did.

I suspected it just might be.

༄ Chapter Ten ༄

I gave David a kiss and stepped away from him, moving back to the window.

"Ellie, don't pull away from me because you're afraid of losing me."

I swallowed the lump in my throat and turned my attention to the wall of photos opposite his desk. "You have a lot of pictures."

He rested his butt against the desk, watching me. "Yeah," he murmured.

"I don't see any photos of naked coeds," I said with a small smile. "When I tried to show you a photo of my tattoo on my phone, you told me that you'd have me arrested if it was a naked picture. Have you really gotten any of those?"

"A few times, which was a few times more than I cared for. I think you know me well enough to know that I'm not really into that sort of thing." A slow grin spread across his face. "Unless you want to text me some photos of yourself."

I snorted. "Not a chance."

"You can't blame a bloke for trying."

My heart was heavy, but I couldn't stop myself from laughing. I stepped closer to the wall, where there were several pictures of David with an older couple. "Are these your parents?"

A soft smile spread across his face. "Yeah. And that's my brother, Matthew."

I studied a photo of a younger David with a guy who looked a lot like him. They were indoors, but the photo was so closely cropped, I couldn't tell much else about the room where they were standing. "He has a nice smile. He looks friendly."

"He is. We aren't close—we're just such opposites—but we're there for each other if one of us needs something."

"So you miss them?"

"Yeah. Particularly my mum, but we get to chat on the phone and Skype."

My head jerked up. "You haven't talked to her very much since you've been with me."

"I usually call during my lunch break at work." He shrugged. "The time difference."

I continued down the wall. The photos were random snapshots of his life. Pictures with friends at parties and a few archaeological sites. And there were several of David with a pretty blonde woman. Even though they weren't showing any signs of physical affection, I knew they were a couple. In one of the photos, they were in the mountains, both of them dressed in ski jackets and carrying poles. "You ski?" I asked.

"Yeah." He shifted nervously.

I pointed to the photo while looking over my shoulder at him. "This is Allison, isn't it?"

"We're still friends, Ellie. As I told you, our breakup was amicable." He pushed himself off the desk. "I can take them down."

"No." I shook my head. "Please don't." I gave him a tentative smile. "I'm not jealous of her."

He flashed a wonky grin. "I'm not sure whether to be worried or relieved."

I turned around so that I was facing him and stared into his anxious face. "Go with relieved. I know you want to be with me, so I'm not worried." Although I still wondered if it was a good idea for me to keep him around. The last thing I wanted to do was endanger him. "Do we know anything about when we're meeting her?"

"She texted earlier. She wants both of us to come over for dinner."

"*Dinner?*"

"We parted friends, Ellie. She's curious about what I've been up to in Manteo." He hesitated. "But we'll only do it if you're okay with it."

I didn't want to, but David put up with so much crap involving Collin, how could I refuse him? I could tell he really wanted to go. "Of course. It's fine."

"Okay." But he didn't sound convinced. "She'd like us to come to her house at seven."

"Okay." I paused. "I still haven't made arrangements to see Myra. I was waiting to see what happened with Allison. I'll see if she can meet me tomorrow."

"Let's grab some lunch and head back to my place. I can pack up some of my personal things before we go over to Allison's."

David led me to the doorway of his office. Before walking out of the room, he surveyed it for a moment, releasing a sigh. Then he locked the door behind us without another word.

"You miss it," I said softly. "Being here at the university."

He looked down at me, his brow furrowed. "Ellie."

"No, you do. I can tell."

He lowered his head close to my ear. "Do you remember when I told you weeks ago that I thought you were my destiny? That I had been moving on a path toward you for years? I still believe that."

"Maybe so, but you didn't answer my question."

He hesitated. "Yes, I miss it. I like teaching, and I miss the interaction with students."

My heart ached and guilt flooded in.

"You just asked me a few minutes ago if I miss my family and I admitted that I do. But I still wouldn't move back home." I started to talk and he put a finger on my lips. "Even if you weren't part of my life. I miss them, but it wouldn't be the same if I went back. I've changed. They've changed. I can't go back to that life even if that's what I wanted, which it isn't . . ." He took a breath. "This situation is exactly the same."

"No, it's not. You've only been gone about two months, not years."

"Maybe so, but *I've* changed. I can't just come back here and pretend like the last two months haven't happened."

I started to respond and he leaned down to kiss me. When he lifted his head, he grinned. "I'm hungry. Let me take you to my favorite Italian restaurant."

I nodded my agreement and we went to lunch, making sure to steer our conversation away from anything related to the curse. We spent so much time in Manteo talking about the curse that I worried our conversation would flounder, but David told me stories about teaching and some of his students. And I told him some horror stories about training new employees at the restaurant. By the time we left to go back to his house, our moods had lightened, even after David stopped at a hardware store to pick up a load of boxes and packing tape.

We spent the rest of the afternoon packing up David's house. I expected it to be sad for both of us, but David seemed to enjoy showing me some of his favorite things from his travels in the States and in the UK. I wanted to take a shower before we went to meet Allison, so I stopped working at around five thirty to get cleaned up while David continued to pack.

When I got out, I dried off and looked around the bathroom for a hair dryer. I couldn't find one, so I wrapped a towel around my body and opened the door, intent on asking David. As soon as the door was open, I could hear his voice in the living room.

"I really don't think that's a good idea, Allison."

Curious, I stood in the bathroom doorway. David's back was to me.

"Because I don't want to overwhelm her." He sensed me behind him and turned, pointing to the phone.

"What's wrong?" I whispered.

He covered the mouthpiece with his hand. "Allison has invited a bunch of our mutual friends to see me and meet you."

"Why isn't it a good idea?" Was he embarrassed about his friends meeting me?

He removed his hand from the phone. "Allison, hold on for a moment." He pushed mute and lowered the phone. "Ellie, you've had a stressful afternoon. It isn't fair to make you deal with a bunch of people who want to ask you a million questions. They know we're together and they're extremely curious."

"Do you want to see your friends?"

"That's not the point."

"It's a valid question. Do you want to see your friends?"

"Well, yes." He shrugged. "I don't know when we'll be back to Chapel Hill, so I would like to see them." He held up his hand. "But this is about you, Ellie. I'm sure you must be uncomfortable with going to Allison's house. I don't want to make this any more awkward for you."

I shook my head. "No. I want to meet them. Don't you see, I want to see as much of your life as possible." And I meant it.

"Are you sure?"

"Positive. I'm excited to meet them."

He took the phone off mute. "Okay, Allison. We'll see you at seven." He hung up and studied me. "You can still change your mind if you'd like."

"No way. But now I really need a hair dryer. I forgot to pack mine."

"Bedroom closet. I'll get it for you."

As I followed him to the back room, a new thought occurred to me. "Are you nervous about *me* meeting Allison?"

He stopped in front of the closet. "Yes, although I'm not embarrassed or ashamed of you in any way. I know that's where your mind is going." He shot me a nervous smirk. "I want you to be comfortable."

"I'm not some fragile flower, David."

"Oh, I know. I'd never accuse you of that. It's just that you deal with so much crap between the curse and your job . . . well, I wanted this weekend to be a chance for you to get away from it all. But tonight could end up being another stressor for you." He pulled the hair dryer down from a shelf and handed it to me. "If it gets overwhelming, just let me know and we'll take off."

But we couldn't, not really. We needed whatever information she had, and I couldn't help wondering if this was her way of stalling so she could spend more time with David. Still, I wasn't about to tell him that. I wrapped my hands around his neck and pulled his mouth to mine. "Thanks."

David took a shower while I got dressed and used a mirror in his bedroom to put on my makeup. Once I was ready, I grabbed my phone and worked past my nerves to call Myra. Our last call had ended on a good note, but what if she'd reverted to her previous indifference?

To my relief, she sounded happy to hear from me. "Ellie. How are you? I take it you're in Chapel Hill?"

"We made it in last night."

"Have you seen David's colleague yet?"

"No, we'll see her later tonight. But David's researching some things related to the curse in the library, and we made some headway there today."

"Really? Good news I hope."

Myra's emotional distance had hurt me more deeply than I'd realized. The fact that she was now acting more like the stepmother I knew brought tears of relief to my eyes. My throat burned and I swallowed before answering. "Yes, we found out something that could help us use the ring."

She paused. "Really? That's wonderful, Ellie. Will I still get to see you this weekend? I'd love to hear all about it."

"I hope so. Would sometime tomorrow work?"

"That would be great." Myra sounded happy. "How about a late breakfast? Were you planning on bringing David?" She paused and her voice lowered. "You know I'm fond of him, but I was hoping it would just be the two of us."

Myra had made no secret of her concern that my relationship with David was moving at light speed, so her request wasn't a complete surprise. I suspected she wanted to make sure I was still happy. I wouldn't be able to answer honestly if he was there.

I cast a glance toward the bathroom door. The shower had turned off, but the door was still closed. I could use this to my advantage. If I was going to sell the bed and breakfast, I owed it to Myra to consult her first. "I'd like that too. There's something important I need to talk to you about."

"Oh." She sounded surprised. "Is it serious?"

"It's about the inn."

"Is everything okay?"

"I'd rather talk in person."

"Of course, Ellie. How about I text you directions to my apartment? Can you be here around ten?"

"Yes, sounds perfect. Thanks, Myra. I love you."

She paused. "Me too."

A few moments later, the bathroom door opened and David

emerged, walking into the bedroom completely naked. I felt warm just looking at him, my fingers itching to touch his still-wet skin.

He caught me watching him and grinned. "You having second thoughts about going tonight?"

"No, but I'm wondering if we can be fashionably late."

"Nope." He laughed. "Let's go on time, stay as long as we feel like it, and then you can bring me home and ravish me."

I smirked as he brushed past me. "You think you can turn me down?"

"I will tonight. I'm always on time, so my friends will wonder why I'm late. And the guys will take one look at you and know." He gave me a passionate kiss and then lifted his head to smile at me. "And I'd prefer not to give them a reason to think about you like that."

I lifted my eyebrows in amusement. "You're jealous?"

"Not typically, but tonight I'm feeling a bit protective. I confess, it's caught me a little off guard."

"You act like you've never had a girlfriend before," I teased.

He turned serious, his hand cupping my neck, his thumb brushing along my jawline. "You know you're the only one I've ever loved."

For some reason, his words were my undoing. He'd said those three magic words to me weeks ago, and I had wanted to say them back. At the time, something had stopped me, even though all the signs were there.

"Ellie?" He was watching me, a strange look in his eyes.

I didn't want to keep holding back. I had no idea how long I had left in this world, and I didn't want to waste another minute without letting David know how much he meant to me. I kissed him softly. "I love you, David Preston."

His eyes widened in surprise.

I smiled as the truth of my words washed over me. "I love you."

His arms wound around me, pressing his naked body against my clothes. He started to unbutton my shirt and then dropped his hands and groaned. "*No.* Later."

I gave him a sexy grin. "Are you sure?"

"No." He laughed. "But I've resolved for us to be on time and now I'm determined to see it through."

I reached my hand behind him and cupped his ass. "And you do know that makes me even more determined to break your will."

His mouth lowered to my ear and he pulled my earlobe into his mouth, biting gently, then sucking. "You are an evil woman, Ellie Lancaster." His warm breath fanned against my neck, sending shivers down my spine.

"And you like me that way." I laughed, but I dropped my hold on him. "You better get dressed if you want to be *on time.*"

I picked up the hair dryer and went into the bathroom, drying my thick hair until it was only slightly damp. After pulling it into a loose French braid, I studied my reflection, worried I wouldn't be good enough for David's friends. I was probably younger than all of them and far less educated, but David loved me. That had to mean something, right?

I shook my head at the mirror, a slight smile on my face. A slew of evil spirits and demons roamed the earth, and I was worried about impressing David's ex-girlfriend and his professor friends. I obviously needed to get my priorities straight.

David appeared in the bathroom doorway wearing a dark green shirt and a pair of jeans. I took one look at him and my breath caught in my chest. More unneeded confirmation of what a gorgeous man David was.

"You look beautiful, Ellie. Don't look so worried. My friends will love you."

I followed him through the house and out the front door. "You're not just saying they'll like me because you think it will set me at ease, are you? I'd rather prepare myself for the worst."

"What's not to love about you? You're beautiful, kind, thoughtful, and funny." He gave me a gentle kiss. "Besides, they aren't pretentious stuffed shirts. You get along well with Steven and the researchers who stay in the house. My friends will love you."

"Okay."

The drive to Allison's house was short, only five minutes. Several cars were already parked in front of the cute two-story home. I smoothed my skirt, trying to get control of the fluttering in my stomach.

David grabbed my hand and interlaced our fingers. "It's hard to believe you're so nervous. Last night you faced a wind god and back-talked him like he was some punk on a street corner."

"That was different."

"Yeah, it is. Which is why it's so shocking you're this anxious over meeting a few academics."

We stood in front of the door and I took a deep breath, pulling my hand free of David's grip. I didn't want to look like I couldn't walk into the room without his support, even if I wanted it. "Okay. I'm ready."

Chuckling, David rang the doorbell. Seconds later a cute blonde I recognized from the pictures in David's office opened the door. She had on a light pink ruffled shirt and white capris. Her face broke out into a huge smile. "David!" She threw her arms around him and squeezed him tight.

He returned her hug, but with a much looser hold. "Good to see you, Allison."

She stepped back and eyed me up and down, still smiling. "And you must be Ellie."

I returned her smile. "Thank you for inviting us."

Her face tightened a bit. "David knows he's always welcome."

I resisted a sigh. So it was going to be one of *those* nights.

But David wasn't one of those oblivious men, thank God, and he put his arm around the small of my back. "I'm eager to see everyone. Thanks for inviting them."

"Of course. You take a two-week trip to Roanoke Island and the next thing we know, you're taking a semester's leave. We never got a chance to say a proper good-bye."

David's arm tensed.

She turned her head to the side and coughed before looking back at us. "Excuse me. My summer allergies have kicked into high gear." She stepped to the side, opening the door wider. "Everyone is in the back. We're grilling. I've been marinating steaks all day and I hoped you'd take over your official duties as grill master."

David had stepped inside the house, but he stopped short in the entryway. "Allison."

She turned around to see why he wasn't moving, and they had a stare-off for several seconds until I looked up at David. "You grill? I can't wait to see you in action."

Allison's eyes widened in surprise. "David hasn't grilled for you?"

"The bed and breakfast doesn't have a grill, Allison." David's voice was tense. "And I've been working late at the colony site most nights."

I wasn't sure if David was defending his behavior to Allison or me or perhaps both. He had nothing to apologize for as far as I was concerned. "Well, thanks to Allison's thoughtfulness, you can grill tonight," I said, forcing myself to sound pleasant.

David beamed down at me and took my hand. "Let's go see everyone." He walked past Allison, leading me through the entryway and a renovated kitchen. I gasped when we reached the open

French doors leading into the backyard—although calling it a back-yard was like calling the Atlantic Ocean a body of water. The steps led to a cobblestone patio that held about ten people, some standing, some sitting in chairs by a koi pond with a waterfall. Multiple flower beds surrounded the perimeter of the yard. It looked like something straight out of a decorating magazine.

"It's gorgeous," I said before I could stop myself.

"David did a wonderful job, didn't he?" Allison asked from behind me. Then she sniffed and reached for a tissue. "He's very gifted."

I glanced up at him in awe. "*You* did this?"

His face reddened. "It was nothing."

"This isn't nothing, David."

"I'm sure he misses puttering around since he moved into his rental house," Allison said. "He tried to make up for it with all those pots, but it's not the same."

I turned toward her, unable to stop myself.

"We had just started dating when I mentioned I wanted to landscape my yard," she went on. "He was eager to help. I teased him that he should have been a landscaper." She cocked her head with a pensive look. "He got so much more accomplished after he moved in with me."

My stomach dropped. He hadn't told me that he and Allison had lived together.

David's hand tightened around mine. "That was a long time ago."

"It was only last summer," Allison said in a smug tone.

"David!" called out one of the men on the patio. "Get over here and tell us how it's going out in Manteo."

David pulled me away from Allison and leaned down into my ear. "I had no idea she'd act this way. We can leave if you like."

"No." I shook my head. "I want to meet your other friends."

The group of people turned to face us as we approached, and their genuine smiles helped soften the tension that was building in my shoulders.

A man in his thirties reached out his hand to David and pulled him into a hearty handshake. "Congrats on the Roanoke assignment."

"Thanks," David beamed.

"And who have you brought back with you?" the woman next to him asked.

David smiled down at me, then glanced back at her. "Cheryl, this is Ellie Lancaster. Ellie, Cheryl Dalton. Her husband, Noah, works in the English Department." He gestured toward the man who had just greeted him.

"Hi, nice to meet you," I said.

Cheryl grinned. "Noah might be asking about the colony, but what we really want to know is how you met Ellie. We hear it's quite serious."

The group of six people around us turned their attention to David.

"And who tells you that?" David asked, brushing off her question.

"Please." She waved a hand. "Noah knows Charles Ditmore at Duke, who knows Steven Godfrey. When Steven came back from Roanoke Island, he told Charles that you found the lost colony *and* the love of your life."

I shifted uncomfortably, but David wrapped an arm around my back and held me close. "I found a lot of surprises in Manteo." He grinned down at me, setting me at ease. "But I'm sure everyone would love to hear more about the colony. Especially what's been found in the Dare house."

Someone brought two chairs and we sat while David and his friends spent the next ten minutes talking about the colony and the things that David had seen, before Allison walked over with a bottle of beer and a plastic cup. "Where are my manners? You two don't have drinks yet." She handed the bottle to David and the cup to me. I took it hesitantly, wondering if she'd done something to it.

She smiled, but I could see the bitterness in her gaze. "I made sure to have your favorite beer on hand, David. I wasn't sure if Ellie was legal to drink, so I brought her lemonade."

David stiffened next to me and started to say something, but I patted his arm. "Allison, how thoughtful of you. Thank you."

Confusion flickered in her eyes and her mouth parted as if she wasn't sure how to react. The group around us hushed, their expressions shocked.

After a couple of seconds, Allison's smile returned. "David, the grill's ready." She pulled a tissue out of her pocket and wiped her nose. "I really need you to help out. I shouldn't come into contact with raw meat with this runny nose."

David glanced over at me, then back at Allison. "Ellie, why don't you come over with me and I'll teach you the fine art of grilling, something I've picked up since moving to North Carolina."

Allison shot me a challenging look that said she firmly believed I couldn't handle her on my own. I'd dealt with her kind before back in high school. For some reason, I'd expected better manners from a college professor. Well, I wasn't about to back down. I could take demonic badgers. This bitch was nothing.

I leaned back in my chair and took a sip of my drink. "No, I think I'll stay here and chat with the girls."

David's eyes widened, so I leaned over and placed a kiss on his mouth, lingering for a couple of seconds before brushing my mouth against his ear. "Go. I'll be fine."

He pulled back, worry in his eyes.

A smile spread across my face. "Make my steak medium-well."

The guys in the group cast nervous looks between me and Allison and hopped up, following David to the grill. The four other women who'd been left behind looked as though they wished they could join them. Instead, we all settled in our chairs on the patio. I turned my attention to a woman who had been talking to David. "So, Trina, how long have you known David?"

She and the other women all told me how they'd met him. Trina was a professor of Native American studies, and the other three were married to professors David knew from the university.

After a while, there was a pause in the conversation and Allison leaned forward. "Don't you want to know how I met David?"

I offered her my sweetest smile. "Of course."

Sipping from her wine glass, she leaned to the side of her chair. "We met in the library. Penelope, the archivist there, was sure to introduce us."

"I met Penelope this morning at the Wilson Library," I said. "She seems very sweet."

She gave me a conspiratorial grin. "She can be quite the match-maker. She hooked up Trina and Phil too."

Trina glanced over at the men and grinned. "She sure did."

"David had been at Chapel Hill for over a year and Penelope thought he needed a girlfriend. He doesn't cook very much, so she suggested I invite him over for a home-cooked meal. He protested that he didn't want to be a bother, but he came over and then the next thing you know, we were dating."

Trina narrowed her eyes. "I thought it was several months after you cooked for him before you two started dating."

Allison shot Trina a glare, then turned her attention to me. "*In any case*, he moved in and helped me with this old house. He's really quite handy." She took a drink of her wine, watching me over the rim. "Like I said, he landscaped this entire backyard."

"It's very beautiful," I said. "You're lucky he shared his talent with you." She wanted me to act like a jealous lover, but I wasn't going to fall into her trap. For one thing, I wasn't jealous. David had left her, not the other way around. If he wanted to be with her, he would. If anything, I felt sorry for her. David was a wonderful man, and I knew it had to be hard for her to see him with me. I didn't appreciate her bitchiness, but I understood it.

I crossed my legs and smiled. "I hear that you're a history professor. My parents and stepmother were all history majors. My father was the park ranger at the Fort Raleigh National Historic Site for many years until he became ill. My mother died when I was a girl, but she was an archaeologist at the site and specialized in sixteenth- and seventeenth-century artifacts. Their names were John and Amanda Lancaster." I tilted my head to the side. "Perhaps you've heard of them?"

"Your father was John Lancaster?" Trina asked in awe.

I nodded. "He was very passionate about the early colonies."

"He's a legend, but he had stopped lecturing by the time I started my undergraduate work. Do you know why?"

I pushed down my sorrow. "My mother's death was hard on him and he found it difficult to leave me after that. I had no idea how respected he was in academia until I spoke with Steven while visiting the colony site."

"You visited the site?" Trina asked.

"I did." I told her my impressions of the reemerged colony and how hard it was seeing tiny baby Virginia's skeleton in her cradle.

Allison shifted in her seat and I could tell she didn't like that the conversation was steering away from her. "Allison, David said you specialize in weaponry from the Middle Ages. I'm curious about what prompted that interest."

The color left her face. "David's mentioned me?"

I took a sip of my lemonade. "Yes, very fondly."

She eased back in her chair. "My parents and my older brother were participants in our local Renaissance festival. We spent every weekend in October there, and I became fascinated with it. But once I went to school, my passion turned to the Middle Ages. So much has been lost over the years, and I've always been fascinated with the idea of discovering lost things."

"What happened with that exhibit you were invited to preview?" Trina asked, crossing her legs. "You were so excited to see it."

Allison took a sip of her wine, then frowned. "I signed a nondisclosure agreement when I went to Charlotte. You know that."

Trina leaned forward. "Come on. It's *us*. Who are we going to tell? Did you see any Native American artifacts? I'm dying to know."

Sucking in a deep breath, Allison's mouth puckered as her gaze rotated to David before returning to her friend. "Yes, there were several."

Trina waited for several seconds. "You can't stop there. Tell us more."

Allison shifted in her seat. "I'm really not supposed to tell anyone, but I agreed to tell David what I saw." A wicked smile twisted her lips. "Well, I guess you two work in the same department and share information anyway . . ."

I was sure an attorney would be able to point out any number of flaws in her logic, but Trina's face beamed with excitement.

"You know I don't know much about Native American weaponry, but I can tell you that there were multiple spears that looked to be quite old based on the warping of the shafts. There was also a large collection of arrowheads and ax heads."

"We all know you were asked to examine something else," Trina prompted.

"There was a large collection of pocket watches. One was identical to the watch in the photo David sent to all of us weeks ago. It's really quite a find. I'm amazed there are two in existence."

"Allison," Cheryl said. "You said you were invited to see something that you were sure would provide the source for your next paper. Stop being so mysterious. Did you see it?"

For the first time since she started spilling details about the collection, Allison looked hesitant. "Now, that I'm *really* not supposed to talk about. Not yet anyway."

The woman turned her attention to me. "Ellie, why is David so eager to find out about a bunch of English pocket watches and swords?"

My eyes widened in dismay. I hadn't planned on having to answer questions about the Ricardo Estate. I shook my head while my tongue stumbled for an explanation. "I . . . David . . . since the majority of the colony site is composed of English artifacts, he's found a new appreciation for them. In fact, the majority of Manteo's hut consists of English items."

Allison frowned. "Then what on earth is he still doing there? He's a professor of Native American studies."

Trina rolled her eyes. "Don't be so shortsighted, Allison. David's studying Manteo's residence. What's actually in there is less important than the fact that Manteo lived there. And even if some of his things are English in origin, they must still say a lot about how he lived his life." Her eyebrows rose. "Am I right, Ellie?"

"Uh . . . yeah." I never could have come up with that answer in a million years. I owed Trina big. But if Allison was willing to discuss the collection, I wanted to get as much information out of her as I could. "So did you see anything else that was particularly interesting?"

She cocked her head to the side.

"Well, did you?" Trina asked.

"Yes." She licked her lower lip and grabbed the arm of her chair, looking nervous. "But if the Guardians find out . . ."

The blood rushed from my head. "Did you say the Guardians?"

Allison's face paled and she stood. "I've said too much. I've never been good at keeping secrets. I better go check on the baked beans."

Allison hurried into the house. I was dying to tell David our new information, but he was deep in conversation with his friends. This could wait a few minutes.

"Wow. That was weird," Trina said, watching Allison slip through the kitchen door.

Cheryl cast a glance from me to Trina. "She's been out of sorts since she started planning tonight's get-together."

Everyone was quiet and I shifted in my seat, wondering if I should get up and check on David, when one of the women addressed Trina in a serious tone. "The campus police say there hasn't been any trouble here, but they're being extra vigilant."

My attention perked up. "Why would the campus police need to be vigilant?"

The three of them were quiet for a long moment, and then Trina spoke up. "There have been some missing person reports in Durham. Duke students."

"Missing?"

"Yeah, three in the last two weeks."

"Just students?" I asked, suddenly worried about Myra. What if some of the spirits had followed Myra to Durham? What if they went after her to make me suffer? "No professors? My stepmother just took a position there."

"No." Trina shook her head. "Two guys and a girl, all students. Just vanished."

"And the police have no idea what happened?"

"Not a clue. But I'm sure you have nothing to worry about. Your stepmother will be just fine."

She was right. These could very well be garden-variety disappearances, but I had begun to take the stance that anything unusual was supernatural until deemed otherwise.

I needed to protect Myra, no matter what it took.

⋅: Chapter Eleven :⋅

I wanted a few minutes alone to sort through all the cards I'd been dealt in the last half hour. I stood. "I need to use the restroom. I'll be right back."

"It's the first door on the left," Cheryl called after me.

My movement caught David's attention. He turned to look at me as I walked toward the house, an anxious glint in his eye. I smiled at him—even if I didn't feel like it—and the tension in his face instantly eased.

"He loves you," Allison said, her voice matter of fact.

I jumped at the sound of her voice, surprised to see her standing in the doorway to the house. I could lie to her, but I didn't see the point. "Yes. He does."

Tears filled her eyes and she forced a smile. "How wonderful for you both." Her lip quivered, but she kept right on smiling. "These stupid allergies." Then she pushed past me into the yard.

I didn't have to go to the bathroom, but Daddy had always taught me to go when I had the opportunity, whether I needed to or not, and old habits died hard. It felt invasive walking through David's ex-girlfriend's house, but I couldn't restrain my curiosity. While her kitchen was generic with white cabinets and laminate counters, her living room was lined with glass display cases filled with knives and swords. I abandoned my original plan and wandered into the living room, stopping in front of one of the cases.

"Impressive, isn't it?" Allison asked. She must have changed her mind and turned around to follow me.

I jumped again. *Damn it.* Some super-stealth sneak I was. Collin would be horrified. "I didn't mean to snoop."

"It's not snooping." She shrugged and a soft grin lifted the corners of her mouth. "If I were in your shoes, I'd do the same."

Guilt slammed my chest. "Allison, I never meant to hurt you in any way. I considered not coming—"

She shook her head. "No, I specifically asked David to bring you. I wanted to see who had finally managed to win David Preston's love and devotion." She turned to face the case, her expression painted with sadness. "I'm not surprised he fell for you."

My mouth parted. That was the last thing I'd expected her to say.

"Why does he really want to know about the collection I saw?"

"I told you."

She turned to study me. "That's a bullshit answer and we both know it."

I resisted the urge to stiffen my shoulders in defense. "I can assure you that it does have something to do with the colony site." When she didn't respond, I decided to take the offensive. "You mentioned the Guardians. Were they the ones who contacted you?"

She glanced around and moved deeper into the room. I followed. "Yes. I wasn't sure who they were until I got to Charlotte. They contacted me through the university and said they needed to consult with someone who had my expertise. But they told me I couldn't tell anyone and made me sign and scan an NDA before they'd give me more details. After they received it, they gave me an address and told me to show up there the next day at one p.m. I almost told them no; it was the day before classes started and I really couldn't afford to leave town for the day. Plus I wasn't sure I could trust them."

"But you went anyway?"

She released a short laugh. "They told me they thought they had the Sword of Galahad. Of course I went."

I gave her a blank look.

"It's a legendary sword rumored to have been blessed with the ability to kill demons."

I held my breath, then forced it out. This was the one she'd mentioned to David. "Was it?"

She laughed again, the sound deeper and richer this time. "Are you asking if it was the actual Sword of Galahad or if it can really kill demons?"

I decided to go for broke. "Both."

Her smile fell. "You're serious."

"David said the sword was blessed by a priest in the Middle Ages for a knight to use as a weapon in the Crusades. Would they really have used a sword that old? King Arthur's court would have been centuries before the Crusades."

Allison watched me intently for several seconds. "You're not what I expected."

"I hear that a lot." Although it was usually from gods and spirits.

She shook off her musings. "You're correct. If King Arthur were real, historians would place him between the fifth and seventh centuries. The Sword of Galahad is mentioned in relation to King Richard the Lionheart and the Third Crusade. That would have been 1189 to 1192, making it highly doubtful it could be the same sword, even if Galahad *were* real. Most historians think the sword was created specifically for King Richard and only modeled after a sword they attributed to Galahad. Still, the styling of swords had evolved—not surprisingly—over several hundred years. An Arthurian sword would have had a wider, bulkier blade, while one from the twelfth century would have been more tapered and lighter in weight." She moved to another case, staring at the jewel-encrusted handle of a small knife. "But calling it the Sword of Galahad makes sense symbolically. Galahad was entrusted with the job of finding the Holy Grail. King Richard was on a holy mission too. People weren't happy when Richard raided the treasury to support his quest. Saying he carried the Sword of Galahad into battle would have elevated him in people's eyes."

"Did you see it?" I asked. "Do you think it was the sword King Richard attributed to Galahad?"

"Now, that is the question, isn't it?" A sly grin spread across her face. "I showed up in Charlotte and was met by an older woman. She told me her name was Miriam and she was with a very old organization called the Guardians. When I asked her what they were guarding, she laughed and told me I wouldn't understand. Then she took me into a back room. They had enough antique weapons there to fill a museum and then some, along with a collection of pocket watches."

"No other jewelry?"

Allison looked surprised by my question. "No."

I involuntarily fingered the ring on my right hand, but Allison's gaze followed my movement. "They wanted you to authenticate the Sword of Galahad?" I asked, to divert her attention.

"Yes, but they had other swords and knives as well. Miriam gave me a few moments to examine several of them. I asked to take photos, but they only allowed me to take one picture of the sword in question. After I told them there was no way I could verify on the spot whether it was authentic or not, they relented and allowed me to take one more. Photos aren't enough, but they're a start. I'm supposed to go back on Monday with some conclusions."

"So what's your gut reaction? Is it the Sword of Galahad?"

She stared at me for a few moments, her friendliness fading. "I don't have to help you, you know. I don't have to tell you a damn thing."

"I know," I said quietly. "Why *are* you telling me?"

Her eyes burned with intensity. "Because I have a feeling you're putting David in some kind of danger."

"*What?*"

She moved closer and grabbed my arm. "These people—the Guardians—I get the impression they don't like it when people get into their business. But that's exactly what David's doing, isn't it? Tell me I'm wrong."

I didn't answer. She was right.

"I also have a feeling you're a huge part of this thing; otherwise why would you be hanging on my every word? Call it woman's intuition, but David is doing this to help you."

Again, I didn't contradict her.

Her face softened and her eyes turned glassy. "So I'm begging you, Ellie. I'll tell you everything you want to know, but leave David out of this."

I shook my head, "Allison . . . I . . ."

"Ellie?" David stood in the doorway to the living room. "Is everything okay?"

My head spun around to face him. "Yeah. Fine."

Allison put her hands on her hips. "I was just showing Ellie my collection. Who knew she'd be so fascinated with dangerous things?"

David hesitated before responding. "The steaks are ready."

"Then let's eat." She brushed past us, but before she stepped into the kitchen, she turned to look at me. "Ellie, think about what I said."

I walked over and pulled David into a hug. "What did she say?" he whispered in my ear.

"More than I expected." I glanced up into his worried face. "You were on the right track. The Guardians are behind this. They have a large collection of antique weapons and pocket watches, which I highly suspect is part of the Ricardo Estate. Allison went to look at a sword that is rumored to have belonged to King Richard the Lionheart, not just some random knight in the Crusades. It's also known as the Sword of Galahad." I filled him in on everything she'd said about the sword and its rumored history.

"Did she tell you what she originally wanted to show me?"

"No, but she confirmed she has two photos of the sword. She didn't show them to me, and I suspect she's holding them for ransom."

"What's the reward?"

"You. She's figured out that I'm the one who needs the information. She's worried for your safety, so she hopes that if she tells me what I want to know, I'll leave you out of this mess."

Anger darkened his eyes. "That's bollocks!"

"She cares about you. She's trying to protect you. I'm not sure I wouldn't do the same thing if our roles were reversed."

His gaze softened. "Ellie."

Voices filled the kitchen and irritation pinched David's mouth. "We'll talk about this later. And I'll set her straight."

"Don't be angry with her. Please."

He gave me a gentle kiss. "You're an amazing woman, Ellie Lancaster."

I wished I were as amazing as he thought I was.

"We'll ask her about it after everyone else leaves."

I released a sigh. "I think she's told me everything she plans on sharing unless I agree to give you up, and I refuse to lie. You'll probably get more out of her if I'm not with you."

He scowled. "I don't think that's a good idea, Ellie."

"David, I know that you love me. I trust you."

He looked torn.

"You trust me when I see Collin." Guilt stabbed me through the gut. I had every reason to trust David, while he had every reason *not* to trust me.

"That's different. He's the other Keeper. You're tied to him whether you like it or not."

"If we want more information—and we definitely do—you need to see her on your own. After dinner. I'll go back to your place and come back to pick you up later."

He grumbled his acceptance and we went off to join the others. Several of David's friends teased him about going off into the other room with me, but he laughed it off good-naturedly. We filled plates with food from the buffet on the kitchen island and then headed outside to eat. I listened in rapt attention as David's friends told me story after story about him. He had some wonderful friends, and it was obvious that they both liked and respected him. Even Allison seemed to loosen up after a while.

When the sun went down, David offered to start a fire in the fire pit. To my surprise, I felt slightly awkward that he felt so comfortable here at Allison's house. But of course he would if he'd created this backyard oasis. Maybe when we moved closer to the ocean and found a place that was ours, David could grill and look as relaxed as he did here. But part of me knew that would never happen. As long as he was with me and demons roamed the earth, David would always be on guard. The thought made me sad.

Trina came and sat next to me while Allison helped David search for a lighter.

"You're a better person than me."

"What?" I asked in surprise. "Why do you say that?"

"Allison is determined to win him back. She always assumed their breakup was temporary. She thought David just got cold feet and would come back to her in good time. Then he went to Manteo and met you. I can tell you one thing—he never looked at her the way he looks at you. And she doesn't like it."

Trina must have read the surprise on my face. "You seem like a sweet girl," she said. "I just wanted to warn you."

I met her gaze. "Thank you. I appreciate it, but I trust David."

"I'm sure you do. I just wouldn't trust Allison." She got up and returned to her friends.

David got the fire started and came back and sat next to me, draping his arm around my shoulder.

The sun had set, and I cast a glance up at the stars. The darkness always made me nervous now. And as our midnight visitor from the previous night had proven, we weren't too far from Manteo for the Croatan gods to find us.

Allison sat across from us, her eyes glued on David for the next half hour. Dark clouds began to roll in after a little while, and the rest of David's friends decided to call it a night.

David stayed back and said good-bye to everyone, promising to come back soon to see them. Once they were gone, David walked me to the front door while Allison started cleaning up the kitchen.

"I'll wait at your place for an hour, and then I'll come back and get you. Do you think that's enough time?"

David took his keys out of his pocket. Worry filled his eyes, and it struck me that his smiles were becoming like a rare ray of sunshine on a cloudy day.

What if Allison was right? Once I had enough information to survive on my own, maybe I should set David loose so he could go back to his job and his friends.

I reached for the keys, but he held them tight. "Why do you have that look on your face?"

"What look?"

"The look that says you're about to do something you don't want to do."

I reached up on my tiptoes and kissed him. Even if setting him free was the right thing to do, I wasn't sure I could do it. Especially now that I loved him. But wasn't that reason enough to let him go? Even so, the whole idea was preposterous. David Preston would *never* willingly walk away from me, and it only made me love him even more. "I'm just being sentimental. If you get done sooner, let me know. I'm eager to *show* you how much I love you."

He wrapped an arm around my lower back and pressed his forehead to mine. "When you talk like that I want to say screw it all and take you home."

I laughed and broke free. "Find out what we need to know, and then I'll give you a special reward later."

"I like the sound of that."

I snatched the keys out of his hand and hopped into his car, driving off before I changed my mind. While I trusted David, Trina's warning looped in my head.

When I got back to David's house, I got out of the car and promptly tripped over something on the driveway. I nearly fell flat on my face but managed to catch myself with my hands. Just as my right hand hit the ground, my palm started to tingle. But it was gone just as quickly as it came, replaced with the pain of a scrape. I hurried to the front door to make sure the marks weren't smudged, and after I went inside and turned on the lights, I went out the back door to do the same.

Just as I was about to go back inside, something moved at the edge of the yard. Since the property backed up to the woods, I figured the creature was probably a raccoon or an opossum.

No. My hand was tingling again. It was supernatural.

A tiny dark figure streaked across the yard and scampered behind a tree ten feet away.

I resisted the urge to shriek. Whatever it was, it was no more than two feet tall. It was probably an animal, just as I first thought. My hand had been randomly itching for weeks, so there was no reason to believe this was any different.

The creature ran to the far edge of the house and the porch light made it easier to get a good look at it. I couldn't ignore the fact that it wasn't covered in hair or fur. It looked like it was covered in skin.

Holy shit, it was a tiny person.

The mark on my hand began to burn.

Shit. It was a demon.

I held out my arm, flexing my wrist so that my palm was aimed at the creature. "Demon, come out and face me." But I was on the edge of the porch and I lost my balance, falling the two feet to the yard. After landing on my feet, I stumbled around to face it.

"I'm not a demon," a voice grumbled. "You know nothing."

I took a breath, holding up my hand. "Then what are you?"

"A guardian of sorts."

"Like the Guardians who are collecting all those old weapons?"

He scoffed. "They may call themselves guardians, but they are thieves and liars."

He obviously knew about the Guardians and I considered asking for more information, but finding out about him took priority. "What or whom do you guard?"

"You, you idiot, now lower your hand."

Rebuked, I lowered my hand without even thinking about it. "Come out and let me see you."

"No."

Whatever it was, it thought it was superior to me. I could use its arrogance to my advantage. "You mustn't be much of a guardian. You tripped me in the front yard, didn't you?"

"You've been too stupid to even notice that I've been tripping you for over a week. I needed to do *something* to get your attention."

"Well, now you've got it. Come out and see me."

A tiny head poked out from under the bush. The face reminded me of a gnome's—round with big brown eyes. But his mouth was turned down in a pronounced scowl. Dark brown, scraggly hair hung around his face.

"I'm not going to send you away," I said. "I just want to ask you a few questions."

He stepped away from the bush and I could see the rest of his body. My first impression had been correct: he was a tiny person. He looked to be the same height as those American Girl dolls a lot of tourist girls brought into the restaurant, but I was sure he'd be offended by the comparison. An animal-skin tunic covered his stocky body, though his slightly hairy feet were bare.

"I'm Ellie," I offered, hoping it would introduce itself.

"You are Curse Keeper, daughter of the sea and witness to creation."

So much for my plan working. "And you are?"

"Tsagasi."

"Tsagasi." I let the name roll off my tongue.

He shook his head in disgust. "You are careless. Some of the salt on the threshold of the western window isn't thick enough."

"How do you know that?"

"Don't insult me," he said, sounding annoyed.

"Who sent you?" If he was one of Ahone's lackeys, I was going to send him away as soon as I was done getting information from him.

He curled his upper lip in disgust and took a step toward me. "No one sent me. I came on my own. You're the Curse Keeper, are you not?"

"Yeah. So what are you protecting me *from*?"

"The baddies. The ones who want to see you gone forever."

A chill shot through my body, making me shiver. "Does that mean you're a good spirit?"

He gave me a smile, but it was more ornery than friendly. "I'm not a demon or a god. Many people consider me to be a fairy, but that's not true either. I prefer little person."

"You still didn't tell me whether you're good or not."

His grin grew wider. "I'm not going to harm you."

"Why do I find that hard to believe after you tripped me?"

"For being the Curse Keeper, you're remarkably dense."

I released a sigh. Great. Now I was being insulted by a good spirit. "How long have you been watching me?"

"Two weeks."

"You say you're here to protect me. What do you plan to do?"

"I'll know when another spirit is close and I have some magic of my own I can use."

"Okay," I said, still trying to process this in my head. "*Why* do you want to help me?"

"You are the salvation of the world."

And we were back to the Raven Mocker's prediction. I was in big trouble, all right.

He crossed his arms, a stubborn frown settling on his face. "Now that you know I'm here, I'm through with hiding."

"So you're here because I'm the salvation of the world?" I repeated.

He nodded.

I moved over to the porch and sat down. "Three nights ago I met an old woman on the road home and she told me my future. What was she?"

He shrugged and walked over to stand beside me. "An elderly woman?"

"Very funny. Her eyes glowed red. She was definitely a spirit of some kind."

"She was a Raven Mocker. But you already know that."

A chill ran down my back. "Why would she come see me?"

"Kalona has his own plan for you, and it is different from what Okeus wants. But Kalona fears facing Okeus and Ahone until he is stronger. He has entrusted his children to another's guidance until he is ready to face the wind gods. The Great One."

So Okeus wasn't the Great One after all. I bet he'd be pissed to hear that. "How do you know?"

"I know many things." He looked bored. "The gods are all working against each other in an effort to control you and what you know. The spirit world is in chaos. You think you need to face Kalona to stop the Raven Mockers, but you need to find his proxy. The Great One."

"Who is the Great One and where do I find him?"

"I do not know the answer to that yet." The way his nose scrunched, it looked like it pained him to admit it. "But I *do* know Kalona's proxy has the Raven Mockers at work tonight. They are in the process of taking the heart of the woman who hates you."

"*Allison?*" I shrieked in shock.

Allison had been sniffling from allergies. Was that serious enough for the Raven Mockers to stalk and kill her?

Oh, shit.

I ran inside and found my phone, discovering I had two missed calls from David.

Grabbing David's keys, I ran out the front door. After I jumped behind the wheel of the car and started for Allison's house, I dialed David.

"Ellie," he answered, his voice breathless. "Something evil is here."

∿ CHAPTER TWELVE ∿

Terror filled my chest. "A Raven Mocker."

"Yeah, I think so. How did you know?"

"Something clued me in." I turned the corner, the tires screeching. If I weren't more careful, the police would pull me over. For once, I found myself wishing Tom was around. "Can you see them?"

"No, but Allison is lying on the floor screaming, telling something to leave her alone. I don't know how to help her." His voice was frantic.

"I'm only a couple of blocks away." I hung up and drove faster, skidding to a stop in front of her house. Three large black birds circled the roof, releasing loud cries.

The Raven Mockers in their bird form.

I could hear Allison screaming inside the house from the front yard. Terrified, I didn't stop to knock; I just threw open the front door.

David kneeled in the middle of the living room floor next to Allison, who was lying on the floor, thrashing around in hysterics.

I could see why.

Two old men and two old women were circling the room. Their faces were grotesque, with deep wrinkles and long hooked noses.

Their mouths opened in unison to laugh, revealing their pointed fangs. Their shrunken, hunched frames were covered in loose, gray linen fabric. The men wore pants and tunics and the women wore old-fashioned housedresses.

Allison's body was covered in bloody gashes. Her previously crisply pressed pink shirt was ripped and drenched with blood. The Raven Mockers took turns swiping at her with their long claws. Then they stopped in the same eerie unison and spun around to watch me.

Great. Possessed geriatrics.

David kneeled at her side. He looked up at me, his eyes wide with fear. "I can't see it. Is it a Raven Mocker?"

"There are *four* Raven Mockers inside and three outside."

"*Seven of them?* They don't typically travel in packs." He shook his head, helplessness filling his eyes. "I haven't been able to do anything to help her. She just started screaming about ten minutes ago, and she hasn't stopped."

"The ones outside are flying around the roof, screaming. Can you hear them?"

"Yes, but legend says all people can see and hear them when they're in their bird form. Just not when they appear as humans."

Which is why he couldn't see Allison's attackers. I stepped closer as one of the women swiped at her leg, drawing fresh blood.

Allison screamed again.

"Why is she screaming, Ellie?"

"I know you can't see them, but don't you see the gashes all over her body?"

"No. I only hear her screaming!" His voice was frantic.

His clothes were covered with splatters of her blood. How could he not see it? "They're clawing at her!" I shouted, running toward one of them as it reached out to slash her arm. The old woman backed away, smiling.

"Get rid of them!"

"How?" I asked, freaking out. I could see them, but I still felt helpless to stop them.

"They're supposed to flee if they encounter someone powerful enough to see them."

"Yeah, well they're looking at me right now and they don't seem to be going anywhere." Panic crawled up my spine and burrowed at the base of my throat, clogging my airway. I had no idea how to handle this. I pinched the ring with my left thumb and middle finger. Even if I decided to use the damn thing, it would be worthless here. According to the letter at the library, I had to be standing next to the gate to use it.

The old men and women had resumed their strange circular dance, but my comment seemed to have renewed their interest in me. They stopped and turned to face me, all four laughing in tandem. I was officially freaked out, particularly since all of them were equipped with vicious claws and razor-sharp teeth. "Welcome, Curse Keeper. We've been waiting for you."

One of the men lunged toward Allison.

I had no desire to throw myself into the path of his claws, but I had to protect her. I dove for her, grabbing a decorative china vase off an end table as I threw myself over her body. I twisted around just in time to smash the vase into his head. His claws narrowly missed sinking into my back as I landed hard on Allison's bloody legs. Thrown by the sudden pain of her knee jabbing my stomach, I cried out in surprise.

"Ellie!" David cried out in a panic. "What happened?"

"It tried to claw me," I grunted, scrambling to my knees. I was fair game on the floor.

"That's impossible. You're not sick."

"What happens if they claw you?"

"I don't know," he answered. "I've never heard of them clawing anyone."

"Add this to the *not acting in character* list." My breath came in quick pants as I climbed to my feet, searching for a weapon, any weapon. Then I shuddered at my stupidity. I was surrounded by them. The wall behind me was filled with swords and knives. The question was if they would work.

I searched out the old man whom I'd attacked with the vase. He'd rejoined the group, which was once again pacing in a large circle, blocking any exit out the front door or window. Thick black blood trickled down the creature's face, but he looked unfazed otherwise.

"How do I kill these things?"

"Other than the seven-day rule, I don't know." His voice was calmer and more reassuring. The fact that he had regained control settled my anxiety. "What about the ring? I know we're not next to the gate, but it might do something."

I shook my head. "No! I'm not using the ring." I glanced at the wall behind me. "Can I hurt them with any of Allison's swords?"

He shook his head. "I don't know."

My other alternative was to stand back and do nothing. I quickly scanned the wall of display cases, looking for a weapon. "David, drag Allison over to the corner."

He looked dubious. "Why?"

"Because there are four Raven Mockers, and right now they can attack us from all sides. If you're in the corner I can protect you both."

"Ellie. Then we'll be trapped!"

The Raven Mockers laughed derisively.

I ignored them and the implication of their amusement. "*Do it!*

I'll get rid of them, but if we don't protect her, they might kill her before I send them away."

I picked up a laptop off the end table—the only hard object I could find in close proximity—and narrowed in on a display case containing a large sword.

Grunting, David grabbed Allison under the arms. "No, not that sword. It's too heavy and will wear you out. Go for the smaller one on the right."

"No." A small gruff voice spoke up from the other side of the room. "You must use a warded sword."

My head jerked up to the still-open front door. Tsagasi stood in front of it, his face contorted in anger.

"Are any of these warded swords?" I shouted back at him.

The Raven Mockers stopped their pacing and turned to face the little man. "Stay out of this, *fairy*," one of the women hissed.

"You know how much I hate that name," Tsagasi sneered. "That's reason enough to help her."

David leaned forward, still standing next to me, his arms supporting Allison. "Ellie, what the hell is that?"

"It's Tsagasi. He's here to help me."

"Tsagasi? *A little person?*"

"The sword on the end, next to the doorway. At the top," Tsagasi grunted as he moved into the room and shut the door.

The Raven Mockers' eyes glowed red. Their heads swiveled to face me, but none of them made a move to attack. "The fairy can't help, Curse Keeper. We will kill you."

I found the sword Tsagasi had pointed out—a thin-bladed weapon with a narrow hilt and curved guard to cover the back of my hand. As I rushed toward the case and broke the glass, David dragged Allison across the floor, knocking over a table and lamp in the process. The light bulb in the lamp flickered and went out, plunging the room into a murky, shadowy darkness.

The Raven Mockers continued to watch me as if they were waiting for something. I was shocked they hadn't intervened and couldn't help but wonder what they had planned. Nothing good, I was sure.

Taking a deep breath, I lifted the sword off the hooks holding it in place and pulled it out of the case. I spun around to face them, hefting the weapon in my hand. I'd never held a real sword before, let alone used one. This thing was hundreds of years old. I hoped the blade was still sharp. "Only Raven Mockers will die tonight," I growled, putting my back to David and Allison.

I considered lifting my hand to say my words of protection to send them away, but that would only be a temporary solution and I was tired of all my problems coming back to bite me in the ass. Not to mention the fact that they were so close they could attack and kill us all before the vortex even opened. I'd also have to switch the sword to my left hand. I was right-handed and wasn't sure I'd be able to use the thing with my nondominant hand. I'd try the sword first.

Light from the moon shone through the windows, casting the room in shadows, but I could still see the Raven Mockers' slumped frames. They broke into a collective grin, and the woman who had done most of the talking looked happiest of all. "She is ready. Let us begin."

A male Raven Mocker rushed me while the others stood back and watched. His claws gleamed in the moonlight as he swung for me.

I had to protect myself, but more importantly, I had to save David. A surge of protectiveness rose up inside me as I swung the sword at the creature. It sunk into the demon's shoulder and dug into bone, spraying demon blood into the air and all over my arm. The Raven Mocker screamed, his eyes glowing bright red as I pulled on the sword, trying to free it. I put my foot on his stomach and jerked backward, narrowly missing a swipe from his claws. My kick sent him halfway across the room with more force than I should have possessed.

"Good," Tsagasi said. "*Good.* It gives you strength, just as I presumed."

"We're warning you, fairy . . ." one of the male Raven Mockers said.

". . . stay out of this," one of the women finished.

Allison had stopped whimpering and was now quietly sobbing in the corner, her eyes wild with fright. David had crouched down in front her in a protective stance.

I'd fought off one but hadn't killed it. There were *four* of them. What if they all rushed me at once? Was I fooling myself by believing I could actually kill them? "I need the ocean," I whispered. Collin was right. That was the source of my power, and I was hundreds of miles away.

"No," Tsagasi said, his voice firm. He had moved closer to David and Allison while I was busy grabbing the sword and fighting off the first Raven Mocker, and now he stood behind me. "You get part of your power from the sea, but why do all the gods want you? Why do they search out *you* and not the son of the earth?"

"I'm the witness to creation."

"Yes. Your greatest power is as the witness to creation, and you haven't even tapped it yet. Dig deep. It's there."

Finding my power was easier said than done when I was being stalked by four demons. But Tsagasi was right. How had I never realized it before?

I thought about the vision I'd had in the ocean with Collin, the one in which I'd relived the creation of the universe and the world. Suddenly, I wasn't just remembering the *vision*; I was remembering what it felt like to watch the event millions of years ago. Power coursed through my blood and filled my body.

"Yes," Tsagasi said. "Now."

When the next demon, one of women, leaped at me, I was ready. Crouching low, I let her get close before lunging toward her, using all my weight to shove the sword through her chest. I embedded the blade between her ribs and up through her back as her scream pierced my ears. I started to pull the weapon out, but her body evaporated into a ball of smoke.

"Did I kill it?" I asked, breathless. Thick black liquid coated the dull metal and dripped onto the floor.

"Yes," Tsagasi answered.

I nodded. Three more to go. I could do this.

David was talking behind me, but I had no idea what he was saying. I concentrated on the three creatures in front of me. Two had changed from cocky to wary while the older woman beamed. One of the men glanced toward the door.

"Don't you fuckers even think about leaving," I said through clenched teeth. I had no idea how to correctly wield a sword, but I held my arm close to my body, the blade pointed forward. If one of them rushed me, it would run into the blade. Their claws looked vicious, so I wanted to stay out of their reach. But thinking of the number of times I'd been clawed by demons only pissed me off more.

I was done taking crap from demons.

"We aren't going anywhere. We haven't completed our assignment," the two men said as one.

"And what's that?"

"To kill you." They laughed, but the woman—whom I was beginning to suspect was in charge—remained silent.

"How did you know that I'd be back here tonight?"

"You are predictable," one of the men answered in disgust.

"If that's true, why do I get the feeling that what I did to your friend was totally *unpredictable*?"

The creatures didn't answer. Instead, the injured old man bolted toward me with both arms raised, ready to claw me. I shoved the sword into his stomach, but he laughed and skimmed his claws across one of my shoulders.

Trying to ignore the burning pain of the wound, I leaned backward and jerked the blade out. But he continued to come toward me, his mouth open, his teeth ready to sink into my neck. Pulling my arm back so that the sword was next to my body and parallel to the floor, I threw my weight into it, impaling his heart with the weapon.

Surprise and fear flickered in his eyes before his body turned into flames and a cloud of smoke.

Two left.

But I was already out of breath, and I lost the advantage of surprise now that they realized I could kill them. The remaining two would be prepared to put up more of a fight.

I held the sword out to my side and leaned over, sucking in a deep breath. "Are you so sure you're going to kill me now?" I sneered. But even as I said the words, I realized that their plan made no sense. The Raven Mocker I'd seen in Manteo had told me that I was a vessel who would either save or destroy the world. How could killing me now achieve that? The future was supposedly unchangeable, and the Raven Mocker had committed suicide to deliver her prediction . . .

"We will shred your abdomen and watch your intestines spill out onto the floor," the man said, laughing.

"While that sounds fun, I think I'll pass."

"What's going on, Ellie?" David asked, terror in his voice.

Crap, he couldn't see or hear any of this.

"I've killed two and two are left. They've threatened to gut me. I took a rain check."

"You've killed *two*?"

Before I could answer, both Raven Mockers attacked me at once, coming at me from opposite sides. I'd been lucky to take out the first two, but I was in real danger this time.

Tsagasi's voice echoed in my head. "Listen to your power, witness to creation."

I dove out of their path, away from David. One followed me, but the woman moved toward David and Allison. Tsagasi shot in front of the Raven Mocker, blocking her path with his body and a flash of light.

Grabbing the sword with both hands, I ran forward, sinking the blade deep into the chest of my attacker. The weapon hadn't hit his heart, but I'd used so much strength that its blade was embedded almost to my fist. As I struggled to pull it out, I pressed my foot on his stomach and kicked, jerking my weapon free.

The Raven Mocker growled, swiping at me from the side, but I twisted in the opposite direction and spun in a circle. I used the momentum to move behind the creature and plunge the sword into its back, under its left shoulder blade. The demon screamed loud and long before bursting into flames and smoke.

I spun around to face the remaining demon. The old woman stood in the center of the room, watching me. "And then there was one."

She'd had a chance to kill me from behind and hadn't taken it. Why?

I cast a glance at the group huddled in the corner. David was still squatting in front of Allison, while Tsagasi stood in front of him, bathed in a soft yellow glow. The perpetual scowl on his face was deeper and made him look fierce.

"You've been lucky, Curse Keeper," the elderly woman cooed. "My brothers and sister were careless, but I am not."

"You just keep telling yourself that if it makes you feel better."

She advanced as I took a step into the middle of the room. "You're not supposed to have the power to kill us. You need the other Keeper."

"Surprise," I singsonged.

"It matters not. You will soon be in Popogusso. After you fulfill your role."

Rather than answering, I just watched as the demon inched toward me. I moved closer and closer to the front door. If I could lure it outside, hopefully David would think to pour salt across the threshold.

"Where is your sharp-barbed tongue now, Curse Keeper?" she asked.

I ignored her, digging deep inside, trying to find the well of power that had faded along with my physical strength. I was desperately out of shape and it was now biting me in the ass. I could tell this Raven Mocker was smarter than the others, more patient. She'd wait all night for me to make a mistake. There would be no defeating her in a defensive maneuver. I'd have to take the offensive.

Power surged through me again, swelling and filling me, but I held back, waiting for her to show weakness.

"Ellie, what's going on?" David shouted, but I ignored him.

I heard Tsagasi's low voice in the back of the room, and I hoped he was filling David in on what was happening.

"I'm going to kill your pet." The Raven Mocker gave me a wicked grin.

David? Panic raced through me, but I forced myself to remain calm even though the Raven Mocker stood between us. She could have meant Tsagasi for all I knew. I couldn't let anything happen to either one of them.

She spun around and kicked Tsagasi with the side of her foot, throwing him across the room. His body hit the wall and slid down it with a sickening thud.

I was too terrified for David's safety to even stop to check on my little protector. David couldn't even see the Raven Mocker, so he had zero chance of defending himself.

"David, she's right in front of you! Jump to your side!"

The Raven Mocker leaped for him, her claws extended.

He dove to his left, but she kicked him, sending him flying into the wall beside Tsagasi. He landed three feet from Allison, clutching his stomach with a groan.

A metallic taste coated my tongue as fear sent my heart rate sky-rocketing. I couldn't give in to my panic. "You want to fight defense-less humans who can't even see you? Come fight me."

Laughing, the Raven Mocker rushed me with her hand raised. She was faster than the others, and I had no hope of killing her yet. I knew I would be lucky just to defend myself. Her arm slashed toward my chest as she cackled, sounding every bit as crazy as she looked. I swung the sword as hard as I could, the blade connecting with her biceps and slicing diagonally through muscle until bone stopped my swing. The thick black blood splattered on my shirt and droplets landed on my face. I resisted the urge to wipe it off as nausea roiled in my stomach.

She pulled herself free and lunged at me time and time again, ignoring the blood that poured from her arm. It was easy to see her goal—wear me down as I kept swinging the sword to defend myself. My arms ached from the unaccustomed activity, and my swings and thrusts became sloppy and wild.

"You are full of surprises tonight," she said, looking thoughtful. "You are stronger than we thought. You are almost ready." Suddenly she twisted to the side and kicked my stomach and shoved me backward, using enough force that I landed on the sofa. Then she spun around until she was standing directly between David and Allison.

"I've seen enough." An evil smile spread across her face, her sharp teeth gleaming in the moonlight. "But *someone* must die."

Then she turned toward David and thrust her hand at his chest. "*David!*" I screamed.

But at the last moment, her body pivoted and her hand plunged into Allison's chest instead.

Allison's eyes widened in surprise before she screamed in pain and terror.

The Raven Mocker's arm rotated as her mouth twisted into a wicked smile, her hand still buried deep inside the other woman's body.

Allison gave one last scream and then fell limp as the Raven Mocker pulled her heart from her chest. The creature spun around and held the organ in front of her, smiling.

"It's a pity. If you had not seen me this night I would have gotten many years from this one."

Then her mouth opened wider than I would have thought possible as she lifted Allison's heart above her head, then brought it to her mouth, taking a huge bite. Blood squirted all over her face and body. She grinned as I gasped in shock and disgust, stumbling backward as she took another bite.

Fury rose inside me as I leaped for her, thrusting toward her chest with the sword, but she just laughed and turned into a flame that shot into the air and out the window.

And the Raven Mockers above the house released their haunting screams of triumph.

❖ Chapter Thirteen ❖

"What happened, Ellie?" David shouted, crawling over to Allison and feeling for her pulse.

"It took her heart." Black dots danced in front of my eyes and I felt like I was going to pass out, but there wasn't time for that. "Tsagasi!" I ran over to the little figure that was still slumped against the wall.

His eyes were closed, but he cracked them open when I leaned over him.

I dropped to my knees beside him. "Are you okay?"

He climbed to his feet, tilting his head back and forth, the bones popping. "Fucking Raven Mockers. Nasty sons of bitches."

I closed my eyes, trying to keep control. I was about to lose it. "I failed."

"No," Tsagasi said in a hard voice. "You never accessed your power as a witness to creation until tonight, and yet you still killed three of them."

"They killed Allison." My voice broke as I crawled across the floor toward David.

Allison's head lay in his lap, and he looked up at me with tears on his face. "She's dead, Ellie. She's really dead."

"I know. I'm sorry." I started to cry. "I tried to save her. I promise." I had failed both of them. I might have tapped into my power as the witness of creation, but what good was it if I couldn't even save people?

I relived those last moments in my head, remembering how terrified I had been when I was sure the Raven Mocker was going to kill David. "It almost killed you." I threw my arms around his neck, clinging to him. "She almost killed you."

"What are you talking about?" His voice was emotionless.

"The Raven Mocker was reaching for your chest, but then she swerved at the last second and took Allison's heart instead." My last words choked on a sob.

"*How could they kill her?*" His voice rose. "It doesn't make any sense! Raven Mockers only take a victim's heart after they're dead."

"I know what I saw, David. Allison was alive when she pulled out her heart." I looked around the trashed room, battling my rising hysteria. "What are we going to do?"

"We have to call the police."

I couldn't believe the police hadn't shown up already. I'd heard Allison's screams from the front yard when I pulled into the driveway. "How are we going to explain this?"

He shook his head, his jaw set in determination, but he looked dazed and in shock. "I don't know, but we can't just run off, Ellie."

I knew he was right, and if we were in Manteo, I would have felt better about the whole thing, especially since Tom knew there was something supernatural going on there. But the police here didn't know anything about me, and David's reputation could be on the line. I climbed to my feet and tugged his arm. "You have to go."

He looked up at me, his eyes wide with bewilderment. "What are you talking about?"

"You're her ex-boyfriend. You'll be a suspect." I continued to pull his arm, but he resisted.

"Are you crazy?" he asked in dismay. "I can't just leave. And I won't be a suspect, Ellie. She just died. There's no sign of trauma, no blood."

"What do you mean 'no blood'? Her body is covered in claw marks! There's a giant hole in her chest!"

"There's nothing there, Ellie!"

"The wounds are magical." When I looked down, Tsagasi was standing next to me, staring at Allison's body. "Only those who belong in the spirit world can see them."

"So you can?" I asked.

"Yes."

David sucked in a deep breath and released it. His eyes looked vacant. "There's no reason to worry. There's no sign of foul play. Just like with the other victims in Manteo." His voice broke. "I'll call the police."

"You and the police might not see the blood, but there's no hiding the fact that her heart is missing. And this room is trashed, David. You have to leave."

Tsagasi turned to David. "The Curse Keeper is right. You must go."

He shook his head. "How am I supposed to *leave*? I can't do that."

"She's already gone," Tsagasi said. "There's nothing more you can do for her."

I pulled on his arm again, crying. "David. Please."

"What about you, Ellie?" David asked, pulling out of my grasp. "Do you really think I'm just going to leave you here?"

"You both will leave," Tsagasi said.

"There are too many things tying us to what happened," I said. "David needs to go home, and I'll clean everything up."

Tsagasi crossed his arms with a scowl, his feet shoulder-width apart. "I may have been locked in Popogusso for hundreds of years, but I'm capable of cleaning this up."

I wavered. I didn't want to send David home alone, but I wasn't sure I could trust Tsagasi either.

The small man stepped closer to me, lowering his voice. "You cannot leave him alone. The Raven Mockers might return for him. He is a target now."

The image of the Raven Mocker reaching for David's chest filled my head. He was right. "David, let's go."

His body stiffened in anger. "You're just going to trust him? What if he's evil, Ellie? What if he's setting you up?"

"He helped me, David. He helped me kill the Raven Mockers. He was the one who told me they would be here. He was the one who told me which sword to use."

"But it wasn't enough, was it?" he asked bitterly. "He didn't save Allison."

I was the one who had failed to save her, but I wasn't sure bringing that up would be a good idea. Still, the guilt was overwhelming and my shoulders sank under the weight of it.

"You can't save them all," Tsagasi said, looking up into my eyes. "This battle has only just begun. There will be many deaths on both sides. But each time you must move forward, not back."

David cradled his ex-girlfriend's head in his lap, his body shaking as he fought tears. His grief was my undoing, and not because I felt jealous or threatened. I knew he still cared for her. He just hadn't loved her enough to commit his life to her. I couldn't expect him to get up and brush off his hands and pretend this meant nothing.

I couldn't help but wonder how I would have reacted if David had died and not Allison. Or Collin. I wouldn't have been able to leave without looking back. I couldn't expect any different from him.

I gently removed David's hands from Allison and guided her head to the floor, trying not to look at her poor body. I couldn't believe he couldn't see the torture she had been through. The poor victims in Manteo must have suffered for hours. Why hadn't I seen their wounds in the photos? "I need my phone," I muttered, digging for it in my pocket.

"Who are you calling?" David asked.

I hadn't considered calling anyone other than the police. But then a thought popped into my head, an unshakeable one. I needed to tell Collin. Just not yet.

"No one," I said. "I need to take a picture."

"You're going to take her picture?" he asked incredulously, his eyes widening. "You want a *memento*?"

I opened up my camera app. "David, just trust me on this one."

Thankfully, he didn't try to stop me. Instead, he climbed to his feet and walked over to the sofa and sat down, cradling his head between his hands.

I centered the screen over her face and upper body. I could see the wounds on my screen, but when I snapped the photo, she looked like she was sleeping, which explained why I hadn't seen any disfigurements in the photos Tom had shown me.

"Curse Keeper, you must leave," Tsagasi said, his voice firm. "The longer you stay, the more danger you are in."

"You mean of getting caught by the police?"

"The human police are by far your lowest concern." He turned his focus to David. "The Raven Mocker was on a mission. It was obvious she didn't intend to kill you, but she took pleasure in taunting you. She could come back to finish the job." He tilted his head toward David.

I knew he was right, but it felt so wrong to leave her like this. Allison hadn't liked me, and it wouldn't surprise me a bit to learn that she'd done everything in her power to win David back tonight, but that didn't mean she'd deserved to die. "Tsagasi, thank you."

He nodded, looking solemn and serious. His ever-present scowl still puckered his face, but it had softened. For the first time I noticed a wound on the side of his head, black blood trickling down his cheek. He'd risked his life to help us. Why? But trying to reason it out was like pulling on a loose thread—everything just kept unraveling. My poor brain couldn't handle another puzzle at the moment.

I grabbed David's arm and pulled him toward the front door, stopping to peer outside to see if anyone was around. When it looked clear, I dragged him to the car and opened the passenger door, pushing him inside.

"We can't just leave her like that, Ellie," he said as I got in and started the car. But his voice sounded like it was drained of fight.

"Tsagasi will take care of her."

He turned to me, the pain raw in his eyes. "Can you really trust him?"

"He has given me every reason to trust him in the little time that I've known him."

"And how long has that been?" There was accusation in his voice. "Have you known about him for weeks without telling me?"

"No," I said, trying to keep the hurt out of my voice. I deserved his questions. "I found him in your backyard after I left you with Allison."

"Can you blame me for asking? You went to see Collin yesterday without telling me. And you avoided giving me any details about seeing Okeus so you could keep it secret. What happened when you were with Collin in the ocean, Ellie? When you were *touching marks*?" His voice was ugly. He knew what had happened, what I was refusing to say. "What other things don't you want to tell me?"

"David, please. Let's not do this right now."

"Why not? Now seems like the *perfect* time, with my dead ex-girlfriend being 'taken care of' by your new friend."

"No, you're hurting." I swallowed my tears. I deserved all of his accusations and more. And it would be easy for him to push me away in his anger, but I couldn't let him do that. He needed me whether he wanted me or not. I had to be calm and strong for him, just like he usually was for me. "But you have every right to ask me if I kept him from you. I'll admit that I've kept things from you while trying to protect you."

"Even though you promised not to do that." Bitterness laced his words. "You promised no secrets, Ellie. You *lied* to me."

"Yes, I'll admit that I've tried to protect you. *I love you, David.* I've put you through enough hell . . . I thought that I was doing you a favor if I could save you from some of it. But I was wrong, and I'm sorry for that."

He shook his head and stared out the window, his shoulders trembling. "She didn't deserve to die."

"No, she didn't. I'm so sorry."

"*We* did this to her." His voice was drenched in self-disgust. "We killed her."

I wasn't sure how to answer, mostly because I couldn't deny his claim. There was a good chance that we were the cause of her death, one way or another.

"I keep seeing her thrashing on the ground, screaming and begging for me to help her." His voice broke and he choked back a sob. "There wasn't a bloody thing I could do about it. I brought those fuckers to her door and I couldn't save her."

"I'm sorry."

"What the hell am I doing with you, Ellie?"

I gasped, the pain of his words sinking deep into my heart. My throat burned and I couldn't hold back my tears.

"I couldn't help Allison. I can't help you. What bloody good am I?"

"That's not true, David! You help me more than you know. I need you." I reached for his hand, but he shoved me away.

"No. You need Collin." His words were hateful. "You went to Collin yesterday because you need *him*, Ellie. You spiritually and emotionally and *physically* need him. You don't need me."

I pulled into his driveway and turned off the car, sobbing.

"Every time you're with him, you have to fight some primal need buried deep inside you. Why are you fighting it? Your soul is bound to him, Ellie. You should be with Collin. Not me."

"I don't want to be with him. You know that! I need *you*. I want *you!*" I grabbed his hand, but he shook me off again. "David, I need you for your knowledge about the gods and the spirits. And if not for you, I wouldn't know the story behind the ring or the spear. I wouldn't know that Ahone had plotted that too. I wouldn't know about the Guardians and I wouldn't have found a warded sword." Oh, God. In my panic, I'd left the sword at Allison's house. "I can't do this on my own. I need your help. I love you." I choked on the last sentence, hoping my words were enough.

He turned to face me, his eyes filled with anger and hatred, and my heart broke even more. My worst fear was coming true. I was losing him too.

I wiped the tears from my cheeks. David's safety was more important than my hurt feelings, and we were sitting outside in his car. "But right now, we need to get inside. Tsagasi and I think the Raven Mocker might come back for you."

He released a bitter laugh.

By the time I opened my door, he had already gotten out of the car and was walking toward the porch. I hadn't had time to lock the front door, but David didn't seem to notice or care when I just pushed it open.

We stood in his living room and I wondered what we were

supposed to do. It's not like David could watch his ex-girlfriend die in agony and then come home and turn on the television.

I looked down at my arms and clothes, which were caked in demon blood and smelled of sulfur and tar. I suspected that I'd have to throw my clothes away. "I need to wash the Raven Mocker blood off."

He swung his gaze to study me. "What are you talking about?"

"I killed three of them and their blood is on my skin and clothes, even if you can't see it."

He turned to look out the window.

"Do you want me to get you something?" I asked, worried about leaving him alone.

"No." His voice was cold.

"I'm going to take my shower. Don't go anywhere."

He looked at me with a vacant expression. "Where am I going to go, Ellie?"

I pressed a kiss to his lips, cupping his cheek with my hand. "I love you. I'm so sorry."

He didn't answer and he didn't kiss me back. I fought new tears. He looked so broken, and it was all my fault. Was I keeping him with me out of selfishness? Was the answer to let him go? I pushed down the panic that accompanied that thought.

"I'll be right back." I went into the bathroom and turned on the shower, stripping off my clothes. I needed to hurry back to him.

I climbed into the steaming water and quickly washed my hair and body, fighting the sorrow that permeated my heart like the demon stink that clung to my body. I scrubbed my skin until it was raw. As I rinsed off, the curtain parted and David stood in the opening, naked and watching me.

I held out my hand to him. He grabbed it and stepped into the tub, pulling me to his chest, his hands digging into my shoulder blades. I wrapped my arms around his back and held him close, nearly crying with relief. He had come to me. He still wanted me.

We stood there for several seconds, the warm water beating down on us, until I lifted my head and looked up into his face.

His eyes were squeezed shut, pain etching lines on his face.

I had done this to him. I had brought this upon him.

His hand slowly slid up my shoulder blade to my neck, and he grasped the back of my head and tilted my face up so he could search my eyes. Whatever he saw there must have been what he needed because his mouth lowered and he gave me a hesitant kiss. I tangled a hand in his now-damp hair and held him tight.

Letting loose any of the reserve that held him back, his grip on me tightened and his kiss became more demanding. He turned and pressed my back against the cold porcelain tile as his hand found my breast.

"Part of me hates you," he murmured before kissing me again, his mouth punishing before it lifted again. "You've ruined everything. I can never, ever go back to the only life I've ever known."

His words stabbed my heart, and my grief and guilt threatened to suffocate me.

"But I love you more than I've ever loved anyone or anything in my life, and the thought of living without you is inconceivable."

"I'm sorry," I choked out, tears burning behind my eyes.

He lifted one of my legs and wrapped it up around his waist so that his erection prodded my entrance. Then he plunged in deep.

I gasped in surprise and he stopped, holding me up with my leg and his other arm, still buried deep inside me.

"You're my soul mate, Ellie. I never believed in soul mates until I met you. You're the one person I was destined to be with forever. I know that as clearly as I know that winter follows fall and the sun will rise every morning. But fate is a fickle, fickle bitch." His words were harsh as he pulled back and plunged into me again, pressing my back hard against the wall. "Because while you are my soul mate, I'm not yours."

"*David.*"

He grabbed my right hand, spreading my fingers open to reveal the circle and the square embedded in my skin. "You belong to *him.*"

I shook my head, crying. I couldn't deny it. "I don't want to belong to him."

"But you do anyway, don't you?"

"David, please."

"Tell me who you want, Ellie." His voice was harsh.

"You know who I want."

"*Say it.*"

"I want you, David," I said in desperation. "I want you. I only want you."

His eyes searched mine. "But is it enough, Ellie? Is wanting me enough?"

"It *has* to be."

His mouth covered mine and he lifted my ass up so my legs straddled him. He threw the shower curtain open and stepped over the side of the tub, carrying me out the bathroom door and the few steps to his bed. The cool air hit my water-drenched skin, raising goose bumps.

I kept my legs wrapped around his waist as he dropped me onto the mattress, climbing on top of me and entering me again. I clung to him, trying to keep up, trying to give him what he needed from me, but I realized the only thing he needed was for me to be there, holding him and proving that I was staying with him. That I chose him.

When he finished, he rolled to his side and pulled me up next to him. I started to cry softly on his chest and he pulled back, horror on his face. "Oh, God. What have I done? I hurt you."

I shook my head adamantly. "No, David. I hurt *you*. I'm so tired of hurting you."

"Shh." He brushed kisses along my cheek and hairline. "I love you, Ellie. Do you have any idea how much I love you?"

I nodded, fresh tears streaming down the sides of my face and running into my wet hair. "I love you too."

His mouth found mine, and I held his head in place. I needed him. I needed this. I needed to know he wasn't giving up on me.

"We left the water running in the shower. I'll be right back."

He left me naked on top of the bed. I realized how easy it would be for him to walk away and leave me alone and vulnerable, despite his protests that he had nowhere else to go. Anywhere he went would be safer and saner than staying with me.

When he returned moments later, I was curled in a ball on the bed, sobbing.

He pulled me into his arms. "God, Ellie. I'm so sorry." His voice broke. "I just treated you like—"

I shook my head, my mouth finding his, but I continued to cry and had to pull away to catch my breath. "I can't lose you. I can't lose you."

He pulled me against him, holding on tight. "I'm not going anywhere, love. I'm here."

∽ CHAPTER FOURTEEN ∽

I cried for several minutes and was finally starting to calm down when the image of Allison's abused body pushed to the front of my head. "Oh, God, David. It was so horrible. What they did to her." I released a fresh sob. "All I can see is her blood. I keep hearing her scream."

He sucked in a breath as he realized whom I was talking about.

"That last Raven Mocker was different than the others; I knew she would be harder to destroy. And then she lunged for you." I tried to catch my breath. "I was sure she was going to kill you, but she took Allison's heart instead." I took a shuddering breath. "It was the most horrible thing I've ever seen. Until I saw what she did next."

"What?" he whispered.

I shook my head. "You don't want to know."

"Enough secrets, Ellie." His voice was harsh. "Enough."

"The Raven Mocker held Allison's heart in her hand and ate it. Like it was an apple."

His body stiffened.

I jerked out of his arms. "I'm hurting you. I just keep hurting you."

"Not you, Ellie. You're not doing this. Ahone. Okeus. The Raven Mockers. They're the ones who are responsible."

"But they would leave you alone if it weren't for me."

"You don't know that, Ellie." He sounded weary. "Countless people have died who have no ties to you at all."

I jumped off the bed, still naked, and began to pace. "Oh, God. You're right. All those people and animals—they're all dependent on me to save them and I'm failing." I started to cry again.

"Ellie, that's not what I meant."

I shook my head. "Maybe not, but it's true."

He was silent for a moment, and then he slid off the mattress and opened one of his drawers, pulling out a T-shirt. Grabbing my arm, he tugged the shirt over my head and helped me put my arms through the sleeves. He leaned down to kiss me before pulling me into a hug.

"You're doing everything you can. You can't do any more than that."

I took a deep breath and tried to pull away, but he led me back to the bed. He pulled back the covers and sat with his back against the headboard, my body pressed to his side.

"Now tell me about Tsagasi."

I told him about finding him in the backyard. "He said he's my guardian."

"And you trust him?"

"I don't know. He helped me, so I suppose that I have no reason not to trust him other than the fact Ahone was supposed to be helping me too. Have you heard of Tsagasi?"

"He's part of Cherokee legend. He and Tsawasi. They are both mischievous, but they're not supposed to be evil . . . not as far as I know, anyway. I wouldn't be surprised if they were brothers."

"If he hadn't helped, we'd all be dead."

"You could have sent them away with your mark if he hadn't shown up."

Was David right? Should I have just sent them away instead of trying to destroy them? I still wasn't sure I would have gotten the vortex open in time to protect us all, and I couldn't have done both. But my decision had led to Allison's death, even if it had probably saved many other people. "I'm sorry."

He held me close. "You did everything you could, Ellie."

"Did I?"

"You can't second-guess yourself. You managed to tap into your power as a witness to creation by trusting your instinct, right?"

"Yes."

"Then that's all you really have to rely on—instinct. I suggested that you use the ring and you automatically dismissed it."

"I'm sorry."

He tipped my chin up. "Don't even think of saying you're sorry again. It's good that you've been following your gut. My suggestions are merely suggestions. I had no other idea to offer. Thank God for Tsagasi."

"I never even considered that I might have additional power from being a witness to creation. It's stupid when I think about it."

"Don't be so hard on yourself, but you're right. Everyone wants you for that very power, so it makes sense. But you need to practice with it and see what else you can do."

I nodded, relaxing into his chest. I rested there for several moments, listening to the soft rhythm of his heartbeat in my ear.

"I'm sorry," he said softly. "I treated you so badly tonight."

I tilted my face up and kissed him. "It's okay."

"*No.* It is *not.*"

"David . . ."

"I said some ugly, hurtful things that I wish I could unsay."

"You had every right to say them. They're all true." He started to protest. "No, I have ruined your life. I killed Allison."

"*Ellie.*"

"It's true. I wish it wasn't, but it is. I'm giving you a last out, despite what I said earlier. I need you, and the thought of living without you . . ." I swallowed the lump in my throat. "But I don't want you to stay with me out of guilt or obligation. Things got real tonight, and I suspect it's only a preview of what's to come. I won't hold it against you if you decide that this is too much."

He slowly shook his head. "I can't go back now. I told you that earlier, even if it was in the most hateful way possible. Even if I could go back to my old life, I wouldn't want to." He lightly rubbed my arm. "Nothing of great worth comes without a price."

"The cost is too much."

"That's for me to decide, love."

I rested in his arms, both of us nearly asleep. "Did Allison show you her big secret? The reason we came to Chapel Hill in the first place?"

"No." His arms tightened around me. "She refused to tell me. She said she'd only tell you if I broke up with you. I have no idea what it was."

"She died for nothing." My voice broke again.

"Ellie, enough." His words were sterner than usual. "This will eat you alive if you let it. There's enough guilt to go around, but I'm not blaming you. And if you continue to blame yourself, you could jeopardize our safety. Get it all out of your system now and let it go."

"It's not that easy."

"Nothing about this is." He kissed my forehead. "Try to get some sleep."

I lay in his arms, terrified as he fell asleep. The doors were marked. We were safe. But for how long? How long would I be able to protect him?

I fell asleep, David's arms chasing away the nightmare of Allison's screams. But I blinked awake in the middle of the night, sensing that something was off.

David slept next to me, his breathing soft and even. I waited to hear the familiar banging on the door followed by my slurred name, but it didn't come. There was no angry god waiting for me. Still, a slight itch tickled my right hand.

I carefully sat up and slid out of bed, trying not to disturb David.

I padded through the house and into the kitchen, pouring myself a glass of water. While I was midsip I heard a noise outside, so I set the glass down on the counter and cracked the back door open.

"Took you long enough to check on me." I heard Tsagasi's voice but couldn't see him.

I walked out through the door and sat on the step, tugging David's T-shirt down to cover my bare ass. "I'm sorry. I was dealing with a crisis of my own."

"Human feelings are such fragile things," he grunted in disgust.

I wasn't sure how to respond to that. There was definitely no arguing his point. "Did you have any problems?" It seemed so wrong to ask it that way. Allison had died and Tsagasi had stayed behind to cover up her death. Goose bumps broke out on my arms. When had I become so callous?

"No, but the Raven Mockers returned, looking for 'he who guides the Curse Keeper.'"

He who guides the Curse Keeper? *David?* He has a title?

"Everyone and everything has a title. Sometimes more than one."

Like me. I had three. "David said Raven Mockers are only supposed to go after people who are on their deathbeds. Even then, they wait until the person's dead to take their heart. But that Raven Mocker took Allison's heart while she was still alive."

"Being locked up for centuries changed the Raven Mockers. And not in a good way."

"So they aren't following the rules anymore?"

"Many things aren't." Tsagasi crawled up the steps and sat next to me. "I thought you would have realized that by now."

I stared at him longer than intended, but I still wasn't used to talking to a one-and-a-half-foot-tall man. "You said you're my guardian."

"I said a guardian *of sorts*. Perhaps 'coach' might have been a better term."

"Coach?"

"I can guide you and point you in the right direction. I can watch you train. But I can't volunteer information. I can only answer direct questions, but I can't tell you what to ask. I can only steer you in the correct direction. Tonight you asked the right questions."

I shook my head. "It wasn't enough. I didn't save Allison."

"While you must try to save the world, you cannot save everyone in it."

My head knew he was right, but I wasn't sure how many more people I could watch die. "That's depressing."

"It is what it is. Once you accept your circumstances and your fate, you will truly be ready to take on your adversaries."

"You think I haven't accepted my circumstances and fate?"

His head tilted to look up at me. "Have you?"

"I suppose not." I sighed and leaned my temple against the side of the house. "So what did you do after we left?"

"I straightened up the house. I asked my friends to help me lay the woman out on the sofa."

"Your friends?"

"There are many beings in the spirit world. Many are my friends."

"Are they good spirits?"

He groaned and shifted his legs. "There you go again with categorizing things as good and bad. The rightness or wrongness of a situation depends on which side you lean toward. The same with people."

"I'm not sure I like that answer."

Tsagasi's shoulders slouched. "It is the way of the world, Curse Keeper."

I sucked in a deep breath, surprised by how relieved the little man next to me made me feel. Still, even though I was grateful for his help, I wasn't sure I could totally trust him. "How do I know that you aren't trying to trick me or use me?"

He shrugged, looking unconcerned. "I suppose you don't."

"Then how can I trust you?"

"Maybe the question is why wouldn't you trust me?"

"Ahone."

He pursed his lips and nodded. "Good reason."

"I asked you earlier, and you wouldn't tell me. Who sent you to work with me? Okeus or Ahone?"

"Why are you so sure that someone sent me?"

I expected him to look at me, but he kept his attention on the back of the yard. Was he purposely avoiding eye contact to hide something from me? "Because the spirit world is run by Okeus or Ahone. So which one do you side with?"

"Neither."

One thing I'd learned over the last couple of months was that most supernatural beings were cagey with their answers. I wasn't sure what to make of him. "So you're on your own?"

"Few beings are truly on their own."

Yep, he was being cagey all right. "Who told you to come to me?"

"No one. Although I did discuss it with my friends."

"And do your friends side with Okeus or Ahone?"

He laughed. "Neither of the gods pays much attention to me and my friends. We are considered too small, too far beneath the gods for them to concern themselves with *lesser beings.*"

I knew I wasn't imagining the bitterness behind his words.

"Still, we are many, and some of us are smart enough to recognize that while this is a game played by the gods, we will be affected one way or another."

"So you were elected to come to me?"

"No. I volunteered. Most think this is a fool's errand. Especially after tonight. Many are upset with me now. They believe that I've put them in danger."

"Why?"

"Because the Raven Mockers now know I'm involved."

I closed my eyes. "And several got away."

"Why do you think the Raven Mockers engaged you tonight?"

I shrugged. "I don't know."

"Don't be so dense."

I shook my head. "You don't hold back, do you?"

"Do we have time to waste?"

"No." The facts came hurling at me like projectiles. They had waited for me to get the sword before attacking. Then they'd only come at me one at a time, and the final woman hadn't killed me when she had the chance. Why? She'd said I wasn't ready. "It was a test," I murmured. "She said I was stronger than she expected and I would be ready soon. But ready for what?"

"Do you think that's the only reason? Then why would the Raven Mockers seek out that woman?"

I shook my head. "No, I thought they targeted Allison because killing her could hurt David, thus hurting me." My gaze stayed on his face. "But that was just a bonus. The main reason they killed her was because she saw the Ricardo Estate, and more importantly the Sword of Galahad. It's the real thing, isn't it?"

"It depends on what you mean by 'real thing.'"

"The sword the Guardians possess can kill demons."

He shrugged, looking unimpressed. "The sword you used tonight has the power to kill demons." He hopped off the step and waddled over to a bush, pulling out the sword I'd used earlier, the blade wiped clean.

"You took Allison's sword? Did she know what it was?"

He laid it on the porch next to me and resumed his original seat. "I doubt she had a clue. It belongs to you now."

"Do I still need the Sword of Galahad?"

"You need every tool at your disposal." But the end of his sentence lifted up slightly.

My eyes narrowed. "What's so special about the Sword of Galahad then?"

His face spun to look at me, a genuine smile spreading across it. "*That* is the right question." He leaned forward. "The sword they call the Sword of Galahad has the power to subdue gods."

It took a full two seconds for his words to register. "Subdue but not kill?"

"You can never kill a god. But you can remove its power. The sword the Guardians possess has that ability."

So were the Raven Mockers trying to keep me from finding out about the sword? It made sense that the gods wouldn't want me to have it. But it appeared the Raven Mockers weren't following Okeus. The real question was what would they all do to stop me? "So it was a coincidence that Allison just *happened* to have a sword on her wall that was warded to kill demons when the Raven Mockers showed up to attack us?"

He shrugged again.

"Who's in charge of creating all these coincidences anyway? Ahone?"

"That is for you to determine."

I groaned my frustration, then we sat in silence for several moments. But the more I thought about how my life had been manipulated, the more my anger grew. "That stupid collection has killed so many people."

"More than you know." He sounded weary.

How many were there? "I'm sure my mother was killed because of it."

He was silent for a moment. "Your life is like a spiderweb. There are many connections, finely woven, only there is more than one spider spinning your web. You have more tangled threads than I have ever seen."

"Who has woven the threads? Ahone and Okeus? And can I burn the web and make my own?"

He laughed. "Surprisingly, I think I will like working with you."

"You didn't answer my question."

"Maybe it's the wrong question."

I shook my head. "I'm too tired for riddles."

Tsagasi chuckled softly.

"Why are you helping me?" I asked, rubbing my forehead with one hand. He was making my head hurt with all his talk of tangled webs. "You still haven't really answered that."

"I want to ensure your success."

I released a heavy sigh. We sat next to one another on the porch and listened to crickets chirp all around us.

"You did well tonight, witness to creation. Better than I'd expected."

I turned to him, my mouth gaping. "Why are you so surprised?"

"Your sex for one. You're a female. A curious choice."

Were the spirits all misogynists? "There have been female Curse Keepers in the past."

"Yes, but not very many. Less than the number of fingers on my hand."

I glanced over to see how many fingers he actually had. Five. "Why?"

He shrugged. It was a wonder he didn't have a muscle spasm from all his shoulder rolling. "There is another question that is more important."

"What question?"

"You must figure it out on your own."

I groaned. "You're talking in riddles again."

"Try to figure out what that question is and ask me tomorrow."

"Now that I have the power from being a witness to creation, do I still need to use the ring and the spear and the sword?"

His eyes narrowed and he leaned toward me, his gaze piercing mine. "As I already said, you need *every* tool at your disposal. What works in one situation might not work in another."

"So you'll answer every question I ask?"

He laughed and sat back. "It depends on what you ask."

"Ahone was there on the night of my mother's death. Do you know why?"

"I was locked away in Popogusso with the others. How would I know?"

"That's not an answer."

He grinned. "This is why I like you, Curse Keeper. You pay attention. I knew he was there."

"And he let my mother die?"

He remained silent, his gaze intent on the woods behind the house.

"My memory of that night is coming back in bits and pieces."

"Many things happened that night. You must try harder to remember. It is important."

I nodded, picking up the sword next to me and laying it across my lap. I'd never been a proponent of citizens arming themselves, but holding the weapon gave me a confidence I hadn't felt seconds before. "A Raven Mocker told my future and called me a vessel," I said. "Does it mean that Okeus will get his way?"

"Fortunes and prophecies are purposely vague so that they can be interpreted in many ways."

"You didn't answer my question again."

He sighed. "Sometimes there is no answer, Curse Keeper. Sometimes there is only the question, and it is up to you to supply your own answer."

"I think that's bullshit," I said, even though there was a certain Yoda-like wisdom in his response. "I think that's your answer because you don't know and you're not willing to admit it."

He laughed and climbed to his feet. "Enough questions for one night. I need rest to face your next interrogation. You are like a human toddler with your endless questions."

"How long will you be around to help me?"

He stood next to me, inches separating us, but I still had to look down at him. His head didn't even come to my shoulder. "I will help you as long as you need me, but once you don't, I will be gone."

"Okay, *that's* vague."

He hopped off the porch and started walking toward the woods.

"Tsagasi, one more thing and then I'll go inside." He twisted at the waist to look back at me. I needed an answer to a question I'd already asked and he'd left unanswered. I took his previous advice and rephrased it. "What do you get out of helping me?"

His grin faded. "Survival."

CHAPTER FIFTEEN

The next morning I gasped in shock when I reached the door to Myra's apartment.

There were marks on it.

Myra had never shown any interest in the markings I put on the doors to the inn each night other than concern for my safety. But the most perplexing part of it was that these marks weren't the same ones I used. While they were primitive, they were mostly lines and circles. What were they, and why had she started using them?

I lifted my hand to knock, but Myra opened the door before my fisted hand could connect with the wood. A smile spread across her face. "Ellie, I'm so happy to see you."

My palm burned when I crossed the threshold, but the sensation stopped as quickly as it had started. I turned around to check behind me. Myra's apartment had an inside entrance, and the hall was completely bare.

"Is everything okay?" Myra asked with a worried tone.

"My mark tingled."

"Do you think something's out there?"

"No, doesn't look like it." I turned to face her. "It happened when I walked through the door. What are those marks?"

The Curse Defiers

"Oh!" She grimaced and looked embarrassed. "I confess that once I got here, hundreds of miles from you, I got a little paranoid. Steven found a Native American shaman to come by and start marking my door."

"These marks aren't Croatan."

"No, but I figured the gods and spirits this far inland were more likely to be associated with another tribe." She shut the door and headed to the small kitchen that was separated from the tiny living room by a short bar.

"So are they Cherokee?"

Myra grabbed a pot of coffee and poured some into a mug. "I'm not sure. Steven called a Cherokee shaman, but he told me he blended in some other local tribal signs to be safe."

Worry knotted my stomach. "Maybe I should mark your doors before I leave. Just to be sure. I heard about the missing Duke students." That was the only reason I was here instead of with David after all we'd been through the previous night. In light of Allison's death and the missing students, I had a possibly not-so-irrational fear that Myra was in danger. I needed to see her for myself. A phone call wasn't good enough.

She shook her head, tsking. "Everyone on campus is quite upset about it, justifiably of course." She poured creamer into my cup and handed it to me. "That's why I decided to mark my door. Steven thinks I'm crazy." She rolled her eyes with a grin. "In Manteo, we explained the marks on the doors as part of the colony experience, but here . . ." She looked up and chuckled. "I told him it was because I was homesick."

"Good thinking."

Myra grabbed a basket and moved past me to set it on the table. "While I'm grateful for your offer to re-mark my door, I think I should keep these ones. Yours will fade, but the shaman can come back and redo his work every week."

"Okay . . . I just want to make sure you're safe."

She offered me a soft smile. "Ellie, that's what I love about you. You'll do anything to make sure the people you love are safe." She spun around and returned to the kitchen, leaving me standing on the opposite side of the bar.

"Can I do anything to help?"

"Nope. I've got it." She pulled a bowl of cut-up fruit out of the refrigerator and a hash brown casserole out of the oven, then scooped a generous helping of both onto a plate and handed it to me.

"Good heavens, Myra. Are you trying to fatten me up?"

"You look like you need meat on your bones," she said, scooping her own plate. "Isn't David making sure you eat?"

"It's not his job. I'm a grown woman, capable of monitoring my own caloric intake," I teased, giving her a wink as we sat down at the small table.

She held up her hands in surrender. "Point taken, but worrying about you is part of my job description. You can't expect me to give that up just because I live a few hundred miles away."

"Fair enough."

She picked up her fork, her mouth puckering with worry. "I hope David wasn't upset that I asked you to come alone. You know I'm quite fond of him, Ellie, but he gets to see you all the time. I wanted an hour or so with you all to myself."

"No, he wasn't upset at all. I just told him that I wanted to talk to you alone about the B&B." In reality, it had never come up. One of David's friends had called around seven in the morning to tell him about Allison's death. She was supposed to have gone running around six with Cheryl. When she didn't answer her phone or the door, Cheryl peeked in the front windows. She could see Allison lying on the sofa, surrounded by tissues and cold medicine. Frantic, she called 911, and the emergency personnel declared her deceased upon arriving at the scene. The coroner had already declared the death an illness—a sudden onslaught of the flu—and decided an autopsy was unnecessary. Devastated, her friends had all gathered to console one another, David included. And since I would have felt like an outsider in their group, I'd decided to keep my date with Myra. But I didn't want to tell my stepmother any of that. She worried about me enough.

"I want to hear about your new job," I said, forcing myself to sound cheerful.

Myra spent the next fifteen minutes telling me about the classes she was teaching, along with some humorous encounters she'd had with students. I was happy to see how animated and excited she was, but something seemed off. I knew people changed—look at David and me—but I still felt sad. Myra had moved on without me.

That was a good thing, right?

"So how's Claire?" Myra asked with a wide smile. "How was her honeymoon?"

"She's good." I paused, unsure what to tell her. "She had a great time."

Myra's smile froze, then faded. "What are you keeping from me?"

I gave a half shrug and shoveled hash browns onto my fork. "Myra, it's nothing."

She reached over and covered my left hand. "Ellie, something's worrying you. I'm still your mother. Don't shut me out."

Tears filled my eyes. "So much has happened in the last two months. Some days it's just so overwhelming."

Myra scooted her chair next to mine and pulled me into a hug. "Oh, Ellie. It's just so much responsibility for one person to carry. I so wish you could give this up. You have no idea how much I worry about you." She cradled my head to her shoulder. "Maybe I should come back home."

I jerked out of her hold, panic racing through my body. "No. Don't. Please don't give this up. This is your dream. I want you to have it."

Her hand cupped my face, her skin feeling warmer than normal. "But Ellie, you're my daughter. I want to be there for you."

"The best thing you can do for me is stay here." I still thought she was safer here than at home, particularly if Claire was right about the inn. "Myra, are you feeling sick? Your hand is warm." Any sickness would make her fair game for the Raven Mockers.

Laughing, she pulled her hand free. "I'm fine. I've been *cooking*. It's made my hands warm."

"There are things out there killing people who are sick. They rip their hearts out after they terrorize their victims. If you're sick, I'm not leaving you alone."

"Oh dear." She paused, then shook her head. "Ellie. I'm fine. You have enough to worry about without worrying about my welfare. Besides, my door is marked and the windows are sealed. There's no need to be concerned." She offered me a soft smile. "Enough about me. How about you explain your cryptic message about the inn?"

I put down my fork and sighed. "We both know it's a hopeless cause to try and keep it open. I quit the New Moon, but I'm still struggling to keep the inn going with my other . . . activities."

She frowned. "Hasn't Becky been stepping up?"

"She's been a huge help, but she can't work seven days a week like you and I did." I paused, close to tears. "I think that the best thing would be to close the inn and sell it."

Myra stared at me for several seconds. "Ellie, I think this is an impetuous decision. You need to wait. The Dare Inn . . . well, it's been in your family for over one hundred years." Her expression softened. "I would hate for you to make a decision you'll regret."

"Myra." I reached across the table and covered her hand with mine, still amazed by how warm her hand was. "Look me in the eye and tell me that you think the inn can be saved."

She stared into my eyes for a moment, but then looked down. "You can probably hold on to it for another six months, possibly a year."

"Not if I keep paying Becky's salary. That's a strain too."

"It would give you time to adjust to the idea."

"I've already adjusted to it. I'm ready. I just wanted to talk to you about it before moving forward."

Her gaze returned to my face, but her face had hardened slightly. "It's a huge job, Ellie, dismantling the house and the inn. I don't have time to help you right now, and it wouldn't be fair for you to do it on your own. I think you should wait." Her tone made it clear she didn't approve.

My mouth gaped in surprise. "I can close the inn and take a month to sort through everything. Of course, you're welcome to anything in the house you want, Myra. It's your home too."

"There's nothing there I want." She shook her head and sounded angry.

Tears strangled my throat. "I'm sorry. I thought you'd be on board with this. You know the inn's been in trouble for ages. This shouldn't come as a surprise." I tried to swallow the burning lump in my throat. "Please don't be upset with me. I'll keep it for now if you feel that strongly about it." Myra was the only family I had left. I couldn't lose her too.

Her face softened. "I'm sorry I've been so harsh, Ellie, but I do think you're being hasty." She leaned forward. "Maybe it's being immersed in the history of the university that's made me appreciate the history we have at the inn. Once you sell it, you can't turn back. I think you should wait a little while."

"Okay." I disagreed, but there was so much turmoil in my life that I couldn't bear to fight Myra too.

"That's a good girl." She stood and headed for the kitchen. "Let me get you more coffee." She brought over the pot and the creamer and set them on a placemat in the center of the table. "But this brings up the real reason I wanted you to come alone." She paused. "I'd like to talk to you about David."

My back stiffened. "What about him?"

"As I said, I'm very fond of him, but I've also made it clear that I think things are moving much too quickly with you two. I have a feeling he's influenced you in this decision about the inn. Am I right?"

"Well . . . yes . . ."

Anger filled her eyes. "Frankly, he's making decisions he has no right to make. I think you should slow things down, and the first step is for him to move out."

My chest tightened. "How can you say that?" Myra had disapproved of several of my previous relationships, but she'd never been this forthright. "You know I need him. And not just because we have a relationship."

"All the more reason to put some distance between you two. I think you're still upset over your father's death and you're transferring those feelings onto David. You're confusing your need for information with your need for someone to take care of you." A small smile lifted the corners of her mouth. "You've gone from one man to another since your father became ill. Anyone with any sense can see that, and I've allowed your behavior to go on for far too long." Her back stiffened. "As your mother, I'm telling you to end your relationship with David and learn to stand on your own two feet."

I gasped at her bluntness. "I can't do that, Myra. I love him."

She shook her head. "You only *think* you love him. It's not real, Ellie."

My phone buzzed in my pocket and I pulled it out to see if David was calling. When I saw Claire's number, I declined the call and set it down.

"You were checking to see if it was him, weren't you?" There was a snotty tone in her voice I'd never heard there before. "See? You can't even have a conversation with me without letting him interfere with it."

I wanted to cry, but I was too shocked and dismayed to let any emotion slip through the massive fissure in my heart. "I can't believe you're doing this, Myra. You've never been . . . hateful before."

Her expression softened. "I don't mean to sound hateful, Ellie. I just worry about you. With all the responsibilities of the curse . . ." Her gaze landed on my right hand. "I see you've taken to wearing the ring. Do you think that's a good idea?"

"I . . . David . . ."

Myra's eyes narrowed. "Ellie, do you hear yourself? All you can say is *David this* and *David that*. You are a grown woman, and you need to make your own decisions without his influence." She stood and picked up her plate. "You said you're not working at the New Moon anymore. I take it that you quit because of your horrid new boss?"

I numbly nodded.

She set her plate on the counter and smiled. "Perfect. I think you should leave the inn in Becky's care and come stay with me for a while. Maybe we can get you enrolled in some classes. I know how much you regretted not going to college. It could be a fresh start for both of us."

I shook my head in confusion. "But just a few minutes ago, you said I shouldn't sell the inn. And the semester has already started. Not to mention the fact that it's *Duke*, Myra. I'd never get accepted."

"I didn't say sell it. I said leave it with Becky and come stay with me."

My phone went off in my pocket again. I glanced at the screen and saw that it was Claire again. She wasn't usually this persistent. I wasn't sure how much more I could take of Myra's planned reboot of my life, so I decided to use Claire's calls to my advantage. I stood. "Myra, I hate to leave like this, but Claire has a crisis going on and I need to go help her."

"You're going back to Manteo?"

I didn't want to lie to her, but I needed to get out of there as soon as possible. "Yes."

She emerged from the kitchen and walked closer to me. "Ellie, I beg you to consider what I've said. I think if you're honest with yourself, you'll see that I'm right." She pulled me into a hug. "Just know I care about you and my door is always open."

"Okay." Her body felt piping hot next to mine, and no matter how upset I was with her, I was still worried about her health. "Are you sure you're not sick? You feel like you have a fever."

"I'm fine. It's just hormones. I've been having hot flashes, embarrassing though that is." Her smile tightened. "You scoot and take care of Claire." She moved toward the front door and opened it.

"Okay." My breakfast weighed ten pounds in my stomach. I couldn't bear to leave with things like this between us, but I wasn't sure how to fix the situation. "Take care, Myra."

"You too."

I walked through the door and my hand burned again as I passed through the threshold. I turned around to mention it to Myra, but she'd already closed the door.

Whatever was on the door was messing with my mark.

I pulled out my phone and took multiple pictures to show David, then practically ran out to the car and slid behind the wheel. Once I had the door shut, I gave in to my storm of emotion and let the tears flow freely down my cheeks. I wanted to dismiss everything she'd said, but the problem was that I could see some truth in it. But how much was truth and how much was overprotectiveness?

My phone buzzed again.

I answered this time and Claire sounded beyond irritated. "Ellie, I'm sorry, but she's bugging the shit out of me. She won't leave me alone until I talk to you."

I shuddered in confusion. "Who's bugging you?"

"My ghost." I could practically hear her roll her eyes. "The one that thinks you need to move out. She won't leave me alone until I tell you something."

I wiped the tears off my cheeks and started the car. "And what's that?"

Claire paused. "She says you need to leave your house and you need *him*."

"Him who?" I asked as I started to pull out of my parking space.

"David. She's very upset. She insists that you need him."

My head grew fuzzy, so I pulled back between the lines, shifting the car back into park. "How did she know?"

"Know what?"

"That Myra was giving me a huge guilt trip about selling the inn and being with David. She asked me to move to Durham with her and start taking college classes."

"*What?* That's the craziest idea ever. That doesn't sound like her at all."

"I know . . ."

"She's probably lonely, Ellie. Sure, she's got an exciting new job and a boyfriend, but she's left her entire life behind. I bet she misses you and this is her way of trying to get you back."

"Maybe . . ."

"Plus, my ghost is adamant that you need David."

I laughed even as tears burned my eyes. "Too bad your ghost isn't Myra." I sucked in a deep breath to get control. "Can you see your ghost yet? Do you know who she is?"

"No." She sounded frustrated. "And I still struggle to understand her. Her words are often garbled. But I do know it's a *her*, and she's quite persistent in regards to you."

"And you think we can trust her?"

"Yes. I can feel her concern for you. So put Myra's words out of your head."

"Easier said than done, Claire. She's my mom."

"I know, but she's still human like the rest of us, which means even Myra is fallible from time to time."

I smiled. "Yeah, you're right. Thanks."

"What's a BFF for?"

I filled her in on everything that had happened since I'd talked to her last, which took up the whole twenty-five minute drive to Chapel Hill.

David wasn't home yet, so I resumed packing but wondered if I was overstepping my bounds. He sent me a text saying one of his friends had dropped him off at the library and he'd call me to pick him up later.

My encounter with Myra, along with everything else that had happened over the weekend, had been overwhelming. After I heated up a can of soup for lunch, I went into David's room and crouched next to the bed, pulling out the sword Tsagasi had given me from between the mattress and box springs. Sitting on the edge of the mattress, I held the blade in my hands. It needed to be sharpened, although I had no idea how to do that, but it had proven effective nevertheless. Still, I couldn't ignore how quickly I'd gotten worn out in my fight with the Raven Mockers. If I was going to start using a sword regularly, I needed to learn how to wield it. And build up my upper-body strength.

But first I needed a nap. I lay down, setting the sword on the comforter next to me. Then I grabbed David's pillow and wrapped my arm around it, breathing in the scent of him—the clean smell of his shampoo, with a hint of musk. Myra's admonishment was still fresh on my mind, but so was the message from Claire's ghost. Did I trust the woman who had been my mother for the last ten years or some nameless ghost?

I roused out of my dreamless sleep and blinked my eyes open as I felt movement on my arm. "David?" I murmured.

He was sitting on the bed next to me. "Hey."

"How did you get home?" I asked, still groggy.

"I ran into a friend who gave me a ride. How was your visit with Myra?"

I rolled onto my back to face him. "Don't ask. Moving to Durham has changed her in a lot of ways."

"I'm sorry."

I told him about the whole incident, and when he heard what Myra had said about him, pain flickered in his eyes. "It's not you, David. She thinks it's all me."

"What do you plan to do about her advice?"

I sat up and placed a gentle kiss on his lips. "I'll hold off on selling the inn for a few months. But I'm not giving you up. Even Claire's ghost agrees that I shouldn't."

A grin spread across his face, even if his eyes were slow to catch up. "Well, there you go. It's a good thing this ghost likes me since you follow her lead so much."

I shook my head and smirked. "It just so happens Claire's ghost and I think a lot alike. Anyway, I wanted to show you the marks on Myra's door. They're really different." I dug the phone out of my pocket and pulled up the photos. "Have you seen anything like this before?"

He enlarged the photos and scrolled through the images. "I can honestly say I don't recognize any of the marks. Forward them to my phone, and I'll see what I can dig up."

"Thanks." I texted them to him, then put my phone on the bed. "Now tell me about your day."

David had spent several hours with his friends, helping Allison's parents arrange for her body to be moved to her hometown of Asheville for her funeral, and then Phil had dropped him off at the library.

"I read the letter Penelope recommended, and it helped confirm a lot of what we know." It was written by a man claiming to be part of a group of Keepers whose duty it was to watch for a curse to break. The man spoke of a gold ring and a spear that could be used to rid the world of demons. Both objects had been lost for over fifty years, but he'd discovered that the prominent Middleton family in Charleston, South Carolina had gained possession of them. He had gone to the plantation to confront the current heir, but had never made it past the caretaker. He'd tried to talk to the sheriff in Charleston, but the man had refused to listen because the Middleton family was so respected, not only in Charleston but in the entire nation.

"Middleton," I said. "I've heard that name before."

"Are you sure? Could it have been from a history class or book?" He winked. "Or perhaps a *People* magazine story about Kate Middleton?"

"Very funny." I shook my head. "It's a memory, trapped in my head. I'm sure it's associated with the Ricardo Estate. I don't know how, but I am."

"Okay," he said, nodding. "Somehow the Middletons got possession of the ring and the spear. And we suspect the ring you're wearing came from the estate through your mother. But what happened to the spear?"

"Allison told Trina that the collection also had Native American spears. Some were so old that the shafts were warped."

"So the Guardians might have the spear. That's good."

"Tsagasi says that there are things from the night my mother died that are important. I need to remember what happened."

David grabbed my hand and stroked the back of it with his thumb. "I know you weren't keen on the idea before, but do you want to try hypnosis?"

"I don't know. Maybe." If I were back home, I could ask Collin to go into the ocean with me. But that would hurt David. He might not ask questions, but he knew my encounters with Collin were far from innocent. Yet if I could get necessary answers, didn't that justify it?

Didn't Tsagasi say that the right- or wrongness of a situation depended on which side you stood on?

But there had to be another way. Hurting David was an absolute last resort. Some of the memories had already emerged. I just needed to tap into the others.

He lowered his voice. "Ellie, there's one more thing the letter mentioned."

"What?"

"The writer of the letter—a man named Samuel—said the Middletons were part of a secret group. But when he tried to appeal to the sheriff, he was just laughed out of the station."

"Secret group?"

"The Guardians."

I sat up straighter. "Oh, crap."

"Samuel found out they had the ring and the spear because he'd heard they were seeking weapons created to fight supernatural creatures."

"It's them."

"I think so." He paused. "There's one more thing and it's the best news of all." His grip on my hand tightened, counteracting his words.

My breath stuck in my chest.

"This afternoon, I received a phone call from a woman associated with the collection. She had heard about Allison's death, and she asked if I knew anything about the research Allison had been doing. When I said yes, she asked me to come to Charlotte in Allison's place. I'm meeting them at ten tomorrow morning."

My eyes widened. "How is this good? It's creepy enough that they knew about her death this soon, but they specifically sought you out. I don't like this . . ."

"Ellie, this is my chance to see the weapons for myself."

"And look what happened to the last two people we know who saw them."

"Don't be so superstitious."

"Superstitious? My mother and your ex-girlfriend were both murdered less than a week after they saw the collection. You're the one who keeps claiming there are no coincidences in any of this."

"This will be different. I'm not going in blind. I have an idea of what I'm looking for."

"But you have no way of knowing what their plans are. They might be waiting there to kill you."

His back stiffened. "Ellie, I'm doing this with or without your approval."

I hopped off the bed and headed for the kitchen, David on my heels. "Don't be angry with me."

I placed my hands on the counter and squeezed my eyes shut, trying to smother my panic. "I'm not angry, David. I'm terrified."

He stood behind me and pulled my back to his chest. "I have to do this, love. And you know it too, deep in your gut." When I didn't answer, he bent his mouth to my earlobe. "This could be the big break we need. We have a sword that kills Raven Mockers, but I suspect they have many more weapons we can use. This is our chance to not only protect you but to go on the offensive. To save the world."

He was right, and it killed me to admit it.

We hung around his house and ordered a pizza. He said he had more research to do to prepare for his visit the next morning, so I told him I was going to sit in his backyard in the hopes that Tsagasi would come to me. I hadn't seen him since our middle-of-the-night chat.

"This is going to sound quite bizarre," David said, glancing up from his laptop. "But I think you should take the sword with you."

I put my hand on my hip, my eyebrows raised. "What will your neighbors say about a woman walking around your backyard with an antique weapon?"

"We'll deal with it if it comes up. But the sun will set soon, and I'd feel better if you could defend yourself with more than the mark on your palm."

"Okay." Minutes later I was behind his house, heading for the woods as the sun hung low in the sky, my nearly three-foot sword in my hand. I hiked a good thirty feet before calling out Tsagasi's name.

Moments later he walked out from behind a tree.

"Why are you in the woods, daughter of the sea?" But he wore a smirk.

"To find you, of course."

"Did you bring a list of questions? I haven't had my nap yet."

"Very funny."

He gestured to my hand. "You are carrying the sword."

"David thought I should bring it in case I needed to defend myself."

He nodded solemnly. "He who guides the Curse Keeper is wise."

It was good to know that Tsagasi thought I needed David too. "You're right. I need to remember what happened the night my mother died."

The little man leaned his shoulder into the tree. "And?"

"I need you to help me find the memories."

He shook his head. "You must figure that out on your own." His scowl deepened. "The loss of your memories isn't normal."

"Because of the trauma?"

"Because of magic."

I was an idiot. "I can use my power as a witness to creation to remember," I whispered.

A hint of a smile flickered at the edges of his mouth, then just as quickly disappeared. "They will come rushing back once you tap into them. You will be vulnerable."

"Like when I'm with Collin in the ocean." I considered waiting until we returned to Manteo. I could ask Collin to watch over me in case something supernatural showed up, but I needed whatever information was trapped in my head now, so David would be more prepared for his visit tomorrow.

My gaze narrowed on Tsagasi. He had protected us last night. "Will you protect me?"

"I'm not sure I can do it on my own."

"Will your friends help?"

"They are reluctant to get involved." But he shifted his weight as his voice trailed off, hinting that they could be convinced.

If I'd learned anything since this mess began, it was that everything had a price. "What do they want?"

His eyes met mine. "They want peace, but more importantly, they are frightened of the power you wield. They want your blood oath that you will never banish them to Popogusso."

"Blood oath?" I shook my head. I'd had one blood oath too many to suit me. "No way."

He crossed his arms and turned to look toward the setting sun, barely visible through the foliage. "Then you must take your chances."

This had to be negotiable. "If I swear this oath, what guarantee do I have that they won't do something evil, something that earns them a place in Popogusso?"

He shrugged. "You don't."

"How many are there? Do I have to promise this for all the creatures that don't follow Ahone or Okeus?"

"No, only those who will agree to guard you."

"Can I meet them first?"

He nodded his approval. "It is a wise request."

The leaves behind him rustled and another little man appeared next to him. While Tsagasi resembled one of Snow White's dwarves, this man looked much more proportionate to his height. His face was smooth and wrinkle-free, and his long, dark brown hair hung down his back, the ends brushing the plant life at his feet.

Tsagasi stood straighter. "This is my brother. Tsawasi."

"Hello," I said. I wasn't sure it was the correct greeting for a supernatural creature that wanted to protect me for a price, but it was better than "hey."

The little man gave a tiny nod.

"And this is Gawonii and Ama."

A man and a woman appeared out of thin air behind the little men, both dressed in deerskin clothing and carrying bows on their backs.

I gasped in surprise.

They looked like the Native American warriors I'd seen in drawings and the occasional photo, and they were the size of normal humans. The woman watched me with interest, but the man looked wary.

"They are Nunnehi," Tsagasi said, as though that explained their sudden appearance.

I shook my head, still staring at them, even though I knew it was rude.

"The Nunnehi are 'the people who live anywhere.' They are immortal beings who can appear and disappear at will. They have long been friends with the Cherokee."

"And they want to help me?"

"If you agree to the blood oath. But before you decide, you must understand that you are not the only one who will be making an eternal pledge." He looked over his shoulder. "We will agree to come to your aid whenever you need us. But only seven times."

"Wait, I'm being asked to *never* send all of you to Popogusso, but you're only agreeing to help me seven times. That hardly seems fair."

He shrugged his indifference.

"And how will they help me?"

"They will defend you to their deaths."

Maybe it was a fair trade. "Okay." I was nervous. Making another bond seemed like a bad idea, but David had urged me to go with my instincts. I had never felt comfortable taking Ahone's mark, but somehow I was sure that making this blood oath was the right thing to do.

Tsagasi dug a hole next to the base of the tree, uttered words in a guttural language, and pulled a short, sharp-pointed knife from his belt. He pierced the palm of his right hand with the tip, then let the several drops of black blood fall into the hole and said, "Upon my life I swear."

He repeated the process with the other three. Once that was done, he turned to me.

Shifting my sword to my left hand, I held out my right hand and he quickly pierced the exact center of the circle of the mark, where I had the scar from the blood ceremony Collin had completed. The pain was minimal as I watched the red drops emerge from the cut. When the blood started to pool in my hand, I held it over the earthen hole and tilted my palm to let it fall.

"Upon my life I swear."

The moment my blood hit the earth, a billow of white smoke rose and a blast of energy shot from the hole, rushing through my body and stealing my breath away.

"Her blood is more powerful than I believed," the woman said in awe.

Fear strangled my throat. Had they tricked me?

"I told you she had the power to defeat the gods," Tsagasi murmured. He turned toward me, looking at me with something I hadn't seen on his face before: respect. "Together we will defy the gods and bring peace to all creatures. Mortal and immortal."

All four of them watched me.

Feeling uneasy, I took a step backward. "Let's get started." I sat on a log and laid my sword beside me. Taking a deep breath, I curled my fingers around the rough tree bark and then released it as I closed my eyes. "Okay."

Taking several slow and even breaths, pulling up my memories of the birth of the world, I found myself immersed deeper in them than I'd ever been. I was the first drop of water to hit the earth. The memories of the changing and evolving world sped up to warp speed, a dizzying display of images that left me disoriented and anxious until it all stopped, dumping me into the memory of a cool winter day.

I was eight years old again, sitting under the oak tree with Claire. The wind was cool and crisp as I stared into her tear-splotched face, desperate to make her feel better. She had just told me that her father was thinking about a divorce. So I shared with her the one thing I knew would distract her—the story of the curse. As soon as I shared the information, I realized I was already forgetting things about it that I should have remembered.

Momma came home and made a phone call to Steven, asking him to help her access the archives at Chapel Hill, and she mentioned calling the police. But whatever else she said was confusing to the little girl me. I only knew she was hiding something from Daddy and she thought he'd be unhappy when he found out.

Since I was upset, Claire decided to share another secret of her own—that she heard voices. She said one of the reasons her family had moved to Manteo was that she was teased at school. But the voices had begun to quiet over the last few months, even though they all still said the same thing: *you must help her.* Only Claire didn't know whom she was supposed to help.

The next two days seemed to be on fast-forward as I traveled through my memories, and the action only slowed again when I was working on my homework after school. Momma and Daddy were still fighting about Momma's visit to Charlotte the week before and how she wouldn't tell him about what she'd seen. They went into Daddy's office to argue, but I hid around the corner, listening to their raised voices and getting peeks through the French doors. Finally, Momma relented and showed him a ring that she wore around her neck on a chain. It was an artifact from the Middleton collection that had been stolen and lost during the Civil War. The ring had been lent to her in good faith with the request that she discover its significance. Daddy became very excited when he recognized the engraved Croatan symbols on the ring. He told her it was the ring Ananias's great-grandson had created with a Croatan priest. He'd had it made so that he could banish demons on his own if necessary.

She reluctantly gave him the ring, but only after he made an agreement: if he couldn't find the gate to hell within a week, he would completely give up the curse for the rest of his life and stop telling me about it. Then he went back to his office at Fort Raleigh to get papers that would help him translate the markings on the ring.

After Daddy left, Momma told me she'd read me a story before I went to bed, but she needed to check on the guests at the bed and breakfast first. I went upstairs and put on my favorite nightgown, a lacy, white cotton, billowy gown that made me feel like a princess. After brushing my teeth and picking out the story, I started downstairs to tell Momma I was ready.

That was when I heard glass break.

A man was downstairs, threatening Momma, asking for the ring. But Momma pretended not to know what he was talking about until he threatened to hurt me if she didn't give it to him and started to hit her.

I wanted to help Momma, but a man's voice in my ear told me it was too dangerous. I sat on the stairs crying. When the intruder told another man to go upstairs and find me, my mother begged them to leave me alone. The voice in my ear told me to hide.

So I ran to my closet and burrowed into the back, hiding even though I was desperate to help Momma.

Momma and the bad men came upstairs. One was looking in the rooms while the other asked Momma questions.

Then there was scuffling in the hall and I could see shadows moving along the wall. A smaller shadow jumped on a larger one, and then I heard my mother's screams.

I sobbed in the closet, anger rising up inside me. I needed to protect Momma, but some unseen force pinned me to the wall.

The bigger shadow grunted and growled as his arm swung over and over toward the smaller shadow. My mother screamed and screamed.

I tried to burst free, but the invisible hold kept me in place and the voice in my ear whispered, "Not yet, Ellie."

A figure stood in the doorway to my bedroom, his head concealed by the hood of his sweatshirt. He held a large knife in his hand, the metal shining in the lightning flash outside my window. I stopped crying and held my breath, terrified.

He moved into the room and around the bed, crouching down to check underneath. Then he rose and moved past the closet door. Just as I thought he was going to leave, he spun around, squatting in front of me. Blood dripped from his knife onto the floor. He reached for me and I screamed, but a bright light filled the room. The man covered his face with his arm.

"*I claim her as my own, Curse Keeper. You will not harm her.*" The angry words belonged to the voice that had told me to hide.

Curse Keeper?

I tried to break free of the memory but it pulled me back down, smothering me with renewed grief.

"Do not think me *stupid*, son of the earth. You wish to break the curse. You are not the first, nor will you be the last," Ahone said.

The Curse Keeper still held his knife, ready to attack, and Ahone's light shone brighter in warning. "You are mistaken if you think that I will let you hurt her. I need her for another purpose. The curse will be broken, but not today. It will happen when *I* deem it so."

"I'm sick and tired of being at the mercy of the curse," the man said, his voice gravelly. "I want this to end. *Tonight.*"

"It began at *my* will and will end when *I* wish it. I do not condone you forcing my hand, Curse Keeper, and you will *pay* for this transgression, just like the others before you." The light glowed bright white. "*This girl changes everything.* If only you had shown patience and restraint, you would have seen this. You will get what you want, but not during your tenure. At a time of my choosing, I will find your son and help him break the curse." Ahone's voice lowered and sounded more menacing. "But because of your treachery, he will rue the day I sought him out, and he will curse you for the sacrifices he must make as penance for *your* betrayal."

The Curse Keeper climbed to his feet. "With the help of Okeus, my son will defeat you, Ahone."

"He will try, and he will fail. The girl will be his downfall."

"No!" The man grunted, lunging for me.

I screamed and the light burst brighter than before, blasting the man out the door and onto the floor in the hall.

The Curse Keeper's hood had fallen off his head, and his wavy dark hair and dark eyes resembled Collin's. But when this man's eyes locked with mine, the ugliness there was nothing like the expression in his son's eyes. He shouted at the other man and hurried down the hall and then the stairs.

The little girl me tried to break free from the invisible band holding me back. "Not yet," Ahone said, his anger now gone.

"What are you?" I whispered.

"Not what, but *who*. And you will find out soon enough."

Finally, the hold broke free and I stumbled as I ran out of the closet and landed in the pool of blood in front of the closet door. I screamed.

"Ellie!" Momma called out in fear.

"Momma!" I got to my feet and rushed to the hallway.

She lay on the floor, her clothes covered in blood. I called out her name, light-headed with fear. Her head turned toward me and I gagged as I took in the puddle of blood around her.

"Ellie, call 911." But I was too terrified to move, so Momma told me to sit with her. I stared at the blood on the floor, feeling like I was about to throw up.

My mother comforted me, and although I knew she was dying, I could only hold her hand and listen to her last words of advice and love. Her voice broke and fear filled her eyes. "There's so much to tell you and not enough time."

"Momma, please," I cried. "*Pleasssse . . .*"

"*Oh, Ellie*," she whispered. "I wanted to protect you from the ugliness of the world, and I brought it to your front door." Her eyes fluttered and her grip on my hand loosened.

The next thing I knew, the shadowy figure of an older man with white hair and a white beard floated over the staircase. Ahone.

"Ellie, you are strong and brave. When it is your time, you will make an excellent Curse Keeper."

"You said the man who killed Momma was a Keeper," I said, lifting my head to look at him. "I don't want to be a Keeper anymore."

"Elinor, you are *destined* to be a Keeper. It was foretold from the beginning of time. You are more special than any Keeper before you. I've been waiting centuries for you to arrive. The forces of nature have finally heard my plea and sent you so that I may finish the job I began with your ancestor, Ananias Dare. Tonight begins a chain of events that brings us to the end."

"*I want my momma*," I wailed.

"Daughter of the sea and witness to creation, your first sacrifice has been made." His light faded slightly, and he sounded sad.

"It will be the first of many. The unraveling of the curse begins tonight, but I will take all memories associated with the curse from you, so that the events of tonight will be locked deep in your mind. I need you to be willing to accept your role when the time comes." He moved closer and his voice softened. "But you will also lose all other memories of the curse. They've already begun to slip away. You will believe it is because you told Claire, and you will be filled with a heavy burden of guilt. I'm sorry, but it is the best way."

I looked up again, shaking my head in confusion. "I don't understand."

"I know, but one day you will. When the time comes for you to know, you will remember everything."

And then I began to scream.

⁓ Chapter Sixteen ⁓

I was back in the forest, lying across the log, my face covered in tears.

"Did you see it all?" Tsagasi asked, standing next to my head, his knife in his hand. My other guardians stood at four points, their backs to me. Their weapons were in their hands, ready to be used if necessary.

"Yes." I sat up, still in shock. "Collin's father killed Momma."

He didn't respond.

"You knew?" When he still didn't say anything, I asked, "How could you know? You were locked away."

"We are not clueless to the events that have occurred over the past four hundred years, at least the ones that affect us."

I knew his answer was the best I was going to get.

Disappointment made his mouth droop more than usual. "Out of everything you learned, that is what you focus on?"

He was right, but it was still a kick in the gut. Did Collin know? I thought back to when I'd told him about my mother's murder. The look of horror and concern on his face. If he didn't know, he suspected. But even so, could I hold it against him? There was a lot I didn't know about Collin, but I knew he'd never condone my mother's murder.

"I have to call him."

"I agree. You are half of a whole. While you have great power on your own and you must learn to defend yourself and fight alone, you need the other Keeper."

After everything I had heard and seen over the last couple of days, finding out that I needed to spend more time with Collin instead of less was not what I wanted to hear. "I can't. For one thing, Collin has pledged himself to Okeus. We're on opposite sides."

"Are you? Do you align yourself with Ahone?"

He had a point. "Second, if I spend more time with Collin, it will kill David. I can't do that to him."

His eyes narrowed. "More fragile human emotions. They say humans are made to resemble the gods, and every time I deal with one I understand why. Your egos and emotions rule your lives. There are more important things in the world than your *feelings*."

I closed my eyes, resting my face in my hands.

"You are going to Charlotte tomorrow?"

I looked up. "How did you know?"

He rolled his eyes. But if Tsagasi knew, did that mean other supernatural beings did too? What danger did that put us in? I suspected that the Raven Mocker had killed Allison to keep us from finding out whatever she'd kept from us about the collection. What would they do if we actually went to see it?

"You need the other Keeper to go with you."

I shook my head. "He'll never come."

"He will if you ask him."

The more I thought about it, the more I realized that Tsagasi might be right. Collin had ties to the Ricardo Estate. I couldn't imagine that he'd want me to waltz right in and see it on my own. Besides, I didn't think he knew where it was, and David had a location.

"What else did you learn?"

"Ahone has been scheming to use me for longer than I realized, but Okeus had already told me that two days ago."

He nodded.

"My father lied to me. He knew why my mother died."

"Perhaps he wanted to protect you."

I swallowed a lump in my throat. "I don't know what to believe anymore."

"Follow your instinct. Trust only yourself."

I forced a teasing grin. "Are you telling me not to trust *you*, Tsagasi?"

"I'm telling you that every being is interested in one thing: self-preservation. I am no different. Pick the being that has your survival foremost on its mind—you."

I wanted to argue that his opinion was selfish and egocentric, but wasn't that the point?

"The Nunnehi wish to return and Tsawasi and I will go with them. You may use us six more times for protection. Choose wisely."

"And how will I find you?"

"We will find you. Simply call my name." Then the Nunnehi warriors vanished and Tsagasi and his brother walked behind a tree.

I pulled my cell phone out of my pocket and checked my reception, grateful to see I had so many bars. I found Collin's number and pressed send.

He answered on the second ring. "Ellie."

A shiver ran down my spine when I heard him say my name, and I almost hung up. "Collin, I'm sorry to bother you."

"I figured it must be important. That's the only reason you call. When you want something that's important to you."

Ouch. But I couldn't deny it, and his statement only confirmed Tsagasi's words. "What do you know about Raven Mockers?"

He hesitated. "They're Cherokee."

"Well, they seem to be equal-opportunity terrorists."

"You've met a Raven Mocker?"

I told him about my encounter with the Raven Mockers at Allison's house.

"You fought Raven Mockers? *Are you crazy?* Was this *his* idea?"

"If you're referring to David, then no, it wasn't his idea. I think he wishes I would have just sent them away instead of killing them."

"What do you mean you killed them? That's impossible."

I shook my head before realizing he couldn't see me. "Tsagasi helped me."

"Tsagasi? The little person?"

For someone who was dedicated to Croatan culture, he sure knew a lot about the Cherokee.

"Oh, Ellie. What have you done?"

I shoved down my anger. "I've saved countless people, that's what I've done." Even if I didn't manage to save Allison. "But that's not why I called you."

"Then why *did* you call?"

"I remember what happened the night of Momma's murder."

He paused. "You do?"

"Did you know about your father?" I choked out.

He waited several seconds before answering. When he did, his voice was thick with emotion. "What do you remember?"

"Did you know your father killed my mother? Answer the question, Collin."

It took him several seconds to answer. "I didn't know for sure."

"But you suspected?"

"He went off to do a job for Marino, and then he disappeared. We literally never saw or heard from him again. Marino was so attentive in offering his help after my father's disappearance. It wasn't until years later that I figured out that something permanent had happened to my father, and Marino was directly involved. But I wasn't about to say anything. Hell, I was a kid. I was ten years old."

"So why did you think your father killed her?"

"Because my father had found out about the Ricardo Estate. He knew of the ring and spear that were tied to the curse. He had no idea what they did, but he was determined to end it. I heard him tell my mother he was going to destroy the weapons. Maybe he considered you a weapon too. It sounds like your mother got in the way." His voice broke. "God, Ellie. I'm sorry."

I took several breaths to control my tears. "So how does Marino come into this?"

"Marino has no idea about the curse. I suspect my father found out about the Ricardo Estate, but it was too big of a job to do alone so he brought Marino on board. Marino only wants the loot from the estate. Hell, it's not even about the money anymore. It's the one big heist he's never completed. It's his ego that's on the line."

"Which is why he was so intent on finding me."

"Yeah." He paused. "All the financial aid Marino has offered my family over the years makes me think he was involved in my father's disappearance, but at times I've wondered. My grandmother never condoned my father's insistence on breaking the curse. Honestly, part of me has always suspected she may have killed him herself. Her own son."

"Are you serious?"

He didn't answer.

"I know where the Ricardo Estate is right now."

He didn't answer for several seconds. "How do you know that?"

"A professor at Chapel Hill saw it last week, but she was killed by Raven Mockers last night. My mother saw the collection and a week later she was killed by someone who was looking for the ring she'd taken. Apparently your father and Marino." I tried to keep the accusation from my words. I couldn't hold Collin responsible for his father's actions.

"The one you wear now." He cursed under his breath. "Ellie, you're messing with shit you shouldn't be messing with."

"Tsagasi is helping me."

"And you do realize Tsagasi is known for his mischievousness, don't you? He could be setting you up."

"It doesn't matter, Collin. We're going to try to see the collection tomorrow."

"We? You mean you and your professor? Do you plan on just walking up to the door and asking to see it?"

I didn't answer.

"Are you fucking kidding me? Is that your plan?"

"No. The woman who was killed, Allison, was supposed to meet with the proprietors of the collection tomorrow. They've asked David to go in her place."

"Do *not* go to see that collection, Ellie."

"You can't stop me, Collin."

"No fucking shit. When have I ever been able to stop you from doing something you've set upon doing? But I can't let you go alone."

"I won't be alone. I'll be with David."

"Like I said," he growled. "*Alone*. I know how to handle these people. What kind of criminals have you two dealt with lately?"

"I've met more than my fair share thanks to you."

He sighed. "True enough." His voice softened. "Don't go without me, Ellie."

"Don't pretend your motives are purely altruistic, Collin. I know you want to see it again."

"Again? I never saw it in the first place. But I won't deny that I've tried or that it's part of the reason why I want to come."

"So why does Marino think you've already seen it?"

"Because I lied to him."

"Why would you do that?"

"I was trying to get more information. The timing was so coincidental. Ahone approached me about breaking the curse just when Marino started talking about the Ricardo Estate resurfacing. I knew it held curse-related artifacts. I wanted to find them."

"Only it backfired all the way around."

"Sometimes you have to play the hand you have."

"Which is why you never play poker."

To my surprise, he laughed. "I miss you, Ellie."

I didn't respond.

"So do I get to go on this little adventure with you?"

"You have to promise me something first."

"What?"

"David's going to be with us. I need you to promise that you won't be ugly to him. That you'll treat him with respect."

"You've got to be shitting me."

"Unfortunately for you, no."

He hesitated. "Ellie, I'm sure you've noticed, but the more we're together, the more we're drawn to each other. I'm not sure there's any hiding that. For either of us."

"I know, but I love him, Collin. I'm begging you to try."

He took several breaths. "But I love you too, Ellie."

"I know." My voice broke.

He was silent for so long I was sure he'd hung up. Finally, he said, "I'll do my best. That's all I can promise. But I'll only do it because I don't want to hurt *you*, Ellie. Make no mistake, I don't give a fuck about him."

"Thank you."

"I think it's a big mistake for you to be with him. He's more of a hindrance than a help."

"He's more help than you could possibly know. And even if David weren't part of my life, you and I would never work out. Not as long as you keep picking Okeus over me."

"And what if I picked you, Ellie? What would keep us apart then?"

My breath caught. "Collin."

"I don't expect you to answer. All I ask is that you think about it. And the next time I ask, if you don't give me a good answer, I'm going to break my promise."

"What promise is that?" I asked, breathless.

"My promise to myself to leave you the fuck alone."

⌒ CHAPTER SEVENTEEN ⌒

I found David at the kitchen table, huddled over his laptop. He looked relieved to see me. "I was getting worried about you. You were gone for over an hour."

"I saw Tsagasi. He watched over me while I remembered what happened the night my mother was killed."

He took off his reading glasses and put them on the table. "You remembered? How?"

"By using my power as a witness to creation. And there's something else I need to tell you before I tell you what I remembered. I have my own quartet of protectors now."

His eyebrows lifted. "You have *what*?"

I told him about the blood oath I'd made in the woods.

He grabbed my hand and pulled me into the chair next to him. "Are you sure that was a good idea?" There was no recrimination in his voice, only genuine curiosity.

"You've taught me to trust my instincts. So far it hasn't let me down. I had a moment of worry when Ama—the female Nunnehi warrior—commented that my blood was more powerful than she expected, but Tsagasi said he was certain we could work together to defy the gods." I released a heavy sigh. "That's what we're doing, isn't it? Defying the gods and the plans they want to use me for?"

His hand gripped mine and held on tight. "Yeah, we are."

I studied his face. "Very few people in the history of mythology have ever defied the gods and survived."

His mouth shifted to one side. "Then they've finally met their match."

My love for him blossomed even more. He truly believed beyond a shadow of a doubt that I could do this.

I told him how I'd tapped into my power and relived Momma's murder. I stood and paced while I spoke, too antsy to sit still.

When I got to the part about finding my mother on the floor, he stood and pulled me into a hug. "Oh my God, Ellie. That's horrible. No wonder you forgot. You were traumatized."

I leaned back. "No, I forgot because that selfish asshole Ahone didn't want me to remember. He stole my memories from me." I told him the rest of the story, and then we stood in silence for several minutes.

"David, there's more."

"Okay . . ."

"Tsagasi told me I needed to call Collin and tell him about his father and our plan to go to Charlotte."

"And did you?"

"Yes."

His left eye twitched as he searched my face. "And what happened in your conversation?"

I stood and took a deep breath. "He claims he didn't know the truth about his father until a couple of months ago. He put it all together the day we got the cup back."

He looked skeptical. "And you believe him?"

I resisted the urge to turn away from his scrutinizing gaze. "Yes, I completely trust him in this instance."

He stiffened and turned toward the sink.

I followed him. "He's the other Keeper, David. Tsagasi's right. I can do some of this on my own, but at some point, I'm going to need Collin."

He pulled a glass out of the cabinet and filled it with water from the faucet, refusing to look at me. "He doesn't want to help you, Ellie. Have you forgotten that part?"

"He wants to come to Charlotte."

"Of course he does. He wants to see the collection." His face lifted. "What did you tell him?"

I paused. "I told him yes."

His eyes hardened. "And what if I disagree?"

While I presumed David wouldn't be happy with Collin's involvement, it had never once occurred to me that he would try to prevent it. "Why would you disagree?"

He set the glass on the counter with a loud thud. "He's using you, Ellie. Just like he's used you every step of the way since he walked into your restaurant and purposely put you in danger."

Could I really argue with that? "So you want just the two of us to check out this collection? We're in over our heads. Two people have died for it, someone close to each of us. We both know how dangerous this is. Do we even have a plan other than just show up at ten?"

He slammed the cabinet door shut, anger radiating from his body. "Yes, I realize it's dangerous, but your solution is to add another dangerous element. Collin is not to be trusted. He's proven that time and time again. Why would you want to involve him?"

"He's betrayed me and deceived me, yes, but he would never try to purposely hurt me."

David rested his back against the counter, looking out the window over the sink. "Are you even listening to yourself right now? You just admitted that the wanker deceived you"—he suddenly turned and grabbed my right hand, jerking me toward him and exposing my palm, pressing his thumb to the scar from the knife wound Collin had inflicted, my wound from the blood oath ceremony still fresh—"that he bloody *betrayed you*, Ellie, and yet you say he would never purposely hurt you." He dropped my hand and looked into my face. "No."

My eyes widened. "*No?*"

"No." He shook his head. "Not just no. Hell no. Fuck no. No fucking way, no."

I put my hands on my hips, trying to keep my anger in check. "I'll take your suggestion under consideration."

He stepped away from the counter, his eyes burning with fury. "It's not a fucking suggestion, Ellie. It's a statement. *No.*"

I shook my head. "That's not the way this works, David. I'm in charge when it comes to the curse. You make suggestions. I consider them. Then *I* decide."

He shook his head, his mouth twisting in anger. "Not anymore. Not after last night. I'm as much a part of this as you are. I have just as much to lose as you do."

My mouth parted in surprise. "We had an agreement. You can't change the rules, David."

He spread his hands wide. "Well, guess bloody fucking what, Ellie? *I just did.*"

I shook my head. "No. I agreed to take your suggestions under advisement, but *I* get to decide. We both came up with the rules. We *both* agreed on them."

"Forgive me if I was too naïve to realize what I was getting myself into. Last night made it perfectly clear that we're playing a very deadly game. It's one thing to talk in abstracts, but this is *real*."

"And Ukinim and Ilena were real too. You didn't try to change the rules then."

"This is different, Ellie!"

"Why? Because you lost someone you care about?" I shouted. "Well, welcome to my world! I've lost both my parents to this curse!" But even as I said the words, I realized how unfair I was being. I was asking him to put his life and the lives of people he cared about completely in my hands. How would I feel if I was in his position? All my fight fled and I sagged against the wall.

His voice softened. "I'm your in to the Ricardo Estate. I'm the person they're expecting. I know what to look for. This is my area of expertise. You need me to do this, Ellie, but if you involve him, I won't take any part in it."

I gaped at him. "You're serious?"

"I am unless you can give me a really good reason to change my mind. And the fact that he has experience with breaking and entering isn't about to sway me."

I could argue that I needed Collin to fight supernatural beings, but we were dealing with humans in this situation. And David had just admitted Collin's criminal past wouldn't convince him we needed his help. "Okay. What's your plan?"

"As you know, I have an appointment with the Guardians at ten tomorrow morning. They're calling themselves the Henderson Foundation. I told them I know everything Allison knew about the collection and that I have the research she conducted."

"Do you?"

"No."

I stared at him, my eyes wide.

"Don't look so surprised. Collin isn't your only boyfriend who's capable of deception."

I bit back an ugly retort. My temper never resolved anything. "David, this could all go so wrong." I lifted my chin. If he wanted to do this alone, we could still make it work. "But I can think on my feet too, so I think we'll be able to get the information we need."

"There is no we, Ellie. Me. I'm going alone."

"No." I shook my head. "No way."

"They're only expecting me."

"Tell them I'm your assistant or something."

"No. They told me to come alone."

"And that doesn't make you question the situation?" My voice rose. "Why would they want you to come alone if it wasn't dangerous?"

His cold eyes pinned mine. "There's something important enough in these pieces that people are dying for them. I want to find out what it is. I owe that to Allison."

"You didn't kill her."

He brushed past me into the living room and I grabbed his arm, but he shrugged me off.

"David, she would have died whether we were there or not. I think she died because she went to see the collection."

He spun around to glare at me. "You don't know that for sure. Those *things* made sure to prolong her torture until you showed up. There was definitely a personal tie there."

I swallowed the lump of guilt in my throat. "I'm sorry. I don't know what else to say. I'd do anything to change it."

He released a heavy sigh and then pulled me against his chest. "I'm sorry, Ellie. I know this isn't your fault. If anyone is to blame, it's Collin Dailey. He fucked up everything when he walked into your restaurant and broke the curse." His voice hardened. "Her death is on *his* head." He leaned back and looked down into my eyes. "So, no. We will *not* be using that wanker's help."

I nodded, biting back tears. "Okay. No Collin."

His eyes softened. "Thank you."

Fundamentally, I disagreed with his request, but he was right about Collin's culpability. Ultimately, Allison was dead because Collin had broken the curse. But I could take it a step further and say I was partially responsible for not learning enough to stop him. Ahone may have stolen my memories of the curse, but I flat out refused to relearn anything about it. And after Collin had confessed that Ahone had convinced him to do it, I couldn't help but feel sympathetic. I wondered what I would have done if a duplicitous god had approached me and tried to convince me that breaking the curse was best for all concerned. Would I have fallen for it too?

But I couldn't make David endure Collin's presence. I'd already put him through enough, and he alone had an invitation to see the collection. We didn't need Collin for that. While I struggled to convince myself it was a good plan, I knew in my gut it wasn't. I needed Collin there—*we* needed him, whether David wanted to admit it or not.

David was right about one thing. He'd graduated to a new level last night. He was no longer a tagalong assistant; he was a partner, whether he had magical powers or not. A good team was made up of people with various skills and talents. We needed to focus on David's strengths and put them to the test the next morning.

"So what's the rest of your plan?" I asked.

"Tomorrow morning, you'll stay here while I go to Charlotte."

I put my hands on my hips, glaring at him. "I'm going to Charlotte with you, David. If you even think about trying to go without me, I'll just rent a car and follow you." He started to protest and I held up my hand. "And I know the address now—I saw it over your shoulder when you were looking up the driving directions—so don't think I won't do it."

"I'm supposed to go alone, Ellie."

"It doesn't mean I can't go to Charlotte with you."

He looked unconvinced.

"Do you really want me to be two hours away from you? We both know how many of these creatures are out there right now. What if they attack me while you're gone?" I purposely avoided reminding him about my new protectors, purchased through my blood oath.

And that was what finally swayed him. My safety, not his own.

Since his meeting was at ten in the morning and the drive to Charlotte was two and a half hours, we decided to get up early and leave by six thirty to make sure he wouldn't be late if we ran into traffic. We looked up the address online and checked out satellite images of the office building and the surrounding area.

The office was in an industrial area, which made it sketchier. When we looked up the addresses of the offices around it, we discovered that many of the businesses had closed.

I sat next to David on the sofa, staring at the screen of his laptop. "I don't like it, David. It's isolated for a reason. It's not safe."

"I'll be fine, Ellie."

"I can't let you do this. I'll worry too much."

He offered me a soft smile. "Now you'll know how I feel when you run headlong into dangerous situations."

"That's different. I actually have powers I can use to protect myself."

"And I have a power too." He tapped his temple. "Don't sell me short. I can go in and inventory items and determine if they're potentially important or not. If you go in, you'll have no idea what you're looking at."

I couldn't argue with his line of reasoning. "It doesn't mean I have to like it."

His eyebrows rose with a hint of teasing. "I know a thing or two about that."

He'd been so solemn all day that his momentary playfulness gave me some reassurance. "So are you and I going to be okay?"

"You mean *us*?" His eyes widened slightly. "Ellie, we had a fight, but it doesn't mean we're going to break up. Every couple fights."

"But this is different." I tried to settle the anxious feeling in my chest. "This is so very different."

He put his arm around my back, snugging me against the side of his body. "I reacted badly last night and I'm not proud of it, but I'm only human. I'm glad I told you how I really felt instead of bottling it up inside. We need to know where we stand with each other."

I nodded.

He grabbed my hand and laced our fingers together. "Tell me how *you* feel, Ellie."

I sat up straighter. "About what?"

"About anything."

"I'm not happy that you're going into that office building without me."

His mouth tilted into a lopsided grin. "I knew that already. Tell me something I don't know."

"There's nothing."

"That's shite and you know it. Tell me how you feel about not including Collin in this trip to Charlotte. *Really.*"

I looked at our joined hands, unsure how to answer. But he wanted the truth. "I understand why you don't want him there and I can't argue—you have valid points, after all—but I still think we should include him. Call it a gut instinct." He stayed silent, though it was obvious he wanted to say something. "But I want to give you more input in how we do things, which is why I'm going along with your request."

"But you resent me for it."

"No." I took a breath to steady my voice. "I resent myself for letting this happen."

"Are you sorry you're involved with me, Ellie?"

I looked up into his worried eyes. "Not in the way you think. You may have acted like my connection to Collin didn't bother you in the beginning, but I knew it was something we couldn't ignore. Still, I don't regret a single minute I've spent with you. Selfish or not, I can't imagine having gone through any of this without you. But if I were a better person, I would have done things differently. I would have protected you from the pain I'm putting you through right now."

His gaze dropped to our joined hands, and I realized how tenuous our connection was. My connection to Collin was eternal and out of my control, but my connection to David was like a thread that could snap at any second.

"David, you made me a promise not to leave me, but just like when we set the rules, you didn't know what you were getting yourself into." I lowered my face so it was underneath his. "I'm telling you that you aren't bound by that promise."

He shook his head, sadness filling his eyes. "Ellie, I'm not going anywhere."

"Neither am I."

We stared into each other's eyes for several moments before I squared my shoulders. "I want to know more about your plan for tomorrow."

He released a heavy breath. "I don't really have one. Like I said, I just want to inventory what they have for now, and if an opportunity arises that I can take advantage of, I'll do it."

"How will you know what to look for? I had no idea which one of Allison's swords to use until Tsagasi helped me. From the sounds of it, there are lots of weapons in the collection."

David turned my right hand over and traced the circle on my palm with his fingertip. "Our only course of action is for me to go in and check it out; then you and I can figure out where to go from there."

"David, I'm scared."

He tugged me against him, fitting my head under his chin as he held me close. It was a warm and familiar contact that felt natural, like coming home. I wrapped my arms around his back and held him tight.

"I know, Ellie, and so am I. And I know you'd probably be more comfortable if we had an elaborate plan like whatever Collin would come up with, but in this case, I think the simpler, the better."

I forced a smile and glanced up at him. "Actually, Collin seems to go for simple too. So maybe you two aren't such opposites after all."

He didn't look happy with the comparison.

"Just don't take any unnecessary risks," I said, "and don't ask too many questions either."

He nodded, then let go of me and stood. "Let's get to bed. We have a long day tomorrow."

David fell asleep within minutes, but I lay awake for at least a half hour, staring at the dusty ceiling fan. Finally, I carefully slid out of bed and grabbed my cell phone. After all the time I'd spent thinking in bed, I'd realized that Tom still expected me home tonight. I needed to let him know I was going to be delayed for at least another day. And I needed to find out if the Raven Mockers had left Manteo when I did. And I still hadn't called Collin to let him know about the change in plans.

I went out the back door and sat on the step, staring up at the starry sky. It felt so peaceful out there, alone in the dark. But the feeling was an illusion and I couldn't forget that.

I found Tom's number on my phone and pressed send. He answered right away. "Ellie, tell me that you're back in town."

I cringed. "I'm still in Chapel Hill and we're going to Charlotte tomorrow." I paused. "I take it things are still bad."

"Worse. There were two deaths last night. I have no idea how to prevent them. It's not like we can tell people who are sick that they need to put salt across their thresholds."

"I know." I sighed. "But the victims have all been sick, right? No one healthy?"

"Yeah, all sick." He hesitated. "Why?"

"They're here in Chapel Hill too. They killed a woman who had allergies, but they also went after a man who was completely healthy."

"What the fuck am I dealing with, Ellie?"

I didn't say anything.

"Ellie."

"Tom, you're going to think I'm crazy."

"Ellie, I'm long past thinking any of this shit is crazy. What am I dealing with?"

Having an ally in the Manteo Police Department would be beneficial, and he had already made the leap to the supernatural. "Okay, I'll tell you what I know. It's up to you whether you choose to believe me or not."

"Okay."

"They're Raven Mockers."

"Cherokee," he whispered.

"Yeah. They weren't recorded in Croatan history, but that doesn't necessarily mean anything. I've encountered several Cherokee spirits here in Chapel Hill."

"Croatan?" I heard him exhale. "What are the symbols on your doors?"

"Protection, just like I told you. Against demons and spirits. And Croatan gods."

He was silent for several seconds. I expected him to start accusing me of lies and deceit, but instead he asked, "Okay, how do I get rid of them?"

"You believe me?"

"Call *me* crazy, but I do. There's no logical, scientific explanation for all the shit that's been happening here over the past couple of months. So what do I do? Put the marks on people's doors?"

"I don't know if it works if just anyone does it. Claire uses salt when I can't mark her doors, and it keeps them out."

"But that still doesn't answer my original question, does it?"

"How we can save people from the Raven Mockers?" I leaned my head back to look at the starry sky and whispered, "I wish I knew."

"There is a way," Tsagasi said from next to me, and I jumped, caught off guard by his sudden appearance. "It won't kill them, but it will keep them at bay."

I covered the mouthpiece with my hand. "What is it?"

"They must gather seven smooth stones. Have the person lay with their head facing north and their feet facing south, then put a stone at the top of their head, one on either side of their head, and one at each of their hands and feet. It will hold off the Raven Mockers until morning." His eyes narrowed. "But you are correct. Salt will keep them out in the first place."

I relayed Tsagasi's message to Tom. "Last night there were four of them, but they were lying in wait for me, so I'm not sure if they usually attack in groups or not," I said. "They're invisible to people without magical abilities, but they slash their victims with claws. They attacked David's ex-girlfriend and he couldn't see the wounds. After they tortured her, one of them reached into her chest, tore out her heart, and ate it. I could see the wound, but David couldn't see anything."

"Why do you know this? How can you see these things?"

"Because I'm a Curse Keeper. It was my job to make sure a four-hundred-year-old curse didn't break. The curse is the reason the colony of Roanoke disappeared. Only I didn't believe in it and it *did* break. Now all of these things have broken loose from hell, and I'm trying to send them back."

"You can't be serious."

"I wish I wasn't," I sighed.

"How many of these fuckers are there?"

"I don't know," I breathed out, suddenly exhausted. How was I going to kill all of them? "David thinks the Raven Mockers will be easier to destroy or subdue if we go after their leader—Kalona—only Kalona seems to be in hiding. Another supernatural creature told me they are currently under the control of a proxy. I'm trying to figure out what that is."

"*Can* you destroy them, Ellie?"

I looked into Tsagasi's stern face. "Yes," I finally said. "I killed three last night."

"Thank God," Tom muttered.

"But we've found the Ricardo Estate and we think there's a spear and a sword in the collection that will help us destroy the spirits. So we have to go to Charlotte first to try to get them. I won't be home until tomorrow at the soonest."

"The Ricardo Estate? The one you got mixed up in? Why did you *really* go see Marino back in June?"

"I told you the truth. Collin took me to him to sell my candlesticks."

"Collin Dailey," he said as if he'd just figured out where to fit a puzzle piece.

"Yes, he's the other Keeper."

"Why didn't you just tell me this weeks ago? I begged and pleaded with you to tell me what was going on when that thing was ripping out hearts across town. What was doing all that killing?"

"Two demons—giant badgers who had once been people until a Croatan god named Okeus cursed them. They wanted to kill me to get even with Okeus, but Collin and I destroyed them instead."

"In Festival Park?"

"Yeah."

"Wow." He released a low whistle. "That's a lot to take in."

"Do you think you were ready to believe in it when you first asked me?"

"No, probably not. But I am now. The giant snake in Wanchese?"

"Mishiginebig. I call him Big Nasty for short. He's bad, but he protects me for Okeus."

"Okeus, the evil god?"

"He wants to use me. Long story."

"Okay." But he didn't sound so sure. "Thanks for trusting me, Ellie."

"Thanks for believing." I hung up and glanced at Tsagasi.

"You're making a mistake," he said gruffly.

My eyes widened in surprise. "You mean telling Tom? I think he'll help me in the long run."

"Yes, you need more human allies. I'm talking about the other Curse Keeper. You need him. I told you that earlier."

"I know, but—"

"Are you planning to go to Charlotte without him?"

"Yes, but—"

He shook his head, his forehead furrowing so much that his bushy eyebrows became a unibrow. "Then we are done."

He turned to leave, but I grabbed his tiny arm, surprised to find the hair on it so wiry. "What? Why?"

"You have all this power, yet you refuse to use it. When you are ready to fight the gods, call on me and I will help you. Until then, I refuse to waste my time."

But to do what Tsagasi wanted would hurt David. "What am I supposed to do?" I asked quietly.

"Witness to creation, you are the hope of *all* creation. You are letting the emotions of one man cloud your judgment. What do your instincts tell you to do?"

I shook my head, frustrated. He was right and I knew it. "Collin's untrustworthy. Even if he comes, there's no guarantee he'll really help. Collin Dailey looks out for Collin Dailey. Helping humanity—helping *you*—is very low on his priority list."

His gaze remained unwavering. "Not everything is as it appears with the other Keeper."

"You're asking me to risk my life and David's by trusting Collin."

"Do you really fear for your life when you are with the son of the earth?"

No, but I didn't trust him to protect David. And as difficult as it was to admit, David was the most qualified person to look over the pieces in that collection.

"You know what you need to do," the little man said. Then he disappeared into the woods.

I stared at my phone for nearly a minute before I made my decision, but deep in my heart, I knew I'd never really changed my mind in the first place. Otherwise I would have already called and told him not to come.

I ended up texting him. It was stupid. David was going to find out, but I wanted to be able to deny calling Collin, even if it was a technicality. I texted him the address and told him that David was the only one who could see the collection and that I was going to wait for him somewhere close by.

That's better, Ellie. Stay away from it if possible. Will he know what to look for?

I was surprised he was being so cooperative.

He's looking for weapons we can use against the supernatural beings. We know there's at least one spear and one sword. Anything else you know of that he should look for?

It was a full minute before he answered.

No.

Liar. *He doesn't want you there, so stay hidden. I'll text you once he's in.*

Okay ;)

I was in so much trouble. He was definitely up to something.

❧ CHAPTER EIGHTEEN ❧

I was nervous the entire drive to Charlotte, so much so that when we were halfway there, David blurted out that he wished he'd left me in Chapel Hill.

"You don't mean that," I said, swallowing my nausea.

"Only partially. I'm feeling fairly calm, but your jumpiness is turning me into a nutter. Stop."

"Sorry."

He reached over and covered my hand. "Deep breath, Ellie. No one died right when they went to see the collection. They died days later."

I twisted in my seat to gape at him. "Is that supposed to make me feel better?"

"It was my lame attempt at a joke."

I spun around and pushed my back into my seat, crossing my arms. "Not funny."

"You're right, but it was also my way of telling you that it's safe for me to go in there. We'll deal with the rest later." He squeezed my hand. "Now let's talk about what happens when we get to Charlotte. I'm going to need the car, so I'll have to drop you off somewhere. There was a coffee shop a couple of miles away from the office."

"No way. You can drop me off at the corner of the building. You didn't bring those binoculars for nothing."

"I brought them in case I wanted to check out the building before the meeting, not for you to play Nancy Drew. And don't even think about taking that sword with you."

We'd brought the sword I'd used to kill the Raven Mockers. It was currently in the trunk, wrapped in a towel. David insisted it was a last resort. "Look, I agreed to let you go in alone," I said, "but the only way I'm getting out of the car before we get to the business park is if you physically kick me out."

"Ellie, it's all strip mall offices and warehouses. It's going to look suspicious if you're just standing around."

"I don't care, David. I'll find somewhere to hide out of sight. But I'm not going to be two miles from you."

"Fine," he groaned. "But you need to stay away from the front of the building."

"Okay." But I'd already figured out a plan. After texting Collin, I had looked up the location on the Internet again, paying close attention to the buildings around the office. There was an abandoned warehouse next to it, as well as a couple of businesses I could possibly visit in the guise of a customer.

Exhausted after my mostly sleepless night, I dozed off after our conversation and woke up an hour later when David patted my arm. "Ellie. We're here."

I bolted upright in the seat and took in my surroundings. We were parked in front of a strip mall with several cars parked out front. At least there were witnesses.

"Is one of those offices it?" Most of the complex looked abandoned.

"No. We're on the east end. We need to head toward the center of the industrial park. I'm having second thoughts about you staying here, though. Where are you going to go? It'll be much safer if you wait somewhere more public."

"No, I'm not leaving you here. Besides, there's a flooring show-room a little bit down from where you're going. I'll go in there and pretend to look for carpet."

He turned to me with narrowed eyes. "Why didn't you tell me that earlier?"

I gave him a haughty look. "I didn't want to give you several hours to come up with reasons to stop me from doing it."

He released a heavy breath. "I just want to make sure you're safe, Ellie."

"You forget that I'm the one with powers."

"Sure, against supernatural beings. I'm dealing with humans."

"That you know of. And you're unarmed and unprotected. And what are they going to do when they find out you don't have the research information Allison was supposed to bring?"

"Ellie. We have a plan."

"Which is sketchy at best. You're going in alone while I'm hang-ing out in the carpet store. End of discussion."

We drove through the semideserted park in silence. David pulled up in front of the flooring store and glanced down the alley in the direction of the office. I leaned over and gave him a kiss, then stared into his eyes. "Please be careful."

"I'll be fine. Wait here."

Rather than answering, I opened the car door and climbed out before he could realize I hadn't agreed. I gave him a small wave and walked over to the showroom, going inside without looking back. The car drove off and I pushed down my fear. He was right. He would most likely be safe.

I wandered around the showroom, staying close to the windows. The building he was visiting was close enough that I could see him park and get out of his car. When he disappeared inside, I took a deep breath.

"How long do you want to give him before we start to get worried?"

When I spun around, Collin was standing three feet behind me, his trademark cocky smile on his face.

"What are you doing here?"

His eyes shifted to the windows. "You gave me the address and the time, Ellie," he said with a snort.

"I know that. I mean *here*. In this showroom."

He walked behind me, his chest barely brushing my back as he passed. "It's such an *obvious* place. You must have missed the class on stakeouts when you were getting your degree in entrapping a billionaire bachelor," he whispered into my ear, reminding me of how he'd thought I was out to marry for money when we first met. "Or how to seduce a man. You would have gotten an A plus in that. Although I think I need to spend more time with you to be sure."

My breath caught in my throat and my hairs stood on end. "One could argue that I spend too much time with you," I forced out.

"I don't know, honey," Collin said a little louder, wrapping an arm around my back, resting his hand comfortably on my hip. He ran his free hand slowly down a carpet display. "I was thinking something more brown for the family room."

I tried to ignore the flutter in my stomach. "I know what you want, sweetie. But Aunt Melba has a nice cream color in her bedroom that I just love."

Collin's grip tightened when I mentioned the word "bedroom" and he lowered his mouth to my ear. "I can assure you that I wouldn't notice the carpet color if I was in your bedroom."

My mouth went dry and I broke loose of his hold, moving on to another display rack. "Or maybe we should go with hardwood." I immediately jerked my head up, my eyes widening in warning when I realized I'd set him up for the perfect sleazy comment. "Don't go there."

His eyes twinkled. "I didn't say a word, Ellie. You're the one with your mind in the gutter." He moved next to me again but kept his hands to himself this time. "I say we give him fifteen minutes before we get worried."

I nodded, guilt washing over me. David was in danger and my hormones were getting all wonky while I was talking to Collin about flooring choices. Some girlfriend I was.

"I know a place where we can watch the building. Let's go." Without waiting for an answer, he headed for the door.

I glanced at an employee who stood several rows away. "Thank you."

She nodded, and I followed him out the door. He stood at the corner of the building, looking in the opposite direction of the office. When I approached him, he put an arm around my back and led me around the corner.

I took two steps away from him. "Is all the touching necessary?"

"Just trying to make us look like the happy couple so we don't arouse anyone's suspicions."

"Well no one's watching us here, so it's not necessary. Besides, David dropped me off. Doesn't that look more suspicious?"

"I can guarantee you that no one noticed him dropping you off. But you're a beautiful woman, Ellie, which means they definitely noticed you coming into the store."

"Knock it off, Collin."

"It's true. If you're going to learn the art of the stakeout, you need to learn the art of blending in. *You* do not blend in. You shine, demanding attention."

"Cut the bullshit."

"*Ellie.*" He stopped at the corner of the building.

I reluctantly turned around. "What?"

"I'm serious. I suspect you're about to dig yourself into a shit-load of crap, and you're going to need to be more careful." The earnestness in his eyes told me he was telling me the truth. "If you're going to try playing private investigator, you need to stick to the background and make sure no one notices you."

"Okay." What he said made sense, as hard as it was to admit that he was right.

"Come on, this way." He turned down the alley, heading in the direction of the office. We were on the backside of the strip mall, a warehouse on the opposite side of us.

I followed. "Where are we going?"

"Somewhere we can get a better view without being seen."

We walked in silence halfway down the long building until we approached a Dumpster. "This is where we go up."

I looked from the Dumpster to the roofline five feet above it. "Okay." It made sense to be on the roof across from the office. In fact, it was brilliant, not that I was about to tell him so. Collin had a big enough ego as it was.

He stood next to the trash bin and squatted, lacing his hands together and glancing at me with a grin. "Too bad you don't have on one of those skirts you're so fond of wearing."

I was suddenly glad I was wearing a pair of denim shorts. I put my foot in his hands and reached for the edge of the metal box so I could pull myself up as he boosted. When I was on top, he grabbed the edge and hoisted himself up with little effort. Once he was on the trash bin, he repeated the process, helping me up onto the roof first before pulling himself over the edge.

We stopped when we reached the edge at the front of the building, and I was surprised to see he already had a blanket spread out, topped with a bottle of water and binoculars.

"You've already been up here?"

"For a couple of hours, actually. I wanted to keep track of how many people were in the warehouse in case your professor got into trouble."

"He has a name. David." At least Collin was proving to be useful, which made me feel better about going against David's wishes. "So what have you seen?"

"Two guys showed up at around nine. I've been watching since seven and hadn't seen any other activity until then, so I think it was empty. It looked like they turned off an alarm when they entered. There's a front office and they entered the code to get into the back. The front door only requires a key."

"So just the two men?"

"No. A woman showed up around nine forty-five. Very well dressed—heels, expensive skirt, and blouse. I'd say her purse cost more than your car and my truck put together."

I chuckled. "That's not saying much."

"True enough."

"Allison said she met a well-dressed older woman named Miriam. I bet that was her." I narrowed my eyes mockingly. "And for the record, may I state that I'm more than a little concerned that you recognize a high-quality purse."

This time he laughed. "Fancy purse or not, the two guys were expecting her."

"Any idea who they might be? Had you heard of Miriam?"

"No."

"Would you tell me if you knew?"

He glanced over at me, his grin fading. "Yes."

I believed him, but it surprised me that he was being so forthcoming. That wasn't exactly characteristic of the Collin I had come to know.

"What about the back?" I asked. If he'd staked out the front, he'd definitely know about the back.

"There's a warehouse next to the office. The public record says it's available for rent, but I think they're using it for short-term storage. The office has been leased to the Henderson Foundation for less than a month."

"The people who called David to set up this meeting said they were from the Henderson Foundation." The fact we were finally connecting dots made me feel like we were making progress. "So they're using the warehouse without paying for it?"

"No. The warehouse is owned by the same corporation that owns the office. I called this morning to ask about seeing the warehouse for my imaginary business, and they told me it was under renovation and wouldn't be able to be seen for another week. Which tells us two things . . ." He turned to me with a grin. "How about giving it a guess, my little prodigy?"

"They rented the building to the foundation, but it was an under-the-table deal."

"Exactly. If they rent a warehouse, it draws suspicion. Now, what's the other?"

"If you can see it in a week, they're planning to move the stash soon."

"Exactly. I should have texted you to have Dr. Preston try and find out where it's going and when."

"The less he knows, the better, Collin. He's out of his element in there. David grew up in highbrow London. He's not used to people like this."

"Then what's he doing down there?"

I lifted my eyebrows. "You and I both know that he knows what to look for better than either of us do. We need him. Admit it."

He scowled and turned to look back at the building.

I took his lack of comment as an admission of truth.

"I wish we had a better view of the back." He picked up his binoculars and scanned the front of the building. "It's been ten minutes and there's no one in the office. I say we give him five more minutes, then I'm going to do some investigating of my own."

"And how do you propose we do that?"

"Not we, me." When I started to protest, he interrupted. "I want to go out back to make sure nothing's going on. I need you to stay here and watch the front."

"Why don't we just try to get on top of that building so we can see both exits?"

He grinned. "Good question, young apprentice. I'm saving that for a last resort. It's harder to access, and I honestly think all the action is going to take place in the front." His grin turned wicked. "Kind of like how you enjoy all the action on top."

I flushed. "Shut up, Collin."

Still grinning, he turned back to his stakeout.

I took a deep breath, preparing myself for a fight. "I don't want David to know you're here."

He kept his gaze on the building. "I'm no relationship expert—"

"*Obviously.*"

"—but I think that's an unhealthy sign."

"He has a large amount of disdain for you."

"You mean he hates me?" He chuckled.

"Yeah, you could say that."

"Again, I'm no expert, but he must not be very secure if he feels so threatened by me."

"He doesn't trust you. On my behalf." I held out my right hand, the pink scar reflecting in the sunshine.

Collin looked from my palm to my face, all teasing gone from his expression. "You know I wish things had gone differently."

No apology. No regret for his actions. Only the outcome. Typical Collin. "Nevertheless, in David's eyes you betrayed me after vowing to protect me, putting me in unnecessary danger and risking my life."

He remained silent.

"No witty retort?"

He shook his head. "No, he's right."

It took me a second to recover from the shock of his admission. "And on top of that, multiple innocent people have died since you released the spirits."

He swallowed.

"No rebuttal?"

"No. Like I said, he's right." He turned back to his surveillance.

I wasn't sure what to do. I had been prepared for a fight.

We were silent for several moments before he asked, "Did you really fight Raven Mockers?"

His question caught me off guard. "Yes."

"They could have killed you, Ellie. Your Manitou is safe, but they can still kill you."

"What do you expect me to do? I can't sit around and let those things torture people."

"I know," he whispered.

"People have died because of the objects inside that building. I want you to tell me what you know about them. And quit the bullshit about how it's better if I don't know. We both know it's too late for that."

His back tensed; then he set the binoculars on the blanket. "I told you that my father found out about the estate and then brought Marino on board. That's pure speculation, but I'd bet money I'm right. Rumor has it that the collection disappeared soon after my father did. The next time it was heard of was when the family of the private collector, Emilio Ricardo, announced it was going to New York for auction a few months ago. Then it disappeared again. Marino got preview photos from Ricardo's attorney, but it was gone before he could see it. Marino asked me to find out what had happened. I wanted to know the truth because of my father's involvement. And, like I said, the Manteo Keepers knew a couple of weapons had been created by a Dare Keeper, but I never knew the specifics until I asked my grandmother."

"And what did she say?"

"She said it was a given that the curse would eventually break. The real question was when it would happen. The Dare descendant realized the spirits and gods would be upset and had weapons blessed at the gate to Popogusso that would help defeat the demons."

"The letters David found insinuated that Ahone was the one who instigated the creation of the weapons. He knew the curse would break, and they were his way of sealing the gate permanently."

Collin shook his head. "We already did that."

"Ahone wants me to use this ring at the gate." I held up my hand, the gold glittering in the sunlight. "And I'd bet money it has something to do with my power as a witness to creation."

Collin's mouth twisted as he considered what I'd said.

"Did you know that a group called the Guardians owns this collection? That they've been collecting weapons for centuries to fight demons?"

He scowled. "No."

"David pieced it together. They've been preparing for the end of the world, but Tsagasi says they're thieves and liars. I don't trust them."

"It's safer not to trust *anyone*, Ellie."

"Including you?"

He looked up at me. "I used to tell you *especially* me. I'm trying to change that."

"And yet you still keep a shitload of secrets from me. What do you know that you're not telling me?"

A grin spread across his face. "That could fill an entire encyclopedia set."

"What aren't you telling me about the curse? What Ahone really has in store for me?"

"I'm completely clueless about what Ahone has planned. I had no idea that he wanted you to use the ring next to the gate. But I'm not surprised he wants to use you for his own purposes. Both he and Okeus have their own agendas. They always have."

I believed him, not that I liked it. If he didn't know, who did? Maybe I needed to press Tsagasi more. "Then I'm just as clueless as I was before. Everyone wants to use me for something, and I'm not sure how to stop them."

"I'm sorry."

I looked up into his face. "You keep telling me that you're sorry, and while I realize that your apologies are as rare as a full solar eclipse, what exactly are you sorry *for*?"

He swallowed, his eyes turning glassy, his right hand grabbing my left one. "How about I tell you what I'm not sorry for? I'm not sorry you were persistent about getting me into bed. And I'm not sorry I gave in. And I'll never be sorry that our souls are bound together. I'm sure that makes me a bastard, but you want honesty, so there it is."

I fought my warring emotions.

"I'm not sorry I met you, and if it took breaking the fucking curse to do it, I'd do it again in an instant."

I tried to jerk my hand from his hold, but he held tight.

"Now how about what I *am* sorry for? I'm sorry I met the one person in this world who makes me believe I'm actually worth a shit, but I completely and hopelessly fucked it up." He dropped my hand and narrowed his gaze at the building. "And I know how much David means to you, so I'm going to go down there and make sure he's okay."

"He'll be upset if he sees you."

He grinned. "Would he rather get killed or see my ruggedly handsome face?"

"He's going to be upset with *me*."

"I may have put you in danger in the first place, but haven't you noticed I've spent the rest of my time trying to keep you *out* of danger? This falls under the same category. I'll cover for you. I'll tell him I used my questionable resources to figure out where you were."

My mouth parted in surprise. If anything, I would have suspected that he'd cause trouble between us in the hopes of breaking us up.

"I'm going to head around to the back of the building. I need you to watch the front. If you see any movement or activity, text me. Only call if it's an emergency." He paused. "You have your phone with you, right?"

I nodded.

"How about a kiss for luck?" he teased.

"Not on your life."

He sighed. "Let's hope it's not on David's." Then he crawled across the roof and disappeared.

CHAPTER NINETEEN

David had been inside for more than twenty minutes, and there was no sign of any activity in the building, nefarious or otherwise.

Was Collin serious about protecting David, or was he just saying that to placate me? One thing was for sure—having Collin's help was better than having no help at all. Without him, I'd still be perusing carpets.

I kept my eyes trained on the front door, seeing into the small front office, which was empty besides a metal desk and two plastic chairs. What was going on behind that secured door?

I checked my phone to see if I'd missed a message from David somehow, but my screen was glaringly empty.

Several minutes later Collin texted me.

I'm in the back with no signs of trouble. Anything in the front?

No.

There was a pause before he texted back.

I'm going to do a bit of snooping. Text me if you see anything.

I hesitated before texting back.

Be careful.

I expected a smart-ass response, but got nothing. I wished I knew what he was planning to do. Instead, I was forced to sit there helpless, watching the building where the two men I cared about might be in serious danger.

Several minutes later, a black limo pulled up in front of the building as the secured door to the back of the front office opened. A sharply dressed woman emerged, her snow-white hair perfectly coiffed. She walked with an air of confidence and power. I expected David to follow her out the door, but she was alone.

I quickly texted Collin.

The woman came out as her limo pulled up. She's alone. Anything?

He quickly responded.

Nothing.

Shit. The driver got out and walked around the car to open the door for her. She was about to climb into the back when the secured door opened again and a well-built guy wearing jeans and a dark T-shirt who looked like he was in his twenties walked out to talk to her. My binoculars were trained on them, so when he lifted his hand to his face I could see that his knuckles were bloody with fresh wounds.

My heart threw itself into my rib cage. *David.*

I zoomed the binoculars in closer and noticed flecks of blood on his arm. I called Collin and he answered on the first ring.

"Collin, they've done something to David." My voice shook with panic.

"What? What do you see?"

"One of the guys came out behind the woman. His hand is covered in blood and it looks like he's hit someone."

"Ellie, calm down. You don't know that he hit David."

"Why would the woman let him hit David? What's her part in this?"

"*Calm down*, Ellie." He lowered his voice. "Panicking isn't going to help anyone."

"That man has David's blood on his hands and arm, so don't you tell me to calm down!"

I lifted the binoculars back to my eyes. The man's face contorted with anger and the woman pointed a finger at his chest before spinning around and getting into the back of her limo.

"You have to get him out of there, Collin. *Now.* I'm going to find out more about the woman in the limo. She must know something."

"Ellie, what the fuck are you doing?" He sounded furious.

I got up and ran across the roof and then tried to come up with an off-the-cuff plan while I stood at the edge, looking down at the industrial park. "Collin, I'm begging you. Get David out of there."

I hung up and jumped over the edge, landing on the Dumpster with a loud thud. My knees buckled to absorb the drop. Once I managed to steady myself, I leaped off the trash bin and landed on my feet.

I took off running toward the south entrance to the industrial park. Since I'd studied the area the night before, I knew that while the main entrance was to the east, there was a smaller one to the south. It was a gamble. Using the south entrance would require me to pass some dubious-looking buildings that anyone with a sense of self-preservation would avoid, but I was betting that that woman in her expensive clothes and limo didn't want anyone to find her here. It made sense that she would opt to use the alternate entrance.

My phone vibrated in my hand and I answered. "Did you get David?"

"Ellie! You need to think this through. *What are you doing?*"

"Did you find him?"

"I won't do a goddamned thing until you tell me what you're doing."

"I'm intercepting her car at the south entrance. *Now get him.*"

I hung up as I turned down a road opposite from the east entrance, hoping I'd made the right gamble. I stuffed my phone in my pocket and bolted down a side street that—if I calculated correctly—would connect to the south entrance street. I skidded to a stop at the corner when I saw that the black car was several blocks away and headed in my direction.

I reached up and grabbed the collar of my pale-blue cotton shirt and tugged, ripping it slightly. Then I grabbed my upper arms and rubbed them vigorously. As the car approached, I ran out into the middle of the road, waving and screaming, "Help!"

For a brief moment, I thought the car was going to run me over, but it slowed down and then pulled to a halt. I ran up to the driver's window and banged on it. "Help me! Please!"

The window rolled down and a man's irritated face glared at me.

"Thank God! I was attacked and he was chasing me . . ." My voice broke as I looked back over my shoulder. I didn't have to fake my terror.

The man continued to stare me down.

"Marco, where is your sense of propriety?" The cultured female voice came from the back of the car. "Offer the poor girl assistance."

He lowered his gaze. "Yes, ma'am."

"Have her sit in the back with me so she can catch her breath."

He pushed the car door open and I stepped out of the way as he reluctantly slid out and opened the back door.

I peered into the dark interior before sliding into the seat next to the woman. I forced myself not to claw her. Instead, I said, "Thank you."

"Are you okay, my dear?" She sat primly in her seat. She wore a long-sleeved white blouse, the top button left open to reveal two short strands of pearls. Her hands were neatly folded on her knees, partially overlapping the hem of her gray linen skirt. Her black heels rested flat on the floor. Her short white hair had been slightly fluffed and, although she was obviously older, her face was mostly wrinkle-free. *Kudos to her plastic surgeon.*

I hesitated, surprised by how concerned she appeared to be. "I'm just shaken up."

"What were you doing out here all alone?"

"I . . ." Why hadn't I come up with a story before now? "I was at the carpet store with my boyfriend and we had a fight over which color to pick. But he got really mad and got physical."

She glanced down at the red marks on my arms, then up into my face. "That must have been very frightening. Where is he now?"

"I don't know. I got scared and took off running."

"Marco," she called out the door. "Why don't you call the proper authorities? And shut the door so our guest can have a bit of privacy."

"Yes ma'am," he said, then did as she requested.

"That's really not necessary," I said. "If you could just take me back to the carpet store, I can call my friend to ask her to come pick me up."

She nodded. "If that's what you'd prefer, dear. We'll just sit here for a moment so you can catch your breath."

"Thank you." I was suddenly at a loss. While I'd succeeded in getting her to let me in the car, I couldn't just ask her why she had been at the warehouse.

"What's your name?" she asked before I came up with an appropriate line of questioning.

"Ellie." I said, wishing I'd come up with an alias.

She nodded slightly. "Such a sweet nickname. Is your given name Ellen?"

"Elinor."

A slight smile tugged at her lips. "A family name?"

"Yes." I rubbed my arms. "I'm so lucky you happened to drive by. Don't take this the wrong way, but I can't imagine why someone as nice as you would be out here."

"Business," she said without emotion. She shifted and unfolded her hands, revealing blood splatters on her skirt.

Keep it together, Ellie. But what if David was lying in the warehouse right now bleeding to death and I was sitting here chatting with one of the people who had injured him? I forced out a slow, deep breath. "You must be a successful businesswoman if you have a limo and driver."

"So you live in Charlotte?" she asked, ignoring my statement. Her question had the tiniest amount of bite.

"Yes."

"What neighborhood? We can just drop you off at your home. No need to call your friend."

"I'm sure you wouldn't know it."

"I've lived in Charlotte my entire life and I know this city like the back of my hand. Try me."

I stared at her.

"Ellie, why don't you tell me why you're really here?"

My racing heart nearly flung itself from my chest. "Excuse me?"

"You're right. I am a businesswoman and my time is valuable. I'm sure yours is too. So why don't we skip all of this tedious deception and cut to the chase."

I sat up straighter and looked into her light-gray eyes. "Agreed."

"As with every business transaction, we must come to an arrangement that benefits us both. You haven't made any attempt to rob me, so I must surmise that you have some questions for me."

"And what do I have that you want?"

"Ellie," she said in a stern voice. "Or should I call you Elinor Dare Lancaster?"

My stomach dropped to my feet.

"I was going to find you soon enough, but it looks like you found me first."

"Why would you want to find me?"

She smiled, but her eyes were cold and calculating now. "All in good time, Elinor." She grimaced. "Forgive me, but I do hate nicknames. So uncouth."

"It hardly seems fair that you know my name but I don't know yours."

"Miriam Peabody," she said with an air of superiority, and I wondered if she expected me to take her hand and kiss the big diamond ring on her right ring finger.

Not bloody likely, as my Brit would say. But I'd do it if it would save him. "I'd say it's nice to meet you, Ms. Peabody, but I'd be lying. You didn't answer me before: I might want answers, but what do you want?"

"We'll save that for later."

"You basically want me to give you a blank check."

A deceptively sweet smile spread across her face. "I think you really want the information I can give you. You'll owe me something for every question you ask."

It was tempting.

"I'll give you one question for free."

One question. What should I ask? "Why are you collecting weapons?"

Her smile widened. "Cut right to the heart of it, don't you?" She laughed softly, then reached into her purse and pulled out a handkerchief. "There's a war brewing, Elinor. It's been predicted for over four centuries. It's important to be prepared. And to pick the right side."

"And which side is that?"

"The side that benefits us the most." Her eyes twinkled as she dabbed her nose with the handkerchief before lowering it. "And that was question number two. We only agreed to one free one. You are now in the deficit."

Oh, fuck it. "Why were you coming to find me?"

"You are a key player in the outcome of this battle."

"You know about the curse?" I asked, incredulous.

Confusion flickered in her eyes. "What curse?"

What the hell was she talking about if she didn't know about the curse?

She shifted slightly in her seat. "My turn."

My heart sped up. Her answers had only given me more questions, and now I was supposedly in her debt. Well, I'd learned a thing or two from Collin. There was no honor among thieves, and this bitch was definitely a thief. I gave her a cocky grin. "Go for it."

"Where is your friend, Collin Dailey?"

I lifted my eyebrows. "First of all, Collin-fucking-Dailey is not my *friend*."

She cringed at my vulgar language and I fought to keep from smiling. Ms. Uptight Pants didn't even like nicknames, so I hoped I was offending her prudish sensibility.

"And second, I don't keep tabs on the bastard. We spent a week together and then we were done."

She dabbed her nose again, then glanced out the window before returning her gaze to me, her eyes hard. "That's not what my sources say. I know he protects you and that you two are capable of great things together."

I shook my head. "I don't know what you're talking about."

The corners of her mouth lifted slightly. "I think you do. In fact, I'm counting on it."

The smugness in her voice sent a shiver down my spine. "What are you talking about?"

Her head tilted slightly. "Unfortunately for Dr. Preston, he was quite uncooperative."

My chest tightened and the blood rushed from my head. *Focus, Ellie. Focus.* "Funny, I've found him to be quite the opposite. He's proven himself entirely useful."

"I know that you're fond of him, Elinor."

"What does that have to do with anything?"

"You sent him to see the collection, didn't you? You're curious about what we possess. Dr. Preston was sent to evaluate it." She tsked and shook her head. "It's a pity what happened to his ex-girlfriend." Her eyes lit up. "Have you noticed that the collection seems to be quite unlucky? When outsiders come to see it, foul play usually befalls them. You know this firsthand. On multiple counts." She shook her head. "Your poor Dr. Preston was doomed from the moment he stepped into the warehouse."

I forced myself to remain calm, at least on the outside. Time to pull more Collin Dailey tricks. I was playing the role of an aloof bitch who was about to kick an old woman's ass. Or maybe I wasn't pretending. "And where is Dr. Preston now?"

She grinned. "Somewhere safe." Her mouth twisted in amusement. "Well, safe for my purposes. I shall not comment on his physical state. And no, he's no longer in the warehouse."

I forced a wry smile. "I'm going to need him back. I'm not done with him yet."

"I'm counting on that."

"If your time is so valuable, tell me what you want."

"An exchange of a sort. Your Dr. Preston for your cooperation."

"With what?"

"We want to locate the gate to hell."

I blinked, certain that I'd heard her wrong. "What?"

"We want you to provide us with the location of the gate to hell. We'll meet you there and then we'll hand over Dr. Preston."

"That's it?"

She smiled. "We want the location confirmed. We'll need Mr. Dailey to be present to ensure that."

My heart sunk. There was no way Collin would go for that. "I want something in return."

She laughed in surprise. "You'll get your valuable Dr. Preston. Isn't that reward enough?"

"No. I want more."

"You're not exactly in a position to negotiate."

"I think I am. You need me and you need Collin. Collin can't stand David, so he'll never agree to cooperate. He'll gladly see him gone. You'll need to make it worth his while as well."

She pondered my statement. "Obviously, you have something in mind."

"There's a seventeenth-century Croatan spear. I believe it's in your possession. He'll want that as well as the Sword of Galahad."

She shook her head. "No."

I sighed, reaching for the car door. "Then I guess we're done here."

She laughed. "You haven't fooled me. I know you care more about Dr. Preston than you're letting on. You're not going to just walk away and leave his life in my hands."

I narrowed my eyes. "You're right. I do care about David, but I also know Collin. There's no fucking way he'll agree to this unless he's getting something in return. Something big. So if you won't offer anything up, I don't see any point in wasting more of either of our *valuable* time."

"The spear. Not the sword."

I shook my head.

"That's the best you'll get, Elinor. Take it or leave it."

"It's not my call to make, *Miriam*. It's up to Collin." I opened the car door, but she surprised me by grabbing the handle and pulling it closed.

"If you are going to leave without reaching an agreement with me, then I'll need a deposit to pay for the care and well-being of your beloved Dr. Preston. Otherwise we'll deliver him dead."

I couldn't contain my shock.

She smiled and almost looked pleasant, like an overly polite grandmother. "I thought that might grab your attention."

"What do you want?"

"The ring on your hand."

I instinctively raised my hand, my left hand fingering the band. "Why?"

She tilted her head to the side, irritation flickering in her eyes. "*Why*? Because it doesn't belong to you. It was given to your mother in good faith and never returned. It belongs to the Guardians."

"Did you play any part in my mother's murder?"

She rolled her eyes in disgust. "Why would we want her killed? We wanted her expertise. She was killed by barbarians. We presumed they stole the ring."

"Why do *you* want it?"

"Seeing how it is my property, I don't feel the need to tell you. Why do *you* want it?"

"Sentimental reasons."

She chuckled. "You are a very gifted liar."

Collin would be so proud.

"I need you, Elinor, and I'd prefer for you to be cooperative. I'm told you need a bit more time before you're ready, so I'm happy to let you go prepare. But make no mistake: I have no problem taking you with me right now. So I'll take your ring as a down payment for Dr. Preston's care as well as insurance that you'll meet me tomorrow night."

Did I really have a choice? Could she or someone else in her group use the power of the ring? Did they even know what to do with it?

Her eyes narrowed. "*Now*, Elinor."

With shaky fingers, I slipped the band off my finger and placed it in her open palm. While I'd never planned to use it, my finger felt naked, and I worried about what she'd do with it. But I'd do anything to save David, even if I was trying to project otherwise.

"That's a good girl." She thrust a cell phone toward me. "You'll want this. Call the most recent number with your answer. But don't take too long. Dr. Preston's current hosts aren't very civilized, if you catch my meaning." She leaned toward the door and called out, "Marco, Ms. Lancaster has recovered enough to take her leave."

He opened the door and I started to get out, but before I did, I turned around to stare at her.

"You messed with the wrong person," I said after a long moment passed. "You might get what you want this time, but in the end, I will hunt you down and make you sorry you ever messed with me."

She laughed. "You *are* quite entertaining."

I cocked an eyebrow. "The last demon I killed thought the same. Disposing of you will be ten times easier." I climbed out and slammed the door on Miriam's stunned face.

Unfortunately for her, it wasn't an empty threat.

✌ CHAPTER TWENTY ~

The limo pulled away just as Collin rounded the corner.

"Ellie!"

I turned to him, my anger surging. "Did you get David?" I asked, hoping Miriam had been bluffing even if I knew better.

"No! I came after you!" He watched the limo drive away and then looked down at my torn collar. His eyes hardened as he clenched his fists at his sides. "What happened?"

"Nothing. I'm fine."

His gaze drifted to my still-red arms. "You don't look fine. Why did you run after them? What happened?"

"I'm *fine*, and I got some answers." My voice quivered on the last word and I started to break apart, but I pushed down my panic. "She said they have him."

"You actually talked to her? What else did she say?"

I tried to step around him, but he blocked my path. "I'm not telling you a goddamned thing. How does *that* feel?" I shouted, shoving his chest with the heels of my hands, the phone she gave me still in my grip. "Now get out of my way."

He stood his ground. "Why'd she let you go?"

I gritted my teeth, anger surging through my veins. I latched on to it, because I couldn't let myself think of the worst-case scenario. "Get out of my way, Collin. *Now*. I have to find David."

He studied me for several seconds before stepping to the side. I took off sprinting, but he easily fell in step beside me. "We have to stick together, Ellie. You need to tell me what you found out."

I shook my head, worried that I'd burst into tears if I tried talking. There was little chance that David was still in that building—after all, she'd flat out told me that he wasn't—but I had to make sure before I let myself accept it.

I skidded to a halt in front of the glass door to the front office, grunting in frustration when the door wouldn't open for me. Out of breath, I leaned over my legs and sucked in lungfuls of air, willing myself not to cry. "I have to get into this damned building." But when I scanned the street for something that would break the glass, I came up empty.

Collin had stopped next to me, but he took off down the road and rounded the corner while I continued to futilely pull on the door. David surely had a jack in the back of his car, but he had the keys. I pounded my fists on the glass in frustration.

"You've got quite the temper, but I don't think that's going to get it open," Collin called out. He came back into sight with a crowbar in his hand. "This will come in handy all the way around. Step back."

I took several steps away and he swung the steel rod at the door without any hesitation, creating a hole that fractured the entire pane but left the glass in the frame. Several quick taps knocked the shards to the floor.

As far as I knew, Collin never carried weapons—other than the crowbar currently in his hand—but I wasn't about to go in there unarmed. Not after Saturday night. I grabbed the bar out of his hand and strode toward David's car as I shoved the phone I held into my pocket.

"Ellie. What are you doing?" he called after me.

I swung the bar into the driver-side window, but it bounced off.

"Ellie! Now's not the time to have a fit."

Ignoring him, I jerked the bar back and swung it two more times before the glass in the window shattered and fell onto the seat. I tossed the crowbar onto the pavement in front of Collin. While he bent down to retrieve it, I reached into the car and popped the trunk.

"*Ellie.*"

I stomped around the back of the car and lifted the lid, then pulled out the sword.

"What the fuck is that and what do you think you're going to do with it?" Collin asked as we headed back to the office, a hard edge in his voice.

My gaze hardened. "Protect myself."

"You're going to get yourself killed with that thing."

"This *thing* saved my life two nights ago, so I'll take my chances."

He looked doubtful but kept his opinion to himself as he ducked under the door handle, the only barrier to the now-gaping doorway. "We don't have long, so let's hurry."

I followed after glancing down the street to make sure no one had noticed us, even though it was too late for that. Luckily, the area was completely deserted. I only hoped no one in the flooring showroom was watching.

We stood in the small foyer, the keypad on the secured door mocking us. "Will your crowbar get us through that door too?" I asked, some of my anger fading.

"Why? Eager to try your new toy?" he asked with a sneer.

"Shut the fuck up, Collin." I was ready to kick someone's ass and if Collin wanted to volunteer for the position, more power to him.

"No, my crowbar won't open it, but *this* will." He punched in a code and then tugged on the door.

I gasped when it opened. "How do you know the code?"

"I watched them with binoculars, remember? It wasn't hard to figure it out. I planned to check it out later anyway."

I started to walk past him, the tip of the sword pointed toward the floor, but he grabbed my arm and held me still. "Slow down. I know you want to find him, but we need to sneak in before we start eviscerating people," he whispered sarcastically. "Let me go first."

I almost pointed out that breaking the glass door and my attack on David's car had ruined any chance at stealth, but instead I nodded. And I had no problem letting Collin take the lead. There was no denying he had more experience with break-ins than I did, even though I seemed to be racking up a fair amount of experience the more time I spent with him.

He stuck his head through the opening and peered around the corner before slipping through the door and motioning me to follow. We entered a dim six-foot-long hallway with stark white walls and a single flickering fluorescent overhead. At the end of the hall was another door with a keypad.

Collin lifted his hand to punch the buttons, but stopped and turned at the waist to stare into my eyes. His irritation softened. "Ellie, I know you're upset, but don't do anything stupid with that sword when we get in here."

"We'll just have to wait and see what we find." I hadn't grabbed it with the intention of protecting myself from human attackers. Even though it was daylight, I wanted to be equipped to defend myself against supernatural foes. But if David was inside and using the sword would help me save him, I wouldn't hesitate, not even if the threat came from a human. Still, I hoped I wouldn't need it.

Scowling, Collin entered the same code he'd used before, which—to my surprise—worked. He slowly opened the door and scanned the room before motioning to me. We stood in a large space that reminded me of some type of distribution center. Two rows of empty stainless steel tables that resembled the ones in the kitchen of the New Moon filled the space. Collin tossed the crowbar onto one of the tables with a loud clang, then walked down one of the rows and spun around in a circle. "They're gone."

"No shit." Anger surged through my body again, burning away the tears that stung behind my eyes. My grip on the sword tightened. "How did this happen?" My accusation was clear.

His mouth dropped open. "How did *what* happen?"

"How did they manage to take him away without us even noticing? We were both watching the building!" I shouted.

Collin walked over to me and snatched the sword out of my hand before I could stop him. He dropped it on a nearby table and then grabbed my shoulders, his face firm. "I know you're upset right now, and if it makes you feel better to blame me for this along with everything else, go right ahead. But I need you to focus and tell me what that woman said to you."

I took several deep breaths.

His face softened. "If you want me to help you find David, you have to give me whatever information you have."

I hated to admit it, but he was right. Now was not the time to be petty. "Her name is Miriam Peabody. I'm sure she's the woman Allison met. She confirmed they've been collecting weapons. She said there's a war brewing and they've been preparing for centuries. According to her, it's important to not only be prepared but to pick the right side."

He frowned. "What's the right side?"

I gave him an ugly smirk. "The side that benefits them. Whatever the fuck side that is."

Collin placed the heel of his hand against his temple, looking bewildered.

I nodded. "I ran in front of her limo and pretended I'd been attacked so she'd let me in the back. She did, but she knew who I was from the start. She called me by my full name—Elinor Dare Lancaster—and told me she had been about to start looking for me."

His face tensed as his gaze jerked to my face. "Why?"

"She said I'm a key player in the outcome of the war. She also knows about you and the fact that you've been marking my doors. She called you by name."

"They've been watching us?"

I didn't answer his question. I didn't know how. "They took David." My voice broke and I stiffened my shoulders. "She offered me a trade."

He lowered his hand. "What does she want?"

"She took the ring and she wants me to show her the gate to hell."

"She wants *what*?" His eyes widened and he took a step back. "*Why*? And how does she even know about Popogusso?"

I shook my head. "I don't know. But she wants both of us to show it to her and prove it's real. She seemed confused when I mentioned the curse."

He rested his butt against a table, looking like he'd been blindsided. "The only people who know anything about the curse on my side are my grandmother and my brother. And I *know* they didn't tell anyone."

"The only people who know about it on my side are Claire and Drew, and they would never tell . . . And I told Tom last night," I added as an afterthought.

He bounced upright, his face red. "You did *what*?"

Who the hell was he to judge me? "You've been out on your boat frolicking with all your demon buddies while I've been stuck in Manteo dealing with the fallout of their extracurricular activities. Which brings me face-to-face with Officer Helmsworth on a regular basis." I took a breath, my irritation softening. I couldn't blame Collin for being upset—this affected him too. "Look, he's not stupid, Collin. He knows there are supernatural forces behind what's happening in Manteo, and he knows I'm square in the middle of it. The Raven Mockers are killing people every night and he's trying to save them. Tsagasi told me what to do, so I told Tom. Was I supposed to keep that from him?"

He heaved a sigh and closed his eyes. "What a fucked-up mess."

"But I only told him late last night, so there's no way they found out from him."

He stood upright and turned toward me, his eyes gleaming with determination. "We need to figure out how they know about us."

"I can't think of anyone else."

He stared at the floor for several seconds before looking up. "You're forgetting about Myra."

I shook my head. "There's no way Myra would tell anyone."

"She's seeing someone now, right? Didn't she move to Durham to be closer to him?"

"Well . . . yeah . . . but she wouldn't tell him."

"What if she slipped? You and I both know how easy it is to get caught up in the heat of the moment and say something you don't mean to."

My face burned with the memory of the things I'd said to him. Things I should have kept to myself. Yet despite his betrayal and the fact that the man I loved was in mortal danger, my body responded to the memory of being with Collin. I hated him a little for that, even though it wasn't his fault. "Steven's an old family friend. He would never put my life in danger."

The pain in his eyes told me that he noticed the venom behind my words. "Maybe he accidently told someone, Ellie. We need to talk to him and find out."

I just couldn't believe Myra would tell him, let alone that Steven would sell me out. "What if it wasn't someone human? What if a supernatural creature spilled the beans?"

"To what end?"

"I don't know!" I shouted in irritation. "Maybe it's Ahone. Miriam took the ring. She knows it does something."

He pushed out a breath. "Let's presume you're right about Ahone wanting you to use the ring at the gate, and I suspect you are—why would he encourage them to take it from you? That doesn't make sense." He paused. "But if my grandmother was right about the Dare line being the only ones with the power to use it, they won't be able to do anything with it anyway."

None of this speculation changed the fact that David was in danger *right now.* My fears pushed to the surface, but I buried them again. I didn't have time to cry. "I told her that you hated David and you'd need some other incentive to cooperate. I said that you needed the spear and the Sword of Galahad."

He shook his head. "What's the Sword of Galahad?"

"It's a sword from the twelfth century that was blessed for King Richard the Lionheart to take to the Crusades."

"And why would they want that?" He squinted in confusion. "Why would *we* want that?"

"It was blessed to kill demons."

His eyes widened. "You're shitting me? They think they have a sword that can kill demons?" he scoffed. "What idiots."

277

"Collin, they *do* have a sword that will kill demons. Tsagasi confirmed it. Hell, I have a sword that kills demons. I killed three of them two nights ago. But that's not all the Sword of Galahad does. Tsagasi says it can subdue gods too."

His face paled. "How can such a thing exist?"

"I don't know, but I need it."

He shook his head, clenching his jaw. "No, Ellie. That's the *last* thing you need. You'll become a target."

"Wake up, Collin! I already *am* a target!"

He paced for several seconds looking like he was about to be sick. "So you told her the only way I would show was if she gave you the spear and the sword. What did she say?"

"She only agreed to the spear. I told her I had to check with you." I suddenly remembered the phone and dug it out of my pocket. "She handed me this and told me to call her when you had your answer. She said to use the most recent number."

He reached for the mobile. "That's no burner." I handed it to him and he frowned. "It's an *iPhone*. How much money do these people have?"

When he tapped the screen, I recognized the screen saver and instantly felt like I was going to throw up. "Oh, God, it's David's."

I reached to snatch it back, but Collin refused to release it. "Ellie. There's a video on it."

My breath caught. "I want to see it."

He held it close to his chest, pity in his eyes. "I think I should see it first."

His pity only made me angrier. "Why? Are you trying to *protect* me? Too goddamned late for that. I've had to face more shit in the last couple of months than I did in my entire life before meeting you."

"Ellie."

"You can't protect me from this, Collin. You can't protect me from *anything*."

He looked devastated. "I know."

His hold loosened and I grabbed the phone with shaky fingers, holding it out so we both could see it.

Then I pressed play.

The video started with Miriam's face. "Hello, Elinor. If you're watching this, then you've discovered who I am. I want you to be completely aware of what you're dealing with." She stepped away from the frame, revealing David. He was tied to a chair, his face bloody.

My stomach jolted and I sucked in a breath. Collin snaked an arm around my back, pulling me to his side.

David looked at the screen, and I could tell that one of his eyes was starting to swell.

"Tell Elinor what we instructed you to say."

"Go to bloody hell." He spat blood at her and it landed on her skirt.

The man next him—the man who had gone out to talk to Miriam before she left—hit David in the face and his head slumped to the side.

I felt wobbly, but Collin's hold tightened.

"I expected better manners from you, *Dr.* Preston," she reprimanded in a disapproving tone. "Now tell Elinor what she needs to do."

He looked at the camera, anger radiating from his body. "Ellie, don't listen to her. Don't do it."

The man hit him again.

Miriam released an exaggerated sigh. "Dr. Preston, we really don't want to have to do this, but you leave us with no choice."

Blood dripped from his nose and down to his light-blue dress shirt. The one I'd ironed for him that morning, even though he'd protested he could do it himself. Hysteria bubbled below the surface and I struggled to keep it under control. "All right, but I want to give her a message first."

Miriam hesitated. "Fine. But then you must deliver the message you were instructed to give."

He looked into the camera, his face softening. "Ellie, listen to me."

I released a soft whimper. They were beating the shit out of him and he was still only thinking about me.

He leaned forward as though he could get closer to me. "If something happens to me, don't blame yourself. I wouldn't give up a single minute with you. Give Myra's boyfriend my regards. And remember that I love you, Ellie. I'll always love you. Not even death can separate my love from you."

"Enough," Miriam shouted. "Deliver the instructions."

"They want you to meet them in the Manteo aquarium at eleven on Tuesday night." His gaze dropped as though he was ashamed, then he looked up again. "I'm sorry, Ellie. I didn't want to tell them where the gate was, but they forced me."

"He lied to them," I blurted out.

His uninjured eye widened and his back stiffened. "But don't do it, Ellie! Don't meet them. They'll kill me anyway, and they won't let you go when they're done."

The man punched him twice more and David slumped in the chair. The camera turned back to Miriam. "Elinor, I hope I haven't underestimated your attachment to young Dr. Preston. Meet us tomorrow night or we'll deliver him to your front doorstep. And you won't like the way he looks when we're done with him." Then the video ended.

I stared at the frozen frame on the screen. A sob broke loose and I reached back my hand to throw the phone across the room, but Collin grabbed my fist and pried the device loose before I could do it.

"I know you're pissed, Ellie, but we need this phone."

I leaned over my knees, my heart cracking into pieces as I finally let myself break down. What had they done to him? What more hell would he have to go through because of me? I struggled to catch my breath. No, the fucking Guardians were the ones who had beat the shit out of him. I needed to blame them. I choked on a sob again, remembering how his sweet face had looked in the video—bloody and bruised. My threat to Miriam wasn't a bluff, and her video only made me hate her more. I stood up straight, my chest heaving as I fought to regain control. "*Pissed?* You think I'm only *pissed?*"

"Ellie." He grabbed my shoulders and stared into my eyes. "I swear to you, I'll do everything in my power to get him back. This is not done."

My control broke again and tears clogged my throat. "I begged you to save him when I went after her. You told me you would and you didn't . . . you came after me instead. Why should I believe you now?"

His hand cupped my cheek, his thumb brushing away my tears. "Because you'll always come first. Above everyone and everything. Every fucking time, you'll always come first."

I shook my head and sagged into his chest and sobbed, some of the fight draining out of me.

His hand moved to the back of my head as his other arm wrapped around my back, holding me gently against him. "He was already gone by the time I got out back, Ellie. There wasn't anything I could do. I'll help you save him."

His words filled me with hope. But I suddenly realized that I was back to where I was when all of this began—blindly following Collin. Well, I was no longer that naïve, stupid girl who'd followed him like a lost puppy. I was stronger now, and I knew things he didn't. I jerked out of his grasp. Nothing good ever came from letting Collin take control. "Then you'll have to tag along with me, because I'm going after him myself."

Resignation filled his eyes and he took a step back. I reached over and grabbed my sword off the table and strode toward the door.

"Ellie, hold up."

I spun at the waist and stared at him, my gaze cold. "Are you coming with me or not?"

"Hey, I'm all for going on a recovery mission, and you seem hell-bent on taking over," he said, his tone light as he held his hands out at his sides. "And fine, I'll let you. But what's your plan?"

Asshole. I didn't have one and he knew it.

He took a cautious step toward me. "Can I just make a suggestion?"

"*What?*"

"Before we leave, let's look for clues." He took my nonresponse as a sign to continue. "If they moved the collection out, they would have needed a big truck. Maybe someone noticed."

I put my hands on my hips. "Who? This building is completely unoccupied except for this section. And the back faces a field. Who would have seen anything?"

A wry grin lifted his mouth. "Someone most people would ignore."

Chapter Twenty-One

"Come on." He brushed past me as he moved to the back door, unlocked it, and then pushed it open.

I followed him out and down the steps next to the loading dock. A puddle of water sat in the middle section of the drive.

"I noticed this earlier, but it's directly under an overhang and it rained last night. But now I think it's condensation from a car or truck's air conditioner." He pointed to it. "This was how they took David."

Fear rushed through my bloodstream, making me light-headed. *Get it together, Ellie.* "And it was gone when you got back here?"

"Yeah, I suspect they didn't waste any time before starting their interrogation, and then they hauled him off before anyone could investigate. If they are really watching you—or me—then they probably even knew we were here."

I put my left hand on my stomach to ground myself. "So what do we do with that?"

"Come here."

I followed him down the stairs and around the corner, telling myself that following him didn't mean I was giving him control. "Where are we going?"

"To talk to someone I noticed earlier." His gaze drifted to my sword and he scowled. "You might want to keep that hidden. It doesn't exactly make us look friendly." Without waiting for an answer, Collin walked toward the end of the building and stopped next to a sunken doorway. An older man in dirty jeans and a faded army fatigue jacket lay on his side, curled into a fetal position on a piece of cardboard. He wore a stocking cap even though it was already at least eighty-five degrees.

I kept to the side and put the hand that was holding the blade behind my back. But I was carrying a three-foot sword—if the guy paid any attention to me, he would see it. I'd make it work, because there was no way Collin was questioning the guy on his own, and I wasn't about to put the sword down.

Collin looked down at him. "I need your help."

The man blinked, his clear blue eyes focusing on Collin. "I ain't got time to help you. Can't you see I'm sleepin'?" Then he closed his eyes again, curling up tighter.

Collin reached into his pocket and pulled out his wallet. "I'll make it worth your while."

The homeless man cracked one eye open.

Squatting next to him, Collin set a five-dollar bill on the concrete stoop. "Have you noticed anything unusual here in the last few weeks?"

The man pushed himself up into a sitting position and grabbed the money in his fist. "I keep to myself. It works better that way. That's why I hang out back here."

"I need to know if a big truck has been back here this week."

The man eyed Collin's wallet, his fingers fidgeting.

Collin put a ten on the pavement.

The man snatched it up. "Yeah, it was here last night. Big white truck with no words on the side. I had to hide in the corner because they've kicked me out before and I was comfortable in this spot."

"So they've been here for a while?"

"Yeah, for about three weeks. The big truck came in and they unloaded lots of silver boxes. But last night another big truck came and took all the boxes away."

Collin pulled another bill from his wallet and placed it in front of the man. "Tell me what you know, not what you think I want to hear."

The man nodded and snagged the bill, bolder this time.

"Do you remember any defining characteristics about the people who came and went? Anything different about any of them?"

"The guys movin' it all were just regular guys, but the cars were fancy, usually two of them. Two different men would come, both dressed in suits. Once there was a woman, all hoity-toity."

"Was she older? Did she have white hair?" Collin asked. "A long stick up her ass?"

The man cracked a smile. "Yeah, that was her."

"Did you hear anything they said?"

The old man shook his head. "Nope. I kept out of the way."

"What about this morning?" Collin asked, shifting his weight and glancing toward the loading dock. "Did you see any activity back here?"

"Yeah, I saw a silver car leave just a bit ago. Didn't see it come earlier, but like I said, I was sleepin'."

The cry of a bird came from overhead. A shiver ran down my spine, but I took comfort in the fact that it was late morning and the sun was beating down on the pavement. My imagination was getting carried away.

Collin rested his forearms on his knees, balancing on the balls of his feet. "Did you see who got in it?"

When the man hesitated, Collin started to pull out more money.

Another bird cawed, joined by a third. Anxious, I spun around, the sword still in my hand, and moved into the center of the street.

Collin stood and narrowed his eyes. "Ellie?"

Screaming filled the air and three large, black birds started to circle over our heads. "Raven Mockers. What are they doing here?" I asked, shading my eyes to look at them.

"That's impossible. Raven Mockers don't come out in the daylight. They're nocturnal."

"Well, someone forgot to tell them that . . . that and everything else they're not supposed to be doing."

Two of the birds swooped down, landing in the middle of the road before they transformed into an old man and woman—the same woman who had killed Allison.

The old woman tilted her head to the side and studied Collin with a sly grin.

A shiver settled at the base of my neck and I lifted my sword, ready to defend him. My action caught her eye and she laughed, her eyes sparkling. "Curse Keeper, we meet again."

"What do you want, Raven Mocker?" I asked.

"What I always want. To eat." Her gaze was drawn back to Collin, while the male stood behind her. "Son of the earth," she said with a smile. "I've been curious about you."

Collin glanced from me to the Raven Mocker, clenching his fists at his sides. "Ellie is protected by Okeus. You can't harm her."

The Raven Mocker laughed and then lunged toward me, but she was purposely slow, as though she was taunting me. I jumped out of the reach of her claws, raising my sword.

Collin moved closer to me as she retreated.

The woman and man split apart, the man moving toward the building and the woman toward the field. We all stood about fifteen feet apart, facing each other.

"Okeus wants her protected," Collin snarled.

"Okeus wants her *alive*," she said. "And we don't care what Okeus wants. We answer to another."

The homeless man had climbed to his feet, though he was still in the sunken doorway. "Who are you talking to?"

The male Raven Mocker rushed toward the homeless man, sinking his claws into his shoulder, dragging down. The man screamed in pain and fright as blood soaked through his jacket.

Not again. I couldn't watch them kill someone again.

The homeless man shrank back into the corner, grabbing his arm while he moaned. The male Raven Mocker paced back and forth in front of him, taking swipes at his face and arms, leaving surface wounds.

I started to rush to his aid, but Collin grabbed my arm, his fingers digging deep. "Ellie, stop."

My mouth dropped open in shock and horror. "You'll let them kill him?"

He didn't answer, his face pale.

Disgust washed through me in hot waves. "Maybe you can stand back and watch him suffer, but I can't."

I jerked out of his hold and lifted my sword as I took several steps toward them. I needed to get between the Raven Mockers and the homeless man.

The bird overhead still circled and cawed.

The old woman lunged as I passed, purposely missing again. She laughed when I jumped out of her way and wielded my sword in a defensive position.

"Ellie. Goddamn it! *Stop this!* You're going to get yourself killed!" Collin shouted.

The male Raven Mocker released a loud caw and the black bird overhead joined in, as though they were chanting a taunt.

The old woman grinned, her lips pulling back to reveal her yellowed razor-sharp teeth. She stood six feet away but she reached her hand toward me, rolling her fingers as if she wanted to dig them into my skin. "You are slow today, Curse Keeper. I think the Great One is wrong about you after all."

"Okeus?" I asked, sliding closer to the doorway, and the old woman moved with me. Tsagasi had already said it wasn't, but it didn't hurt to get confirmation from one of the Raven Mockers.

She spat on the ground as she matched my movement, keeping her sharp eyes on me. "Someone more cunning than Okeus."

"Ahone," Collin grunted as he positioned himself closer to the male Raven Mocker.

"A thousand curses on Ahone's head." She spat again.

A glob of spit landed on the homeless man's arm and sizzled. Smoke rose from the spot and he screamed.

Her eyes narrowed with hatred. "Soon he will pay for his transgressions."

So if they weren't working for either of the gods, who *were* they working for and why were they here now?

The only way to defeat them was to take the offensive. I stood at the corner of the doorway, the homeless man shrieking in pain behind me. He grabbed at the hem of my shirt, pulling me backward.

"Help me!" he screamed.

Collin was a good fifteen feet away from me now, with the male Raven Mocker circling around and separating us. Collin's gaze shifted from the male Mocker to the female one and then to me, his eyes flying open in horror as I fought to untangle myself from the homeless man's grasp. I jerked free and moved several feet to the side, but the injured man fell face-first on the street.

The old woman took advantage of my distraction and rushed toward us, clawing the man's back. The angle was wrong—her side was to me—but maybe an injury would slow her down. I grabbed the sword with both hands and lifted it like a bat, swinging with all my strength and embedding the blade into her back.

She shrieked and bolted upright, nearly pulling the weapon from my grasp. "You will pay for that, Curse Keeper." Thick black blood spilled onto the pavement as I wrenched my weapon free.

Collin's face hardened as he glanced from me to the Raven Mockers, the homeless man still screaming in pain. Fear and anger filled his eyes as he ran between the demons and then turned to face me, lifting his palm. The mark on his hand began to glow.

"*I am the son of the earth.*"

The wind howled and a pinpoint vortex appeared.

"No, Collin!" I shouted above the gusts. "Let me destroy them!"

The old man's face contorted in anger and he ran toward me, lashing out as a bird's scream came out of his mouth. I held the sword in front of me with both hands and planted my feet, bracing myself. It was a risky move. Even if I dealt a killing blow, there was a strong likelihood he'd be able to claw me before he succumbed.

"*. . . born of space and heaven.*" Collin's firm voice boomed through the open space and my head.

The vortex widened and the suction increased. The old man was struggling to reach me while the old woman turned her attention to Collin. I decided to take the offensive and surged forward, sinking the sword deep into his chest. But even as I pushed the blade in with the continued momentum of my lunge, I knew it was too low. I had missed his heart. With the sword embedded in his chest, I was close enough for him to wrap his arms around my back. His claws sunk deep into my shoulder blades. A maniacal laugh escaped his mouth, followed by a putrid odor. The scent and the pain overwhelmed my senses, and the edges of my vision turned black.

Who would save David if something happened to me?

"*I am black earth and sandy loams . . .*"

I could hear the panic in Collin's voice. The pure terror in it registered as a sticky warmth coating my back, plastering my shirt to my skin and trickling down, seeping into the waistband of my pants. How I separated his voice from the chaos going on around me was a mystery. But somehow it gave me strength. I couldn't leave him either.

The wind grew stronger. The monster still had his claws embedded in my back, and they sank deeper yet, digging into my muscles and dragging outward toward my sides. I gritted my teeth to keep from giving him the satisfaction of a scream. His feet began to slide and I realized he was being pulled into the vortex.

And he planned on taking me with him.

"Don't kill her, *you fool!*" the old woman shouted in anger. "The Great One needs her!"

"*The mountain ranges and the rolling hills.*" Collin's voice faltered as he realized what was happening. The vortex shrank slightly and the wind lessened.

Fighting to keep conscious despite my pain, I instinctively bent at the knees and forced the sword higher into the monster's chest, then to my right.

The old man's eyes widened and he screamed before sinking his teeth into my shoulder. Then his body evaporated into a plume of black smoke.

I fell to my hands and knees, the sword tumbling from my hand and clattering onto the pavement. The old woman moved deliberately toward me, stopping only a few feet away from the screaming homeless man. He still lay on his stomach, his jacket ripped open, the muscles and skin of his back ripped into ribbons, blood covering his clothes and the street beneath him.

I realized my own back must look the same. Probably worse.

"I am the foundation of life and the receiver of death . . ."

The woman laughed, only it sounded like cackle. "So the Great One is right after all. You are a fighter."

I looked up at her, my hair hanging in my face, my blood dripping into alarmingly large pools around me. "Go to fucking hell," I snarled, trying to summon the strength to grab the sword and kill her, an unlikely act given the fact I was moments away from passing out from blood loss.

". . . and everything in between . . ."

The wind was hurricane force now, and the woman struggled to resist its pull.

Caught in the gusts of wind, the sword spun back and forth on the asphalt before starting to slide toward the hole. I lunged for it, stretching out my arm. But my coordination was gone and my arms flailed like a rag doll's, sending intense pain searing through my back. I screamed as my fingers closed around the handle and I fell the rest of the way to the ground, my cheek scraping the pavement as I watched the Raven Mocker turn toward the homeless man.

"I compel you to leave my sight," Collin shouted, fury in his voice.

In one movement, she thrust her hand into the homeless man's back. His screams pierced my ears, only stopping when her wrist twisted with a sharp jerk. The wind swept her feet out from beneath her and pulled her backward as she ripped the man's heart from the gaping hole in his back. Holding it up in triumph, the Raven Mocker took a bite as she disappeared into the vortex. The hole closed, but her evil laughter still rang in my ears as everything fell away and faded to black.

I was dying. I'd failed them all.

❧ Chapter Twenty-Two ❧

I was plunged into the blackest darkness I'd ever experienced and surrounded by an icy cold. Was this Popogusso? I fought to breathe, but my chest resisted the simplest command to draw in a breath. I was suffocating.

Collin called my name and I tried to answer him, but nothing came out. Instead, I felt myself falling and his voice became fainter and fainter.

Desperate, I reached out for anything to hold on to. My hands felt nothing but the dank, heavy air around me.

Was this how it would end?

The moans of countless creatures filled my ears and my panic resurfaced. I couldn't spend the rest of eternity in Popogusso. Hysteria took over and I searched for an escape. But it was like I was running on a treadmill; there was nowhere to go. The moans and screams grew louder.

"*Collin!*" I screamed.

Then a searing pain exploded in my hand, shooting straight to my back, and a bright, blinding light flashed in front of my eyes. My spine arced as electricity shot through my body, jolting my nearly still heart and sending it racing. The band on my chest loosened and I sucked in a deep breath.

The Manitou of every living thing rushed through me with an intensity I'd never experienced. The sensation had always been peaceful and reassuring before, but this time it burned through my blood, filling every cell, and I cried out in pain and surprise. I was me, but not me. I was part of all living things, both in the sea and on the earth. I was everywhere and nowhere.

I was in Collin's arms. His touch had brought me back.

Our connection was stronger than it had ever been before, and I not only felt his emotions—intense, overwhelming grief and panic— but my racing heart slowed down to synchronize to the rhythm of his, the rise and fall of our chests matching to the millisecond.

I felt his arms loosen around me as he realized I was not only alive but that we had a deeper access to each other than ever before.

We were literally two halves of a whole, separated by a thin veil. We stood on either side of it, our conscious minds aware of each other but neither one willing to make the breach.

I dragged my eyelids open and took in his pale face and his red, glassy eyes.

"Ellie," he murmured in relief as he bent forward, resting his face on the top of my head. "Thank God." His voice cracked with emotion.

Without releasing my hand, Collin sat on the ground with me draped across his lap. His grip on me tightened and his body shook with emotion.

"Oh, God, Ellie. I thought I'd lost you." His grief and gratitude pushed through with his words, and I knew without a doubt that Collin had never been more frightened or more thankful in his life.

I stared up into his face, realizing that something about our connection had changed. I had always been able to feel him before, and while the veil between us was still intact, a wall I hadn't known existed was gone.

"Thank you," I murmured, but my mouth was dry and my tongue struggled to form the sounds. "You saved me."

He let go of my hand, shutting down our connection, and pulled me closer. His eyes sank closed and he kissed my forehead. "You were dead, Ellie. You had no pulse."

"I'm not dead now." I didn't want to think about what I'd experienced before Collin saved me. Nor the implications of where I'd be spending eternity.

I tried to sit up but realized my energy had faded now that we were no longer touching marks. I sagged into him, limp and useless. If a Raven Mocker were to attack us now, I wouldn't even have the strength to lift my hand and recite the words of protection.

He felt my movement and released a heavy breath, searching my face. "How do you feel? Does your back hurt?"

"There isn't any pain. I'm guessing our connection healed me?"

A soft smile barely lifted the corners of his mouth. "Yeah, but I thought I was too late." His mouth pinched with anxiousness. "We have to get out of here. It's not safe."

"The third Raven Mocker?" I asked, looking for the bird.

"It was sucked into the vortex with the woman."

At least those two would be gone for a while. I tried to move again, but my body was slow and sluggish.

Collin climbed to his knees and pulled me with him, but when he got us to our feet, my knees buckled and I fell against him. The front of his T-shirt was drenched in my blood, and a large puddle was still pooled in the street. How much blood had I lost?

"Don't look at it, Ellie. You're safe now." He scooped me up in his arms and started for the corner of the building, but something shiny caught my eye.

"Collin, wait. The sword." It lay on the pavement, several feet from the bloody body of the homeless man. He was one more person

I had failed to save, but I couldn't think about him right now. I was lucky to have survived myself.

Collin's body tensed. "Fuck that *goddamned sword*," he forced through gritted teeth as he kept moving toward the front of the building.

Some of my strength returned and I squirmed in his arms. "No! I need it!"

His feet froze and his face contorted in anger. "I'm not taking that fucking sword with us! It almost got you killed!"

"No!" I protested, still struggling, but I didn't have the energy to fight him. I was barely hanging on to consciousness. "Collin, please. I need to be able to defend myself. You know there are countless creatures that have me on their hit list. Okeus's protection isn't enough." I leaned my head on his shoulder. "You can't leave me unprotected, Collin."

I felt his resolve soften. "You won't be unprotected, Ellie. I'll be here for you."

"You can't be with me every minute of the day. I need to learn to defend myself." I forced all my strength into lifting my hand to his cheek.

His gaze drifted to my face and I saw the terror in his eyes.

"Collin, *please*."

He lowered his head until his forehead rested against my hair. "I'll get it, but it doesn't mean I'm just going to give it back to you."

At least it was something.

Grumbling, he turned around and squatted next to the sword, then picked it up with me still in his arms. He carried the weapon in one hand, the blade pointing away from us. Collin's truck was parked two streets over. He opened the passenger door and set me gently on the seat and buckled me in when I struggled to reach for my seat belt. The physical exertion from fighting him had sapped what little energy I had left, and sleep was quickly overtaking me.

"I'm tired."

He cupped my cheek, searching my face. "You just fucking bled out, Ellie. I can't believe you're sitting here talking to me. You need sleep. Hell, you probably need a transfusion." His gaze drifted from my shirt to his. "Do you have anything to wear in David's car? We're going to get a shitload of unwanted attention in these blood-soaked clothes."

I nodded, or at least attempted to.

He shut my door and the truck engine turned over. My awareness faded, and when I came to again, he was back on my side of the vehicle. He stripped my shirt off and leaned me forward to look at my back. His fingers trailed down my spine, sending sensation shooting through me. "I can't believe it. Not even a scar. Your back was ripped to shreds." Then he tugged another shirt over my head and gently rested my head on the back of the seat.

"We have to save David," I said, but my words were slurred like a drunk's.

"We will," he whispered next to my ear. "I promise."

The truck began to move again, and I pried my eyes open. "Where are we going?"

His gaze turned to me, serious and protective. "Chapel Hill."

Sleep took over before I could ask why. And when I awoke hours later, we were parked in front of David's house and Collin was watching me with a guarded look.

I was on my left side, my back slumped against the door. At some point Collin had rolled the open window halfway up. "David's house? Why are we here? How did you know where it was?"

"We need somewhere to clean up before heading to Durham. And I found his address in his bag."

I pushed myself into a sitting position. "You had his bag?" But I also noticed he was wearing David's short-sleeved button-down shirt—David's favorite, a white and blue plaid. Anger raged to life inside me, accompanied by the irrational desire to demand he take it off. But Collin's shirt had been soaked in *my* blood. It was smart for him to change, and I was sure that Collin hated wearing David's clothes.

"I got all your personal belongings out of David's car before we left Charlotte."

"Why Durham?"

He hesitated. "I want to talk to Myra and especially her boyfriend. David wouldn't have mentioned him for nothing."

"Oh." After my encounter with Myra yesterday morning, I wasn't sure how well she'd take it if I showed up at her doorstep with Collin in tow. But Collin was right. David's message had to mean that Steven must know something. Had Myra told Steven anything about the curse? Had he sold me out?

"I called the number on the phone while you were sleeping and arranged the meeting for tomorrow night at eleven. They agreed to give me the spear, but not the sword. But I want to know what these people know about us and how they found out. We need to figure out a way to get the three of us out of this alive and unharmed, so the more we know going in, the better."

"The three of us?"

He nodded, looking solemn. "I promised to help save him, and I intend to make good on my word. We *will* get him back, Ellie."

I couldn't answer without breaking down again. Instead, I looked at the clock on the dashboard. It was close to two o'clock. It was hard to believe that so little time had passed since David and I first arrived in Charlotte. "So what's your plan?"

"Let's go shower, change clothes again, and try to set up meetings with the both of them for this afternoon. Then we'll head back to the Outer Banks. You need the ocean."

I couldn't argue with him.

"I considered driving straight to the shore, but we really need to talk to Myra and her boyfriend in person. I'm pretty good at reading people. I think I'll be able to tell if he's lying." His eyes hardened. "And if he is, I'm going to find out the truth."

I couldn't stomach the thought of Steven betraying me, but at this point I could count the people I trusted on one hand. "It's a good plan."

He wove his fingers through mine. "Do you know where a spare key to the house is? I can pick the lock if you don't."

"I don't think he has one."

"Wait here while I take care of it and I'll come back to get you."

He was out the door before I could answer.

My eyelids felt heavy again and I let them close for a moment before jerking them open. I didn't have time to sleep. We needed to get this information. Now. I couldn't leave David with those people. What were they doing to him?

Tears squeezed through the corners of my eyes and Collin's voice surprised me.

"I'm going to carry you inside."

I tried to lift my forehead so I could look him in the eye. "I can walk."

"I know you can, Ellie." But he scooped me up anyway and carried me into the house, setting me down on the sofa. "You really need to shower. Do you think you can stand for long enough?" He sounded worried.

"Yeah." I sank back into the cushions, letting my eyes close again. "Just give me a minute." But when I opened my eyes, it was dark and the air around me was cold.

I was really dead this time.

I bolted upright, screaming Collin's name as hysteria swamped me. He pulled me into his arms in an instant.

"Ellie. It's okay. You're safe."

"It was dark and cold," I forced out between sobs. "I thought I was dead again."

"No. It's nighttime. You're safe." He held me for a long time until I calmed down, and then he unwrapped his arms from me and slid off the bed. Seconds later a light turned on in David's bathroom and Collin cracked the door before coming back and sitting next to me.

I was in David's house. On his bed with Collin.

This was so wrong.

"I thought we were going to Durham," I said, confused.

"Ellie, you passed out. I almost put you back in the truck and drove you to Nags Head, but Tsagasi convinced me to wait. We decided the best thing was to let you sleep."

"You met Tsagasi." My mouth cracked with the hint of a grin.

"Stubborn little ass, isn't he," Collin grumbled.

"You could say that." I was already tired again. How was that possible? "What time is it?"

"Two thirty."

"In the *morning*? So I wasted a full day."

"No. You died or came damn near close. Your back might be healed, but you need the ocean to fully recover. But Tsagasi thinks it's too important for us to meet with your stepmother and her boyfriend for us to leave now."

"I'm surprised you listened to him."

"Well, I didn't at first." He ran a hand through his ruffled hair, a sly grin spreading across his face. "But the little shit got my attention when he jolted me with a bolt of electricity."

"He has a way of getting his point across."

Collin's shoulders tensed. "Ellie, I've watched the video a few more times."

My head jerked up. "Why?"

"To see if I missed anything. We were both pretty spooked the first time we watched it."

I fought my rising tears as the memory of David's battered face filled my head. I refused to break down. I was already weak enough. "And did you figure anything out?"

"No, the only thing that stands out is David's message about Myra's boyfriend." He turned to look at me and took my hand in his. "Who *is* her boyfriend? I take it David knows him."

Of course Collin wouldn't know. I hadn't thought to tell him earlier. "Um . . . yeah. Steven was a researcher at the colony. He invited David to Manteo to spend two weeks at the colony. They both stayed at our house because the bed and breakfast was full."

His face lowered closer to mine. "He invited David? So they're friends?"

"Yes, but David hasn't talked to him lately, and I know he hasn't told Steven about the curse." I looked into Collin's eyes. "He's always very careful."

"But Steven could have gotten information from Myra."

"Yeah . . . I guess . . ."

"Is there anything else tying Steven to this collection?"

"Oh, God." I nearly passed out as the truth hit me. "Momma. After she saw the Ricardo Estate, she called Steven. She wanted to call the police, but he convinced her to wait." I couldn't stop the tears this time. "I don't understand. When he told me about this a few weeks ago, he seemed genuinely upset." I shook my head. "He's been part of this all along."

Collin sucked in a breath. "Maybe. Maybe not. But we'll find out. I promise."

"Okay."

We sat together for several minutes before he stood. "I'll be back in a minute. Are you okay?"

I nodded. I knew he was asking if I was okay with him leaving me. There was no way I was *okay* in general, and we both knew it.

He got up and left the room, returning less than a minute later with a plate and a glass. "You need to eat to help regain your strength." He set the plate on my lap and clicked on the bedside lamp.

"A hamburger? Where did you get this? I know for a fact David didn't have any."

He scowled. "Your little friend forced me to get you takeout. I refused to leave you unprotected, but three of his friends showed up to stand guard while I was gone."

I groaned. "His brother and two Nunnehi warriors?"

"Yeah . . . actually . . ."

"Oh no." I leaned my head back against the headboard. "I only had six more times. Now I've wasted one."

Collin shook his head. "You lost me."

I explained my blood oath and our agreement.

"You didn't lose anything, Ellie. Tsagasi told you to call on him when you need to use their protection."

"But you said they showed up and guarded me."

"Yes, but they volunteered."

"Why would they do that?" I shook my head in confusion.

"Ellie, they call you the salvation of the world. They think you're going to save them."

I swallowed the lump in my throat. "Then they'll be bitterly disappointed, won't they?" I asked with an acrid laugh. "Shall we run through the very long list of people I have not only disappointed but gotten killed?"

"Ellie." Collin's voice was soft and gentle. "Stop."

When I looked into his face, I was grateful to see no pity there, only understanding.

"You need to eat. We need you to be strong enough to go to Durham tomorrow."

I nodded and took a bite of the hamburger. "This is cold," I mumbled through a mouthful.

"I can't help it if you slept for hours and hours," he teased, but it was forced.

"Ever heard of a microwave?"

He laughed and took the plate from me. "Glad to see you're feeling better. I'll be right back, Diva Princess."

"Cold hamburgers are disgusting," I called after him.

He'd been gone for several seconds when I heard a pounding on the front door.

"*Curse Keeper.*" My title floated through the house with authority, rippling through the air as though it were smoke. This was different from any other time I'd had a house call. I could feel it in the simmering burn in the mark on my hand.

Pure unadulterated panic shot through my body. After my most recent experience, I definitely didn't feel prepared to face anything supernatural. But I scooted to the edge of the bed and put my bare feet on the floor.

Halfway across the living room, I heard the pounding again.

"What the hell do you think you're doing?" Collin asked in disbelief, standing in the kitchen doorway.

"Getting this visit over with. It won't go away until I answer, and they usually last for less than a minute."

"You need to go back to bed." He sounded angry. And scared.

I stopped in front of the door, the knob in my hand. I turned to him, wariness washing through me. "You re-marked the doors, didn't you?"

"Will you stop this madness if I tell you no? You're in no condition to deal with a supernatural visitor."

Collin had marked my doors for over a month when he thought I was safe. There's no way he would have left them unmarked when I was in this state. Before he could stop me, I pulled the door open.

I gasped when I saw who was on the other side.

Okeus.

His eyebrows lifted in a bored expression. "Ellie, you have a penchant for finding trouble."

"Uh . . ." I was literally speechless. I'd had plenty of visits at my door since the curse broke, but never from Okeus. He always had me brought to him. His terms, his location. My eyes shot to the door. Had Collin tricked me? No, the familiar symbols covered the door in heavy charcoal, joined by ones I'd never seen before.

"May I come in?" the god asked with a wry grin.

At least I was starting to regain my senses. "No."

"No?" he asked equally amused and irritated. "I'm surprised the spirit world hasn't given you another title to add to your growing list."

"And what's that?"

"Defier of the gods."

When I didn't respond with one of my usual barbed answers, Okeus became more serious.

"I sent Mekewi to warn you about the Raven Mockers."

"The wind god of the south?" I grabbed the side of the door and leaned into it before I fell over. "Yeah, his warning was pretty vague. You might want to start sending more helpful messages. A copy of *Killing Raven Mockers for Dummies* would have been a nice place to start."

A smirk lifted his lips. "And if I gave you such a manual, would you let me in?"

"Hell no."

His grin fell. "You nearly died, witness to creation. You're no good to me dead."

I put a hand over my heart. "That is one of the sweetest things anyone has ever said to me. I suppose you want me to say I'm sorry?" When he didn't respond, I snorted. "A big powerful god like you didn't send one of his abominations to protect his potential brood mare. Sounds like somebody messed up."

Okeus's eyes glowed bright red, and he released a loud roar that shook the house and made my ears ring.

Collin was behind me in seconds. "It was my fault. She was in my care. I tried to stop her from engaging with the Raven Mockers, but she's persistent. She was attacked before I could stop her or them."

Okeus turned his evil gaze on Collin. "If a Raven Mocker comes anywhere near her again, you are to get rid of it without hesitation. Is that understood?"

Collin's body stiffened. "Yes."

"Good."

I'd never seen Collin so subservient, and I had to admit I didn't like it.

"Elinor," Okeus said with an air of authority. "Tomorrow night you will receive a very powerful weapon. Ahone wants you to use it to help him."

"Let me guess—you want me to use it to help you instead?"

"Ahone will use you again and he will demand another sacrifice. I'm sure you can imagine who."

"David," I whispered, fresh terror washing through me.

"Ahone has distanced himself from his children for so long he no longer knows how to show them love and mercy. He wishes to separate you from all that you love so that you will be dependent on him. But Ellie, I assure you that I wish to show you my kindness."

"For a price," I said, but my fight was gone. Only horror was left.

"Everything comes with a price. You pay for everything you own and use, from your clothing, to your food, to the shampoo that makes you smell of spring flowers."

I wasn't sure I liked that Okeus was so familiar with my scent.

"You wear Ahone's mark, yes, but you can still choose me. I will give you what he chooses to take: I will protect the people you love."

My heartbeat thudded in my ears and Collin pressed his chest into my back. I felt him tense.

"I know you don't trust me, and I understand why," Okeus said, placing his hand on his chest. "I give you my word, Curse Keeper. If you agree to my arrangement, I will save the people you love. You only have to name them, and they will be protected."

"From everything? The demons and Ahone?"

"Yes, if you agree."

Could it really be that easy? I could make sure David, Myra, Claire, Drew, and Collin were kept safe from all the threats around us.

Then he added, "But the arrangement has changed."

Weariness washed over me. Of course it had. "You and I both know that you can forcibly impregnate me anytime you want. So why is my cooperation so important to you?"

"Because I see the potential in you. And let us not pretend that if I forced you to carry my child, I wouldn't then have to imprison you to make sure you didn't harm it. To do so would break your spirit, and it's that spirit I need to create the perfect children that would result from our union."

"Before, you wanted me to have your baby. What do you want now?"

"For you to be my partner."

This couldn't be happening. "What does that mean?"

"Ellie, you will be my queen, the mother of a new race. You will be revered and loved for all eternity. And the humans you love will be protected."

My mouth opened, but no words came out.

"I will save David from the Guardians. If you agree right this moment, I'll have him retrieved and delivered to you within the hour."

I shook my head in dismay. "Queen? What does that mean?"

He grinned. "Ellie, you are a bright woman, which is one of the things I most appreciate about you. You know what it means."

I stared at him, trying to wrap my head around his words.

"You will be an excellent queen. Our many children will love you, and you will never be alone again."

Many children?

"I sense your reluctance to make such a big decision so hastily," he said, his voice lowering. "So you have until tomorrow night to decide. While considering your answer, think about this . . ." He leaned closer to the doorway. "I am not the only one who wants you for your power, but I'm the only one who's offering you something in return. Who's the malevolent one now?"

Then he was gone.

❧ CHAPTER TWENTY-THREE ❧

Collin pulled me backward into the house and shut the door. "You need to go back to bed."

I was still numb with shock. "I could have saved David—right now—and I didn't do it." My voice broke. "*I didn't do it.*"

He grabbed my shoulders, his eyes penetrating mine. "Ellie, you can't make a decision like that on the spot, not even to save David."

I started to protest, but he shook his head. "Ellie, I know you love him. I can feel it when we're connected; your love for him fills me until I'm choking on it. This isn't some crush. It's the real fucking deal. Do I like it? No, I hate it." Anger blazed in his eyes, then just as quickly faded. "But I love you. I'm the one who made your life this hell"—he grabbed the side of my head, his fingers digging into my hair—"but I'm going to help you fix it."

Being this close to him sent my hormones into overdrive, and I pressed my chest against him, lifting my mouth to his before I could stop myself. Fresh horror washed over me. I might love David, but I was still irresistibly drawn to Collin.

"Ellie, don't be ashamed," Collin murmured. "We can't help the way we feel. It's part of the curse. I think Ahone's plan is that my overwhelming attraction to you will be my downfall."

I blinked up at him through tears. Collin's destiny had been determined by Ahone just like mine was. Only Collin had been set up for destruction because of what his father had done and because I was a witness to creation. I was just as responsible for Collin's predicament as I was for David's. "I'm sorry."

"You didn't do anything wrong. You called it hormones and magic. Maybe you're right. Maybe this connection between us isn't real. Maybe it's all an illusion. So we'll just keep trying to fight it."

He was right. So why did his words make me feel so lost?

He took a deep breath and released his hold on me. "I mean what I said. I'll help you save David. The offer still stands."

The weight of his words settled on me. "You mean you'll help me if I choose not to accept Okeus's offer?" I shook my head. "He won't like it."

He put an arm around my back and steered me into the bedroom. "You need to get more sleep. You need your energy for tomorrow."

"Will you stay with me?" I asked. I knew it was a bad idea, but I couldn't be alone.

A war raged in his eyes before he gently pushed me to a sitting position on the bed. "I'll bring your once-again cold hamburger and sit with you until you go to sleep."

"Thank you."

When he returned with the rewarmed food, he sat on David's side, fully clothed, his back pressed against the headboard. He watched me eat half the hamburger before he shifted on the bed. "Tsagasi helped put some things in perspective earlier."

I put the burger on my plate and turned to face him. "Like what?"

"My role in all of this." He looked into my eyes. "Ellie, I'm going to help you."

"You mean tomorrow night? You already told me you would, and I know the sacrifice it entails. It means more to me than you know, Collin."

"No. Not just tomorrow night." He paused. "From here on out."

I inhaled sharply and jerked backward to get a better view of his face. "What?"

"You're not seriously considering Okeus's offer, are you?"

"I don't know," I whispered. "I have the chance to save everyone I love. How can I reject it offhand?"

"You don't want to be his queen."

I shrugged and looked away from him. "There are worse things than being a queen." Thinking about being his queen was preferable to thinking about mothering the new race he envisioned. Would they be monsters like his other biological children? Could I love them?

"You know he's not telling you everything." He grabbed my hand, wrapping his fingers around my palm. "Okeus is a tricky bastard. He might save the people you love, but that doesn't mean you'll get to be with them. You might never see them again if he has his way."

I took a deep breath. "I know. But to really love someone means that you're willing to give them up to save them, right?" My hand tightened around his. "Maybe this is the one last good thing I can do before . . ." Before I became the mother to monsters.

"Do you really think David wants you to sacrifice yourself to save him? *Seriously?*" There was no recrimination in his voice, only insistence. "And Claire. Hell, she'll track you down to wherever Okeus lives and drag you back herself."

I laughed, but it had to squeeze past the lump in my throat. "And what about you?" I asked.

"What *about* me?" He sounded gruff.

"Your name will be on my list, Collin. What will you do?"

He grabbed my chin and tipped my face up so that our eyes met. "If you give yourself over to him to save me, I will find the fucking Sword of Galahad, hunt Okeus down, and neuter the bastard myself."

I gasped at the intensity in his gaze. I had no doubt that he meant it.

"Ellie, you've decided to turn your back on Ahone. What if I turn mine on Okeus? Tsagasi and his friends declare no allegiance to either god. What if we follow their lead and make our own side?"

I stared at him in disbelief, wondering if I'd heard him wrong.

"We'll find another way, Ellie. I promise. Just trust me. We'll find another way to save everyone."

I nodded, too tired to fight.

He took the plate off my lap and set it on the bedside table. Still sitting up, he pulled me against him, resting my head on his chest. "Get some rest. We have a long day ahead of us. Don't you worry. We're in this together. We'll get David back, and we'll get the weapons too. After we get through tomorrow night, we'll start worrying about the future."

I shook my head slowly. "I can't believe I'm hearing this from you."

"I know. It goes against everything I've been saying since we met, but Tsagasi made a lot of sense. I think he's right."

I fell asleep against his warm chest and woke up to the sunlight streaming through the bedroom window. I was still in the same position, and when I looked up, Collin was sleeping.

He felt me stirring and his eyes cracked open. "Please tell me there is coffee in this house."

"I think there is somewhere."

He leaned to the side to check his phone. "It's already eight. Why don't we get ready to go. We'll find out Steven's schedule so we can ambush him at the university."

"You don't even know that he's guilty." I couldn't believe the seemingly sweet, kind man who had been friends with my parents—and was dating my stepmother—might have arranged for David to be kidnapped. But I couldn't ignore David's suggestion that he was involved somehow.

"I'm going to presume he's guilty until he proves otherwise."

"That's not how the United States works, Collin," I said.

He lifted his eyebrows. "Obviously you've only been on the right side of the law, or you'd think differently."

"Maybe you can take this opportunity to get on the right side of the law."

He laughed. "I think it's too late for that. Now get ready. I need coffee."

Sleep and food had helped restore some of my strength, but I was still slower and weaker than normal. I was definitely in no shape to fight demons, let alone gods. Hopefully, when we got back to the Outer Banks, the ocean would revive my strength.

I was still caked in blood, so I showered and then dressed in the clothes I'd worn on Sunday. Myra would be sure to notice, but everything else I had was covered in gore—my own, Allison's, and Raven Mockers'. I hoped this wouldn't become a trend.

When I emerged from the bathroom fully dressed, towel-drying my hair, Collin filled me in on his progress. He had called Steven's office, claiming to be a student, and asked about his office hours.

"He has an eight-thirty class, and then he's going to have office hours from ten until eleven-thirty."

"So when do you want to go?"

"The earlier the better. I want to cut him off before he makes it to his office after his class. He'll be in his own environment there, which will give him an edge. If we catch him on the go, it'll shake things up in our favor."

"Okay." I still felt wrong about not warning Myra that Steven could have betrayed us, but we had no proof. At this point it was a wild guess. And unlike Collin, I really did believe in the presumption of innocence.

"Let's drive over to Durham now. It might take us a while to find parking."

It turned out that Collin was right. We spent twenty minutes looking for a place to park and another ten minutes locating the history building. The campus was bustling with the excitement of the new school year, but I was full of dread, especially since my palm started to itch as we walked past the library.

"Did you feel that?" I asked, turning to Collin.

"Yeah," he mumbled with a scowl.

"I've had that same itch off and on for a couple of weeks. Like something's there but not."

"I think the smarter demons are figuring out how to camouflage themselves," he said as we approached the door to the history building. "We'll have to be more careful."

"Great." But I could see the truth in his words. If there was a way to hide from us, it made sense that some of them had figured it out.

Collin held the door open and followed me inside. "Back to Steven . . . our biggest question right now is if he typically keeps his class the entire time it's scheduled or if he likes to let them out early," he said, watching the students pass us in the hall. "Does he enjoy hearing himself talk?"

I glanced up at him with a scowl. "What kind of question is that?"

He tilted his head to the side with a smirk. "Does he talk a lot or not?"

I shook my head and admitted, "He talks a lot."

"Then we go to his classroom."

When we reached the second floor, I peered into his classroom, which was still full. Students furiously typed notes into their laptops while Steven stood at the front of the class.

"Good call," I said. "He's still lecturing."

Collin shrugged with a smug grin. "So now we need a plan. We'll catch him by surprise. Introduce me as a friend."

"He knows that David's living with me. He's going to think it's weird for me to be here with you."

"Then tell him I'm a colleague of David's."

I looked him up and down, taking in his T-shirt and faded jeans, which hung on his hips in a very alluring way. I felt myself flush.

"Eyes up, Ellie. Focus."

I cringed.

He chuckled. "You don't think I look like a college professor?"

"Not just that. I'm sure Steven probably knows anyone who's important enough to work on anything Roanoke related."

"Then tell him I'm a family friend and don't elaborate."

"If he tells Myra, she'll instantly know who you are."

"I don't care what he finds out about me after we leave. Right now we need the upper hand."

"Okay." This still felt wrong, but if there was the slightest chance he knew something that might help David, it was worth it, consequences be damned.

Collin put his hand on my arm and lowered his voice. "Don't tell him anything about David being taken. Let's see if he shows any signs of knowing it when we start asking questions. I'll be able to tell if he feels guilty about something."

I nodded. That sounded smart. "But he's going to wonder why I'm not with David. And Myra knows I was in Chapel Hill with David this weekend. I had breakfast with her on Sunday."

His head lowered closer to mine. "Was Steven there?"

"No, she wanted to talk to me alone. I was fine with it since I wanted to consult her about selling the inn."

He froze. "You're selling it?"

I sucked in a deep breath, the pain of my decision stabbing me with guilt once again. "Now's not the time to discuss that."

"Ellie," his hand tightened on my arm. "You gave up everything for that place. You hawked the cup on multiple occasions to get money to keep it afloat. How can you just let it go?"

Now he sounded like Myra, making me once again question my decision. "Sometimes you have to know when to let something go. Just like this topic." I heaved a sigh. I had enough to worry about without adding the inn to the mix. "I'll tell Steven you're a family friend; then what do we do?"

"Tell him you have a question about the colony. He's an early-American history buff, right?"

I couldn't hold back a smart-ass grin. "If you want to call a master's and a PhD in the topic a *buff*, then yes."

He laughed. "Ask him if he found any weapons when he was there, particularly swords, and we'll see how he reacts."

"But we're not interested in weapons at the colony."

"Right, but it will provide a natural segue into the work of the Guardians. If he's involved with them, he's going to know about them collecting the artifacts. Once you get him talking about weapons, let me take over."

"Okay."

Five minutes later, the door to Steven's classroom opened and students poured out of the room as Collin pulled me around the corner to another hall. We waited several minutes and I was starting to worry that we'd missed him when I saw him round the corner, looking down at a stack of folders in his hand.

"That's him." I moved toward him, Collin following close behind me. My heart raced, and I forced myself to breathe normally. If Steven was involved, or if he at least knew something, I needed to get as much information from him as possible. Freaking out wouldn't help a thing.

"Steven!" I called out, sounding bright and happy. I had no idea how I pulled it off when I felt like I was about to throw up. Maybe Collin was right about me being a natural con artist.

Steven looked up, confusion flickering on his face, then smiled when he caught sight of me. "Ellie, what a wonderful surprise. What are you doing here?" He didn't act like a man who was wracked with guilt over the kidnapping of his colleague and the boyfriend of his girlfriend's daughter.

"David's in Chapel Hill doing some research. I'm surprised Myra didn't tell you."

"She did, but she said you were headed back yesterday."

"We got delayed."

Steven's gaze had turned to Collin, not that it was surprising. Collin had a commanding presence, despite what he said about his ability to go unnoticed. I was far from convinced that he was capable of blending in anywhere.

"Steven, this is my friend, Collin."

His eyes flickered with uncertainty for a moment before his mouth stretched into a smile. He extended his hand. "Hello, Collin."

"Nice to meet you Dr. Godfrey," Collin said, shaking his hand.

"What are you two doing at Duke? I believe Myra has a free period this morning if you're hoping to see her."

I smiled up at him. "Actually, I wanted to see you."

"Me?"

"David has come across some interesting information in his research. I was hoping to ask you a specific question about what you found at the colony while you were there."

"Why didn't David just call?"

Oh, crap. *Think, Ellie. Think.* "There was a departmental staff meeting today. Since he's been out of town, he felt he should go." I leaned closer. "He wanted to cross-reference some information he found in the library, which is why he asked me to talk to you." My smile widened. "I hope that's okay."

His forehead wrinkled and he looked unconvinced. "Sure, but can we talk on the way to my office? I believe I have a student waiting for me."

"Of course."

I fell into step beside him, with Collin on his opposite side. Steven cast him a quizzical glance and then turned to me. "What do you need to know?"

"Did you find any weapons at the site? Maybe some spears or swords?"

"Or any other weapons of significance," Collin added.

Steven slowed and his face paled. He glanced at Collin and back to me before he continued to walk. "Of course, Ellie. It was a colony on the brink of a war. We expected them to have weapons, and they did."

A heaviness filled my heart. It was obvious from Steven's reaction that he was involved, and although Collin said he'd take over the questioning, I saw another way to draw Steven out that wouldn't occur to Collin. "David's ex-girlfriend was an expert on weapons from the Middle Ages. She told me about a special sword from the Crusades. She showed me a photo of it too."

He rubbed his forehead, breaking eye contact. "Myra mentioned that you were in Chapel Hill this weekend because David's ex-girlfriend had seen a collection of weapons and he wanted to speak with her about it."

Sweat broke out at the base of my head. I only told Myra David was meeting a colleague—no other details.

Collin moved in front him. "Dr. Godfrey, do you happen to know anything about the Ricardo Estate?"

His mouth opened then closed like a fish's.

"Ellie's mother spoke to you about it fifteen years ago. I'm sure you remember it. It happened shortly before her murder."

Steven took several more steps before stopping and turning back to look at him. "And who are you again?"

"I'm Ellie's friend." His face hardened. "And you didn't answer the question."

Steven turned to me, anger tensing his shoulders. "Ellie, what is the meaning of this? Does David know this man is here?"

"Steven, I'm sorry." I tried to look contrite, but I had to force it. I wanted to punch him in the face myself, but we were already showing too much of our hand. We'd be lucky to get him to give anything away. "Collin is a family friend."

"You didn't answer the question, Dr. Godfrey," Collin repeated. "What do you know about the collection that got David's ex-girlfriend killed on Saturday night?"

Obviously, Collin had assumed the bad cop role.

Steven's face turned white. "I don't have to answer anything." He swallowed. "In fact, I'm going to call security."

"Steven, please," I said.

He looked around, his eyes wild, before pinning me with his gaze. "Ellie you need to stay out of this."

I grabbed his arm. "I can't . . . because of David. Please."

"I'm sorry. I can't help you." He shrugged off my hand and took two steps down the hall, which had gotten more crowded in the last minute.

"We know about the Guardians," Collin said.

Steven stopped and turned around, his face expressionless. "What did you say?"

"We know about the Guardians." Collin took a step closer and lowered his voice. "And we know what they're doing."

He spun around, hurrying toward the open elevator car at the end of the hall. We ran after him but had to push our way through a group of students, and the doors closed before we could reach it.

"Now what do we do?" I asked.

"He obviously has information we need, so we'll stake out his office. He said he was meeting with a student, although that might have been a ruse to get rid of us."

"Do you think he knows about David?"

"No. If this group has levels of membership, he must be at a very low level. He sucks at subterfuge. He gave away so much without even saying a single word, but he asked if David knew you were here with me and he didn't look like he was being coy. He doesn't know what happened."

"So what is his involvement?"

"I suspect they use him to get information, but give him little in return."

Just as I pushed the elevator call button, the doors opened and Myra walked out. Her eyes widened and she stopped in her tracks. "Ellie! What are you doing here? I thought you left yesterday."

"We had to come back. I needed to ask Steven a few questions."

She moved to the side, grabbing my hand and pulling me with her.

My palm tingled.

I looked up at her wide-eyed. Why was my palm burning now? My gaze fell to the base of her throat. She was wearing a round pendant with symbols raised in bas-relief. "Myra, what's that?"

Her hand lifted to it. "This? After Steven saw the markings on my door, he gave me this on Sunday night. Wasn't that sweet of him?"

My stomach dropped. "I don't think it's safe, Myra. You need to take it off."

"Ellie, what's gotten into you? Is this your way of getting back at me for bringing up my concerns about David?"

"What? No!"

"Then what are you doing here? You said you wanted to ask Steven questions. What kind of questions?"

"About something he may have found at the colony site."

"You could have just called him." She cast a glance to Collin.

I considered introducing her to Collin. While she'd never met him in person, she knew enough about him from what little I'd told her to disapprove. Ignoring him seemed the best policy unless she asked. "We stuck around Chapel Hill yesterday, so I thought I'd just come over and see him. And of course you."

"I wish I had more time to spend with you, but I'm on my way to a class. Will you be around for lunch?"

"No," Collin said. "We need to get going."

"Oh." She frowned at Collin. "Well, I guess this will just be a quick hello and good-bye then." She hugged me tight and whispered in my ear. "Be careful, Ellie. Think this through, and don't let poor David get hurt." She pulled back and cast a dark scowl at Collin before hurrying down the hall.

"I don't think your stepmother likes me much." He laughed. "I can usually charm the mothers. It's the fathers who tend to hate me."

"Wow, that's a shocker," I said sarcastically as I watched her round the corner. "She's worried I'm going to hurt David by being with you."

Collin's smile fell. "Let's go find Dr. Godfrey and then get on the road to Manteo. David told them the location was by the aquarium, so I'd like to scope it out and find a possible place to use as our supposed gate to Popogusso."

"Let's make it next to the sound. Who knows, Big Nasty might show up to help me."

"Good idea."

We took the stairs up one flight, looking for Steven's office. When we found it, the door was locked and several students were waiting in the hall.

"Have you seen Professor Godfrey?" Collin asked.

A guy who looked like he should be in high school frowned. "No, but I had an appointment with him and he hasn't shown up."

A woman walked past the group, casting a glance at the closed door. "Dr. Godfrey won't be in for the rest of the day. I just ran into him in the hallway. He was rushing out the door and he told me he was going home sick."

Collin's eyebrows shot up. "Come on. Let's go."

When we left the building and were walking across campus, Collin looked down at me. "Do you have a home address for him? He's sure to have it unlisted to keep students from showing up at his house."

I pulled my phone out of my purse. "I think I have his cell phone number *and* his address from when Myra first started visiting him here." I pulled up my list of contacts. "Here it is. Myra was paranoid about leaving me alone, so she made sure I had lots of contact information for her." I rattled off the street address.

"Good. We'll head over there, but I suspect we might be too late. He's scared and he's running. When a herd animal is scared, it almost always runs to its herd for protection. If we can find him, we might be able to follow him to the Guardians."

The embers of hope kindled, but I kept the feeling contained. There were a lot of what-ifs in following him to the Guardians, and even more what-ifs in him leading us to David. And along with the hope came disappointment. One more person had hurt me. I'd trusted Steven. He'd slept in my house, and he'd convinced Myra to move to Durham. Did he intend to hurt her? My head swam with questions and overwhelming heartache. I wasn't sure how much more I could take.

I turned to look at Collin, now unsure about everything. If I couldn't trust Steven, who could I trust? I stopped on the sidewalk and someone bumped into my back. I stumbled forward as Collin took several more steps before realizing I wasn't with him.

He turned around, a quizzical look on his face. "Ellie?"

Would Collin betray me again too? I was far from certain that I could handle it if he did.

He closed the distance between us, searching my face. "What's wrong?"

"Can I trust you?"

Confusion flickered in his eyes along with something else. Anger? Disappointment? He grabbed my right hand and cradled it between both of his, the mark on my palm tingling from the proximity to Collin's.

I tried to pull away, but he held me in place.

"Collin, if you plan to betray me in any way tonight, whether it's out of your control or not, just leave me here and I'll find my own way back to Manteo." My voice broke.

His face softened. "Ellie."

Tears filled my eyes. "I'm letting you get close to me again, and if you go behind my back to help Okeus or someone else, I don't think I can take it. It will destroy me. So *please*, Collin, I beg you, if that's what you're doing, just leave me here."

He shook his head. "No. I promise you, I'm supporting you all the way in this thing. I won't trick you or betray you." He grabbed my shoulders and tipped his face down to mine. "I know the fact that Steven is part of this is screwing with your head. And if he had anything to do with your mother's involvement—I know it's making you doubt everything. I don't blame you, but I swear to you, Ellie, that I will never again do anything to intentionally hurt you." His hand cupped my face, tilting it up to him. "I finally realize where my real priorities lie."

A fire of lust spread through my body and it took all my willpower not to stand on my tiptoes and kiss him. But if I was asking Collin not to betray me, I owed the same to David. I took a step back and Collin's hands fell to his sides.

"Let's see if we can find Steven and have him lead us to David." Then he turned and started walking again, leaving me to follow.

Why did I have the feeling that I was now betraying Collin?

Chapter Twenty-Four

Steven wasn't home when we got there. I wasn't surprised, but the disappointment was heavier than I'd expected it to be. With no other leads, there was nothing left to do except go back to Manteo.

We were both quiet as we left Steven's neighborhood, and the morning had exhausted me. Collin stopped somewhere in Durham to pick up an early lunch, and I fell asleep as soon as we got back in the car. I didn't wake up until I heard Collin's voice.

"Ellie, we're here."

I blinked and looked around, confused that we were parked on the side of the road and surrounded by sand dunes. "Where?"

"Pea Island. I thought it might be more private here."

"The beach?"

"Yeah."

It was a good choice. I wasn't sure why I hadn't thought of it before. Pea Island Wildlife Refuge was only a fifteen-minute drive from Nags Head, but it wasn't as touristy.

He got out of the truck and I followed his lead, meeting him at the front of the vehicle. "If we hike over the dunes here, we'll be close to the ocean."

I kicked off my Vans and carried them in my hand as we climbed a tall sand dune. I could hear and smell the ocean before I saw it. I stopped at the top and took in the view, surprised and elated that just the sight of the ocean could energize me.

Collin had taken several steps down the other side, but he stopped to look back, his face filled with worry.

I started down, the call of the ocean irresistible. Once I was at the bottom of the dune, I passed him, dropped my shoes on the sand about ten feet from the tidal edge, then waded out into the water. Collin stayed on the shore behind me as a surge of power rushed through my body and I once again experienced the familiar yet always intoxicating sensation of the Manitou of every living thing in the ocean. My eyes sank closed as I gave myself to the moment, letting the vibrant life force remind me of what was really at stake. Not just David or me or Collin; not even just the fate of humanity. As Tsagasi said, the fate of every being in creation was in danger. I wasn't sure what Okeus and Ahone had planned, but I had no doubt that it risked all of us.

I walked deeper into the water, my eyes still closed, unaware of how long I had been there until I sensed Collin in front of me, taking my hand in his before I could think to stop him.

His feelings surged through me, his love, his need to prove that I could trust him. Without thinking, I moved closer to him until I was plastered against his chest. The other half of the Manitou joined with the half I had already experienced. The animals and the plants of the land flooded my head, and while I should have been overwhelmed, I felt nearly complete instead.

I looked up into his face, and the tenderness there caught my breath. His free hand reached for my cheek and his mouth lowered to mine, but then he stopped. "I want you to trust me, Ellie. With everything else you have to worry about, I don't want this doubt to distract you. Do you trust me?"

"Yes."

His hand let go of mine and I stumbled. He wrapped an arm around my back and held me against him for several seconds. To finally be able to trust him was an amazing gift.

Collin offered me a grim smile. "Now let's get ready to save David."

We were quiet as we walked back to the truck, but I was amazed by how much the power of the ocean had helped me regain all my strength. I knew I'd need every bit of it and then some to survive the night.

There was so much against us, not just the Guardians and the challenge of getting David back, but the Raven Mockers and the gods. Okeus's offer, Ahone's plans. Part of me was weary of the whole mess. I had no idea how to fight them all. The best course of action was to deal with them one at a time. Which meant facing the Guardians first.

My cell phone rang as we headed back to Manteo. Tom was on the other end. I plugged my other ear with my finger to hear the call over the wind rushing through the windows.

"Ellie, there were four more deaths last night."

"I'm on my way back, Tom."

"Are you any closer to finding who's in charge of these things?"

I didn't have the heart to tell him that I hadn't even had the chance to look. "No. I'm still working on it."

"We can't tell everyone in town to put salt on their thresholds, Ellie."

"I don't know what else to tell you, Tom," I snapped.

Collin shot a curious look in my direction.

"Look, I'm doing the best I can. David went to see the Ricardo collection and they kidnapped him."

"What did the police in Charlotte say?"

"We didn't call them." Funny how I'd never even considered it as an option.

There was a pause. "Dr. Preston was kidnapped and you didn't think to call the police? What the hell, Ellie?"

I cringed. "Tom, you know that I can't tell the police about any of this crap. Calling the police is at the bottom of my list of resources."

"Were they humans?" When I didn't answer, he continued. "You should have called the police."

I couldn't help but wonder if he was right. "We're getting him back." I shifted my gaze to Collin.

He shook his head, his mouth pursed.

"How?" Tom asked, sounding skeptical.

Even without Collin's warning, I had no intention of giving Tom any information. "Don't worry about it. We have it under control."

"You keep saying 'we.' Who's we? Collin? Is he working with you now?"

"The less you know the better, Tom." I quickly ended the conversation, cursing myself for telling him anything about David. But then I wondered if I should have told him more. The Guardians were human. The police could deal with them, but then again a secret society didn't last hundreds of years by acting stupid. If I involved Tom, it could get him killed.

"What do you want to do?" Collin asked. "It's seven thirty. I think we should get something to eat and then head to the aquarium and scope it out. We need all the advantage we can get."

I was letting Collin take charge again, but I didn't have a better plan. And disagreeing for the sake of being in control was stupid. "Okay."

Collin stopped at a gas station and filled up the tank while I went inside and bought a couple of deli sandwiches, chips, and water. We drove in silence as we ate our food.

My phone rang as Collin pulled into the aquarium lot. When I dug it out of my pocket, I wasn't surprised to see Claire's number on the screen.

"Claire—"

"My ghost is freaking out, Ellie."

Fear shot through my chest. "What are you talking about?"

"She says you're in danger. So much danger."

My mouth went dry and I swallowed. "Hold on, Claire. I'm going to put you on speaker so we can both talk to you." I pressed the speaker button, then held the phone next to me.

"Who? You and David?"

Oh, God. She didn't know. I'd spent most of yesterday unconscious, so I hadn't had a chance to check in with her. "No. Me and Collin."

"Collin? Where's David?" She sounded panicked.

"The people who have the collection kidnapped him."

"Oh, my God, Ellie!"

"Collin and I are in the process of getting him back." I had to believe we'd be successful.

"No wonder Mary's so upset."

"Mary?" I asked, confused.

"Yeah, I finally got a name out of her even though she's still not coming through clearly and she gets pissed when I call her that. Do you have any relatives named Mary? That perhaps went by a *nickname*?" Judging from her mocking inflection, I gathered that the ghost must have been close to her.

"Uh . . ." I rubbed my temple. "I had a great-aunt Mary who went by Bitty." Why were we discussing my relatives when I needed to prepare to save David? We had absolutely no plan at all. This was going to backfire and get all three of us killed.

"Maybe that's her." Claire seemed relieved. "Aunt Bitty says you're in danger. Especially David."

"Then the crazy-ass ghost of Great-Aunt Bitty is Captain Obvious," Collin muttered. "He's been kidnapped and they've threatened to kill him. That's about as dangerous as it gets."

I shot Collin a scowl. I didn't need the sarcasm, and I certainly didn't need the reminder of the gravity of David's situation.

"Aunt Bitty says you need the ring, but not how you think."

My gaze locked with Collin's. "How do I need it?" I asked.

"Each time she tries to tell me, the words are garbled." I could hear the frustration behind her voice.

"If you find out, will you let me know?"

"Of course." Claire paused. "Ellie, there's one more thing. The blackness surrounding your house has gotten worse in just the last hour. And it keeps getting blacker and blacker."

My stomach twisted. "What does it mean?"

"Evil."

I hung up and stared at the phone.

Collin's eyes narrowed. "Do you really trust a crazy-ass ghost?"

I gave him a wry smile. "Okeus says I can."

He rolled his eyes. "Well, if Okeus says so . . . We know how trustworthy *he* is." He opened the truck door and moved to the tailgate and climbed onto the bed.

I got out and followed him. Talk about a total about-face. Only a few days ago he was trying to convince me that Okeus was the way, the truth, and the life.

He started to open the toolbox attached to the rear of the truck bed when he squatted and stared into my eyes. "Are you going to accept Okeus's offer?"

My gaze lowered to his feet. "I . . . I haven't made a final decision yet."

"Can we discuss it right now? Because I'd like to say my piece before you decide."

My eyes widened. "Okay."

He moved to the end of the bed and sat down on the open tailgate, patting the spot next to him. Once I was seated, he didn't waste any time. "*Why* would you accept Okeus's offer?"

"To save you. And David and Claire and Drew and Myra. To save the people I love."

He swallowed but he didn't look at me, staring instead at the small county airport next to the aquarium. "So let's say you become Okeus's queen and you save all of us, but you get pregnant with Okeus's babies. Do you really think you can love them and raise them?"

I shook my head. "I don't know. I can't let myself think about that."

"That's *exactly* what you need to think about. And when your *many* babies grow up and become the monsters their father is, how will you deal with that?"

I closed my eyes.

"Let's go ahead and ignore the fact that not one of us could live with ourselves if you made this decision. Let's even ignore that you'd be lonely as shit. Despite what Okeus says, you will be utterly and eternally alone. And eternity is a fucking long time." His hands curled around the edge of the tailgate. "But let's not ignore what those creatures will do when they are grown. They will kill and destroy. You may have saved Claire and her husband, but you haven't saved their children. And that's the mind-fuck Okeus will play on you. He'll kill their kids. Or, hell, maybe he'll make *your* kids do it."

The truth struck me with mind-numbing horror. He was right.

"So tonight, when he asks you for your answer, tell him to go fuck himself, Ellie. Because not one damn good thing will come from saying yes."

I bit my lip to keep from crying and nodded.

"Promise me. Promise me on David's life."

I gasped.

His jaw set. "I have to be sure. You need to be able to trust me, but I need to be able to trust you too."

"I promise I won't accept his offer."

He stood, stomped to the toolbox, and lifted the lid. "Come here."

I got up and stood next to him, surprised by how serious he looked. "Elinor Dare Lancaster, Curse Keeper, daughter of the sea, witness to creation." He pulled out the sword and handed it to me.

My right hand encircled the grip, and his right hand covered mine, sending a surge of power from his mark into mine. I looked up at him in surprise.

His eyes were trained on my face. "I promise to stand by your side and defy the gods. To forge our own destiny. From tonight and forward, we will work together to defeat the demons and send them back to Popogusso. We will fight to protect all of creation from the evil that we—*I*—set free. And I promise to stand with you until the end, whenever that comes."

I shook my head in shock. "Collin . . ."

"Now let's figure out how to save David, because we need 'he who guides the Curse Keeper' if we have any hope of defeating these guys in the future."

I nodded as he dropped his grip. "Thank you."

"Don't thank me yet," he mumbled, shutting the lid. "We have an uphill battle ahead of us." He walked to the end of the bed and jumped down. "I'm still not sure returning that sword to you is the brightest idea, but I feel better knowing you have some way of defending yourself." When I reached the edge of the tailgate, he grimaced. "Try not to impale yourself when you hop down."

I twisted my mouth into a mocking smile. "Very funny." I held the sword up and away from me as I jumped and landed on my feet.

Denise Grover Swank

"Let's go survey the grounds and come up with a plan."

We walked around the building toward the sound. We stopped at the edge of the trees to the north of the complex. "I think you're right. If we lead them to a fake gate, we should make it close to the water. If Mishiginebig is still watching out for you, he'll come to your defense."

"If?"

He shrugged. "Well, we do run a risk. I suspect once Okeus figures out you've decided to turn him down, he'll remove all protection from you in the hope of forcing your hand. And just like that, Mishiginebig will turn from protector to predator." Collin started to walk into the woods.

"And what will happen when Okeus realizes *you've* defied him?" I asked as I followed him.

He didn't answer.

"That bad?"

"Honestly, Ellie, I don't know. We're making our own rules tonight."

"I need to tell you about the Raven Mocker's prediction for my future."

He stopped and turned around to face me. "A Raven Mocker told you your future? Why didn't you tell me?"

I lifted a hand in frustration. "I don't know. Maybe because I was busy *dying* and all."

"Sarcasm won't help right now."

He was right, damn him. "Look, Collin, I'm sorry. With everything else that's been going on, it slipped my mind. She told me almost a week ago."

"Shit, Ellie." He groaned and lifted his head to look up at the now-darkening sky. "What did it say? It could make all the difference tonight."

"She said I was a vessel that will determine the fate of the world and I will either save it or destroy it. And that it will happen soon."

He watched me for a long moment. "That's it?"

My eyebrow shot up. "That's not *enough*?"

He snorted. "Well, it's vague as shit."

"*Thank you.*" I thrust my hands out from my side. "That's what *I* said."

"What do you think it means?"

"I thought it meant I'd become Okeus's boo. What else would I think?"

He crossed his arms and stared out into the sound. "Remind me of what the ghost of your Aunt Betty said."

"Aunt Bitty. And she said that I need the ring, but not in the way I think."

"Okay." He put his hands on his hips. "How do you think you're supposed to use it?"

"There are letters in the library at UNC at Chapel Hill, and one of them is an eyewitness account of the blessing of the spear and the ring."

"You're kidding?"

I shook my head. "Of course I'm not." I told him about Okeus and Ahone. "So Ahone told my ancestor that a *she* in his line would need the ring and it would save her life. And that if she were to stand next to the tree with the ring that sings and read the inscription, she could permanently seal the gate to hell."

"Is that what you intended to do with it?" Collin asked.

"No," I said in frustration. "I think it's a terrible idea. Ahone's been planning this for centuries, and we both know he's just about as trustworthy as Okeus."

"Your ghost aunt said you need the ring, but not in the way you think. Without her influence, how would you use it?"

"I don't know," I groaned. "I probably wouldn't use it at all."

"Maybe that's the answer. Maybe you *are* supposed to use it."

"Should I really put that much faith in a ghost that's giving me instructions through Claire?"

Collin's shoulders slumped. "Maybe Tsagasi knows something."

"I haven't seen him since Sunday and I'm scared to call him. What if it counts toward the seven times he and his friends agreed to protect me? I don't want to waste the blood oath."

"You just want to ask him a question, so I think you're in the clear. Besides, I think this is important enough to warrant calling him." He paused. "But if you want, I'll try to summon him instead."

"Wait!" My stomach cramped from my nerves. "Let's talk a bit more about this shindig tonight. Maybe it'll help us figure out what to ask Tsagasi."

He nodded. "That's a good idea. And let's figure out where we want the fake gate to be." He stopped next to a tree about twenty feet from the shore. "There's a neighborhood to the north. I'm worried we're too close to people." He ran a hand through his hair. "Maybe we should do this on the dock."

"But what if they expect a tree?" I said. "David tricked them with the aquarium, but what if they know that part? We'll have to find one that's close to the water and hope Big Nasty will help."

"You want a plan, here's one: We lead the Guardians here, we start the words of protection and create a vortex. They won't know it's not the gate. We'll get David and the sword and the spear and then get the hell out of here."

"That's still a sucky plan, Collin."

"And it's the only one we've got."

∿ CHAPTER TWENTY-FIVE ∿

We walked out onto the dock and came up with more details. We'd stand at the back of the dock while Collin used his guile to convince them to show us any warded weapons they had. The threat to my safety would hopefully draw the attention of Big Nasty, and the confusion of a giant snake showing up would help Collin free David and steal the weapons while I added to the chaos. Not to mention I had my own supernatural bodyguard detail at my disposal. And if Big Nasty didn't show, we'd create the vortex and tell them it was the opening to Popogusso.

There was no way in hell it was going to work, but I couldn't come up with anything else.

The sun had begun to set, and I was getting more and more nervous. "We should call Tsagasi now. If nothing else, my four protectors can help us."

"Good idea."

We walked to the edge of the dock when the familiar ringtone of David's phone went off, echoing off the water and trees around us.

I stopped in my tracks, terrified, but I told myself that anyone could be calling him.

Collin was several paces ahead of me, but he spun around to face me as he dug David's phone out of his pocket. He checked the screen and cringed. "Fuck," he muttered before answering. "Yeah." He was silent for several seconds, and then he put his hand on his hip and looked down at the wood planks under his feet. "Fine." After he hung up, he turned to look at me, his face tense.

"What did they say?"

"They changed the location and time."

"What?" I shook my head in frustration. "When? Where?"

"The Elizabethan Botanical Gardens at the five-hundred-year-old oak tree." His eyes locked on mine. "In ten minutes."

I gasped and took a step backward. "But how did they know?"

"I don't know. Does Myra know the location?"

My head was a blur of conflicting emotions and thoughts, but I needed to focus. "No, I don't remember telling her specifically, but it wouldn't be that hard for her to figure it out. Tom found me out there multiple times. He might have told her."

"Or they could have broken David," Collin added, his voice gentle.

"That too." The thought brought me close to the edge of hysteria. But I needed to keep my shit together. Freaking out would get David killed.

"We better get going. We don't know if there's a penalty for being late."

We walked across the parking lot as a small single-engine plane took off from the airport. I was glad for the noise. The eerie stillness of the night made me more nervous.

"What about the sword?" I asked, laying the weapon on the floor at my feet once we got into the truck.

"If we take it, the Guardians might steal it from us. But if we encounter any demons, we'll need it. I say it's worth the risk."

"Do you know how to use one?"

"If you're asking if I'm better with it than you, I'm honestly not so sure. But if you're going to focus on getting the ring back from the old broad, then maybe I should take it. We can still move forward with the plan to form a vortex to confuse them, and once it's open, I'll try to go for David and any weapons they may have."

I nodded. "And Tsagasi?"

"If things get dicey, call him." Collin's hand gripped the steering wheel so tightly, his knuckles were white. "In fact, you should have called him yesterday when we encountered the Raven Mockers."

"You know what they say about hindsight."

"Yeah."

Several other cars were in the parking lot when we pulled in. "Why did they wait so long to call and tell us to come here?" I asked as Collin turned off the engine.

"The same reason we ambushed Steven at the university this morning." He turned to look at me. "To shake us up and throw us off. But we can do this. *You* can do this."

"I still don't know what to do with the ring, Collin."

"You don't even have the ring, so it might turn out to be a non-issue."

"I got the distinct impression she's going to give it back to me to use. What do I do?"

A sly smile lifted his mouth. "You'll figure it out."

I was glad he had so much faith in me. "No pressure. I'm just the salvation or the destruction of the world after all."

"Don't be such a diva." He picked up the sword and got out of the truck while I climbed out on my side. I'd only had the sword for a few days, but I felt naked without it. Still, having Collin carry it was the right decision. He could use it to save David while I created the vortex.

We headed for the back gate, the way we'd gone in almost two months ago. I'd been a different person then. Naïve and blind. My eyes were open to a whole new world now, but I felt as blind as before. I still had so much to learn.

As we entered the gate, a white-hooded figure stepped out from behind a tree and I squelched a shriek.

Collin, on the other hand, was unimpressed. "You've got to be fucking kidding me," he grunted. "I thought you people were the real deal, not some kids playing dress-up."

The man kept his face hidden. "You'll find out how real we are soon enough. Especially since you tried to deceive us about the location."

Clouds blew in and covered the moon. Was it the work of the wind gods? I couldn't imagine the spirit world was happy with these people messing around with the gate. For once, I was actually hoping that demons would show up. Sure, being away from the water meant that Big Nasty wasn't about to come to our rescue, but he wasn't the only creature that went bump in the night in Manteo.

As we rounded the corner to the giant oak tree, I noticed scores of candles on the ground and at least twenty more figures shrouded in white robes. A man was tied to the oak tree, but his face was slumped forward. He was wearing a rumpled blue dress shirt covered in spots of blood and dirt.

David.

He was standing, which meant he was alive. When our guide led us past the tree, I couldn't take my eyes off him, even if I couldn't bring myself to call his name.

Collin moved closer and leaned into my ear. "We're in deep shit, Ellie."

My gaze turned to what he was looking at: a pentagram burned into the grass with candles at the tips. While it looked spooky as hell, I wasn't sure what it meant. But I did have an idea what the rectangular table in the center meant. I looked up at Collin.

His jaw tightened. "They don't want to send the demons back. They want to enslave them."

My head felt fuzzy, especially when I realized they had the weapon to do it. The Sword of Galahad supposedly had the power to subdue gods. Did they plan to enslave Ahone and Okeus? Did they want to use me and the ring to seal the gate shut? If Collin and I were right, we were on our own in this. The demons and spirits might act crazy, but they had to be smart enough to stay away from this mess.

Our guide pointed to a place at the head of the star. "You may stand there."

We had a perfect view of the entire scene. We were directly opposite the tree, and the fifteen-foot pentagram spanned the space in front of us. A golden chalice had been placed at the head of the table, which was covered in a white tablecloth. The robed figures made up two arcs of a circle, the tree on one side, Collin and I at the other.

Terror raced up my spine and I took an involuntary step back.

A man broke free of the circle and moved toward us, staying clear of the pentagram.

"Ellie, Collin, I'm Jeremiah, and I'd like to thank you for joining us this evening." The man's voice echoed off the trees. His chin lifted, pulling the hood back slightly so we could see his pudgy middle-aged face. He wasn't what I'd expected.

David's head jerked up at my name and he looked directly at me. His face was a bloody, swollen mess.

My emotions threatened to overrun my senses, but I had to keep them in check. David—not to mention all of creation—was counting on me.

Collin took a step forward. "Well, an engraved invitation is hard to resist. Only mine didn't mention that it was a white-tie event. Sorry we're not dressed appropriately."

Jeremiah chuckled. "You'll do." He turned his attention to me. "But Ellie, you're the guest of honor tonight." He smirked. "Not to worry, Collin, your presence is still needed."

The man's words elicited a reaction from David, who began to tug at the ropes securing him to the tree.

Collin lifted the sword and moved in front of me, blocking my path. "We were told you'd give me the spear and free Dr. Preston if Ellie and I show you the gate to hell. We'd prefer to play our part, then let you get back to it." He waved the tip of the sword to the group.

"All in good time."

Two figures broke from the group and moved toward me, grabbing my arms. Collin spun around, ready to strike with his sword, but the man on my right lifted a knife to my throat.

Jeremiah pressed his hands together in front of his chest. "Collin, why don't you stand back and give Ellie some room to join me."

My blood pulsed in my head. Collin was right—we were in deep shit. I knew what the table and chalice were for. The Nunnehi had said my blood was strong. Had she been sent to test me just like the Raven Mockers? I'd lost enough blood in the last thirty-six hours, and I really didn't care to share any more. I wanted to call Tsagasi for help, but what if he'd betrayed me too?

Collin reluctantly took a step back but kept his sword in a defensive position.

The man in charge beckoned me with his hand. "Come, Ellie. I'm sure you're eager to be reunited with your ring."

The ring. Surely Ahone hadn't planned for this to happen. Could I use that to my advantage? Plus, I could still use the words of protection. Hell, I'd even ride away with Okeus on his giant snake if it meant getting out of this, because I doubted these people planned to let me live. "Tsagasi," I whispered, reasoning that he was probably hundreds of miles away. If he could hear my regular voice, he could hear a whisper. He and his friends had taken a blood oath to protect me to their death. I had to trust them and their promise. They were one of my last, best hopes.

I took a deep breath and tried to slow my racing heart. "And the Sword of Galahad?"

He laughed. "You'll see it soon enough."

Oh, shit.

David renewed his efforts to break free of his restraints.

"I don't like surprises," I said. "So let's make a deal. I'll be a hell of a lot more cooperative if I know what's going on and what to expect. Why don't you go ahead and fill me in."

His hood had fallen over his forehead again, revealing only his lower face. The image shook a memory free and I was transported to a stormy night fifteen years ago. When Collin's father had worn a hood over his head.

"Collin's father was one of you."

The leader laughed and clapped. "Very good, Ellie."

Collin's mouth dropped open. "*What?*"

Suddenly it was all so clear. "Miriam was lying. You didn't need information from my mother. You needed *me*. Inviting my mother to Charlotte was a ruse."

"At the time, we didn't realize you were too young and wouldn't be ready for another decade. Mr. Dailey came back empty-handed, not to mention quite belligerent."

I remembered Collin saying Steven was a low-level member and would probably run to the group looking for help after we showed up with our questions. Collin's father must have done the same. "You recruited him because you needed him. But he didn't really know why."

"He was needed as a backup plan, just like Collin. We would have considered using your father, Ellie, but we were told to wait for the female Dare Keeper. So we kept waiting, as we had for three hundred years. And once we realized you wouldn't be ready for another ten years, and that Mr. Dailey had a son who was only two years older than you, it was much cleaner to dispose of him and wait for the two of you."

"You killed my father?" Collin asked, his voice gravelly.

Jeremiah released a derisive laugh. "He was hardly an innocent. He murdered Ellie's mother."

"So why wait?" I asked. "Why didn't you instigate this five years ago when I turned eighteen?"

"The timing wasn't right."

Then the answer hit me. "You didn't have the ring. You needed the ring."

The man's mouth twitched. "Admittedly, it was lost. But then Steven told us a couple of weeks ago that you had recovered it."

"He found out from Myra."

He smirked. "Once we knew you had possession of the ring, we could finally achieve our goal."

"To harness the demons to do your will."

Jeremiah nodded. "We will be performing a great public service."

I shook my head. "I don't get it. Why do you need both Collin and me for that?"

"We need you to show us the gate."

I glanced at Collin and gave a slight shake of my head. There was no way I was going to help them. Especially since they planned to kill me anyway.

"But Miriam said you didn't know about the curse."

"Curse?" He paused. "We've never known anything about a curse. But we've known for centuries about the spear and the ring that have power over the demons and gods. And the prophecy has been passed on that the girl who could use the ring would be a descendant of Jonathon Dare, the man who commissioned the Croatan conjurer to bless the objects at the gate to hell."

My mouth dropped open. "How did you know?"

"The letter." He smiled. "The one we sent to the Wilson Library in Chapel Hill several months ago." He took a step forward. "We've watched your family since we stumbled upon the letter. We acquired the ring and the spear in the seventeen hundreds after one of your ancestors became careless with the ring. So we held the weapons for safekeeping and began to accumulate additional weapons that would help us to manage the demons. All in preparation for tonight."

"So we show you the gate, the ring brings all the demons to the yard, and you trap them . . . how?" Their plan didn't make sense. The letter in the library said the ring would seal the gate. From the sounds of it, that was the last thing the Guardians wanted to do.

He hesitated.

So they planned to control the demons with the sword. It didn't take a genius to figure it out, but Jeremiah seemed uncomfortable with how much I'd already deduced. But what about the spear? "Okay, then tell me why you need my blood."

Jeremiah's mouth gaped and he sputtered, "How . . ."

I glanced at the table. "It wasn't hard to figure out."

He swallowed and seemed to regain his confidence. "For the Great One. She has helped us set this in motion, and we have agreed to give you to her in exchange for her assistance."

"Why?"

"The Great One has taken the form of her latest victim, but it comes with limitations. The Great One says your blood will let her stay in one body. She will choose your likeness as an homage."

My blood turned icy and I gaped at Collin. His eyes were wild with fear.

How were we going to get out of this? Why hadn't Tsagasi shown up yet?

"Come, Ellie," the man said, beckoning me again.

"I want the ring."

"All in good time."

"I want the ring *now*." My voice bellowed louder than I anticipated, but I had another resource. These nut jobs might be human, but I suspected they weren't immune to my power as a witness to creation. If only I could figure out how to use it to save us.

He grinned. "Bring me the ring."

A shorter figure stepped forward and placed the ring in the leader's open palm. She looked up with a smirk. Miriam.

Hot anger burned away my fear, and I welcomed it. "I told you I'd make you pay for taking David," I said, surprised to hear how cold my voice was. "I meant it."

A flicker of fear flashed in her eyes. "No need for incivility, Elinor," Miriam murmured.

"Yes, let's keep this all nice and polite. I hope the Great One brought a *napkin*."

Jeremiah released a hearty laugh. "You *are* entertaining."

Miriam shot him a frown of disapproval.

Rebuked, he lowered his chin and then lifted the ring between his thumb and index finger. I held out my left palm and he placed it in the center. As I pulled my hand back, I waited for the singing. Wasn't the ring supposed to sing?

I put the ring on my left middle finger and still nothing. I hoped it was because I held it in my left hand.

"It is time, Ellie."

This wasn't the order things were supposed to take. Weren't we supposed to show them the gate first? But even if I agreed to do that, David was tied to the tree. What would happen if we opened it while he was still tied there? Could we take the risk?

"We need to show you the gate," said Collin, his voice loud and authoritative. And it was obvious to me that he was thinking the same thing I was.

"The Great One believes she only needs the ring. She has opened our eyes since she sought us out a month ago. She wants to help us enslave the wicked spirits, and she has the knowledge and tactics to make our dream a reality at last. You, Mr. Dailey, are here as insurance if something happens to Ms. Lancaster."

"But Ellie needs to be alive for me to show it to you. I can't do it alone." I was amazed how much Collin's voice sounded detached and in control.

I glanced at the table, my heart racing. Had I gambled wrong when I put the ring on my left hand?

The two men who'd grabbed me earlier took hold of my arms and dragged me to the makeshift altar, then lifted me onto the table in a sitting position.

"Ellie," Jeremiah said. "If you'd please cooperate and lie down."

If this wasn't so dire, I'd laugh. So polite. *Ellie, please lie down so we can slaughter you.* But they probably expected me to put up a huge fuss. They probably got off on it.

This was a huge gamble. Probably a stupid one, but David had told me to trust my instincts and every part of me screamed this was the right thing to do. "I'll lie down and I'll let you perform your sacrifice—"

"No!" David shouted.

"—but all I ask is two things. That you don't tie me down, and that you allow me to meet the Great One."

"We'll try the first. The second has already been arranged."

A million butterflies with razors for wings flapped furiously in my stomach. My thumb rubbed the band on the backside of my finger.

"Ellie!" Collin shouted. "What the fuck are you doing?"

I turned to him and stared into his eyes for a long second. "Collin, I'm going to need you soon. To help me finish my sacrifice."

His eyes hardened. "Okay."

He understood. I resisted the impulse to cry with relief. "I have one more request. I want to see the great Sword of Galahad."

The man's voice thinned. "Have no fear, you will see it in a few moments. But I'm curious: Why are you being so cooperative?"

"I've seen what the demons are capable of. I was born and raised to protect humanity. I've proven myself incapable of protecting it on my own. If this will ultimately stop their ravaging, then I willingly make this sacrifice."

"You have proven wise and selfless. We will sing our praise of the martyr who was willing to give herself so others might live. It is good."

The group murmured as one. "It is good."

Goose bumps broke out across my arms.

"Ellie!" David shouted, his arms jerking the ropes so hard it looked as if he was going to dislocate his shoulders. "*Stop!*"

My heart raced and I fought my impulse to suck in deep lungfuls of air as I lay down on the table. I'd never been more scared in my life, but I had to keep control. I had to get out of this and save David.

"Great One, she is ready."

The air stilled as a small figure in a blood-red robe broke through the white-robed Guardians, a golden sword in hand. The hooded figure moved gracefully toward us, stopping at the edge of the makeshift altar. She held the sword parallel to my body with one hand, the other reaching for her hood and pulling it down.

Myra smiled down at me. "Hello, Ellie."

∴ Chapter Twenty-Six ∾

"Myra?" My shock was too great to hide. "*Why?*" I wailed, struggling to sit up and confront her. But I'd broken the rules and the two men were quickly at my side, tying my hands to the legs of the table. I bucked and fought. This wasn't going according to the skimpy plan I'd scrambled together at the last minute.

Grunts and moans came from Collin's direction and I saw three bodies lying on the ground. As I watched, he struck another, ramming the sword into the figure's abdomen. White-clad figures rushed toward him, pulling out knives as they ran.

Where were my bodyguards? This was officially an emergency, and I needed them now more than ever. "*Tsagasi,*" I called out. "*I need you.* Save David and Collin."

Myra had been momentarily distracted by Collin's attempt to free me, but now she turned her attention back to me. Her fingers touched my cheek and trailed down to my neck, lightly pressing my pulse point. "I've wanted your blood for weeks, but I had to wait until the time was right. Until your power was strong and you were ready."

Weeks? Jeremiah had said the Great One had assumed the image of her latest victim.

Did that mean Myra was dead?

Oh, God.

My grief was suffocating and too heavy to bear. This was one loss too many. I lay still as Myra's copy murmured words over my body and then lifted the sword over me. So she had been using the Raven Mockers over the past several weeks to test my strength. Would she kill me the same way I'd killed her pets? Would she run the blade through my heart? Could Collin bring me back from that?

Instead, she grabbed my arm and ran the tip of the blade down my forearm, pressing it deep. I expected pain, but there was nothing, only blissful numbness as Myra, the woman who'd held me when I was frightened and wiped my tears, the woman who knew my greatest fears and greatest triumphs, bent over and began to lap up my blood.

"*Ellie!*" David screamed.

Tears slipped out of my eyes and down my cheeks, drenching my hair. I'd failed her too.

Maybe I deserved to die.

I saw a flash and heard shouting close to the tree. A tiny streak shot toward David. Tsagasi and his warriors were saving him.

Myra grunted her frustration and untied my restraints, lifting my arm higher so she didn't have to bend at an awkward angle. The blade had dug deep and I was losing blood at an alarming rate. If I was going to use the ring to save David and Collin, I needed to do it soon.

I bent my left arm, pulled it back, and smashed my elbow into the demon's nose. She cried out in pain as I reached over to my right hand, the fingers pulling off the ring and enclosing it in my fist, the band exactly in the middle of the circle and square.

An eerie sound filled the air, alternating between harmony and discord. It grew louder and louder, with an ear-piercing hum. The white-clad figures dropped to their knees and covered their ears, releasing shrieks of their own.

Myra's eyes burned bright red and anger contorted her face. She dropped her hands from her bloody nose and reached for my right hand, but I clenched my fist tight. She used her demon strength to try and tear my fingers away from the ring. I resisted, but I'd already lost a lot of blood. Again. I was weakening fast.

Digging deep inside myself, I tapped into my power as a witness to creation and focused all of it on my hand.

The music grew louder and faster. The notes filled my head, and I was spinning and spinning until I was transported to the field where I'd seen Daddy and Okeus. The sky was the same gray and the field was dead and trampled, only this time there were two thrones on opposite sides. Okeus sat on one side in a dark suit, his hair slightly mussed in a sexy way. Ahone sat on the other. His clothes looked like something straight out of a Bible adaptation. His long white hair and beard added to the look.

"You must choose, Ellie," Okeus said, rapping his impatience with his fingers on the wooden chair. "It is time."

I turned slowly, from Okeus to Ahone. "No persuasive speech from you, Ahone?" I asked.

"I do what is best for my children," was his reply.

I was so fucking tired of gods and their bullshit answers. I wanted some real information.

I looked into Ahone's eyes. "The ring. What does it do? Does it seal the gate? Why does the Great One want it?"

Okeus snorted derisively. "*The Great One.*" There was obviously no love lost between Okeus and his offspring.

Ahone sighed. "The purpose of the ring was to give you an advantage over Okeus's children. So you can defeat them on your own without the other Keeper. No more. No less. It was designed for you and you alone."

He sounded convincing, but I had a feeling he wasn't telling me everything. "But it's not doing any harm to the Great One right now beyond pissing her off. Am I doing something wrong?"

A smile spread across Ahone's face, the first I'd ever seen from him. "Choose me and I'll give you the answer." He shifted in his seat. "Besides, you've already chosen. You wear my symbol on your back. This is a mere formality to appease my brother."

Why would I expect direct answers from a god? Everything came at a price. "So I make my choice and that's it? You'll both leave me alone?"

Okeus stood but didn't stray from his throne. "Ellie, you know there's really no choice here. Come with me now and I will save the men you love, who are fighting for their lives right now—who are fighting to save *you*."

But it wasn't that simple. I knew I could never give Okeus what he wanted.

"I make my choice and you will honor it?" I repeated. I wanted confirmation before I played my hand. I turned to look at Ahone. "I want you both to agree to leave me unharmed if you aren't my choice."

"I will honor it for one year," Okeus said, his voice cold. He knew I was up to something. "Ahone," he called past me. "Do you accept this amendment?"

"I do."

Freaking gods. But that meant I'd have a year before I had to deal with them again. "Agreed."

"Enough of the drama, witness to creation. Tell us your choice."

I lifted my chin. "Neither. I choose neither of you."

Okeus shot toward me at lightning speed and wrapped his hand around my throat, squeezing so tight that black dots filled my vision. "*You refuse me?*"

"Let her go." Ahone stood behind me. "You agreed, my brother. And you agreed to leave her unharmed. You must honor your agreement."

Okeus gave one last squeeze and threw me to the ground, where I landed in a crumpled heap. "You will have your year, and then I will take what is *mine*."

And just like that, I was back on the altar. Myra had given up on trying to pry the ring from my hand and had resumed her meal. Her eyes rolled back in her head in pleasure as she licked my arm. "Yes, the power is incredible. I will be invincible now."

The power made it better for her apparently.

The contents in my stomach roiled and I swallowed to keep from throwing up. I pushed what was left of my energy into my wrist and focused on breaking free. The rope smoldered and then burst into a small flame, singeing my skin before it fell off.

Ignoring the pain, I dropped the ring and reached for the Sword of Galahad, which lay across my stomach and legs. When I wrapped my hand around the hilt, a new surge of power shot through me, catching me by surprise. I rolled away from Myra—who'd been so intent on drinking my blood she hadn't noticed I was escaping—and off the table.

Surprise flickered in her eyes when she realized we were now separated by the table. "You are mine," she hissed, crouching down.

A sharp point pressed against my neck and I glanced over at Miriam. "The Great One isn't finished with you yet," she said, her expression smug. Grabbing my upper arm, she tried to push me toward the table.

I had nothing to lose at this point other than opportunity to make at least one person pay for what they'd done. "Maybe not, but I'm finished with you." In one move, I dropped out of range of her knife and grabbed her arm, shoving it behind her back.

"Enough!" Myra shouted and jumped over the table with a squatted hop, landing in front of Miriam. She reached forward and ripped out half the woman's throat, then pulled the body from my grasp and dropped it to the ground.

I froze with shock for a moment and only started to step back when the demon rushed toward me with superhuman speed. I jabbed with the sword, amazed by how it felt like an extension of my arm, lightweight and effortless to hold.

"I will finish you, Curse Keeper." A low growl rumbled from Myra's chest, and she looked more like a wild animal than my mother. But this woman wasn't my mother, I reminded myself.

No, this was the creature that had *killed* my mother.

A white-hot rage flashed through my body and I went on the attack, determined to destroy the monster forever. But the demon jumped out of the way and surveyed the clearing, taking in the sight of the bloody white-robed bodies on the ground, and laughed. "We will meet again, Curse Keeper." Then she took off running faster than humanly possible.

My adrenaline crashed and I collapsed to my knees on the grass, the sword still clutched tight in my grasp. I was dying *again*. Collin was still fighting off a small group of Guardians and I knew I should help him, but my blood was spilling freely from the three-inch gash on my arm. I knew I should drop the sword and put pressure on the wound, but my hand wouldn't release it. It was like the mark on my hand was welded to the hilt of the sword.

My gaze swung to the tree and relief flooded through me when I saw that David had been untied. But he, Tsagasi, and my other protectors were nowhere to be seen.

The world swayed and I fell to my side, pissed that it would end like this, terrified by what I'd find in the blackness this time.

Collin was directly in my line of sight, and I watched him fight the white figures who now brandished swords of their own.

My protectors rushed from the other side and surrounded Collin. Letting the supernatural creatures take point, Collin fell back. After a moment his gaze landed on me, and the way his eyes widened told me a lot about my condition. He was by my side within seconds, trying to pull the sword from my right hand.

"Ellie, let go." He sounded frantic. "We have to touch marks."

"My hand won't let go." I laughed, but I knew it was my blood loss that was making me act like a drunk. "It's the Sword of Galahad."

"Fuck the Sword of Galahad." His fingers dug deep, but mine still wouldn't budge. "Ellie," he pleaded. "Work with me here."

"I'm trying. My mark won't let go." I rolled from my side onto my back. Though I was more tired than I could ever remember being, I forced my eyes to stay open, terrified of the darkness. It would come for me soon enough.

The stars overhead shined in pinpoints that burned bright before shrinking.

"She needs the one who guides the Curse Keeper," I heard Tsagasi say.

"David!" Collin shouted as he stood and took several steps away.

The stars were swirling now, and I realized I was reliving the birth of the universe. The beginning of everything. And the end. *I* was the salvation and the destruction of the world.

"I am the alpha and the omega," I whispered in awe.

"You're a bloody pain in my arse," David mumbled as he dropped to his knees next to me, his hand encompassing my right hand. He leaned over me, his battered face blocking out the stars. "Let go of the sword, Ellie."

I stared up at him, his injuries only adding to my guilt. "They hurt you because of me. They killed Myra because of me. I hurt everyone I love. I can't hurt them anymore. Soon there won't be anyone left."

"I'm too bloody stubborn to leave you alone, so don't you dare leave me, you bloody fool. I need you, Ellie." His voice cracked. "Let go of the sword." His mouth lowered to mine and my fingers relaxed and the sword fell as I felt his love fuse with mine.

Then David was gone and Collin was with me, pressing our marks together. Power surged through my hand and into my body and I cried out, unable to take it all in. The stars filled my vision again, and then I was swept back to the beginning when the universe began. Only this time, I wasn't alone. Collin was with me. An explosion of energy and light ripped through my consciousness, hurling me through time and space as I witnessed the birth of the stars, violent eruptions that filled the black expanse with clouds of reds and oranges, blues and greens. The beauty was almost too much to take in as the massive power of the explosion filled me, consumed me, and then hurled me to the birth of our own star, our own planet. Once again, I was the first drop of water to join with the molten lava on the surface of Earth. Time raced by, and I experienced the birth of Ahone and the other gods, the evolution of the earth, the creation of humanity. It all came to a screeching halt at the gate to Popogusso. I stood in front of it, wearing the ring and holding the Sword of Galahad. Collin was next to me, brandishing a spear, and I was chanting in a language I didn't recognize. Suddenly I was infused with an overwhelming power, and the gate to hell erupted with a blinding white light.

I knew my purpose.

I was the alpha and the omega.

Demons would fall before me.

Collin released my hand, severing our connection, and we both gasped for breath. He fell on his back, next to my side. "My God, Ellie. I was there. At the birth of the universe. I was there watching it with you." He pushed up on his elbows. "How can you see that and be the same?"

I didn't know what to say. I wasn't. Especially after seeing the last part.

"I can usually feel your emotions, but this time I only had a vague sense of being with you, like I was looking over your shoulder. Did you feel me through our connection this time?"

"No." I sat up. "*No.*"

Tsagasi appeared next to us, his face grimmer than usual, holding the ring between his thumb and finger. "You're not done."

ᴄᴠ Chapter Twenty-Seven ᴠᴄ

"The demon that calls itself the Great One has escaped and is returning to the body of its deceased host," Tsagasi said. "If you hurry, you can catch it."

Myra.

She might be dead, but I would destroy the thing that killed her.

I took the ring from the little man and put it on my left hand. Then I scrambled to my feet and retrieved the Sword of Galahad.

Collin jumped up, still wielding his own weapon. When he started to pick up a sword from one of the fallen Guardians, Tsagasi stopped him.

"You don't have time to waste. My friends and I will collect them while you pursue the Great One."

Collin nodded, but I turned back to the little man. "Are all of these weapons warded?"

"No."

"Find me one that is. David needs it." I had no idea what we were about to face, but I wasn't leaving the man I loved unprotected.

Tsagasi waddled over to a group of bodies and pulled a short sword from the pile. "Here. This will work for him."

David took the weapon, and the three of us took off running for the parking lot, but it soon became apparent that David's injuries were slowing him down. "Go without me, Ellie. Get the wanker," he said, holding his side.

"Sorry, Doc." Collin grabbed his arm and pulled him along. "You're one of us now."

We climbed into the front seat of Collin's truck, with me in the middle, and Collin sped down Highway 64 toward the bed and breakfast.

"I saw this thing when they held me prisoner," David said, shouting to be heard over the wind rushing through the windows. "I know what it does. I know how to stop it."

"How?" Collin asked, his grip tight on the steering wheel.

"It's a demon that mimics its host. It kills the host and stores the body in the victim's home. It leaves a token that stays with the body, a stone that hangs from a cord around the victim's neck. It helps slow down decomposition. But once the body has decomposed too much, the demon must retrieve the token and find a new host within twenty-four hours."

"And if it loses the token or doesn't find a new host within that time frame?"

"It dies."

Tears filled my eyes. "I visited the demon in Durham, not Myra. How could I not know? Why didn't the mark on my palm give her away?"

"The marks on her door," David said. "In essence, they cocooned her, protecting her from detection."

I cast a glance toward Collin. "You said they'd figure out ways to hide themselves from us."

He nodded, his mouth pressed into a tight line. "And when we saw her at the university, the pendant with symbols hanging from her neck probably prevented us from knowing she was a demon."

I couldn't let myself think about the fact that this thing had killed

Myra. That I'd slept in the house where Myra's body was hidden. I'd tried to keep her safe, and she'd ended up just like Momma and Daddy. Had she suffered? Did she blame me? Did Steven play a part in Myra's death and possession? Or was it a coincidence? Rage burned in my chest. David was right—there were no coincidences in any of this.

The blackness Claire had seen was the evil stench from the demon. Claire's ghost—the one who was so desperate to help me— was Myra. When was the last time I'd seen the real Myra? Apart from the protective markings on her door, how had I missed the fact that she'd been replaced by that thing that called itself my mother? But I *had* noticed. I'd just attributed the changes in her to the stresses of her move and her new job. Could I have saved her if I'd paid more attention? I sucked in a deep breath to regain control of myself. I could grieve later. First I had to kick a demon's ass.

When we pulled up next to the house, Claire was pacing the porch in a skimpy robe, tears streaming down her face.

I jumped out of the truck, heart racing. Had something happened to Drew? "Claire. What's wrong?"

"Ellie," she choked on my name. "My ghost . . ." Her voice quavered. "It's Myra."

"I know," I said, letting several tears fall. "She's dead. She's been dead for weeks."

"But you just saw her! How?"

"A demon." Those two words explained it all.

She threw her arms around me. "I'm so sorry."

"I think the thing that killed her is in the house right now. It's here to get her body." I wiped my tears and lifted my chin. "And I'm going to make sure it never leaves." Collin had helped David out of the truck and both of them were heading toward us. I grabbed David's arm to stop him. "David, you stay outside."

He started to protest, but I moved my hand to his chest. "I need you to stand watch in case it tries to escape, and I need you to protect Claire." I spun around to face my best friend. "Claire, ask Myra if there's anything else I should know before going in."

Collin, who was standing next to us on the porch now, handed me the Sword of Galahad, keeping Allison's sword in his own hand.

I lifted my gaze to his face, needing his reassurance that we could do this.

"The Sword of Galahad belongs to you, Ellie. Now let's find this thing." Then he held the door open and waited for me, holding his sword in his right hand.

"Ellie," Claire said, her voice still shaking. "She says to look in the attic."

I sucked in a deep breath. The location made sense, and now I knew exactly where to look, but the stark reality of the situation still ripped a hole in my heart. How could Myra have been dead in my house without me knowing about it? What kind of daughter was I?

"Lead the way," Collin murmured as we edged past the kitchen toward the living room. He turned from side to side, checking the shadows as we made our way to the staircase. "Is there anyone else here?"

"Five researchers." I cringed. "They rent the bedrooms upstairs."

"Shit."

We picked up the pace as we headed down the hall toward the staircase leading to the attic. The house was old enough that it had been built with an actual staircase and not a pull-down ladder. Which meant the demon had easy access. I flicked the light switch at the top of the stairs, but the room was still encased in darkness. My breath caught in my chest.

"Ellie, what's wrong?" Collin whispered next to me.

"It's dark." I shook my head, feeling stupid, but I didn't know if I'd ever be able to handle a dark room again. After a couple of seconds my eyes adjusted to the dim interior, and two small dormer windows let in enough light to show the outline of the room's contents. "Let's look around."

The attic was a graveyard for every discarded thing in the house. My father, a notorious pack rat, had saved just about everything we'd ever owned. Halfway across the room, we found a small pentagram, the corners dotted with the bodies of dead animals—birds, mice, and squirrels. We'd smelled something bad off and on for a couple of weeks, and this explained it. A human body would have smelled worse. Which meant there was only one place Myra could be.

I picked my way to the back of the large space, Collin following silently on my heels, until we stopped in front of a chest freezer.

"Ellie, this thing is plugged in and running."

I bit my lower lip and nodded. I wasn't surprised. The demon would have wanted its host's body to last for as long as possible. Freezing Myra's body would have given it an indefinite amount of time. I grabbed the handle.

Collin placed his hand on mine. "Let me look."

I shook my head, trying to work up the courage. "I owe it to her, Collin."

He removed his hand and I lifted the lid. The freezer light blinked on, and there at the bottom was her bruised and broken body, a vacant look in her eyes.

"Oh, God." I took a step back, sucking in deep gulps of oxygen. I was going to pass out. "Myra."

Collin pulled me to his chest. "We'll get the piece of shit that did this. I promise." His arm dropped and he leaned into the freezer as I turned away.

He stood upright and closed the lid. "Ellie, she didn't have the stone around her neck that David mentioned. The demon's already been here."

I closed my eyes and tried to hold back tears. *Damn it.*

"Let's go back outside. I don't feel comfortable leaving Claire and David alone. David may have a sword, but he's not in great shape to fend off a demon." He put an arm around my back and I let him lead me to the staircase. But halfway down the stairs, Collin tensed. "Do you smell that?"

"Smell what?" I shook my head, trying to keep it together.

"Sulfur."

My eyes widened and raw anger surged through my body. "It's still here."

"We don't know that, Ellie. But don't do something stupid if we find it."

Instead of answering, I raced down the stairs and stood in the middle of the hall, spinning around in a circle. "I don't smell it."

When Collin reached me, he lifted his face in the air and just stood there for a moment. "Over here," he finally said. He moved to the second bedroom on the left, his hand on the doorknob. "I hope we don't scare the shit out of one of your boarders if I'm wrong."

That was the least of my concerns. I stood to the side of the door and lifted my sword. My tears were gone, driven away by my strong need for revenge. "Open it."

Collin flung the door open.

Demon Myra stood in the middle of the room, her hands wrapped around the throat of a woman who was on her knees in front of her. The demon had pulled back the rug and scratched a pentagram into the wood floor. Candles encircled the space. When the woman tipped her face up, I could see that it was Sarah, a researcher from Virginia. Duct tape covered Sarah's mouth, and her eyes were wide with terror. Tears streaked down her cheeks.

"Let her go," Collin said, raising his sword.

"I need her," the demon hissed.

Collin moved several more paces into the room.

Myra's eyes flashed red and she released a low growl as she lifted Sarah to her feet. "If you come any closer, I'll kill her *now*."

I had to remind myself this wasn't Myra, the woman I loved. This was a monster.

"You have two choices," Collin said. "You can kill her and I'll kill you. Or you can let her go and I'll let you jump out the window."

"*What?*" I shouted. There was no way in hell I was letting that bitch go.

Instead of answering, the demon shoved Sarah toward me. The poor woman stumbled, struggling to get her balance with her hands tied behind her back. She tripped on the folded-back rug and I caught her before she hit the floor face-first. The demon kicked over several candles and then leaped for the window. Glass shattered, and a gust of wind rushed in as the demon dropped to the grass below. Within moments, flames started to lick up the drapes.

Sarah collapsed against me, sobbing in terror. I pulled the tape off her mouth and then untied the shoestring binding her hands.

"We can't let it get away!" I shouted. "We have to go after it!"

But the flames on the drapes had spread to the wall, and the bed linens were burning too. The fire was spreading fast.

"Ellie, we need to get her and the other guests out of here." Collin grabbed a pillow off the bed and started to beat the flames. "Go wake up the boarders. I'll try to buy us some time."

I almost screamed in frustration. *Goddamn it.* He was right. My need for vengeance was curbed by the need to save the people I could help.

I led a still-shaken Sarah into the hallway and was already banging on the bedroom doors when Claire and David came racing to the top of the stairs.

"We saw the smoke. What happened?" David shouted.

"The demon started the fire," I said. "And it's spreading fast."

A door down the hall opened and one of the researchers stood in the doorway, wearing pajama pants and a T-shirt. "What's going on? I smell smoke."

As if on cue, the smoke alarms kicked in, emitting their high-pitched, eardrum-piercing tones. The other researchers appeared in their doorways, noticed the smoke, and raced for the staircase.

"David, we have to hurry!"

He nodded, then wrapped an arm around Sarah, who was crying hysterically, and asked the man in the doorway to help her downstairs.

Smoke filled the hallway, and flames were now shooting from Myra's open bedroom doorway.

"That's everyone, Ellie," Claire shouted, emerging from a bedroom. "It's moving fast. We have to get out now!"

"I have to get Collin! You and David make sure everyone got out okay." I ran into the bedroom where we'd found the demon. Collin was using a blanket to beat the flames. Half the room was almost completely engulfed.

"Collin!" I shouted. "Come on!"

He turned to me coughing, his face black from the smoke. "Is everyone out?"

"Yes! Hurry!"

Thick smoke filled the hall as we stumbled to the staircase, both of us choking. There was a pocket of clean air halfway down, and I sucked in a deep breath and held it until we reached the dining room. Flames covered the dining room wall, and a cracking sound filled the entire room. The ceiling in front of us caved in, dropping a pile of burning debris onto the table. A plume of smoke rushed through the house, filling my lungs and blocking our exit.

I grabbed Collin's hand, lacing our fingers together, and tugged. "This way." I pulled him to the front door, coughing so hard I could barely see the steps leading to the yard. I dragged him to the edge of the yard and when I released my hold on him, he fell to his hands and knees, trying to catch his breath. Knowing he was safe, that we were all safe, I sat on the grass beside him, exhausted and heartbroken.

A crowd had already gathered before I heard the sirens. They were too late.

"Ellie!" David's terrified shouts rounded the corner of the house. He saw me on the grass and ran to my side, falling on his knees next to me. "Thank God. I was so scared you were still inside." He pulled me to his chest and buried his hand in my hair. "I couldn't find you."

"The ceiling caved in. We had to go this way. I'm safe." But I felt numb. Like none of this could be real.

He held me for several seconds before he looked up at the inferno. "God, Ellie. You're going to lose it all." He sounded horrified.

"No. Not everything." I buried my face into his chest. Not yet.

He turned me so my chest was pressed to his, and I let myself fall apart, safe in his arms. "Myra. We found her." I broke into sobs.

I cried myself into exhaustion before I had the sense to check on Collin. An ambulance was parked on the side of the street now, and an irritated Collin was sitting on a gurney with an oxygen mask on. When he saw me watching him, he tossed it down and, ignoring the shouts of the paramedic who was treating him, jumped out of the ambulance and strode over toward me, his jaw set in determination.

I climbed to my feet as he approached.

"I'm sorry I didn't go after her, Ellie. We'll track her down. I swear to you."

"You did the right thing." I reached my arms around his shoulders and pulled him into a hug. "Thank you."

His hands loosely held my waist before he gently pushed me away. "It looks like your favorite police officer is waiting to talk to you. He's already told me not to leave until we've had a 'chat.'"

Tom made his way toward me, and I looked up at Collin in a panic. "What happened to the swords?"

"Claire," he said as Tom walked up.

"What about Claire?" Tom asked, his hands on his hips, his gaze swinging between the three of us.

"Ellie wanted to make sure her friend was okay," David volunteered, wrapping an arm around my waist.

"I'm going to go check on something in my truck," Collin mumbled as he walked away.

The house gave a loud creaking sound before one side caved in.

"What happened, Ellie?" Tom asked in his official voice.

"Do you want the report-friendly version or the truth?"

He hesitated. "Truth."

"It was a demon. It killed Myra and started the fire." Grief stabbed my heart, but my tears were dry. Tears wouldn't bring her back.

Tom put a hand on my arm. "God, Ellie. I'm sorry."

I nodded, pressing my lips together. "The demon was attacking one of the boarders when we found it." I searched the crowd and pointed to Sarah when I caught sight of her next to a second ambulance. "She was pretty freaked out. The demon has impersonated Myra, so I'd appreciate it if you could do something about that." I cleared my throat. "For the report. Myra deserves better than for the town to think she attempted murder."

"I'll see what I can do." He looked over at the fire, then back at me. "And the Raven Mockers?"

"The demon impersonating Myra was controlling them and it just fled. I hope they're gone too, but it won't be forever."

"Then we'll hope they don't come back for a long time." He started toward Sarah.

"Tom."

He turned back to me.

"You're going to find a total mess at the botanical gardens." Although I hoped Tsagasi cleaned some of it up along with the weapons.

"Again?"

I didn't answer and he turned away, muttering under his breath.

David tugged me tighter to him. "I guess this means we're moving for sure. But we didn't find all of your father's notes."

"We don't need them. We're making our own rules now." I looked up at him. "Collin and I have officially broken all allegiance with the gods. This is far from over." I offered a pained smile. "It's only just begun."

"We'll be prepared. You know I'm on your side."

"What about the Guardians? Do we have to worry about them coming back?"

"I don't know, but I know we pretty much decimated their core group. All the people there tonight were the higher-level members. They might rebuild, but hopefully it will take years."

I nodded. It was the best I could hope for.

David's attention drifted to Collin. He sat on the back of his pickup looking more lost than I'd ever seen him. "He needs you right now, Ellie."

I jerked my gaze up to meet David's.

"You picked me, Ellie. But Collin is floundering right now, and he's your partner. The three of us will be working closely together, and we all have to trust each other. I know your heart. I have faith in you."

I placed a gentle kiss on the corner of his bruised lips. "I love you."

"I love you too. Now go talk to him."

I pushed through the now-thinning crowd, stopping next to Claire, who huddled next to an obviously shaken Drew.

"I'm sorry I didn't know it was Myra sooner, Ellie," Claire whispered through fresh tears.

I pulled my friend into a hug. "You couldn't know, Claire. It's okay."

She pulled back and offered a smile.

"Can you do something for me?" I asked, my voice breaking. "Can you give Myra a message?"

Claire nodded.

"Can you tell her I'm sorry that I failed her?" I started crying as I said the words.

Claire shook her head, starting to sob. "She says you didn't fail her. She's so proud of you and she loves you so much."

I could hardly see Claire through my tears. "Tell her I love her too."

"Ellie, she already knows. She never once doubted your love for her."

I sucked in several deep breaths to regain control and offered her a sad smile. "Thank you." I cast a long glance toward Collin.

"It's okay," she said. "Go to him."

After I made my way to the back of Collin's truck, I hopped up on the tailgate next to him. "You were a hero tonight. Who would have thought?" I teased as I wiped my stray tears, leaning my shoulder into his. "You're just full of surprises."

"I meant it about finding the demon that killed your mother. I don't want you to think I purposely let it go."

"I know you didn't." I slipped my hand in his, lacing our fingers together.

He didn't answer for several seconds, just watching the now-smoldering house. "Our connection is different. It changed tonight. I didn't feel you. Did you really not feel me?"

"No." And my hormones were under control even though we were sitting next to each other. If this lasted, it would make our lives infinitely easier. "Did you mean it about David being part of us now?"

"There's no denying that he can find things we can't. We need him." He glanced over at the man I loved. "If he's open to it, of course."

"He is."

"And Claire?" he asked, turning back to me and studying my face.

"I guess she's one of us too. Part of our team."

A smirk lifted his mouth. "I've never been much of a team player."

My eyebrows lifted and a grin spread across my face. "Why does that not surprise me?"

He turned serious again.

A new thought hit me. "Are you okay with being part of a team?"

He sighed, his gaze on our joined hands. "For the first time, I feel like I belong to something important." His deep brown eyes lifted to mine. "Do you know what I mean? Like we're supposed to save the world even though no one realizes it."

"Yeah, I know exactly what you mean."

His smart-ass grin spread across his face. "We'll need shirts. I think they should say 'Team Collin.'"

I snorted. "Not a chance."

Several minutes later David joined us, and I sat between the two most important men in my life, the two men who would help me fight the evil that was still growing and waiting to rise up and strike innocents.

We stayed until the fire was completely extinguished, wisps of smoke rising as firemen began to poke around the debris. The rising sun shot streaks of reds and pinks along the horizon. A new day was about to begin.

The first day of my new life.

I'd lost my family home and my last remaining parent, and yet the sun still rose. The world still spun. Life went on.

I leaned my head onto David's shoulder and he pulled me close. "Are you ready to leave yet?" he asked.

Was I? No. Something wasn't done. I wasn't sure what, but I knew I needed to stay.

Not long after, Tom made his way over to me, holding a small wooden box. "Ellie, the fire inspector found this in the rubble. Everything around it was practically cinder, but this is in nearly pristine condition."

I took it from him, gasping. The box with Daddy's pocket watches. It was coated in a layer of dust, but he was right—it was completely undamaged. I ran my fingers around the edges.

David sat upright. "Is that what I think it is?"

"What is it?" Collin asked, leaning closer.

I lifted the lid, exposing the contents. "It's from Daddy." The timepieces were in perfect condition, nestled in their velvet beds. Obviously, the watches had survived for a reason. They still had an important purpose.

Did Daddy have anything to do with this? Was this his way of offering his love and support? If someone had suggested it two months ago, I'd have called them crazy. But a scent of leather and cinnamon hung in the air. He was with me right now.

I looked up at Collin. "It's a sign of hope—that we can do this. That we can conquer the demons and make everything right again."

A cocky grin spread across his face. "Hell, we already have that, Ellie."

I chuckled. "Why? Because *you're* on board?"

"No. Because we've got the best weapon we could possibly have." He leaned closer, turning serious. "We've got *you*."

I only hoped that I was enough.

ACKNOWLEDGMENTS

I'd like to thank 47North for their hard work and dedication to the Curse Keepers series. My acquiring editor, David Pomerico, heard the worst pitch in the history of pitches and still asked for a proposal. My first developmental editor, Alison Dasho, came with me to 47North, then left me after the line edits of *The Curse Keepers* to become an acquisitions editor for Thomas & Mercer. Her excitement at helping me create the Curse Keeper world, starting from the very beginning with the proposal, was contagious and inspiring. I was sad to lose her but excited to see her fulfill her dreams. Thankfully, I gained Angela Polidoro, whom I absolutely adore. She jumped in with both feet, not only with the Curse Keeper world, but my Rose Gardner Mystery series as well. She's an absolute joy to work with and puts up with my moments of insecurities. (I'm convinced the poor woman usually sees me at my worst.) And finally, I'm lucky and thankful to have worked with the same copy editor for all three books. Jon has been an absolute joy to work with. I love how he understood me and my style, offering suggestions that were nearly always spot on. I can honestly say I've never enjoyed working with a copy editor as much as I have with him.

This series has had many highs and lows for me, and I'm forever thankful to Heather Pennington, Stormy Udell, Christie Timpson,

Emily Pearson, and Rhonda Cowsert, who always believed in Ellie, Collin, and David, even when I doubted. I couldn't ask for a better set of beta readers and friends.

I'm blessed with amazing readers, who not only read the book in their hands, but devour it and ask for more. You inspire me to keep this crazy pace. You inspire me to keep going even when I'm filled with doubt.

To those of you who have grown to love Ellie, Collin, and David—not to worry, this isn't the end. Their journey has just begun.

ABOUT THE AUTHOR

Denise Grover Swank was born in Kansas City, Missouri, and lived in the area until she was nineteen. She then became a nomad, living in five cities, four states, and ten houses over the next decade before moving back to her roots. She speaks English and a smattering of Spanish and Chinese. Her hobbies include making witty Facebook comments and dancing in the kitchen. She has six children and hasn't lost her sanity. Or so she leads everyone to believe.